# Finding Herself

## MAUREEN REID

EMPEROR BOOKS

*For those who grieve.*
*The journey is your own, but you are not alone.*

# Contents

# Book I

## 1953

My mother may be dead. The telegram read: *Cate. Mam very ill. In hospital. Come home. Joseph.* For Joseph, this was an epistle.

That was yesterday, a morning when I'd awakened with a start. The clock read not yet seven, its alarm waiting to blare the dawn of a new day. The patter of rain against the window was like a lullaby, coaxing me to stay under the covers. Mornings like this remind me of home, Ireland, the rhythm of the drops, soothing and quiet.

I lay in the bed, not willing to force my feet on the ground. I closed my eyes. That is when I saw her. It was my mother, my mam. She was sitting on the bench perched outside my window overlooking Gramercy Park. The morning light captured the floral print of her duster, pale pink with a lace collar; the nightgown underneath would be its perfect match. My first thought was fleeting; it couldn't be her. Mam would never leave the house looking like that; she wasn't dressed to greet the world. My heart began racing; it couldn't be her. Mam was in Dublin. I was in New York City. Mam turned her head. Her eyes, so like mine, looked up, and she gave me one of her half-smiles. Then she was gone.

I blinked my eyes open. My eyes darted around the room, the remnants of my morning dream clinging to me. I expected the room to look different, but nothing seemed to have changed; everything was as I left it the night before. But the uneasiness wouldn't leave me, like a fog that won't dissipate.

I left Dublin for these shores ten months ago. In this sprawling city called New York, I am looking to find myself, to answer the question of who I am, or perhaps who I should become. As I approach a quarter of a century, I am still very much a work in progress.

I made a promise that I would write to her when I came home that evening. It had been over two weeks since I sent a letter. Another one was long overdue.

I summoned my feet to hit the ground and started the day.

That evening, the sun was setting as I made my way home from my job as an editorial assistant in one of the city's publishing houses. My department focuses on technical journals, so the piles of texts crowding my desk aren't exactly thrilling. It doesn't matter. It is the written word I love. I like taking a red pen to a page, my markings are my contribution to the world. The first time I held a published edition of something I had worked on, my pulse quickened. Here is something I helped create, something I can hold onto. My pay isn't much, only a fraction of what my male counterparts are receiving for doing essentially the same work, only with grander titles, larger desks, and more robust egos.

I unlocked the front door of the house that welcomed me the day I arrived on these shores and the place I now call home. I took off my shoes, wiggling my toes free from the three-inch heels that are part of the uniform of a young woman on the rise. My day had been a blur of chasing authors, organizing mountains of paper that seemed to multiply by the hour, and tuning out the office gossip. It was good to be done.

I grabbed the evening paper from the entry table and scanned the headlines. Here was the grinning Joseph McCarthy, the junior senator from Wisconsin, rattling the very structure of the government with allegations of communist infiltrators, charges supported without fact, only deadly innuendo. I couldn't understand how a country that once fought against tyranny could now tolerate such behavior within its own shores. A constant drumbeat of paranoia was echoing throughout this nation, with the press escalating the scare with its bold, black headlines.

I poured a glass of wine, finding refuge in the library, and tossed a log onto the fire. Despite the warmth being cast by the crackling wood, a feeling I couldn't explain began to engulf me. I hadn't thought about my morning dream until I stared into the flames. I shrugged my shoulders at my remembered promise. Not tonight, I told myself. I was too tired, mentally and physically, to write the promised note. Tomorrow, I vowed, tomorrow I would take pen in hand and send an optimistic if not an accurate description of the life I was leading in this, my adopted city.

I opened up the evening paper and was judging both the grammar and the structured arguments presented on the editorial page when the doorbell rang.

It was the telegram from Joseph.

———

The words kept echoing in my head. My mother is ill, very ill. I could hear Joseph's voice telling me what the words did not: my mother was dying. My heart pounded. The room blurred into smudges. I couldn't move. My hands trembled as I read and re-read the words. *"Come home."*

And then the tears came. Slowly at first, like the drip of a leaky faucet, and then sobs from the hollow of a place I didn't know existed.

Nell heard my cries and found me. Nell Walker is a unique human being, a woman hard to describe. She has a presence that doesn't seek attention but effortlessly draws it. Her warmth is combined with elegance, and the same can be said about her home in Gramercy Park. A home that she opened for me to share and where I have stayed. It is a gift—helping me smooth the transition from my life in Dublin to the one I am seeking in New York. Nell is the adoptive mother of my half-brother Teddy. Their story is a labyrinth, one whose details I don't fully know, but the connection between the two of them is powerful.

I stood up, tears streaming down my face, the telegram trembling in my hand. I choked out the words, *Mam is dying. I have to go home to Ireland.* Nell read the telegram; she put her arms around me until I had caught my breath. I collapsed back in the chair.

Her eyes never leaving my face, Nell sat on the ottoman in front of me and handed me my glass of wine. Her voice was kind and practical. *It is Monday. We will have you back in Dublin by Thursday. Air travel now makes this all possible. We will wire Joseph once it's arranged.*

She stood up, strong and straight, and pulled me to my feet. *Rosina left a pot of soup on the stove. You fetch another bottle of wine; I will bring the glasses and meet you at the kitchen table.*

Nell's next words came with quiet certainty, her voice steady. *I knew your mother when she was younger than you are now, before she moved to Ireland, before she had you. She is a fighter. Whatever crisis she is facing, she will meet it head-on. I believe the same can be said about you.*

My tears subsided. Nell always seems to know the right thing to say, at the right time, with the right grace.

Minutes later, we were seated at the kitchen table, our soup bowls filled with the rich scent of a savory broth and large noodles fighting for space with a myriad of red and green vegetables. The warmth swept over me. I lifted the recently procured bottle of wine as if in a toast and smiled, *Dutch courage, I'll need it if you are going to get me on an airplane.*

Courage that took all I could muster as our conversation turned to the logistics of me being locked into a sky-bound mass of steel and glass that somehow defies gravity.

Hours later, I went to my room, but sleep escaped me. I couldn't close my eyes without thinking. Without thinking of what the next days might bring, a life without Mam, a presence I have always taken for granted, always believed she would be there. To think that my life could continue without her, her support, her love, filled me with a terror I have never known. And guilt. I blamed myself. My leaving home made her sick. I couldn't shake that thought. And she must be very sick, or Joseph wouldn't have sent the telegram. My thoughts got darker; she could already be dead. I shook my head. I couldn't bear that notion. I had to be with her.

As the night wore on, my thoughts becoming more and more incoherent, accusation upon accusation hurling at me as if I was caught in a whirlwind. Closing my eyes didn't stop my mind from spinning. *What if* started every sentence. I could find no answers. I gave in. I got up. There were things I had to do. Plans I had to make. I did not know how long I would be gone, or if I would return to this room, this house, this life. My heart was breaking under the weight of questions too frightening to answer.

I had two days to sort my life out.

I got out of bed, found pen and paper, and made a list. The dread and uncertainty subsided as I focused on what I had to do rather than what lay in store. When I finally laid my head back on the pillow, a troubled but uneasy sleep overtook me.

Waking up, it took me a minute or two to remember. My world was falling apart. I took a deep breath. I had to take charge of what I could take charge of. My feet hit the ground and found their slippers. There was no rush to my movements; the sun was still struggling to meet the day. I went downstairs.

Soon, the kitchen and the house would be abuzz, but for a moment, the only noise was the soft whistle of the tea kettle. I looked outside the window; the city outside was indifferent to the turmoil I felt. Cars honked, a distant siren raised its lonely warning. The clock over the table seemed to tick louder, as if mocking me for my idleness when time was precious. I took a slow sip of tea; its warmth could not ease the chill that had settled in my bones. I closed my eyes to steady myself. I reread the telegram. The words felt like they should belong to someone else, someone else's story. Tears began to fall as the realization hit. This story, this story was now mine.

I took my shower and pulled out the wardrobe for the day. I found the sweater I brought with me from Ireland, its soft fabric clung to me like an old friend I hadn't seen in ages. Then came the blue jeans I had meant to wash over the weekend. My tangled hair was left to do as it pleased; it was free to fall anyway it chose. I had donned my suit of armor for the battle of the day. I went back downstairs. The day had begun.

I picked up the phone from its cradle; it felt heavy in my hand. I called the publishing house. I was given a leave of absence from my job with no projected date for my return. I thanked them for their understanding, but couldn't determine how I felt about being so easily replaced. Then another phone call canceling my appointment for a haircut, one very much needed. I am returning to Dublin with a heavy heart, my story still unfinished, and a head full of tight auburn curls.

Then came the hard part—the call to my brother Teddy, my half-brother, to be correct. Teddy is my mother's birth son. I stared at the phone, remembering the day he came into my life. I was eighteen years old, living at home while studying English Literature at University College Dublin. It was a Sunday after Mass when Mam sat me down. *I met someone yesterday that I believe you should meet, as well.*

Mam had never assumed the role of matchmaker in my life, so I felt a bit excited, somewhat apprehensive, and more than just a bit curious. She poured us a cup of tea and put a slice of sponge cake in front of me. I remember thinking, *This is going to be important.* Sponge cake slices were reserved for only the most serious of our discussions.

Mam looked into her teacup, seldom at a loss for words; she seemed to be struggling to find what to say, her voice now serious. *When I was younger than you and living in New York City, I got pregnant. I came to Ireland to have the baby. A baby I gave away without even knowing whether I had given birth to a boy or a girl. About a year ago, I received a letter from Nell Walker, a good friend of mine in those days, and the woman who, along with her husband, raised my baby as their own. It was a boy. This young man, now very much an adult, wanted to meet me. After giving it much thought, I believed it was his right. Yesterday, he and I had tea at the Shelburne.*

My first reaction was one of disbelief and a thousand questions. Mam had a child she had never seen? I had a brother I never knew?

Mam waved away my first question of how all of this came about, with a single sentence, *Best to keep the past in the past.* She continued. *His name is Edward Walker, but he's called Teddy. I told him about you, and he asked if he might meet you.*

A small smile swept over Mam's face. *I think he is quite taken with the newfound fact that he has a sister. I said it would be up to you, but if you agreed, I suggested a luncheon tomorrow. It is your decision, however, your decision alone to make.*

My decision was yes.

I was startled back to the present by the ringing of the phone still cradled in my hand. It was a representative from PanAmerican Airlines. My booking was confirmed. I wrote down the specifics, my handwriting shakier than usual. The thought of surrendering myself to a machine with propellers was filling me with cold terror.

Despite the emotions churning within me, I had to smile, remembering the day Teddy and I met. I recognized him the minute he walked into the restaurant. He was decidedly American, with a casual look that maintains the balance between comfort and sophistication—a look that most Irish men can neither pull off nor afford. Already seated, I raised my hand in greeting. A smile lit up his face as he doffed his newsboy cap, a cap that only such a man could pull off. He took my hand and gave me a smile whose warmth could melt glaciers. But it was his eyes, a mesmerizing blend of blue and green, like the meeting of the sea and sky on a clear summer day, that startled me. We share the same eyes. Mam's eyes.

Since that lunch date three years ago, Teddy has become my champion, my friend, and my guide. He is my brother.

His was the voice I needed most to hear. Teddy left his position as a partner in a Wall Street law firm to work as counsel for a government committee trying to expose McCarthy's baseless claims. I called his Washington office, my fingers drumming impatiently as the phone began to ring. Finally, a voice with a calm tone and a slight southern drawl answered: *Good Morning, Mr. Walker's office.*

I was not inclined to exchange pleasantries. *I need to speak to my brother, Edward Walker. It is very important.*

The reply was polite. *Mr. Walker is in meetings all day. I can take a message and leave it on this desk. Can I have your name?*

My fingers clenched the phone tighter, my voice sharper: *I must get a message to him quickly. This is a family emergency. I am his sister, Cate.*

There was a second of silence at the other end; the polite tone continued. *I will have a page deliver the message. I cannot guarantee when Mr. Walker will be available. He is very busy and his schedule leaves very little time for personal matters.*

I wanted to scream, *He will want this message. It is from me. I need to talk with him*. I took a deep breath instead.

The voice on the other end took the break in conversation as agreement. *I will see that Mr. Walker gets your message. Have a good day*. The line went dead.

I pulled the phone away from my ear and glared at it, as though somehow it was responsible for my not getting through to Teddy.

I couldn't stay in the house another moment without exploding. I called to Nell that I was going for a walk. I needed sun and fresh air. I grabbed my coat, the sound of my shoes on the pavement my only company. With each step, the tension in my shoulders eased ever so slightly. The crisp air filled my lungs, and by the time I found my way back home, I was calmer, steadier.

I walked in to see Nell on the phone. She handed the receiver to me. *It is Teddy. He got your message. I told him about your mother and that you were leaving for Dublin*. She gave my arm a bit of a squeeze and left.

*You know?* My voice trembled.

Teddy's voice was soft, concerned. *Yes. Mam needs you. You'll not be alone. Joseph will be there with you. I'll be here for you. This is hard.*

I was quiet. *So very hard. I don't know if I can do this. Leave New York, take care of Mam.*

*You can. New York will always be here. So will Nell. So will I. For now, Dublin is where you need to be. Stay strong. Write to me as soon as you know more. Call me if needed.*

My voice broke. *Thank you. I love you, Teddy.*

*I love you, too, Cate.* And we hung up.

My last call was to Faith. I had to tell her the news in person; a phone call would never do. She was rushing to or from something, and we agreed to meet for lunch the following day.

Faith is the sister I never had. Nell has known her since she was a child and introduced us the first week I moved to New York. Faith is a flame in a land of cold reality. She wants a world where people care enough to listen, to act, to seek justice. Her convictions aren't mere words; she signs petitions, marches on streets, and fights for the rights of those whom others want to silence. Following her graduation from college, she started working in New York's theatre world, where she was cautioned that her politics and activism could have repercussions. Sure enough, she has become a potential scapegoat and has been subpoenaed by the Committee on Un-American Activities. Their charges are rubbish, yet her age and her support of seemingly socialist theories are making her an open target for those seeking to be hailed in tomorrow's headlines.

Faith needed a good lawyer. Teddy came to the rescue.

I spent the rest of the day deciding what clothes to bring with me, what would stay behind. The windproof jacket and waterproof boots won over the heavy tweed coat that blocked the northeast winds. My carefully procured collection of high heels brought forth only one winner: a pair of red suede heels that, while impractical for Dublin's cobble streets, were simply too lovely to leave behind. The scarf Joseph had sent for my birthday was coming with me, the flimsy sundresses best suited for New York's summer heat staying put. Decision after decision made—the baseball cap from my first Yankees game stayed. My all-purpose black dress coming with me. It was suitable for both weddings and funerals, I reckoned. My hands folded the clothes in a steady rhythm. The suitcase was packed, along with my worries. The heartache I carried with me.

Then it was time to bid New York City farewell. I found my way to Central Park, golden leaves scattered throughout the streets were being tossed by the wind. I smiled; they, too, were bidding adieu. I sat down on a bench and took a slow, deliberate breath, closed my eyes, and listened to the screeching of tires, the clatter of hurried footsteps, the universal language of a child's laughter. The sounds of New York all blended together in a never-ending symphony.

I slowly rose, pulled my scarf tighter around my neck, and turned to make my way back to Gramercy Park. The memory of this city will be coming with me; its promise still calling me.

The next day, I found a booth at our local pizzeria where I was to meet Faith. I relished breathing air filled with the mingling scents of sizzling mozzarella, tangy tomato sauce, and a hint of garlic. She was late, but I didn't mind. I committed the aroma to memory. Of the many things I will miss, New York pizza will make the top ten.

Then there was a bustle, a cold blast of air, and my name being called, all happening at once. Faith had arrived, a whirlwind of energy, her dark hair bouncing every which way as if it was trying to keep up with its restless owner.

*Oh, Cate, I am so sorry. Have you been waiting long? I was on my way and got caught up in a demonstration in Washington Square. Students, faculty, and who knows who else, there were about 30 of them, so full of hope. So impatient to right the wrongs that are taking place. If only McCarthy and his sheep could have seen them.*

She flopped down, the contents of her purse spilling out on the now faded red leather seat. Picking up the menu, she continued without a pause. *This was democracy in action, defiance burning bright against the grayness of McCarthy's witch hunts. I just had to stay.* Faith's voice was hoarse, the fallout from demanding to be heard. The protest was over, but the energy of it all still buzzed in her veins, even if it meant losing her voice.

I shook my head and gave her my first smile of the day. *Oh, Faith, of course I understand. But I need you to take a deep breath and listen to what I have to say. I am leaving tomorrow morning to return to Dublin. My mother is ill, very ill. My brother has wired me to come home. I don't know when I will be coming back to New York.*

Faith cried out, *You can't leave me, Cate. Not now. I need you.*

Then she shook her head. *That was heartless. I am coming with you. Shall we just get a couple of slices and a cola?*

I was laughing and crying at the same time. Faith touches every emotion. A blithe spirit one minute, emoting joy, merriment, and cheerfulness, but her very next breath can exude fire and flame. She is a mass of contradictions, never predictable but always present in the moment. I wouldn't want a lot of people like her in my life, but I am so grateful that I found her.

I was also concerned for her welfare. *Faith, you can't come with me. You have been subpoenaed to testify before a Congressional committee. This is serious. Every word you say can be twisted, every action you take scrutinized, every ideal you embrace challenged. I am worried for you.*

Faith smiled, *Don't worry about me, Cate. I'm not going to back down to those who whisper lies and half-truths about me. I will not walk away. But I know, I* know I can't go to Ireland. I just wish there was something I could do to help. To really help.

You can promise me you will be careful. And you can write to me. And we should share a whole pie.

She gave me her best Faith smile. I'll only promise to write. And to buy lunch.

I was already missing her. And the pizza was delicious.

At 6:00 a.m., I was standing in front of the suitcase that had traveled with me not so many months ago. The plane ticket was in my purse, a one-way flight back to Ireland. The butterflies in my stomach were also ready to take off.

I went back to the library. Nell was sitting there, looking nowhere near her sixty-plus years. She stood up as I came into the room and once again took my hands in hers, sitting beside me.

The days and months ahead of you, dearest Cate, are going to be hard. It will be a difficult journey. My husband, my father, and one of my dearest friends all died quickly. I had to deal with shock as well as grief. Over the years, I have learned that grief is like the weather, changeable but always there. It evolves. At some point, I no longer burst into tears at the memory of them, but the grief didn't go away. It just became an ever-present gnawing ache.

Your journey will be different. You will be with your mother, taking care of her as she took care of you. She has been the rock of your family, but even rocks erode over time. I have no advice for you. This is your journey. Just know that as you walk this path, you are surrounded by those who love you, trust in you, and believe in you. Know you are not alone.

She let go of my hands as she reached into her bag and pulled out the most exquisite journal, handmade light blue leather with parchment pages ready to be written on. A journal for you. You know, I once considered myself a writer.

I smiled, Nell, you were more than a writer, you were a journalist who exposed man's inhumanity to man. The newspapers need the likes of you again.

Nell smiled, a smile that lit up her eyes and the room around her. What I was told all those years ago is the same advice I share with you today. Write down what you feel when you are feeling it. Listen to others, record their words. These notes will keep them with you. I believe the written word is powerful.

A sleek fountain pen was then handed to me. Think of me when you hold this. It will be as if I am holding your hand, as well.

My eyes started to fill with tears. You are so very kind. You opened your home and your heart to me and ... I couldn't get out the last words.

Nell brought me to my feet and put her arms around me. *No more words. You know how special you are to me.*

We sat back down as Nell continued. *So, let's talk logistics. In this new world of taking to the skies, what used to take days is now taking hours. You leave on a 9:00 a.m. flight tomorrow. Joseph has been advised of all of the arrangements. A car will pick you up at 7:00 a.m.*

Nell looked wistful. *I have never flown, you know. Perhaps Teddy and I will come over once you have a better understanding of how your mother is faring. For tonight, I have made reservations for us at Delmonico's. I will spend the evening regaling you with the stories of my life as a 20th Century Nelly Bly.* She threw back her head and laughed.

I couldn't help but join in. *Your life is a story, one that the infamous Miss Bly would have envied. I can't wait to hear your tale. I will be ready in 15 minutes.*

By the time the meal had ended and the plates cleared, Nell had given me one last gift—an evening of reprieve, filled with laughter and vivid descriptions of a world long ago. It was a respite from the uncertainty of what my tomorrow will bring.

Less than 10 hours later, after our return from Delmonico's, I was seated on an airplane.

———

I don't like heights, never have. Yet, there I was, seated in a metal contraption, where the engines rumbled to life with a deep growl, and we moved along at an unimaginable speed. The roar flattened to a steady drone as the plane lifted itself into the air. I put my forehead against the glass and looked out the window. Probably not the best idea, but I simply couldn't resist. The sky turned from gray to white to blue.

Once seemingly safe in the air, the stewardess, all smiles and perfectly coiffed blond hair, put a small bowl of nuts in front of me. She sweetly asked what I would like to drink. I looked at my watch; it wasn't 11 a.m. I shook my head. *I don't like to drink in the morning.*

The gentleman in the seat next to me raised his hand. *What are you talking about? None of us likes it. We just do it. We'll have two Bloody Marys, extra vodka in both.*

I smiled weakly. *That sounds about right.*

He nodded. *Just don't think about where we are and what we are in, and you'll be fine.* And with that, he settled back, pulling out his *Wall Street Journal*.

The vodka infusion did its magic. I slept, waking up only during our stop to refuel in Iceland. Now crossing the Atlantic, the cabin became quiet. Everything around me seemed calm, including the gentle snoring of the man next to me, his paper now askew on his lap.

I closed my eyes, remembering. Remembering where I was, remembering why I was here, remembering what lay in store for me. Ireland. Home. Mam. Memories, concerns, and doubts flew around my brain as fast as this airplane was making its way across the water.

I found the journal and pen Nell had given me and made the first entry.

————

## Finding My Way

I was about to turn 22 when the turning point came. I had finished my university studies with a graduate degree in English Literature. Working as a campus librarian, shelving books and trying to maintain an air of calmness around the place and within me wasn't enough. I didn't know what I wanted to do, but knew this wasn't it. I was merely going through the required steps of life after university.

Then it happened. I was on the tram coming home. The fog was thick and soft, like a veil shielding even the most familiar landmarks; the world outside my window seemed mysterious. The car was mostly full when an elderly man approached, the tapping of his cane silenced as he took the seat next to me. He was bald except for a fringe of salt-and-pepper curls, giving him the look of a medieval monk. He gave no greeting, just half-closed his eyes. As he stood to leave, his eyes met mine, and the etched wrinkles on his face lifted into a knowing smile. *Forge your own path; don't expect others to do it for you. Look for joy.*

He gave a quick salute and was gone. The sound of his cane faded, but not his message.

I got off at the next stop, wondering what the old man had meant.

Maybe it was all right for me to want something else, to search, to find another way.

I wrote to Teddy that night, telling him about the man with the tapping cane and the message he had sent. Days later, Teddy phoned. Other than Christmas and my birthday, he seldom called. It was his message that changed my world. *Come to New York. I will figure out a way to get you work here.*

That is when I decided to give it a go. To leave Dublin. To move to New York. I just had to tell Mam.

I remember the morning of that conversation, we had just come home from Mass, and the skies promised that the only sun we would be seeing was in the day's name. Mam was busy making our breakfast; Joseph had stayed on at the university. The only sound in the kitchen was the soft hum of the kettle.

Mam brought the toast and jam to the table. *There is something you're meaning to tell me, isn't there, my love?*

*Oh, Mam. How do you know?*

She wiped her hands on a towel and gave me her Mam smile. *Because I know you. Ever since you were a bit of a lass, your fingers would tremble just ever so slightly when you were worried or scared. Just like they have been doing all morning.*

She sat down at the table. I clasped my hands and began. *Teddy and I have been writing. I want to go to New York.* Mam frowned, her brow furrowed. *New York? To visit?*

*No, Mam. I want to live there. Or at least, give it a go. Teddy said he could help me get a job.*

*When did you start thinking of this? It is a big step, so far away and so different.*

*I know, and I'm not sure I can explain it. And I know I don't have the answers to the questions you might be asking. I love you. I love Joseph. I'm comfortable. But at 22 years old, that isn't what I want my life to be. I'm not sure what I want, but I know comfortable isn't it. My girlfriends are talking about marriage and babes. That's not me, Mam. At least not now. I want to chase whatever is mine to capture. Wherever it is.*

Mam's eyes softened. She had a look, one mixed with pride and apprehension. *You have never given me a moment of doubt. If this is what you think you should do, then you should do it. You have a bright light about you, one that will shine through no matter what side of the Atlantic you are on. The only advice I can give you is to keep your heart open, stay true to yourself, and never forget the land that you call home. I will always be here for you, cheering you on every step of the way. No matter what path you take. No matter where that is.*

We sat in silence for a moment, both absorbing the conversation we had just had. Finally, Mam spoke up, *Another cuppa, my darling daughter. I love you.*

*Yes, please*, as I held up my cup. *I love you, too.*

Mam nodded. *And Teddy will be there for you. That will ease my worry.*

And plans for my leaving began.

Two months later, I stood on the edge of a bustling pier, the salt air making my eyes water as I looked up at the towering skyscrapers that seemed to touch the clouds. Here was an energy I could already feel. The whole city was alive. I was in New York. My heart was racing from the thrill of it all. I pulled my coat tighter, the January wind biting my face. I couldn't tell if I was scared or excited, or a combination of both.

This was the first step of a journey only I could define.

Then I saw him. Teddy. My steps quickened, my nervousness ebbing away. He waved me over, hugged me, and took my arm. *Cate, so wonderful to have you here. There is a car waiting for us; the driver will come back later to pick up your trunk and bring it to my moth-er's house. She is all set for you to stay with her for as long as you like. Everyone calls her Nell.*

———

I put down the pen.

———

Four hours later, I heard the wheels of the plane come down. At least that is what I hoped the noise meant. I unclasped my sweating hands and clenched my fists, my nails making imprints into my palms. The gentleman next to me was back reading his paper. The plane dipped its nose and drove into a cloud, and for some minutes it was as if we were encased in a bowl of cotton. I couldn't stop looking out the window. Then, suddenly, the ground became visible, concrete buildings and barren trees coming into sight. My traveling companion folded his paper. *We are about to land; it will be a bit bumpy, but that's normal.* He was right. Then we were on the ground. I had made it. I had flown. I was relieved. I was exhilarated.

I remembered I had forgotten to exchange money. As I stepped into the cluttered exchange booth at the airport, the reality of being home, back in Ireland, hit me with an unexpected force. The U.S. dollars placed on the counter were quickly replaced by the rough texture of the Irish punt. I tucked the acquired currency in my bag. The look of the notes, at once known and familiar, brought an unexpected lurch to my heart, a reminder of why I was here and the fear of what tomorrow and all the tomorrows to follow might bring.

I scanned the room, and my eyes caught his. Long and lean, Joseph has an air about him, a quiet thoughtfulness, which tells you he is content with who he is and what he does. His chestnut brown hair matched the color of his checked shirt and neatly pressed trousers. I was certain I had seen the outfit before. He looked older, a bit wearier, or maybe it was just that I was seeing him for the first time in months. And really seeing him, not taking him for granted. We seldom embraced–Joseph is not keen on phys-ical contact. But today didn't count. I dropped the suitcase from my deadly grip, ran to him, clung to him.

*I made it* were my first words. I began to weep. Joseph said nothing, just held me closer until I could find my voice. I muffled into his shoulder, *I won't ask how you are. But Mam?* It was both a statement and a question.

He just stood still and held me. *Let's find our way home. We can talk best there.*

I nodded as he picked up my bag. *You look lovely, little one. All grown up. I'm not sure I would have recognized you if that mop of red hair wasn't flopping all over your head.*

I took his hand, locking his long, slender fingers with my own. I thought to myself, like it or not, Joseph, I need to hold onto you. He said nothing and gave my hand a squeeze. We walked to the car in silence—one that said everything. Whatever the days ahead would bring, I was not alone.

Driving home, Joseph followed the canal along the towpath from the Grand Canal Dock, turning left at Lower Mount Street onto the Northumberland Road. A familiar route, past the moneyed part of Dublin, where the Ascendancy, Irish Protestants who ruled the country for centuries, lived. Houses spacious and handsome bordered the tree-lined streets. Four blocks later, the neighborhood changed, where the houses, along with the privileges of birth, were much less grand. We pulled up to a red brick house, large and inviting, with windows that decreased in size the higher up they were placed. Here was the home I had always known. Mam bought this house when she first came to Dublin some 30 years ago. She started her business here. I was born here. I reminded myself not to ask the event of which she was most proud.

I followed Joseph in. Lamps were turned on, illuminating the rooms I never thought I would leave. And yet I did. Nothing had changed. Mahogany furniture polished to a shine, topped with the finest of Irish lace doilies, a picture of the Sacred Heart of Jesus smiled down from the hallway into the kitchen. There sat the ice box, white and bulky with a motor on top. Across from it and holding itself in the place of honor was Mam's cook stove. It came from America, from Sears & Roebuck, she would proudly proclaim. Patting its white enamel, she would shake her head. *I don't know what allowed me to spend all the money, but I fell in love with its picture, and I love it still today.*

My finger traced the worn oilcloth that guarded the kitchen table from spills and too-hot pans when Joseph spoke. *Found us some bread and cheese, as I didn't know how hungry you would be. I'll put the kettle on for tea.*

*Lovely. Let me get out of these travel clothes, and I will be back down in minutes.*

He nodded. *I put your bag in your room.*

My room. Painted a soft shade of cream, a little faded in places, showing the years of wear, still held my youth. My dresser displayed my school treasures, ribbons of scholarly achievement, the statue of the Blessed Virgin Mary with crystal rosary beads at her feet that Mam gave me on my First Communion Day. Framed pictures of my milestones, religious and academic. Best of all, there was my bookcase, its shelves crammed with novels, spines cracked from too many readings–Jane Austen, the Bronte sisters, Oscar Wilde–all still in their place awaiting my return.

I found my flannel pajamas and robe, slightly worn and most familiar, folded in their usual spot, the third drawer of my dresser. Everything was where it had always been.

I joined Joseph at the kitchen table. He poured our tea. I lifted my cup in mock salute. Joseph returned the gesture.

*Mam?*

Joseph shook his head slowly. *I came home to visit three weeks ago. She looked tired, but I didn't think much of it. One of the women who worked for her in the shop had died the week before, so I figured she was dealing with that.*

Joseph's eyes shut. *I should have known better.* He mumbled to himself, *I should have known better.*

I covered his hand with mine. *Joseph, you know that would have made no difference.*

He opened his eyes, looking a bit bewildered as if he hadn't expected me to be sitting across the table.

I took a bite of the bread. *And?*

*I got a phone call on Sunday from Mrs. Quinn; not sure if you know of her. She and her husband bought the Wicken's place next door about six months ago, and she and Mam are quite friendly. Mrs. Quinn was concerned as it was Sunday, and she hadn't seen Mam at Mass. She found her way in. Mam was in bed. She had a bit of a time trying to wake her up, and when she did, Mam said she was ill. Mrs. Quinn got her husband, a fireman, and he came over with a couple of his mates, and they got her to hospital. That is when I got the call.*

I felt a rush of panic and disbelief. Before I could stop it, my throat tightened, that last piece of bread stuck by a lump, cold and unyielding. I took another sip of my tea, and with a tentative swallow, the knot gave way, but the surge of despair remained.

Joseph failed to notice, he was reliving his own nightmare. *I came home that night and went to the hospital, but I wasn't allowed in; visiting hours were over. I was first in line on Monday morning and found Mam in the women's ward. She was sitting upright in the bed. She had been given some new-fangled procedure where they pump a solution into your veins. She was alert, though still pale and looking very tired.*

My voice started to tremble, my questions spilling out in a frantic rush. *How did this happen? Why didn't she tell us sooner? What did she say is wrong?*

Joseph's fingers tightened around his mug. His gaze remained fixed on the table, his brow furrowed. *She told me she was sick, and it was serious. She had not wanted me to contact you, saying that you were making your life in New York. She didn't want to stop you from making that dream come true.*

I blinked, trying to process the words, but they felt like a blur. *She is sick, and she didn't want me to know?* I was getting angry, raising both my hands and my voice.

Joseph didn't rise to the bait; he just shook his head. *I told her I wouldn't do that. Asked if positions were reversed and she was in America and her mam was ill, where would she want to be? And as only Mam does, she was quiet for a minute and then nodded, quietly saying, "Let Cate know." We agreed that it made no sense to contact Liam until we know more, him being in New Zealand and all, and agreed I would write to Andrew, asking for his prayers. Not sure the monastery where he has taken his final vows would let him leave.*

I cried, wordless. Joseph poured us more tea.

*You need to get your rest tonight, Cate. I have set up a time for us to meet with the doctor tomorrow. I've only had a brief chat, and that was to agree to wait until you came, so you could hear from him and ask your questions.*

I wasn't sure, but I thought I caught a tear falling gently down his cheek. I kissed him good night and made my way up the stairs.

———

In my room, I found the picture I was looking for. It was the only picture I had of the six of us, Mam, my da, and my three older brothers, Liam, Andrew, and Joseph. It was the oldest picture on the dresser, the frame now dusty, the photograph faded at the edges. It was my Baptism, Da was holding me, Mam smiling, Liam and Andrew, together for the last time. And Joseph not quite fifteen. My da had been married once before, so my Mam not only got a husband but three boys when she said her vows. Their mother had died giving birth to Joseph.

I have no memory of my da, he died when I was two in an accident at the mill he owned. Once, when I questioned Mam what he was really like, she responded that I only had to look at my brothers to know him. Liam had his brawn and his passion, and Andrew, his unshaking faith and compassion for others. It was Joseph, she said, that I only needed to know to understand my father. For like him, Joseph has a power within him, one that whispers rather than shouts. He can calm even the most violent storms.

I put the picture back in its place, a rare moment when we had all been together.

I crawled under the quilt and sank into the mattress. I was tired, dead tired. Despite the reason that brought me back, the comfort of being in a bed that understood my every curve melted away some of the angst. Sleep claimed me.

I woke up early the next morning. Joseph had beaten me to the kettle, and he was out for his morning run. Five miles, rain or sun. Most often rain. I looked out the window; a black and gray cloud hung over us like a bruise.

I took the journal out of my pocket, made myself a cuppa, and began to write. To write about the brother who loves Mam as I do. Who loves me. Who is here for me.

———

## Joseph

Joseph graduated in three years from the University College Dublin, where he stayed on to work as a researcher in their Mathematics Department and complete his graduate studies. Puzzles are his passion. He would come home most weekends, bringing me my own number puzzle to complete. There were columns and rows with numbers scattered in some of the blocks. I had to fill in the blanks, never using the same number twice. After Sunday dinner, he would either reward me for a job well done or show me where my logic failed. He would then quietly pass me a Hershey bar, elaborately making facial gestures warning me not to let Mam know such a treat was mine. It was chocolate. It was 1937. It was Dublin. Few could report having such an indulgence.

I was not yet 10 years old when he left the house with his packed bags. I was holding Mam's hand as we watched him walk along the canal, tall and thin, his shoulders squared, never looking back. Joseph was going to London. It sounded far away and extremely exciting to me. Like the adventures of the characters I couldn't stop reading about, even then.

I learned later that he had been sent to London to break German codes. England was once again at war, once again with Germany. Everyone knew that Joseph was the best there was at solving puzzles.

Then the Taoiseach himself, Éamon de Valera, the head of Ireland's government, its prime minister, asked him to help win the war in Europe.

Joseph told the story that at their meeting, De Valera did all the talking. He started with flattery, telling him that he was asked to find the smartest man he could to help the English break the Nazi's codes and chose Joseph. Then De Valera talked about his fear for Ireland. He believed that Belgium and Norway were only the beginning, not the end, of Hitler's tyranny. De Valera said Ireland had to be sure, had to know what the Germans were planning to do, particularly if they were looking to reach our own shores. Joseph said Dev's eyes clouded over as the patriot in him emerged. Joseph would quote his words, mimicking his voice: *We have been ruled by one country for generations. I have no intention of letting another take over our land and our language. I need you to go to London, Mr. Clark, sit with them, break the German code, and prove for the last time that an Irishman's mind and temperament are as good as any who bow and scrape before the Crown. On behalf of your fellow countrymen, thank you for doing this.*

Joseph was dismissed. He had been told, not asked, to go. He came home and packed his bag.

Joseph was miserable from the first day he set foot in London. He wrote that it was too crowded, too sooty, and had too many Englishmen. He wanted to come back home as soon as it was all over. He belonged to Dublin, or at least to Ireland. There was never a doubt in his mind.

And once home, he never left.

Yet he never imposed his views on me. He asked me only once why I was going to New York. *I have to give it a go*, was my response.

He laughed aloud, a rare gift. *That was the same response you gave me when you said you wanted to ride a two-wheel bicycle before you tried your hand at using one of your trainers. You got a few scrapes and bruises, but you figured out how to do it, and soon you were on your way, sailing around the neighborhood like you owned the road. I expect you will do the same there.* And he never asked me again.

Yet it is the same question that I ask myself today.

————

I put down the pen.

————

*Thank you, Joseph*, I murmured. *We will do what is best for Mam. Thank you for believing in me. It gives me the strength I need for whatever lies ahead.*

————

I was finishing my second cup of tea when Joseph came in, damp from both the rain and the run. *Good morning, Cate. Did you sleep?*

*Better than I thought. I think it is the smell of the sheets. Something to be said about a stiff breeze doing your drying rather than a GE contraption.*

Joseph nodded. *Aye, and better for the world around us. We should look to be at hospital around 10 or so. The doctor is expecting us to meet with him at midday. That'll give us time to talk with Mam before we meet up.*

*I'll just finish my tea and get ready.*

My fingers fumbled as I buttoned my blouse, my hands trembling. I was getting dressed to see my mother, my mother in the hospital. Would she notice what I was wearing? She had owned a successful dress shop in Dublin. She knew fabric, she knew color. Maybe she no longer cared, maybe she would no longer notice. I glanced in the mirror and ran my fingers through my hair. This would have to do. I had to get a haircut.

I exhaled, put on my shoes, and went downstairs to start this day.

We rode to the hospital in silence, each lost in our own thoughts. Joseph quietly pointed the way as we entered the building. Greystone on the outside, the inside was painted a uniformly pale green. The air was thick with the sharp tang of bleach. The biting scent stung my nose. I shivered.

Joseph and I continued in silence as we walked our way through the corridor; a reverential hush permeated the chamber. The nurses, clad in white, floated through the halls like angels without wings, making no eye contact. The matron responded to our introductions with a brief nod. Ramrod straight and without a laugh line to call her own, she brought us to the women's ward, reminding us to be respectful as Mam wasn't the only person ill. There was no compassion in her voice, no understanding that we were wrestling with the unfathomable realization that our mother was dying.

My temper flashed, my voice snapped. *Excuse me, I don't be needing you telling me how to behave. Thank you very much.*

Joseph took my arm, thanked her, and said we would be mindful. The matron never flinched, walked away, and never looked back.

Joseph whispered to me, *'Tis her business, Cate. Taking care of the sick and the dying. She's not about sympathy. She's about making sure all is in order.*

I was not to be mollified. *Kindness, Joseph. 'Twas all I needed. Kindness.*

We turned into her ward. My breath caught in my throat when I saw her lying in the bed. It was Mam, but she looked too small, too fragile, her skin too translucent.

Joseph went to her bedside and took her hand. *Morning, Mam, and a fine one it is promising to be. I brought Cate with me.*

Mam's eyes fluttered open. *My dearest children. You didn't have to come, Cate, but I am so glad you are here. It's as if a ray of sunshine has found its way into these dark quarters.*

She looked up at Joseph. *Thank you, Joseph, you always know what is best to do, especially when it means telling me I'm wrong.* Her eyes, now fully opened, twinkled as her hand reached for mine.

I couldn't find my voice. I had never seen my mam like this. She looked so old. So vulnerable.

It was Joseph who kept the conversation going. *Did you see your doctor today, Mam? Cate and I are planning to meet with him a bit later. Has anything changed that we should know about?*

Mam struggled to sit up. I went about arranging the pillows, just to do something other than stare. I still had not spoken.

She grimaced. *I am fine, just takes me a moment to get everything realigned. Thanks, my love. No doctors yet. I want to go home. To my own home. That is the message to be given to the doctor, any doctor. There is no need for me to be taking up space where someone who can get well should be. Do whatever needs to be done. Say whatever needs to be said. Just get me home.*

*You can count on that, Mam*, was Joseph's reply.

I finally found my voice, quiet but clear. *I'm home, Mam. I'm back.* Our eyes met, and Mam nodded.

Something inside me changed with saying those words, finally saying them out loud and to her. I am here for her, to see to her care. I will be by her side. It is more than a promise rooted in love and conviction. It is my vow.

I looked around. There were no chairs for us to sit in. No wonder she wants to come home. Everyone she sees is just glaring down at her as if she were some inanimate object to be scrutinized and discussed. I stood up a bit straighter. We will bring her home, no matter what, no matter how long.

Within the appointed hour, we were in the doctor's office, or a confer-ence room that was designated as such. Mam's doctor came in. He was a short, balding man with a sallow complexion and stern black eyes that were as cold as the coals they mirror. He was the male counterpart of the matron who had greeted us on our arrival. I knew he was from Scotland before he even opened his mouth. Next to him was a younger man by many years, whose complexion and countenance seemed both pleasant and agreeable, but far too young to be the decision-maker over life and death. He looked vaguely familiar, and I recognized the name once the introductions were made. *Timmy Murphy?* I repeated this after hearing him referred to as Dr. Murphy, a recent graduate of Trinity College's School of Medicine.

*Yes, Cate, one and the same. 'Tis lovely to see you after all these years.*

Joseph and the black-eyed doctor glared at both of us. I couldn't suppress a giggle and looked over at Joseph. *Timmy and I, I mean Dr. Murphy and I, went to school together as children. St. Margaret's Academy. He sent me a Valentine in third grade and left at the end of the term. I always thought he left because I broke his heart by not sending him one in return.*

The young doctor shook his head. *Well, break my heart, you did, with your red hair and temper to match. However, it was my father's transfer to head a bank in the States that tore me from your side.* A smile broke out on his face, his eyes merry with laughter.

I gave my first smile of the day. *Aye, though I think both the color and my temperament have cooled a bit these past years.*

Joseph raised one eyebrow.

I shrugged, *Just don't be asking the matron on my mam's floor if she concurs.*

*Well,* the black-eyed doctor commented, *as my countryman Burns once wrote, may auld acquaintance be forgot. Shall we begin our discussion? You are not the only patient's family I am seeing today.*

Timmy's eyes moved down to the chart in his hand, and his eyes returned to me. Their merriment replaced with a look of compassion and concern. The Scot glared, and we began.

The meeting didn't last long. There was not much conversation to be had. Mam was gravely ill. She would not get better. We were to bring her home. A doctor would be dispatched to the house once a week to check on her and give us medication to keep the pain away. That was all that could be done. The doctor started to put away Mam's file.

There was no shock in what I had heard; I had prepared for those words long before I heard them. The ache in my chest was growing more familiar. Joseph remained still.

*Any questions?* the doctor asked.

I choked out mine. *How much time?*

*Less than a year, most likely. You should plan accordingly.* With that, he shook Joseph's hand, nodded to me. We were dismissed.

Timmy gave me a measured look. *Sorry for this news, Cate, Joseph. Your mother has been an icon in the community for many a year. You will have the support of many.*

The Scottish doctor threw him a cold look.

Joseph shook Timmy's hand, *Thank you, Dr. Murphy.*

We were dismissed. We left the room.

I looked at Joseph, shell-shocked by the finality of what I had just heard and how it had been delivered. *So, there is the verdict, delivered by the executioner. If he hadn't made it as a doctor, he could have been a judge condemning folks to death without so much as a prayer or a tear.*

Joseph took my arm. *Let's get some fresh air. Better we talk about what's next before we see Mam.*

The chilly air brought a fresh stab of pain. I closed my eyes, the sting of tears sharp behind my eyelids. *It isn't fair, Joseph. She is too young;* my voice was shaky. *I don't know how I can watch her fade away. And what if I fail her, of not being enough for her in the days ahead?* I began to sob.

Joseph's voice was soft. *You won't do this alone. Not now. Not ever.* His voice broke.

Joseph, too, was grieving. I had been so consumed by what was happening to me, having to leave New York, to come back to Ireland, to care for Mam, that I hadn't noticed. It wasn't until that moment, when his voice faltered, that I realized he had been holding back for me, for Mam.

I whispered, *I know.* I didn't have to say anything more. Joseph was hurting, as I was. We will share the burden of the days ahead, differently but together.

My tears dried up. I kissed his cheek. *I would bet good money you have a plan already factored out.*

Joseph gave a quick smile. *Indeed, my lovely sister. We have to get the house ready. I thought it best to have a bed brought down from Andrew's old room and put in the parlor. Mam won't be able to make it up and down the stairs. There she can have her friends come and visit. After we tell Mam we will bring her home tomorrow, I will go back to the house and, with the help of Mr. Quinn, get the room ready. You can stay with Mam, and I will come back for you later this afternoon.*

*Perfect.* My voice was now my own. *Let's see if we can find a chair to pull next to her bed. I am not sure my standing and staring down at her works for either one of us.*

Mam had finished her lunch, or all she was going to eat of it, when we came by. I told her the good news that we would bring her home tomorrow, and Joseph explained what he intended to do.

Mam nodded. *The sooner, the better for everyone that I am home. That doctor has about as much warmth as the January winds that blow off the Cliffs of Moher.*

She pointed me to the chair that Joseph had miraculously found. *Find yourself a cup of tea and let's have a proper chat, and please, not once are you to ask me how I am feeling.*

She looked me up and down. *The look of that blouse says you bought it in New York. It is a lovely fabric, but you need a bit more color around your face. You are looking pale, love, and the Irish sun isn't going to be giving you any help. In the bottom drawer of my dresser, you'll find a flowered scarf, which will pick up the blue of the blouse and soften the look. There is also fabric left from the shop in the attic, should you be wanting to take your foot to the pedal of the sewing machine up there.*

For a fleeting moment, it was like nothing had changed. Here was Mam offering me advice as to what to wear and how to wear it. Here was Mam egging me to put my own dressmaking skills to work, a skill that had been passed down through her mother and grandmother. Here was Mam concerned with my welfare. For a fleeting moment, my mother was back as I remembered her. It was a fleeting gift and a sharper kind of grief.

I decided not to talk about what was beginning to feel like my "other life," my life in New York. That would be a discussion for a better day. Joseph would be a safer topic. I found my cup of tea and sat down.

*Last night, I got to thinking about the time when Joseph left for London to keep the world safe for democracy, or at least from the Nazis. I remember the day he left.*

Mam smiled *You were so little, and the world was on the brink of what we thought might be the end of civilization.*

*Was Joseph a spy?*

*Joseph?* Mam's eyes brightened. *Naw. I don't think so. Yet you can trust any secret in the world to him, and he'll go to his grave keeping the vow. But never a spy. But I was. Or at least a bit of one.*

I choked on my sip of tea. *Please, Mam, tell the tale.*

Mam settled back on her pillow, a smile on her face. *I am no political pundit, but the war, or the Emergency as the Irish government dubbed it, was closing in. England was being bombed, Paris had fallen, and the United States was remaining neutral. Liam and Andrew were out of the house, your father had died, Joseph was in London. I had you and the shop to look after, both were flourishing despite how the world seemed to be spiraling out of control.*

*I was closing the store when a gentleman I had never seen before entered. He greeted me with manners born of good breeding and proper schooling and handed me his card. He was from one of the government offices, as the address read Merrion Street. I was directed into the now vacant dressing room where another man was waiting. I had not let him in, but a quick look around told me nothing had been disturbed.*

I had to interrupt; Mam was alone in the store. There was no one to protect her. I had lived in New York City long enough to be wary of a stranger approaching. *Weren't you nervous? Shouldn't you have called the Gardaí?*

Mam continued, *Nay. I think it was because the man stood up as I walked in. He seemed polite and dignified. He apologized for having surprised me and hoped that none of my clients were disturbed. I was more intrigued than scared at the moment.*

*I mumbled something about him being correct when he motioned me to take a seat next to him. "Would you please join me?" I sat down immediately. He had the look of someone who was accustomed to having people do as he requested. I kept my gaze on his eyes, crystal clear blue and intense, as he continued. "I know your son is helping us put as quick an end as possible to the sadness that is clouding all of Europe."* I confirmed that Joseph was away working for the government, but we had not seen him for some time.

The gentleman nodded his head, adding, *"I understand that he is highly regarded wherever he goes, and his work is of the utmost importance."*

Mam stopped and smiled. *Do you remember when we used to get a box filled with real coffee, tea, and sugar delivered to the shop?*

I nodded. *How could I forget? A piece or two of chocolate was often included.*

Mam nodded. *There was no sender's name included, but I didn't have to take a guess as to who sent it. Joseph, using his rationing stamps to help feed us. I didn't think that was any information that this stranger needed.* She gave her head a firm nod.

*Then the man started with the reason he was there. Like they did with Joseph, he was asking me to help the government. You were too young to remember all but the chocolate. Though Ireland was neutral, there were still people in our government wanting to help in the war effort. We had declared ourselves an independent country, but were still walking a tightrope as to our standing in the broader world.*

I had to interrupt. *But you never went away. I would have remembered if you had left home.*

Mam smiled. *The gentleman was clear that he was not asking me to do anything that would put me or my family in danger. Having calmed my fears, he stroked my ego. I remember his words now: "What we do know is that your ladies' shop has the highest of reputations and your clients come from the Ascendancy and powerful government and international families."*

*His talking about Joseph had made him less terrifying; his comments on the shop made me want to hear more. I relaxed. But only for the moment, for the next sentence out of his mouth took my breath away. "If I am correct, Mrs. Gray, the wife of the U.S. representative here is a valued client, as is Mrs. Hempler, the wife of the German emissary. And women do talk."*

I nodded, remembering my days in the shop. *That I can attest to. I can remember all the chatter, a combination of gossip and laughter. Along with the repetitive sound of high heels clicking on the tiled floor.*

Mam chuckled. *And that was exactly what my mysterious visitor was asking for. He wanted the gossip. His words were direct and clear. "We are merely asking you to pass on any information that you may hear in casual conversation that could be useful. You do not need to pry or seek clarification. If you hear something, just send a note to Mr. Reilly, whose card you now have in your possession. He will meet you for a cup of tea or a walk in St. Stephen's Green. All in the public eye. And unlike what you see in the cinema or read in novels, there will be no cloaks or daggers. You will simply be giving us the benefit of hearing what you heard. You will be doing your country a favor, one that it will not forget."*

I agreed quickly. To be truthful, I was flattered to be singled out. It proved that the reputation of the shop was well-founded and solid. The stranger thanked me and stood up.

I put my hand out to stop him. "One thing, sir, our Taoiseach's wife is also a regular client. I am assuming that if I learn anything about Mr. De Valera's predilections or predictions, those I should keep to myself?"

My stranger's cheeks turned a bit rosier. "You live up to your reputation, Mrs. Clark. Not only are you clever with a needle, but you are also acutely aware when it would be best to keep certain information for your ears only."

I clapped my hands and got an evil look from one of the passing nurses. I didn't care. This was my mam, and she was sounding just like my mam. *So, what happened next?*

*He shook my hand, Mr. Reilly appeared at his side, and both of them walked out the back door.*

*There were only a few occasions when I thought certain information might be of interest. Most of my clients were more concerned with how they looked and the price of the frock than what was happening in the world around them. I found Frau Hempler to be an excellent woman. I cannot say the same for her American counterpart, Mrs. Gray. That woman dropped more names than I did pins. She was an embarrassment to her country, thinking she was the most important person in the room. Her belief in her own beauty was as obvious as it was misplaced. She blamed the dress rather than her features and her shape for the reflection in the mirror.*

———

When she was finished. Mam closed her eyes and fell asleep. Joseph arrived within minutes, her breathing now regular and relaxed. She was still asleep when we kissed her goodnight and left.

I shared the story with him on our way home.

*Think about doing more of this, Cate. Asking Mam about her life. A life we are a part of but know so little about.*

*Agreed*, my only reply.

I came home to a parlor that had been transformed into a bedroom. A room that was ready for our mother to come home to, and the one she would die in.

*It is incredible, Joseph. You have worked a miracle.*

*Thanks goes to Mr. Quinn and his fire brigade. A team of them arrived and within minutes, furniture was moved, a night table found, and the unneeded remnants of our seldom-used parlor safely moved out of the public eye. Mrs. Quinn brought over two dinners: Irish stew with crusty bread for tonight and a Shepherd's Pie in the icebox for tomorrow.*

*Bless these neighbors,* was my response as my mouth began to salivate and my stomach growled from the smell emanating from the simmering pot of stew. *And did you remember the whiskey?*

*In the cupboard, awaiting our arrival. I will pour. With or without ice?*

I winked. *With. You forget I live in the States now.*

Joseph was breaking the bottle's seal when there was a knock at the door.

*Half-seven, a bit late for callers,* was Joseph's comment as he went to the door holding the bottle. Then I heard his voice, *Well, good evening, Dr. Murphy. Cate and I were just about to open this whiskey bottle. Would you care to come in and join us?*

I looked up to see Joseph leading Timmy, aka Dr. Murphy, to the table. The years have served him well. Well over six feet in height, with eyelashes thick as paint brushes framing his light brown eyes. His dark hair was cut too close, a sure sign that his morning shower needed to be quick with no time for a fuss at the mirror. He had the look of a scholar about him, a man who would be more comfortable reading a book than dealing with a crowd of people. He reminded me a bit of Joseph.

He came over, kissing me on both cheeks. *As I said this afternoon, it is lovely to see you again, Cate, though it took years for my heart to mend.*

My response was equally as merry. *It is good to know that your years in the States didn't keep your Irish tongue from losing the blarney. It is good to see you, as well. Can I still call you Timmy? As long as Dr. Black Eyes and Cold Heart is not within earshot?*

This time it was Timmy's turn to laugh. *You may call me whatever you please, whenever you like. Most call me Tim, but family and friends still revert to Timmy. I am pleased to have you as part of that circle. And you, as well, Joseph,* nodding to my brother who was opening the bottle with a barman's finesse, its neck finding its match with the mouth of the glass. Amber gold liquid poured thickly into the opening.

We clinked our glasses as Tim toasted: *To our mams. A generation of women who will never have their equal.* We took a first sip.

Tim put his glass down. *I can account for Dr. Campbell's behavior. If it brings any comfort, he is like that with all his patients and their families. He is, however, a brilliant physician and teacher for the likes of residents like me. He is brutal to deal with, and one false step and you are removed. Medically, your mam is in the best of hands, and he will be sure that she is given the right medications to ease her pain.*

*I offered to be her attending physician, which translates into my coming to the house once a week to examine her. I wanted to be sure that would be okay with you before the role is finalized.*

I clapped my hands. *That would be perfect. We know you. We trust you. Mam'll be comfortable with you. It would be as if she were talking to the son of one of her chums, rather than someone wearing a white robe. Joseph and I were just about to dive into the Irish stew our neighbor kindly brought over. Would you like to join us for supper?*

Timmy looked at Joseph, who nodded his agreement. *I would love that. It is not often I get a chance to sit down to a home-cooked meal, and with such lovely company.*

*Are your folks in Ireland?* I asked.

*Yes, but not in the house you would remember. When my parents returned from the States, they moved to Dún Laoghaire, a lovely spot but too far away from Dublin proper for me. I live on Pearse Street, so I can walk anywhere. My brother lives near them with his daughter. He is a widower, with a six-year-old wee lass. My folks think she is the sun and the moon. My sister Deidre is a Maryknoll nun and is somewhere in Africa. So, Mary Ellen, whom we call Molly, is the only grand they have to spoil. At least for the moment.*

Joseph refilled our glasses, a golden ember filling Mam's finest crystal. I hadn't realized he was using the 'good' glasses.

Joseph nodded in Timmy's direction. *I remember your brother, a bit older than you. A great hurler, if I recall, even as a young lad. He was large and strong for his age, but could sprint like a deer. He could pluck the ball out of the air and run with it in a single movement that was beautiful to see.*

*That's him, Jack. All sports came easy to him; seems he got all the athletic talent. I found my way to the library and the lab and was content to let him roll in the mud.*

Though smiling, I noticed a small shadow finding its way to Timmy's face.

*Yet now his load is a bit much to carry; his wife died suddenly when Molly was but a toddler. She barely remembers her mam, Jack is both ma and da to her. And once again, he is a star.*

The talk of death was hitting too close. I changed the subject, as we dove into the simmering stew. *Do you miss living in the States?*

*Not at all,* was his quick reply. *Ireland has its own pace, its own sense of time.*

*Much more to my speed and my liking. And you, Cate? I hear you have been living in New York.*

I smiled. *Yes, but I am home now. Home will always be Ireland. Home will always be this house.*

Joseph raised his eyebrows just a tad.

We were finishing up the meal when Timmy offered the best remedy for my nerves about caring for Mam. *If you like, I know one of the nurses at the hospital who is looking for extra work. If you are flexible with your scheduling, she could assist in the evenings in getting your mam down for the night. I can confirm with her tomorrow. Joseph, you could meet with her while you are back there.*

Joseph simply nodded. *That sounds like a plan. Mr. Quinn and his mates are meeting me there at ten in the morning, so I will be there by nine to meet with her.*

Tim mirrored the nod. *That should do. I will find you and make the introduction.*

Two hours later, Timmy looked at his watch. *Best be going. I have a twelve-hour shift starting at 8:00 a.m. tomorrow. If there's any problem about bringing your mam home, just ask for me. The stethoscope hanging around my neck sometimes gives me an authority that others respect.*

I stood up and gave him a hug and a kiss on the cheek. *Thank you, Timmy. Tonight has been great craik. We are going to take you up on your offer to find nursing care for Mam. A couple of hours at the end of the day would be fine. I am quite over my head when it comes to caregiving.*

*I doubt that,* Tim replied, his face flushed with a color like the morning's first light. *I believe you can do anything you set your mind to do. I will see you next week. Good luck tomorrow, and if I can be of any help,* looking at Joseph, *you need only to ask.*

Joseph walked him to the door. He met me at the sink and proceeded to wash the dishes, as I picked up the towel to dry. These were our customary roles. Not much had changed except that Mam wasn't here to supervise.

Joseph looked over at me. *Two things I need to tell you. First, I have hired a couple to come on weekday mornings beginning Monday. Mrs. Murray will cook and clean and give you a hand with Mam. Mr. Murray will keep the house up, run any errands, and do whatever is needed.*

I started to protest. Joseph raised his hand. *I need to go back to the university and will be staying in my own place during the week. I don't want you here all that time with Mam alone. You will need to go out for a walk and get some fresh air, have a luncheon, perhaps even see some old school chums. I will be back Friday afternoon and will stay through Monday morning. All is arranged. The*

*Murrays will be here tomorrow, so I can introduce you to them as they will start on Monday.*

I nodded my agreement. The concern I had about my caretaker role eased with the thought of having others around to assist.

*And the second?*

Joseph chuckled. *You need to go out tomorrow and buy a Valentine.*

*A Valentine? What are you talking about?*

*I am talking about poor besotted Dr. Timothy Murphy, recently of Trinity's Medical School. I fear that you are poised once again to break his heart. Best to have the card bought and stamped.*

He dodged the damp towel I threw at him.

I stayed downstairs after Joseph went to bed.

I walked from room to room, extinguishing lights, trying hard once again to commit everything to memory.

I sat at my desk, the same one where I studied for my A-Levels. Pulling out the journal, I thought about Mam's story. I don't remember much about that time, a time when our government was censoring the press and Ireland was posturing itself as a neutral party, as war was devastating England and Europe. Mam and Joseph had helped. They had been willing to make a difference. My thoughts turned across the sea, to Teddy and Faith. And to the headlines of what is happening there.

———

## Challengers

A war was being fought; men and women were making sacrifices for the world to be a safer place. Joseph left all behind him to help save the world from tyranny. Mam found her own way to help. Nell put herself in danger to expose a world of greed and corruption. Teddy flew a plane into enemy territory and suffered the consequences.

Less than twenty years later, Faith is a victim of finger-pointing and the whispered, damning accusation of being a Communist. Her only crime is that she wants a world where a person is not harangued for what they believe, a world where people can stand for something that matters to them without fear of reprisal. A world where people can disagree without being disagreeable.

These people, so different and so important to me, care about the common good. I am not a staunch supporter of the status quo or those who never question the government. I question pronouncements from the pulpit and societal roles that were defined in another time. But I wonder if I would rise to have my voice heard. If I can be counted on to lend a hand in times of crisis.

Perhaps I will not know until, like Mam, a stranger knocks on my door and needs my help.

———

I put down the pen.

———

The next morning at 8:00 a.m., Mr. and Mrs. Murray arrived. He was a stout man with old-fashioned whiskers and a country accent as strong as the day he left his native Cork. Years of living in Dublin had only changed his girth and the size of his moustache. She had bright red hair, clearly from a bottle rather than the color deemed by the Creator. I couldn't suppress a giggle because she had tucked a feather duster into her waistband above her ample backside. It bore a great resemblance to a tail, giving her the appearance of a mother hen.

She gave me a strong hug. *Such a pretty thing you are. And so heavy a heart to bear for one so young. We will be here for you. I am ready to begin even now*, as she pulled the duster from its nesting place. I already felt I belonged to Mrs. Murray's flock.

This all made sense. I knew it would work, even before Joseph outlined the agreed-upon arrangements. They would be with me Monday through Friday, 8:00 a.m. to 1:00 p.m. We agreed that we would call them Mr. M and Mrs. M, blending just the right amount of familiarity with the respect for elders that had been ingrained in us from childhood.

They left shortly thereafter. They had come to meet me before Mam came home. Joseph then left with Mr. Quinn, whom we now called Sean, for the hospital. Mrs. Quinn arrived at the door with a kettle of chicken broth with rice. *For your mam. I think there is enough there for a couple of meals or so.*

She looked as if she had left the house in a hurry; her hair was a disheveled tumble of raven curls, pulled into a haphazard ponytail that couldn't stay in its clip. Her apron, speckled with the stains of milk, oatmeal, and something unidentifiable, spoke to a morning of unbridled chaos.

I asked her to come and join me for a cuppa, and she ruefully declined the invitation. *If only I could, love, but I fear leaving the boys alone for too long a time is inviting the devil to come callin'. If the three of them are together unsupervised, Saints preserve me, one may end up mangled for life. I grew up with all sisters, so getting your point across with your fists rather than your words is not what I am used to. They're off to school on Monday to see if the good nuns can instill some discipline into them, so let me stop by then.*

*If she's able, I'd love to see your mam. She is the most wonderful neighbor. And please call me Patricia, and I will call you Cate. I heard so much about you from your mam that I know we'll be friends.*

I smiled. *I am sure of it.* The soup now safely placed on the stove, I walked her to the door. *Until Monday. Any time.*

Two hours later, Mam was home, being carried in by Joseph and Sean. I liked him immediately. He looked like a poster boy for the fire brigade, strong jawline, high cheekbones, and a look about him confirming he was ready to leap into action, whether it be a blazing building or calling for a pint at the local pub.

Mam's eyes filled with tears as she sat in her chair. *Home. I am home and never intend to leave. No matter what. I have a clean nightie in my dresser, third drawer. Cate, can you help me put it on? Joseph and Sean, thank you, and please leave us be. The trip has exhausted me, and this bed looks most inviting.*

I retrieved the garment. Removing her clothes took time as she was both tired and in pain. Once I got her settled, Mam laid down and was sleeping before her head hit the pillow. The word home sounding like an amen forming on her lips.

———

### The Parlor

Today, we settled Mam into the parlor. The couch was moved, the chairs rearranged, a bed carried down the stairs, a table put by its side. It is now her place. A place of rest, a place to say goodbye. I helped her into the bed, smoothing the covers the way she used to for me when I was little and afraid of the dark. Sitting by her side,

I traced the bones of her hand, memorizing the shape I have known all my life. I know, with a certainty, Mam will not leave this room.

This is the beginning of an ending that is already breaking my heart.

———

I put down the pen.

———

I woke up the next morning. Joseph having gone to the early Mass and had just returned from his run. I asked if it was the same priest on the altar.

*No, a new one, Father Flanagan. Not much of a preacher, but he knows his Latin, so the Mass goes quickly. He is planning on coming by the house to see Mam on Wednesdays.*

My family goes to Mass on Sunday; it is what we do. Being Catholic is not simply what I believe, or what I was taught to believe; it helps define who I am. The ritual of the Mass is a source of comfort. I follow the Latin passage translations in my missal; sometimes I am spot on, other times either too quick or too slow. I don't think that our Lord cares. I stand, sit, and kneel at the appointed times. Just as I was taught.

Everyone I know here in Dublin, my friends, my classmates, does the same. We graduated from Catholic schools. Our prizes were religious medals. There was no other choice given. It wasn't until I went to New York was I ever asked why I believed what I believed. It was August 15th, the feast of the Assumption of Mary, and I was at work. I left my desk to go to the noon Mass, and I was running late. One of my co-workers asked where I was off to; I explained I was going to church and why. She asked if I truly believed Mary was assumed into heaven, and, if so, what did she look like at the time. *She would have had to be an old woman, so did she go straight up, or had her arthritis set in, and she was bent at the waist?*

I had to laugh. I responded *Never thought about it. Still going, however.* And that is probably how I would describe my faith today. I believe because I have always believed. My brother Andrew is a priest, after all. Though truth be told, he never told me why.

The church stands at the heart of my neighborhood, its grey stone spires reaching for today's overcast sky. I received all of my sacraments in this church, starting with my Baptism. The old wooden door creaked as I pushed it open, the scent of old incense clinging to the wooden pews. Statues of saints, whose names I used to know by heart, line the walls, remaining silent and never aging. The soft rustling of rosary beads and the shuffling of parishioners looking for their usual seats, were the only sounds that broke the stillness. Nothing in the church had changed since I left, except the priest. I knelt down with my eyes lifted to the altar, making the sign of the cross. I smiled, thinking that I was both an anomaly, a returnee from the land of streets paved with gold, and a parishioner needing sympathy as her mam was ill.

Following the last blessing, it was as if I were in the receiving line. Hands, hugs, and nods came from people whose faces I recognized but whose names I couldn't recall. The one, however, I immediately recognized and knew well, was Nora. She had worked in the dress shop when Mam first opened and had stayed on until her eyes and her back would no longer allow.

Nora is not a woman who has aged gracefully. She simply got older, her skin as thin as parchment. Her face not only looks like she has weathered the storm, but that the storm has also weathered her. Her glasses are so thick that they magnify her eyes, making them seem in a perpetual state of surprise. She hugged me. *So good to see you, my lovely. Once your mam is home and settled, I would like to come by. Elizabeth, too. She is visiting her sister in Roscommon and will be back in a fortnight. Would that be good for ya?*

I hugged her back, her arms cradled me like in years gone by. *She came home yesterday, and I am sure she would love to see you both. Let's plan for the week after next. Would Tuesday work? Say around 10 a.m.?*

*Tuesday of that week it is. And if that day and time doesn't work, we'll find another.*

She gave me another quick squeeze and was gone.

The rest of Sunday passed quickly and quietly. I prepared a list of groceries for Mr. M to attend to come Monday. I sat and read. I wrote to Nell, Teddy, and Faith. New York seemed a world away. It was. *This is your new world*, I thought, *a combination of what was, what is, and what is yet to come.*

Mam seemed content. Awake only long enough to take a bit of soup and her medications, she seemed to be catching up on the sleep that had failed her during her stay in the hospital.

Monday morning dawned bright, and I was up and dressed before Mr.

& Mrs. M arrived. Mam had slept through the night and was just waking up when I came into what I now thought of as her room. Joseph had left well before dawn to return to his everyday life. I was now in charge. I neither felt up to it nor stunned by it. The day would bring whatever it was going to bring.

After the couple had been introduced to Mam, Mrs. M immediately took over the kitchen. The kettle was on, and she found all that was needed to make our tea. She was making Mam's soft egg while I opted for toast with jam; the thought of a real Irish breakfast overwhelmed both my mind and stomach. Next on the to-do list was to get Mam washed and cleaned up for the day. Mrs. M once again had it all in hand. She brought a warm tub of water to the table and, with my help, removed Mam's night clothes. Mam's back was softly scrubbed, her hair washed and brushed. She asked for her dark green dress. Within the hour, Mam was looking more like herself, sitting up in the chair, with a touch of lipstick on her lips. I looked out the window to see Mr. M. pruning the overgrown shrubbery.

*Thank you, Joseph, this is all down to you,* I silently whispered.

Mam was alert as I sat in the chair next to her, shaking her head no at the offer of another cup of tea. Remembering what Joseph said about knowing more about her life, I started. *Mam, tell me how you came to live in Dublin. I know Teddy was born here and then went back to New York and was raised by Nell and her husband Edward. But why did you come and why did you stay? You have never told me.*

She gave me the same look she would throw at me as a child when I did or said something unexpected. Mam looked out the window. I thought she was going to stay silent. Then, keeping her gaze fixed to the world outside, she began.

*It was a long time ago. I was not quite 17. Let me tell you first about Billy Conlon, Teddy's father and my first husband.*

I felt that I was about to read an article in *True Confessions*. I knew I couldn't be taking notes, so my level of concentration and attention brought me back to my days sitting in the classroom.

Mam smiled as the years dwindled away. *Even at an early age, I had a weakness for 'bad boys'—tall, dark, and passionate, who believed in a cause greater than who they were. There was a fire in their blood that sparked me. I was a bit of a do-gooder, never one to get in trouble, never crossing the line. After my mother died and later my father, I was basically on my own. So, I had to navigate safely within the lines.*

I knew that my grandmother died on the Titanic. She had been some-what of a heroine. Mam once read me a letter from one of the survivors. *I remember the letter, Mam. The writer was a young pregnant girl on that crossing, and Gran had made the young girl take her own spot on the lifeboat, saving that girl's life and that of her baby.*

*You remember well, Cate. That letter is in my desk. I read it each year on my mother's birthday.* Mam closed her eyes. *My mother was wonderful, kind, and tough all at the same time. Characteristics that have been transferred down to all the women in our family.* I got another smile.

I wanted to bring her back to the story. *So, Billy Conlon was a line-crosser?*

*Oh yes, for sure. A Protestant and a Unionist. In my family, only Satan himself would be any worse.*

I couldn't help but gasp. A Protestant? I had only known a few until I went to New York. They were what the good nuns used to label "a near occasion of sin." I quickly regained my composure. *And you fell in love?*

*Head over heels. Billy was smart, caring, and committed to making a difference in the world. He was charming, intense, and complex. There wasn't a moment of the day that I wasn't thinking about him.*

I nodded. *That sounds a lot like Teddy. I imagine that his father's blood runs through his veins, as well.*

Mam didn't comment. It was as if her thoughts once again were focused on Billy Conlon. *At the time we met, I was employed at one of the more fashionable homes in New York as their seamstress. It was a household of women, and the man of the family had no problem hiring someone to make sure those who bore his name were well clad. I was off on Wednesday afternoons and Sundays. I spent my Wednesdays with Nell Walker and her friends talking about the history of Ireland, a topic that Nell was keenly interested in. My Sundays were reserved for Billy. I never asked how he spent the days when we weren't together.*

*We were so young, so sure of ourselves. In less than two months, we decided we would marry. We both knew what that meant. Neither family would accept us. Billy's family was part of the English establishment in Ulster, loyal to the Crown and taking up arms to defend their right to remain part of the king's empire. My family was staunch Catholics, had no use for the English or the Irish who thought of themselves as such. In deciding to wed, we knew that the road would be rocky, but we were in love and believed we would overcome any obstacles that might be thrown our way.*

I needed to pause, to think about all I had heard. *I could use another cuppa, Mam. And you?*

*No, Cate, I am fine. This is a lot, and I am not even close to finishing. You take your tea, and I will rest my eyes.*

I sat quietly in the kitchen, cradling the warm cup of tea in my hands. Each sip was slow and deliberate. My mind was racing, replaying the words that I had just heard. My mother once loved a man—someone so different, so forbidden. Part of me is in disbelief. The woman she describes is foreign to me. She has a past that I could never have imagined. My feelings were all jumbled. Her story, this story, was not just about love; it is about politics and religion. She fell in love with someone who stood for everything her family opposed.

The tea grew cold in the cup. Maybe it was more than just love Mam experienced. Maybe it was also freedom. And courage. Free to be different. Courage to live another kind of life. Perhaps, my quest is not so different, my searching to find my way.

I need Mam to finish the story. I need to better understand who she was to understand who she is today. And, perhaps, who I am as well.

———

Mam opened her eyes just as I found my way back to her room. I brought her a fresh cup of tea and a small piece of Mrs. M's brown bread. We sat in comfortable silence while she finished both.

I began. *So, you and Billy Conlon were married in New York?*

*Indeed, by a justice of the peace. So, how many lines did I cross that day? I didn't care. I loved him. He loved me. I was convinced that we would rewrite the ending to "Romeo & Juliet."*

*Ah, Mam,* my voice smiling, *my English literature studies would caution that the Bard might well take exception to that.*

Mam smiled back. *Remember, I was young, older than Juliet, but not by much. And trust me, I never was the type to drink a vial of fake poison and hope for the best.*

I nodded. *So, what happened?*

*He was killed.*

*Oh no! In New York?*

Mam's eyes took on a faraway gaze. *No, he had come back to Ireland, and I was to join him once he had found a place for us to live. I read about his death weeks later in an Irish newspaper. He had been shot by the IRA. They were after his uncle, his mother's brother, to whom he bore a strong resemblance. The IRA thought his uncle a spy, while Billy thought him a great patriot. The IRA got the wrong man. They shot my Billy. I was a widow before I could boast that I was a bride.*

Mam's eyes closed.

*Does Teddy know about this?* I couldn't believe what I just heard. This sounded like a tragic romance novel, with my mother as the main character.

Mam's eyes remained shut. *He does now.*

She opened her eyes, her voice trembling slightly. *When I read the news about Billy, my world went black. The only place I could think to go was Nell's. The same house you were living in. She was kind, letting me stay with her and her husband, Edward, and grieve. It was while I was staying with them that I found out I was pregnant. I had nowhere to turn. I couldn't go back to my uncle's house, where I had boarded after my own pa's death, and Billy's family knew nothing about me. I knew I couldn't appear on their doorstep, pregnant and a papist.*

I reached for her hand. *Oh, Mam. You were so young. You had to be so scared.*

*I was, but I was surrounded by women who cared. Nell, Victoria, and Anne were with me when I found out the news.*

I nodded at the sound of their names. Mam had just identified Nell's two best friends.

*When Nell heard the news, she blurted out that she and Edward would take the baby. We were all stunned by the pronouncement. They had been married a long time but had no children. Nell had never talked about wanting a child, so I needed to be sure she meant it. And I to be sure that I could give up the baby.*

*I am not sure any of us got sleep that night. Nell and Edward talked, while I carefully thought through my options. I was single. I was poor. I was pregnant. I had few choices.*

*The morning sun shone brightly that day. I took it as an omen. We had each come to our own conclusion. I would give up my child, Billy's child. Nell and Edward would take our baby and raise it as their own. I had two stipulations: the baby would be born in Ireland, and Nell would take him or her as soon as I had given birth. I didn't know I had a boy until I received a letter from Nell after the war saying that Teddy wanted to meet me. And so, we did. And then he met you.*

I got up and kissed her. *Indeed, we have become remarkably close. He is the best of men. And now that I think about it, he is truly a blend of both you and Nell. Nature and nurture brought together to produce the finest of men.*

Mam squeezed my hand. *Yes indeed. But no one who has ever given away a child can know the bitter desolation and burning guilt of that act.*

Mam pointed to the bed. *I need to rest.*

I helped her back to the bed, saying only to myself, *She has lived more lives than most do in their entire lifetime.*

I sat at the kitchen table, my fingers curled around the rim of the teacup, my thoughts jumbled.

This was a conversation I had not expected. It was one that I couldn't share with Joseph. It was a conversation only women understand. That might not be fair. But then neither was the killing of Billy Conlon. Neither was the fact that Mam had few, if any, real choices.

———

## Mam's Story

What does it mean to love such as Mam had loved? To give your heart to someone, knowing that your worlds could collide. A world not of fairy tales and happy endings, but a world where family histories and prejudices were the very fabric that wove your life.

To give up a child was a memory that still haunted her. The truth was simple and painful. Mam had no choice. Not in this.

I understand, as I never understood before, that there are moments in this world that just being a woman might strip me of the right to do what I want to do. It wasn't fair then. It isn't fair now.

There are rules that need to be rewritten.

I'm not sure what I can do, particularly now. But it is time to take on the red pencil and begin to edit, to change what needs to be changed. To have both the freedom and courage to act as needed.

———

I put down the pen.

———

The aide started that evening. Her name is Bridget Dolley, and she is lovely, the eldest of seven. Her mother was recently widowed, so Bridget is looking for extra work to help the family. It was the same on weekends. I asked if it was too much, seven days a week with no break.

*No, Miss,* was her reply. *We need the money.*

*Well, if you need time off, just let me know. And please call me Cate. I believe we are about the same age and should see ourselves as a team.*

*Thank you, Miss. Best if we still keep it formal, but you are to call me Bridget.*

I paused. I knew there was a difference in our positions, but hearing it so plainly acknowledged struck a chord inside me.

———

## The Enemy in the House

It is when the evening is done and all is quiet that it hits me. My mother is dying. I can barely write the words, lest think about what they mean. There are moments when I see her trying to hide the pain. I want to fix it, to make it all go away.

Cancer is a silent invader, the unseen thief in the night, robbing me of my mother, the woman who could handle anything. This is not an enemy you can face head-on. I watch the woman who once stood so strong begin to fade.

Yet Mam is still with me. I need to focus on what I have—the moments we still have—the touch of her hand, her gentle kiss when we say good night, the stories she can still tell.

I understand how precious these days are.

———

I put down the pen.

———

The next morning, I asked Mam about the shop. *Ah, now there's a story. I am too tired this morning. Later I'll be ready for the tellin'.*

That afternoon, I asked again, reminding her that it was the shop that got her the role of the spy. She closed her eyes. *I need to take you back with me, to a time before the shop.*

Mam's voice grew stronger; she was going back to a time, a time of change not just for her but in the world. *Ireland was at war with England when I first got here. There was fighting everywhere, but I had my own demons to battle and paid little attention. After Nell left with the baby and I found my strength, I made my way to a small village with only a grocer and a pub to call its own. There was a row of cottages, but only one had a roof and a chimney that didn't look as if it had been eaten by the weather. The entire town looked unraveled, like a piece of knitting. I felt at home immediately. That is where I stayed. I was living with one foot in the world of the living and the other in the world of the lost. It made for a ghastly equilibrium.*

*As the months wore on, I began to heal. It was at the same time that Michael Collins and his entourage were in London negotiating a peace treaty, the Anglo-Irish Treaty. I was far removed emotionally from all the controversy that came with its signing in 1922. Though peace was not yet ready to come to this island, I was ready to move on. I was thinking about the future rather than mourning the past. I wanted my own shop. A store with my name on it.*

I needed to understand. I broke in. *And you decided on Dublin to set up the shop?* I was trying to understand why she chose this city, a city where she had never lived.

Mam nodded. *My first business decision, and the right one. I knew it wasn't just about putting thread into a needle. I knew how to do that better than anyone. I needed to be practical. I wanted a business. I had to think and act differently. I had to think about costs. Thanks to Nell and Edward's generosity, I was well-positioned to start the business, but it had to make money. It had to be in a city where the ladies could afford the clothes I intended to make.*

*If there was one thing I had learned growing up in New York, money in your pocket makes a difference. A difference in how you look, how you feel about yourself, and how others treat you. Particularly if you are a woman.*

I made a mental note. Mam wasn't just a woman who had owned a business; she had built it. I had never thought about money; we always seemed to have enough. I thought about Bridget, needing to work two jobs to help her family. More to think about. For now, Mam was continuing with her story.

*First, I had to find a place to live. A place to call my own. I would start the business there and then move on.*

Mam opened up her arms as if in an embrace. *I knew this house was mine the first time I saw it. Like me, it needed to repair itself. It was dark, hollow, and unloved. The front yard was dominated by large, unruly bushes, whose job it was to block any light from entering. Across the street, a pond had been drained, antici-pating the need for future buildings that never materialized. Confused ducks would come by, meandering about while searching for their ancestral home. I could relate to their sense of loss. They confirmed my decision. This was the place. This was where I would begin.*

*Once I signed the papers, I hired men to make it happen, men out of work too long who needed money. I had cash, something few had in Ireland during that time, so most were willing to take the offer I extended. The house needed to look inviting, stylish but not pretentious, modern, while still timeless. The same message I wanted my dresses to make.*

*I drew up the plans I wanted. These gents weren't accustomed to taking orders from a woman. If I found one that paid me no mind or made snide comments about my gender, it was his last day.*

I clapped my hands. *Well done, Mam.*

Mam nodded, and a smile of satisfaction swept her face.

*I spent my days away from the hammering and the swearing by walking the streets of Dublin. Grafton Street, with its thoroughfare of dressmakers, furriers, and jewelers, was my schoolroom. I looked at what everyone was wearing. The men were dressed in suits ranging from Savile Road tailoring to charity castoffs. The prosperous wore shiny top hats; the others sported bowlers; a small few donned the cap. Fashionable women in long, narrow skirts with eye-catching hats and pristine gloves shouted wealth and privilege without speaking a word. These ladies saun-tered arm-in-arm, making their way up towards St. Stephen's Green. Some wore light wool coats, the color of the spring soil that was ready to be turned over; others draped themselves in fine silk shawls in myriads of colors.*

I could see Mam there. Her eyes flitting from woman to woman, assessing, calculating, considering every dress, every detail. She was an artist with a sharp eye, taking in the world around her. A world where her future awaited.

Mam continued without interruption. *I would turn the corner, making my way to Trinity College, where the wardrobes and the posture of the women waiting for the tram changed. Here, the women, with faces marked by determination and grit, their shoulders sagging with the weight of the bag of cabbages and potatoes needed for the evening's supper, were dressed the same as their grandmothers. No fine fabrics pulled together with silk threads, but sturdy, practical clothes, to be worn again and again. I learned they were called the 'shawlies' and you would find them nestled quietly in the snugs each evening, sipping their shandies. I knew who I had to capture to pay my way, and I knew who I wanted to spend my evenings talking with.*

Mam reached out and took my hand. *Cate, could you fetch me a glass of water? I don't believe I have talked this much for this long, in many a day.*

I went into the kitchen, my thoughts focusing on what I was hearing, recognizing that these conversations are a gift. I am seeing my mother as a person I never really knew. A woman of resilience and passion, a woman who was making her own way. A woman with a plan. A businesswoman.

Mam took a sip from the glass I handed her.

*Are you up to finishing the tale, Mam? I love that we are sitting in the very same place that you were creating all those years ago.*

*I'm fine, dear. Let's see, where was I? Ah, yes, at the end of three months, I was ready. These rooms still pay homage to how they began. This parlor was a dressing area and the dining room, home to sewing machines and cutting tables. Only the kitchen wasn't touched.*

*Once it was all done, I sat at the drawing table and poured myself a glass of Ireland's finest whiskey. I needed to draw my first design, in my new home, in my new business. This was the real beginning.*

Mam's eyes told her story; they were bright and alert. *My goal was to be alluring while still practical. This design needed to be the calling card to attract the clientele I was looking to obtain. After almost biting my bottom lip off, the pattern came to life. It was as if it were ready to be born and see the light of day. It was simple yet chic. I remember looking up, the sun was fighting its way to stay in the last minutes of daylight. I felt ready for whatever was next.*

Mam had more to tell, but she was tired. She lay down to rest. Bridget arrived, and we put her down for the night.

———

**Returning**

I went upstairs to the sewing room on the third floor. Once the home of vibrant fabrics and fine stitches, this is the space where she made my dresses that I wore to formal dances, graduations, and Christmas mornings. The door opened with a gentle push.

It was here that Mam taught me her craft. Her hands guided mine the first time I sat at a sewing machine, my feet barely able to reach the pedal. It was here she taught me patience, precision, and the pride of completing something you started.

I picked up a piece of fabric, one that had been carefully folded and forgotten. I stood in front of the mirror, envisioning the dark blue silk on my form, how it would fall, and what would be needed to complete its creation. This is my heritage. I am descended from generations of women who didn't just stitch garments but created them.

Tomorrow I will ask Mr. M to see about the sewing machine. I will try to go back in time to work on the skill that I once had. The skill that Mam once had.

I had the time. There was no excuse.

———

I put down the pen.

———

The next morning, the bright skies called me to exercise my legs. Mrs. M had everything under control, and I wanted fresh air and the sun on my face. I wanted to take a walk like Mam described, one where you were part of a crowd but observing how they looked and conjuring your imagination as to how they lived their lives.

Without any plan, I found myself on O'Connell Street, near where Mam had eventually moved her shop. O'Connell, with its storied past, is now the heartbeat of the city. This was the place of revolution, of moments of pride and pain. My mind turned not to the folks who walked the streets with me, but to the heroes of the 1916 Rising. Here, Patrick Pearse stood on the steps of the General Post Office and declared Ireland free for both men and women. His words were heard by few, but those who joined with him would be brutally executed by the British. It was that act that stirred the patriotic juices of their fellow countrymen and the outrage from others outside their island.

Mam was here during that time, but on the outside looking in. I had never thought of her being in Ireland or even Dublin during that time. I knew the history, had memorized the names of the martyrs, but had never thought about what it would have been like to live through it.

Men and women rushed by me. Sounds of children playing in parks filled the air. I started to think about the "what ifs." What if no one had taken up the cause? What if Ireland were not its own country? What if I had lived during that time?

I need to ask more. I need to learn more. I don't want to know facts. I want to know how it felt.

———

When I came home, Mr. M found me. He said that the sewing machine needed nothing more than a good cleaning and a bit of oil. He deemed it in fine working condition. I couldn't thank him enough.

Mam was sleeping, so I ran up to the sewing room. Mrs. M had done her magic; the dust was gone, the mirrors shone. I was ready to start. First, I had to tell Mam.

I couldn't hide my excitement. I picked up the swathe of silk I had seen yesterday, cradling it in my arms, I ran down to show Mam, who was now sitting up in her chair. I was out of breath, taking the stairs two at a time would do that to me.

*Mam, I think I could make a new dress with this. I love the color. Feel the fabric.*

Mam eyed the fabric, running hands up and down the silk. I had seen her do it many times before, but watching her on this day pulled at my heart.

She nodded her approval. *I remember when I bought this. I had been invited to attend a formal luncheon that was to be the talk of the season. Three weeks before the event, it was canceled. Someone, I can't remember who, got sick. So, this lovely fabric was put aside and forgotten about.*

I pulled the fabric against my face. *Well, it is no longer forgotten, Mr. M has fixed the sewing machine, and I think I will take my hand and see what I can do. I love the feel of the silk.* I undid the cloth and draped it over my body.

*It will be lovely on you.* She peered closely at me. This is what she did with her clients, assessing them, their bodies. *Try cinching the waist so the skirt falls loosely, making it swing when you move. It should look like gentle waves cascading all around you, all grace and understated elegance. You should also look through my closet; there could be dresses there you could alter. They are a bit dated, and most will be too big for you, but with the right cut and a good eye, they could proudly carry the O'Shea of New York label.*

———

## Pieces of Cloth

I went to Mam's cedar closet. There was her collection–tailored dresses that shouted the owner was a successful businesswoman; chic suits in the finest of wools and tweeds that could have been made by the latest Paris designer; hats and gloves neatly stored to complete the desired look. My first reaction was excitement, thinking of what could be done with these clothes, how they could be transformed. Mam had worn them with grace, I remembered seeing her in most of them.

Then a quiet sadness overtook. Mam no longer needs these. The life she once lived is closing; it is now a memory. These clothes were a testament to what had once been.

My updating them, making them mine, is a tribute. These pieces of cloth will continue to live; their past will make way for their future.

———

I put down the pen.

———

True to Joseph's prediction, Father Flanagan came to the door on Wednesday morning. He is tall, his face boyish. His black cassock with its white Roman collar barely reached his ankles, as if it were on loan rather than a permanent part of his wardrobe. He is young, but he has the look of an old soul, his shoulders shrugging as if they carried a burden weightier than one would expect of a man of his years. Even a priest.

Mam gave him a smile as he took her hand. *Father, thank you for coming.*

Father Flangan returned the smile. *Visiting my parishioners is one of the best parts of this job. I am new to the parish, but your reputation, Mrs. Clark, as a woman of faith and charity is well known. I also understand that we have you to thank for the vestments we use on Gaudete Sunday. They are fine indeed, and the color is one of my particular favorites.*

Mam laughed out loud. *Very kind of you, Father, but one of your predecessors, a carrot-redhead to be sure, told me it was too pink. I explained that I knew the rose color when I saw it, even when it was put on a pair of spectacles. I suggested that he may wish to change his glasses accordingly. It could benefit his sermon giving. A little too much fire and brimstone for my liking.*

The priest burst out laughing.

I went into the kitchen to make tea. Returning to the parlor with the pot and Mrs. M's freshly baked shortbread biscuits, I overheard the end of their conversation.

The priest was nodding, *Your faith, like the love you have given all your life, is something you can hold onto in the days ahead. It is with us. God is with us every moment.* His words were simple, but they did more than express comfort. They were a reminder of something greater, something that we couldn't describe but believed was there.

Father Flanagan finished his tea, gave Mam his blessing, and with the promise of seeing her next week, left.

As I walked him to the door, he spoke to me, his words soft. *Your faith is also a part of you, Cate, as is your love for your mother. And remember, you are never alone. Not today, not in all the days ahead.*

The priest left, not having performed a miracle, but bringing a quiet peace to the day and my heart.

———

On Friday, Joseph came home. He was rightly impressed as to the progress that had been made in the five days since he had left. Mam looked better. Having a routine and being home seemed to be the best medicine anyone could have offered. Timmy arrived just as we were setting the table for dinner.

Once again, I offered him the chance to join us, an invitation he quickly accepted.

Joseph shot me a look that I chose to ignore.

———

The next day, I reminded Mam that Nora and Elizabeth would be coming later in the week.

*Lovely,* she said, *we will be doing no talking, the two of them will be at each other from the time they cross the threshold till we say our goodbyes. Yet they are staunchest friends, each willing to go into battle for the other if needed.*

I smiled, bringing her another cuppa. *Joseph, Mam was telling me about how she started the shop. Could you continue the tale, please, Mam?*

Joseph put down his book.

Mam took a sip and started. *At first, it was just me. I was used to designing for one woman, one dress at a time. A luxury that I would not be able to sustain, but was my starting point. I found the fabric. It was the perfect color for every Irish woman, whether she believed in the infallibility of the pope or saw him as a throwback to the 16$^{th}$ Century. It mattered not. Lasses with ginger tresses and freckled skin, ebony-haired colleens who trace their heritage to the Moors, or those whose blue eyes bespoke an English ancestry—all would look radiant. The color not blue, not green, but the blend of both was perfection.*

My renewed appreciation for color and fabric made me interrupt, *Oh, Mam, that sounds so lovely.*

*Well, that was the easy part. Now I then had to find the right person to wear the creation. Not a model. A woman of substance, who would wear the dress and not let the dress wear her. I was at a loss. How to find such a woman in Ireland, in Dublin? It was 1923. Brothers were fighting brothers; families were tearing each other apart over the signing of the treaty. Money was scarce, but not for those who had it.*

*And then I found her, Irish by birth, she had married a German businessman prior to the start of the Great War. She was involved in reviving art and Irish culture. If I could break into that world, I would be launched.*

*Her name was Delia Stein. I summoned all my courage and found my way to her gate. I doubted that anyone would let me in the house, but I had prepared a folder that held my sketch and a sample of the material. I took a chance and left the folder with the maid, along with a note addressed to Frau Stein that I would make the dress for her, free of charge. It would be unique, a fashion statement. Her payment would be to tell her friends, and those who envied her, the name of the woman who had created such a fetching garment.*

Mam chuckled. *That would be me in case you two had any doubts.*

*Not I,* Joseph practically shouted.

*Nor I,* was my response.

Mam took a sip of her tea and continued, *The way I calculated it, this would be a bargain she couldn't pass up—a new dress that wouldn't cost her a penny.*

*I waited patiently, and two days later, I received a note. She was interested. I was to meet her at her house the following day at 11 a.m. and was to enter by the back door. Someday, I vowed, they will be begging me to knock on the front door, but tomorrow would not be that day. I brought my measuring tape and my notebook.*

*I arrived on time. My dress was fashionably low-waisted and worn beneath a long cardigan in the same forest green. A long string of pearls dripped down to my waist. I knew I looked good, too good to be entering through the servants' entrance, but that was not the crusade I was going to take on. I was taken into the sitting room where Mrs. Stein was already seated, and she began the interrogation. Who was I? Where do I come from? Why was I here? All good questions that I was prepared to answer.*

*My new identity was a mix of the old and new me. I became Mrs. O'Shea from New York City. I had met my husband there, an Irishman who had died on the fields of France. I had come to Ireland to deal with my grief and was now ready to once again design for society's ladies. Ladies with taste, decorum, and money enough to pay the price of exclusivity.*

I wanted to break in, ask how she came to have a story such as this. What did it feel like to be telling a tale? But I couldn't or wouldn't interrupt.

Mam was back to that time and that place. *Mrs. Stein, who refused to be acknowledged by the term Frau, was tough as old boots despite the pretty face. She agreed to my terms: if the garment met her standards, she would get a new dress, and I would get her acknowledgement as its creator. An hour later, I had taken her measurements and we had agreed that I would return in five days' time, dress in hand, to do the fitting. I already knew that the dress would be perfect for her.*

Mam closed her eyes, her voice stronger than I had heard in days, she was sounding like the mother I knew. *I remember it as if it were yesterday. It was an early day in May, the air was damp, with intermittent dashes of a wind that broke the promise of a warm spring. The skies beheld the threat of rain to follow. I picked up my pace, practically skipping my way home, my thoughts already on the cutting board. The heavens opened, but not before the key was in the door. Another good sign.*

Mam opened up her eyes and winked. *The next few days were a blur. I forgot to eat and sleep, surrendering only when forced by nature. I also made the decision that I was going to be more provocative than my new client would expect. So, I ordered lingerie. No corsets or stiff bras as undergarments for my creations. The dress and its owner had to be free, to move as gently as the summer breeze, to feel beautiful.*

*For hours unending, I pumped the treadle of my one sewing machine in my stocking feet, the overhead light shining brightly. I licked drops of blood that fell from my thumbs and fingers, cursing when one fell on the fabric. I was driven until at last it was finished, and I was satisfied. It had taken the entire four days to create. I looked at it, and it was good. And I knew it. Now hanging in the doorway, I touched the fabric and spoke to the dress. "We are in this together. You will be a sensation and make me one. No matter what follows, I will always love you best." I remember smiling. I was making love to a dress. It would not be the last time.*

Mam grimaced. I held my breath. I wanted to hear more. She could be tired. This could be too much. I was about to say we should stop for the day when Mam continued.

*Five days from my first visit, I was back at the Stein residence, this time knocking on the front door. I had come by cab, the dress wrapped and cradled in my arms. They would have to tell me to retrace my steps and go to the back door. The maid who answered had the good sense not to make that demand.*

*I was escorted into the grand hall with a stone fireplace and a large wooden staircase. I had never seen the likes of such a place. The whole floor was checkerboard marble, and the walls papered and painted. I was told to wait for Mrs. Stein in the library, a room whose look shouted that the books had been bought by the yard; this was not a collection to be read but one that simply fit the décor.*

*Mrs. Stein came in as I unfolded the dress, laying it out on the couch. I got the response needed. It lasted a brief second, but a small gasp escaped her mouth, and her eyes widened. Her mask of neutrality was soon back in place, but I knew in that second that I had gotten her. My plan was going to work.*

*I instructed her to take off her corset, handing her the delicate undergarments wrapped in tissue. "No need to be bound when wearing one of my creations. Please put these on."*

*She unwrapped the silk slip and panties, looking up at me, her eyebrows arched. "And these are ..."*

*"Lingerie," I answered to the question that had not been asked.*

*She touched the silk to her cheek, her eyes fluttered for a brief second at the softness of the fabric. She looked at me, her eyes now hinting at a touch of humor, "Isn't that just a French word for panties?"*

*I couldn't help but laugh out loud. "Yes, indeed. But fashion is changing, and our undergarments must change with it. It is time for us to feel silk against our skin rather than coarse cotton and rubber."*

*Mrs. Stein nodded. "Come bring the dress to my bedroom, I will change and try on the dress there."*

*Within minutes, I was draping the aqua-blue shantung over her now silk-clad frame. The color matched her eyes. The material clung to her frame, making her look elegant and subtly provocative.*

Mam was looking like her old self. She had a twinkle in her eye, and she was sitting up straighter. It was as if this story was the tonic she needed to dull the savage onslaught of the cancer raging through her body.

*It was the look I designed. It was the look I created. I added a matching stole over the top.* "This dress will catch the light of any sun the Irish skies open to us, and as the evening moon rises, its rays will brilliantly cast their shimmer on this topper."

*Mrs. Stein couldn't keep her eyes from the mirror. She turned and looked at me, appraising me, and I thought, Here it comes.*

*"This meets my expectations, and I will gladly be your ambassador. I would like you to design three dresses and a riding suit for me for the fall and winter seasons. Since you are new to Dublin and have no name, I expect that the price of each will be reasonable."*

*I looked her dead straight in the eyes. "Clearly not as reasonable as this one." I smiled. "Let me take to the sketch board and then we can discuss price and fittings. I may be new to Ireland, Mrs. Stein, but I am from New York. I imagine we can find an arrangement that suits us both."*

*That is amazing, Mam. What happened next?* It was now Joseph asking the question.

*Oh, so very much, my dearest son. Mrs. Stein became, in a short period of time, my biggest supporter and, until the war broke out in Germany, my biggest client.*

Mam pointed to the bed. *I am much too tired to go into that this afternoon. Tomorrow, I will fill in more of the details. But I always think of that day with Mrs. Stein, whom I now call Delia, as the day "O'Shea of New York" was born.*

Sunday came. Mam seemed stronger, more alert. I wondered if talking about the past was giving her a new sense of purpose. An energy to remember what had been and all that she accomplished. This was better than any medicine even Timmy could administer.

Over our first cup of tea, I asked: *What was Ireland like when you first got here? I know what the history books say, but what was it really like?*

*Oh, my dear girl. You will have the best resources at your disposal when Nora and Elizabeth come to call. But be prepared for fireworks. The only thing those two could ever agree on was fabric and thread. But you will hear the truth unvarnished, but different.*

We were both enjoying a slice of Mrs. M's warm soda bread when I asked, *So tell me, Mam, about hiring Nora and Elizabeth. And I was so sorry to hear that Kay died. She worked with me in the shop despite her failing health.*

Mam nodded. *Kay was sick for a long time, but didn't go on about her aches and pains. She got to the point that her legs could no longer carry her, and her being just a mite of a thing. Ended up going back to Kilkenny to stay with her sister. She died about a month or so ago. It was then that I knew I was sick. I didn't have the strength to make the trip to bid her a final goodbye.*

*But take me back, Mam, to the days that you were all working together.*

Joseph made himself a cuppa and joined us.

Mam gazed out the window, as if searching her memories from those days so many years ago. *Well, there was work to be done before I could start. I had a plan. The first thing was to make the designs. Then the tricky part: buying the materials and then estimating the cost of each dress. How many yards of materials, what fabric for the underskirt, what feathers, what lace and ribbons were needed to detail the trim? How many sewing machines? Enough so that deadlines would be met, but not so many, they would sit idle. And then the price, each garment had to cost the right amount. Enough so that the lady buying it would know how unique it was, but not so high that it was out of reach.*

Mam looked over at us. Neither Joseph nor I said a word; this was her story, her memory. These stories of Mam's early career, though seemingly unfamiliar and distant, were really a bridge. A bridge between the successful, determined woman I remembered and the young woman forging her own path. The beginning of it all.

Mam's eyes once again closed at the memory, but she kept taking. *Then last but never least, hiring those with the talent and skill to make it all happen. My team. They were a motley crew, different shapes and sizes, culchies from the west and refugees from Dublin's The Liberties. The one thing they had in common was that they had a wonderful way with a needle and a thread and a love affair with fine fabric.*

*Nora and Elizabeth were my first hires. Much of the success achieved was all down to them. They look the same today as they did when I first met them. Nora, large, pale-skinned, and short-sighted, with glasses that resembled the tumblers at Mooney's bar. Elizabeth was small and sharp with skin the color of yesterday's dried-up puddle. I remember thinking one doesn't look like she could find a needle, and the other doesn't look the least bit Irish. But I liked them. They were smart. They were opinionated. They wanted to work. And they were good. Incredibly good.*

Joseph laughed out loud. *I remember the first time I met them. I'm not sure what I expected, but they looked like one of the sports teams I was put on as a school-boy. We were the ones that didn't get selected to be on the regular teams, and we looked it. We didn't quite fit anywhere except with each other. Yet we became a team, a good one, and they are still my mates.*

*Funny, how I think about that today. And that is what I thought about Nora and Elizabeth that first day.*

Mam chuckled. *A lovely insight, my dear. And so true. For like your raga-*

*muffin sports team, we shared a common mission, a desire to succeed, and a willing-ness to do whatever it took to get the job done.*

*The first outfit I gave them to work on was Mrs. Stein's riding outfit, a light-weight green velvet jacket, form-fitting but flexible, with riding breeches to match. I held my breath as Elizabeth began cutting the cloth on the bias so that the material would actually show you where to place the stitches. Two hours later, she handed it to Nora. I didn't think I could breathe. Nora gingerly fingered the finest green velvet she had ever touched, and then her head and glasses bent down over the Singer, and she started pumping the treadle with stockinged feet. In all our years together, I never saw her wear shoes when she was working the sewing machine. She placed a 4-inch zipper expertly over the grinding needle plate. My breathing became normal. Elizabeth picked up the jacket and started hemming, tracking down the seams, camouflaging hooks, and eyes. There would be no buttonholes to fray in this garment. This pair might not look like much, but they will make Delia Stein's wardrobe the talk of the season.*

*These two became my experts, training others who came in with the precision and dedication that was needed to make the name O'Shea of New York mean some-thing to the fashionable elite in Dublin. Magic with a needle and a thread, all of them. Women with nary a curve would be transformed into voluptuous film stars thanks to padding around the shoulders and starchy fabric around the hips. Those with a bit too much flesh hugging their bodies were softly draped in silk, their curves now accentuating rather than hiding their beauty. No two alike, every one, like the women who created them, unique.*

*I had the pressure of being the designer. I knew my dresses had to be more stylish, more original, and more affordable than those offered by the Grafton Street shops that touted garments from foreign locations whose prices didn't match the low quality of the fabric and the cookie-cutter pattern.*

She winked, *which is why I added "of New York" to the name. And I made sure to keep my American accent and each week read a New York paper so I could keep up with the latest Manhattan gossip. I already knew that in fashion, it is about the image you create, and I was creating my own image.*

Mam spread her arms out in front of her as if she was embracing the whole room. *I can still see and hear what it was like in those days. The floor looked like a mosaic. Scraps of satins, rainbow colored silks, shimmering taffeta, scat-tered about in no order but bursting with color. Then there were the sounds, the dull whir of the Singer, the rattling of the scissors, the dropped off-color word when a needle drew blood rather than made a stitch.*

*I loved every minute of it.*

*Two years after knocking on Delia Stein's door, we were in our own shop on*

*O'Connell Street. It was small enough to feel intimate while large enough to accommodate a growing clientele. Mannequins, a revolutionary concept in those days and an expensive investment, I might add, stood posed in the windows, showing off my latest creations. I hung the sign O'Shea of New York over the front door and said a little prayer.*

Mam looked at me and smiled. *You grew up there. You could tell the difference in shades of blue before you were four. O'Shea's gave me my financial independence. It was who I became. Initially, it gave me a reason to get up in the morning. When I look back on those years, I cannot seem to separate myself from the shop. It defined me at a time I needed definition.*

*And then five years ago, it was time to let it go. You were all grown. It was time to move on. I know longer needed it to tell me who I am. That chapter in my life was now closed.*

When she was settled for the night, I took her hand in mine. *You know you were a woman ahead of your time. You wove together not just fabric but a future you could call your own. Someone else, me included, might have only seen the limits to what they could achieve, you saw possibility. I may have inherited your eyes, but I'm not sure I've your boldness. You carved out your own niche, not just by designing clothes but by daring to live by your own rules. You were, you are, remarkable.*

Mam squeezed my hand. *That is lovely to hear, my darling daughter. But I just did what needed to be done. I needed to survive. I needed to find my life here. And you will find yours. It will look different than mine, for it is your path to follow. You come from a long line of strong-minded, independent women. When the time comes for you, you will be ready. I am sure of that.*

She gave my hand another squeeze and closed her eyes.

I kissed her cheek. I wasn't convinced she was right; my own self-doubt and a blurry vision of what could be next overshadowed her kind words.

———

## A Living Legacy

I always knew Mam was strong. But this story had me seeing her as a woman younger than me. Not yet 20, she was living in a country she wasn't born in, in a city that was recovering from the ashes of a war, beginning a career that no one could have foretold. Her story seemed almost otherworldly; she was the epitome of the heroine of the books that I continue to devour.

Mam found her own way to make her own living, weaving a story of who she was, not doubting what she could do and where she could do it. I am envious and in awe of the confidence she showed, the hurdles she overcame and sacrifices she had to make. Hers is a legacy of strength and determination, fueled by a fire to succeed. A fire that built the life we led.

Mam didn't search to find out who she was. She just became her.

Here is the lesson I mean to learn.

———

I put down the pen.

———

Tuesday came quickly. Nora and Elizabeth would be coming around 10:00 a.m. I told Mrs. M to be prepared, they were Mam's oldest and dearest friends, but she shouldn't be concerned if sparks started to fly.

They arrived dressed in their Sunday frocks; they had not seen Mam in weeks and wanted to be seen in the best light. Mrs. M, having been fore-warned not only about their temperament but their critical opinions of housekeeping meeting their standards, won them over immediately. Not only because of the results of her infamous feather duster but she produced the most delicious scones imaginable, warm from the oven, fragrant with raisins so plump they looked as if they were ready to explode. Nora and Elizabeth approved.

Nora and Elizabeth had finished updating Mam about their comings and goings when she turned the conversation towards me. *Cate here has been asking me what Dublin was like when I first arrived, when we were in the midst of the Civil War. I can recall extraordinarily little, too much going on in my own life to see the world around me. Can you give her a taste?*

Nora and Elizabeth were quiet for a moment.

*Please,* I asked, *I am trying to better understand what the history books don't tell us.*

Elizabeth snorted, *Always remember, my wee colleen, history is written by the victorious who also happen to be aging white men. Caution as to what you read that is labeled truth.*

Nora took her glasses off, squinting as she turned them over in her hand. She paused to look at them before placing them back on her nose. It was as if she were asking them to remember what they had seen. She began, *War is never glamorous. It wasn't then, and it isn't now. But to understand the Civil War, you need to go back. Back to when Black & Tans, British soldiers, and their so-called Auxiliary walked our streets by right of occupation. They were savage and cruel, holding our people in disdain.*

*My older sister was at a dance one evening at the church under the supervision of the parish priest, and having quite the time when the Black & Tans burst in. For no reason. They told the girls to stand against the wall, made the priest give them his collar, which one of them put around his leg like a garter. With rifles posed as if to fire, they made all the boys kneel down in front of them. They poked the young lads with their rifles, calling them pigs and the like, threatening to take the girls out back and show them what a real man could do to them. My sister said all the girls were crying, and some of the boys as well. They were scared, they were young, and for those ruffians called soldiers of the king, it was just good fun. Finally, they left. No one had been physically hurt, but the damage had been done. The girls were shaken, the lads humiliated. The result of such cruelty was a hatred brewing for centuries that was ready to bubble over. The only way to meet their savagery was with a savagery of our own. It wasn't good, me brothers were the first to sign up, and one never came home again. Yet it was time, it was the War of Independence. You have to understand that if you want to make heads or tails of the Civil War.*

Elizabeth broke in. *There'll be no flag waving when your brothers and sons are being blown to bits. Just a few years before this fighting began, these lads had gone to war for the bloody king. Too much Irish blood was left on the fields of France.*

It was my turn to speak. *What about Grace Plunkett? I thought hers was the most romantic and tragic story, marrying Joseph Plunkett in the gaol....*

Before I could finish, Mam added her voice to the conversation. *Grace Plunkett, grieving widow of poor Joseph Plunkett, a hero of the Easter Rising.*

Mam's voice went cold. *The story that is told is that she wed Joseph, but then I heard another story from others. It was their thinking that she never really married him, and I came to agree with them. She bought her own wedding ring and then found some priest to bless their vows. Joseph was at Kilmainham along with Patrick Pearse and the other Rising heroes, and his execution date was announced. Everyone knew that Joseph was so sick, he wasn't going to make it much longer anyway. After this so-called priest finished the sacrament, pronouncing them man and wife, the two of them just sat in a room alone in the gaol, not saying anything, not touching. Then the soldiers take him back to his cell, and he gets shot along with the others the next morning.*

*Grace changes her name, becomes a grieving widow. Years later, she comes around telling me I should give her a discount on her dresses because of all she has been through. And she, only discussing the proposed discount after the frocks have been made and fitted. Gave it to her the first time. Next time she came around, I increased the price by 10 percent and then smiled and said I had taken that amount off their price in recognition of her being a widow and all.*

Mam snorted. *A widow. She was never a widow. To be a widow, you need to be a wife. You need to love, to weep, to laugh, to have his child. To pick up his socks. That is what a wife does. She just doesn't sit and look at her dying husband. She holds him. She cries with him. She mourns him. That is a wife.*

I had seldom heard Mam speak with such passion, and when she had finished, she looked exhausted.

I thanked Nora and Elizabeth for their insights, packing up the remaining scones for them to take home. We agreed to continue our "lessons" in two weeks' time, but not before they underscored how much they enjoyed Mrs. M's scones. I made a mental note to have Mrs. M keep the treats coming; I still had much to learn.

---

## Our Daily Life

In the three weeks I have been home, our daily routines have become oddly comforting. They have a pattern of their own, one that I have no problem following. In the mornings, Mrs. M and I get Mam up and settled in her chair. She has a bit of breakfast, I take my tea.

The cancer is taking its toll, she can no longer focus on small print, so I read the newspaper to her. By mid-morning, her eyes get heavy and she falls asleep in her chair. If the day is fine, I take my walk. If the rain and winds prevail, I go upstairs to the distraction of cutting and sewing. I write letters. I reread the letters I have received.

There are moments when I feel like I am walking through fog, when I look at Mam sitting quietly in her chair, her hands folded, looking out the window to a world she once enjoyed. The house is quiet. It is as if I am a spectator rather than a participant in this life of waiting.

Later, Mrs. M brings tea and we just sit quietly next to each other. If she has the energy, she shares her stories, if she is tired, I read to her. We agreed that Jane Austen is our author of choice and have finished *Pride and Prejudice*, moving on to *Sense and Sensibility*. It is these moments when she shares the memories of life gone by or we escape into a world of witty dialogues and love's triumphs that I cherish most.

Visitors are reserved for afternoons. I greet them with a strange mix of gratitude and helplessness. Gratitude because they are here, not only for Mam but for me, as well. And helplessness, they are the reminders of the journey that we are on, the harbingers of what the future holds.

Tomorrow will be another day. The same but different. I am thankful that I am here. We are together. And for now, that is enough.

———

I put down the pen.

———

It was a Saturday morning, one of those Irish days when the sun looked as if it had planned to stay out and grace us with its presence. After putting

Mam through her morning rituals of bathing, dressing, and eating, I found Joseph in the garden. He smiled as I approached. *Not much for me to do here,* he shrugged. *Mr. M, for all his girth, seems to be able to find his way around the patches of dirt I called a garden. It has never looked better.*

*Would you mind if I left Mam in your care for the next few hours? In addition to getting the sewing machine oiled and functional and the garden blooming, Mr. M fixed my old bicycle. I thought I would take it out to St. Stephen's Green and ride through the park.*

Joseph nodded his head. *Absolutely. And I leave this garden with no guilt; it is clearly in better hands. And you should do the same. Though I am not sure my hands are better than yours, they are at least competent.*

I gave him a brief kiss, an act of affection he was getting increasingly accustomed to receiving.

I changed into my blue jeans and windbreaker, feeling more like a teenager than the adult woman watching my mother die. In my possession were two letters, one from Nell, and one from Faith. Nell's note was chatty, witty, and consoling. She gave me an update on what was happening with Teddy as public sentiment towards McCarthy seemed to be tottering. Faith is still to appear before the Committee in the next Congressional session and Teddy remains stymied on how to create a rebuttal when dealing with accusations that have no substance. Faith's letter is a bit of this and that. In one sentence, she pleads with me to return, and then in the next, berates herself for asking me to leave my mother for her. I love reading it. It is as if she were next to me, fired up and apologetic in the same breath.

I looked forward to reading them again, imagining that they were with me. I began composing my anticipated replies as I pedaled. It had been a long time since I rode a bike, a message my legs reminded me. As I entered St. Stephen's Green, I decided to rest on the first bench I could find. I laid the bike next to me and closed my eyes.

I had turned my face towards the sun when I heard a voice next to me. *Careful of those rays, you may find the freckles on your nose multiplying before the day is out.*

I turned my head in the direction of the sound to find eyes, dark as jets flared with specks of light, looking straight at me.

*I'll take the risk. Closest thing to a tan I ever get.*

His laughter bubbled up as he extended his hand in an exaggerated formal greeting as he stood up. *By way of proper introduction, my name is John.*

I met his gaze and stood up as well. Though close to five foot eight, I still had to look up at him. *And I am Cate.*

*Nah,* he said, *that can't be the name that you were christened with. With all my years under the tutelage of the good friars, there was nary a saint canonized Cate.*

*Well, try Catherine, with a C.*

*Aye, much better. And that is what I will be calling you, Catherine with a C. Let us renounce our surnames as an act of rebellion on this fine day. Will you walk with me, I promise no harm will come to ye. We will keep to the public walkways. Or must you saddle your two-wheeled chariot and disappear into a ring fort?*

I laughed. *Walking is fine, though the chariot must come with me. This is its first outing in many a year, and I am not about to neglect it once again.*

I took a closer look. I had been warned since a child not to go off with strangers. But this felt different. John stood like a man who was comfortable in the world, a world that he could conquer. He looked a bit older than me but not by much. His dark hair, slightly tousled, framed a face that was all sharp angles. His black eyes seemed to know more than they let on. His clothes were well-made and well-worn. I wanted to know more.

He took the bicycle, guiding it with one hand as we walked. *Next time you sip a Guinness, Catherine with a C, you need to give a nod to its brewer, Sr. Arthur himself. 'Twas he who bought and bequeathed this lovely park to our fair city. A staunch Unionist and a proud member of the Orange Order, Mr. Guinness must have rolled over in his grave when 100 years later these very acres were seized by the Irish rebels demanding their rights to be freemen.*

John looked over at me, his eyes twinkling. *You know what they used to call an Irishman on a horse?*

I had heard this before. I winked. *Aye, a Protestant.*

The sound of John's laughter caught me off guard. It was warm and genuine, and for a beat too long, his eyes held mine.

*Didn't expect that,* he said, still smiling, as if the joke had revealed something not just amusing, but intriguing.

We walked through St. Stephen's Green. He was there beside me, effortlessly charming. I remembered not so much what he said but how he said it. How he paused and let a sentence hang in the air, as if he is thinking three steps ahead before he continued. I have a feeling he is comfortable with silence. A man who doesn't need to fill the air with unnecessary words.

The late afternoon sun left bands of color across last night's puddles when we reached the crosswalk on the way back. The man named John handed me back the bicycle. He doffed his cap, *'Twas I that had the luck of the Irish shine on me today, Catherine with a C. A day I shan't forget soon.*

*Nor I, kind sir.*

We were off on our separate ways, my head somewhere in the clouds when I put my 'chariot' back in its stable.

———

## Was It Mischief?

The fairies may be toying with me, weaving the threads of fate that led me to St. Stephen's Green and that bench this day, to be taking a walk with a handsome stranger that calls me Catherine with a C.

I have never fully believed the old tales about how these impish creatures scatter their charms, disrupting your life when you least expect it. Yet today has given me pause.

When I think about today, my heart races. I met a man named John with hair and eyes that match, who laughs easily, and has a voice, low and smooth, with a hint of something playful beneath the surface. I feel a connection, a subtle pull between us. He appears open yet mysterious, a puzzle to be solved.

My fantasies could be shattered. He could be married. He could be Mr. Rochester, whose secret life leads Jane Eyre to heartache and abandonment. For now, and until I learn the contrary, I will have him the hero and I the heroine with a story that is mine to draft.

If the fairies have been spreading their mischief and their charms, then this reverie is their reward. I will dream of him.

———

I put down the pen.

———

Monday came, the day was bright, a gift the weather gods had given us. A post appeared, my first from Teddy. I was impatient for the kettle to whistle, wanting to savor both the letter and my tea. My last letter to him had talked about my trying to better understand Irish history while at the same time asking him to better explain the headlines that Joseph McCarthy was grabbing around the world. A world that Teddy was so involved in. At long last, my cuppa ready, I opened the letter, hearing Teddy's voice in every word.

> *Dearest Cate,*
>
> *You have given me a challenge indeed. It is hard to describe who Joseph McCarthy really is; the American Press has been trying to unravel that mystery for months now. I am not sure how well I will enlighten you, but I will do my best.*
>
> *My pen in hand, I shall try my best to capture what is happening in this part of the world. Be forewarned, my writing is not without prejudice because I find this country to be in great danger spearheaded by people who fly under the flag of patriotism. We have a history of witch hunts, beginning in Salem Massachusetts in the 17th Century and going on today in our Nation's capital. Although the world has changed, some parts remain the same.*
>
> *At the end of the war, we found ourselves a nation stronger, more powerful, and more affluent than ever before. There is a general feeling that the Democrats won the war but lost the peace. A peace that allowed the Soviets to gobble up Eastern Europe. Communism and socialism are our new enemies. Enemies that are ideologies rather than villains with a face and a salute. Radios are giving way to families gathered around a box that dominates their living space with both voice and pictures. The television and its news make a greater impact than anything in print, the audience it reaches, far greater than any news clip that preceded the current box office hit at the downtown*

cinema. The setting was perfect for someone to play a starring role. And that someone is this junior senator from Wisconsin.

McCarthy knows how to play to a crowd, and the television cameras bring his performance into everyday life. His words are deliberately vague. He doesn't accuse with fact but with broad generalizations. Listening to him makes me shake my head. He doesn't say what people did; he says they 'had furthered the cause of Communism.' It is as if he is driving through a fog with no clear direction, yet his followers believe he knows where he is going. He waves a sheet of paper claiming that he has in his hand the names of Communists who work in the State Department. Yet, no names are ever published. When reporters demand proof of his accusations, he falters, saying that the evidence is in another briefcase. I shake my head in disbelief. Admirers claim that whatever his faults, he has the courage of his convictions. My response is that if a man has no convictions, he can scarcely draw courage from them.

There is more light coming to this tunnel, however. I believe the chicanery of McCarthy is going to be exposed in the next few weeks. McCarthy has taken on the United States Army, a formidable opponent indeed. I will report back to you on those proceedings. Until then, it gives me hope. The lady who stands in the New York harbor raises her beacon to light the way into this new world. May its beam find its way south to this small patch of land along the Potomac River.

I think of you and the challenges you face daily. My mother shares your letters with me, so I know the path you are walking. Please take good care of yourself and know that you are loved and supported by so many.

I am holding you close to my heart.

Love, Teddy

---

Mr. M had finished running his errands when he caught my eye. *I hear ye' talking to your Mam's friends about what was happening those years ago. Do you fancy hearing it from someone who was there? I was strong and stalwart man back then, full of piss and vinegar. Believing that I knew what was right, and those that didn't believe the same were wrong. Let me ask the wife to bring us a cuppa and if you have the time, I will tell you what it was like from one who took up arms for the cause. Twice mind you. But let me tell you what happened after that bloody treaty was signed.*

Soon, the tea was poured and Mrs. M sat down next to her husband. Mr. M took a sip of his tea and a drag on his pipe. I thought this must be what their home life is like—quiet, restful, at peace with themselves and the world around them. I couldn't imagine this serenity broken by fighting and killing.

*I'm a Cork man, ya' know. And it was the likes of us who got the Brits out of here. Not them up here in Dublin. Those who wore suits and ended up vowing to kneel before the bloody king. We were the ones fighting in the streets, sleeping in the fields. And we were brothers. We were supposed to be loyal to each other. It was all we had. And we lost it. It was after the Treaty was signed. After Collins offered us up. Those who fought with us, turned on us with guns paid for with the king's shillings. The whole thing was a bloody plot, to my thinking. It was Churchill's divide and rule trick. Split us up, start fights, have us kill each other. Then arrive back on our shores, shouting for the world to hear that the Irish can't govern ourselves and it is up to the British to keep us from brawling on the streets. Then this king and his minions come back and with a wink and a grin, take our land once again. And the world would sigh and let them bloody well do it.*

Mrs. M opened her eyes, and laid a hand on her husband's arm. *Never mind the politics love, just tell the lass what happened. What you saw.*

Mr. M took another sip of tea and shook his head, the memory of it all still grabbed his heart. *I remember it as if it was yesterday. It was a dark morning, one where the sky looked angry even before the day had begun. I should have known then that it wasn't the weather but the shadow of what that day would bring. I started to shiver, I don't think I had ever been that cold either before that day or since. For my blood couldn't warm me. It was a sign of what was to come that day and all the days to come after.*

Mr. M grimaced. *There was a young girl in town, headstrong and beautiful with hair as red as the dawn's first light. We were not blessed with children of our own, and we took her in. Only during the week, mind ya, to help around the farm.*

*We leased a small plot, had a cow for milking, some hens, a rooster, and a dog. The garden had cabbages as well as potatoes. Mrs. M. started a small baking business and started to get quite busy supplying the local pubs with her cakes and pies.* A small smile crept over his face at the memory.

*All in all, we were busy and quite content, but needed an extra pair of hands to keep the load manageable. The lass would go home to her people on Fridays and then come back to us come Monday morn. Well, truth be told, I paid little mind to her comings and goings, though she never went out at night when she was with us.*

Mrs. M interrupted. *She was a good lass but with a mind of her own. The Black & Tans had killed her older brother back in '21, and she was very anti-Treaty. She called Collins a traitor and worse. Then one week, she didn't return. Come Tuesday, we went looking for her. Her folks said she had left as usual the day before, same as ordinary. A couple of the other men were called, and they started a search party. They found her that afternoon. She was in an abandoned shed. Beaten and bruised, her hair cut-off, by her own countrymen, mind ya. Not the bloody British. No one would tell if more had been done to her, there were stories about horrible things done to our girls. It wasn't our place to ask. Her dad brought her into the house to her mother. The lass was limping and crying, her mam weeping. It broke my heart to witness such pain.* Mrs. M turned her face towards the window.

Mr. M's voice grew softer as he looked at his wife, *we never saw her again. We heard from others that she had been seeing one of the rebels, a young man who reportedly was involved in the killing of that no-good British Field Marshal Wilson, a sworn enemy of Irish freedom. Him, considered a hero by the bloody Crown, a scoundrel who had ordered more of our countrymen to death than one could count. Him they put medals on. Those that made sure he would never do it again were considered the enemy and hunted down. It was her lad that they went after, and when they couldn't find him, they took it out on her. She never recovered.*

I couldn't comprehend such violence taken out on the innocent. *Such heartache for so many. No wonder the bitterness continues.*

Mr. M nodded. *In the end this so-called Civil War just withered out. There was no celebration, no claims of victory, no grand gestures of reconciliation. The fighting didn't cease, it dribbled away. We had been fighting for years and there were those among us, particularly the young ones, who only knew how to kill. Even though they lived, they had no future. 'Twas a generation wasted. And the country was in shambles. Mrs. M and I decided to come here; there was nothing much left for us in Cork. We found work, with the only folks who still had a high style of living. The Ascendancy had never gotten their hands dirty during the fighting; they continued their genteel pursuits—horses, politics, and Christ Church. It is their voice that always gives them away. A voice honed by years of feeling their superiority was their right. Never heard it much at home in Cork, but it was a symphony here in Dublin.*

Mrs. M smiled, *You can tell where someone worships as soon as they open their mouths. Anyway, we found work and made a life. And now we are with you, a blessing in so many ways.*

I got up and kissed them both on the cheek. *And you are a blessing for us.*

Mr. M. got up slowly from his chair. *And may this beloved land be blessed with the peace and harmony it so richly deserves.*

His shoulders slumped as he put down his pipe and slowly walked out the door.

―――

## Love and War

I closed my eyes and thought of Mam's love of Billy Conlon, a man whose political beliefs and convictions were not hers. Nor her family's.

My thoughts raced, a chilling realization dawned. Had Ma and Billy Conlon's plan worked, had they returned to Ireland, how would they have survived? Would they have survived? Could Mam, a Catholic with a Unionist husband, been seen as a target? Could she have suffered the same fate as the young woman in Mr. M's story?

Mam could have been at risk, not just from the acts of cruelty rampant during the time, but from the deep-seated divisions that were tearing the very fabric of Irish society apart. Their story's ending could have mirrored the tragedy of Romeo and Juliet, their love overwhelmed by the forces of family, politics, and war.

Perhaps the enemy of love is living in a world struggling for peace. Where lines are drawn. Where love may not conquer all.

―――

I put down the pen.

―――

The following Saturday, I awoke with butterflies in my stomach. I was going back to St. Stephen's Green, back to the bench where I had met John with the black eyes. I braced myself that he might not show up, that he was more a figment of my imagination than a real-life person. That my daydreams would awaken to the reality of what was essentially a one-time encounter. I put my latest letter from Nell in my pocket to read once again, knowing that it would somehow ease the void if my venture for the day was solo.

I found the bench, it was empty. With a heart heavier than I had anticipated, I sat down, and was about to open my letter, when I heard his voice.

*Good morning, Catherine with a C.*

I nodded, *John.*

*Such a lovely day, and I must admit, I am in need of a good walk around. Should we cross the Liffey and make our way to Sackett Street, I mean O'Connell Street?* John threw his head back as he chuckled, *changing its name is one of the few pronouncements our local politicians and our fellow citizens seem to agree on.*

*I have a lock for the chariot, so if you don't mind making a round trip back to the bench, we can begin on foot unencumbered.*

Minutes later, the bicycle now safely secured, we were on our way, circumventing Trinity College, the bastion of learning for any Irishman as long as he didn't see the pope as the leader of his church. No Catholics and no women allowed.

The day was cooperating, the sun was bright, no threat of spoiling the outing with either too brisk of a wind, or a smattering of rain. Crossing the Ha'penny Bridge into North Dublin, it wasn't long before O'Connell Street stretched before us, its great expanse speaking of a world of commerce, shoppers, and strollers. As we made our way down the street, we arrived at our agreed-upon destination, the front of the square mass of the General Post Office. With its big, six-column portico, it still looked like the barracks it became that April day in 1916, the day of the Rising.

I pointed to the building. *I love that the GPO is still a working post office, I often wonder what Patrick Pearse was thinking when he read the Proclamation of the Republic that Monday morning. He has always been a hero of mine, his military credentials practically non-existent for he was a poet, a scholar, and a keeper of Gaelic mysticism.*

John smiled back. *A school master, he was a better poet than a military commander, I can safely say. My thinking is that the Dubliners who were standing in this very same spot that very same day were both baffled and curious. It was supposed to be a holiday, the Easter rituals less than a day old. And here was Pearse and his mates denouncing the centuries of British misrule, overstating our previous rebellions, declaring a republic and provisional government with him as its president, no less. My guess is no one paid that much mind, and most ordinary folks just went back to their daily lives such as they were. Life was harder then that it is now for most, and it is still pretty hardscrabble for far too many.*

I nodded my agreement. *It seems that the only people who got mad were those who didn't want their lives changed.*

John paused, still collecting his thoughts. *I have never understood the British response to it all. The Rising posed no real threat to their rule.* He held out his hand, counting on his fingers. *First, it was not carried out by trained soldiers; second, the communication systems broke down almost immediately; third, most of their fellow countrymen were either angry, amused, or oblivious to the event. And, most important of all,* holding up his fourth finger, *it was over in a week. This post office was an inferno. The Irish flag that the rebels had so proudly hung, whipped by the wind and the fire, ended up in the rumble on this street. Pearse surrendered.* John's voice went soft. *It was over. Heartbreakingly over.*

John pulled his coat tighter around his shoulders, though the day had become quite warm. He gave his head a turn and we reversed our direction, starting back to the river.

Lost in thought as to our conversation, I stopped to take off my jacket, the walk and the sun combining to make the removal of layers of clothing necessary. I wished I had worn a more fashionable jumper, but I was more worried about my hair than what I wore under my jacket that morning.

John, now aware that the sun was radiating more warmth than we had dressed for, raised an eyebrow. *Could I interest you in an ice pop?*

*Today and any day of the week. It is one of my many vices, one that I can never say no to.*

*I will procure us two such treats if you save us a seat on one of the benches overlooking the Liffey.*

I found such a spot and John quickly returned, cradling the promised ice pops in his hands. We sat quietly, looking at the river. John smelled of wood and citrus. When I was with him, I felt none of the uneasiness knowing that my mother was dying. That soon I would be an orphan. The river, its dark waters that gave Dublin its name, was like my memories of my childhood, passing by me without pausing to see if I was ready to move on.

I was lost in my own thoughts when I heard John's voice. *Best if we were moving on. The shadows are making these waters even blacker than before.*

*Oh, yes, so sorry, I was lost in thought.*

*No need to apologize to me, the river can mesmerize, and the last lick of an ice pop brings a bittersweet sense of closure, a delicious farewell to a moment of pleasure.*

*Well, my kind sir, I see I am in the company of both a historian and a poet. A modern version of Mr. Pearse himself.*

John stood up, mocking a formal bow. *As you wish, my lady. And I can hope that I will happen on you once again. I can't make next Saturday but can I book a fortnight from now at our bench?*

I gave my best rendition of a courtesy. *On that, you can rest assured.*

And we returned to St. Stephen's Green and what was now being referred to as 'our bench.'

Unlocking the now rescued bicycle, I couldn't erase the grin off my face. No need to worry, I can count the days off until I see him again. And despite everything, the smile found its way to my heart.

———

Nora and Elizabeth were back for their second visit. Mam was up for the company, and I was looking forward to the diversion. After the initial pleasantries and concern for Mam's health, their eyes greedily looked towards Mrs. M, who had outdone herself when she heard of their planned visit. The apple cake, the crust light and airy, was the center of their attention, its custard topping adding to its perfection. Even Mam was nibbling away.

As they posed their forks, I knew it was the right time to turn the conversation back to a time over 20 years ago, so I began. *I enjoyed our last conversation so very much. Are there more stories from that time you could share?*

Elizabeth took a healthy bite of her cake, and, wiping the crumbs from her mouth, she began. *Savoring this delicious cake made me think of a tale me own mam told about a time when she was working at one of the local restaurants. Granted, this was when me brothers were out of the house fighting for the right for us to have a say as to how to run this land.*

Nora broke in, *Tell the tale before your tea gets cold, Elizabeth. I want the cake story, not the family yarns of your brothers' fighting.*

Elizabeth's voice was sharp. *Nora, you could start an argument in a confessional.*

Nora laughed. *As a matter of fact, I have.*

Mam and I both broke out in laughter.

It was Mam who took control, as she must have done all those years in the shop. *Tell your story, Elizabeth. Your mam's story, to be exact.*

*Very well.* And eyeing the last of the remaining cake, she pointed to the same. *I'll be wanting another piece of that cake when I am finished.*

And she began. *Now me own mother, God rest her soul, was not much of one for politics. She just wanted to go out about her daily life without having me brothers being shot. Did she want things for the better? For sure. She was working 10 hours a day, 6 days a week to put food on the table for those of us still at home. It was the massacre on Bloody Sunday that moved her mind. The Black & Tans slaughtering civilians, one just an eleven-year-old boy. Him and his da were shot in the back as they raced out of Croke Park. And it was those that were supposed to be patrolling us to keep the peace that raised their guns. She said there was a special place in hell for them. But there was little she could do, except say her prayers.*

*Then one day the Lord gave her a chance to seek her own revenge. It was during our fight for Independence that she got her chance.*

*Me ma worked as a server at one of the local shops, one frequented by those that wore the king's uniform. She overheard them regaling each other with stories about how they were torturing our lads in prison, so clever they thought they were. Doing it in ways that wouldn't get caught, thinking they were that smart. That day they told of a lad forced to drink a pint of castor oil and then stand against a wall spread-eagle-like in his bare feet. These so-called soldiers then spread jagged glass all around 'im, so if he moved at all, he would be sliced up. Ma said her hands shook as she poured their tea. They paid her no attention as they laughed about how his insides finally exploded and he fell onto the ground, onto the glass, covered in his own shyte.*

Me ma cried when she came home that night and told the story. *One of our neighbors was at the table as well, and they decided they would seek their own revenge. The two of them, now working with some of the women in the tenement, pulled together all their sugar and cocoa and made an extra special chocolate cake to bring to the restaurant to serve these same soldiers. What made it so extra special is that they added all the borax they could gather to the mix. Their targets never suspected a thing, complimented them on how tasty their dessert was. A dessert that quickly backfired on them, so to speak. It was days before any of them showed their face again. They never figured out it was the cake that had done them in, blaming their malady on something in the water. No thought at all given that these Irish women could have figured out how to do them in.*

*Mam was sure the poor lad's mammy would be thanking her and all the ladies in our tenement if she knew what they had done in her son's name. A name they never knew.*

It was now Nora's turn to speak up. *There're many stories just like this one, Cate. You can talk to the shawlies in the snug to hear more. The grannies' desire for independence wasn't revolutionary as it was for the lads. Nay, it built up over time, born of a holy hatred of foreign domination. Once you feel it, there is no going back.*

*And that is why our lads picked up the guns and fought to have a free state, And why feelings were so strong when Collins came back with that blasted treaty. Feelings that have left their scars on this nation's soul.*

Elizabeth nodded her agreement. *And let me end with, given my mother's tale,* she moved her plate in front of her and pointed to the remaining slice. *I have turned down many a slice of a chocolate frosted cake with all the trimmings. But I am more than ready for that slice of Mrs. M's apple cake.*

After Elizabeth had devoured every crumb, Mam smiled and shook her head. *You need to excuse me, my friends. I am quite tired. I need to rest.*

Mam laid down and closed her eyes.

Nora and Elizabeth left with no date set for the next visit.

———

Bridget was just finishing getting Ma ready for night, she was having one of her better days, when there was a knock on the door. It was Timmy, earlier than his usual arrival time. After Bridget left, he looked over at me but asked Mam the question. *Mrs. Clark, do you think you and Joseph could spend Friday night without Cate this week? There is a new film at the Grafton I have been wanting to see, and I am off for the day. I was thinking about asking her to join me for dinner and the movie but wanted to be sure you'd be okay with me extending the offer. After all, you are my patient, and your needs come first.*

Mam laughed. *I have never been one to step between my lovely daughter and a night out with a handsome lad. As long as I knew his family.* Mam winked. *Now it is up to her to say yea or nay; she has a mind of her own, ya know.*

*Indeed, I do, don't forget, I knew her when we were but little.*

He then looked over at me, *Cate, would you go to the cinema with me this Friday? Dinner first, then the film and with a promise that I won't have you out too late.*

In retrospect, I had no choice but to agree. It wasn't as if I didn't want to go. I like Timmy, I really do. But I kept thinking about Joseph and the valentine. I decided I would just manage his expectations, make sure Timmy understood that the last thing I was looking for was a relationship, particularly now.

Friday night came quickly. Joseph registered no surprise when I said I was going out with Timmy, merely said, *You need a night out.*

It was a pleasant evening. I looked at Timmy over dinner and thought to myself, *Why can't you fall for him? He is smart, considerate, kind, and more than just a little good-looking. But it isn't what I want.* I tried to send the message that I wasn't interested in having a boyfriend, particularly a boyfriend who lived in Ireland. Not sure if Timmy received the message, nor was I being totally truthful. For a little voice inside me said: *Unless you are a tall, dark-haired stranger named John.*

———

The following morning, I was up and ready to go when Joseph came back from his run. He said nothing as he poured himself his tea. I got Mam ready for the day. Mrs. M always left meals in the refrigerator for us to use on the weekend, so Mam was taken care of. I reminded Joseph that Bridget would be arriving around 4:00 p.m. and that I should be home by then or shortly thereafter.

I saddled up the bicycle, checking my makeup for the fifth time, and was off. It looked as if rain could very well fall on my parade. The mirror assured me that today's choice of jumper and jeans was more stylish and flattering than my togs of the previous two weeks, but I slipped on my slicker, a cautionary move.

John was already on the bench reading the paper when I arrived.

He stood up. *Good morning, Catherine with a C.*

*The same to you, John.*

We started walking with no particular direction in mind, sometimes pointing out what we were seeing along the way, sometimes just walking in step. After a bit, John looked up to the sky; the day was becoming increasingly darker. He smiled. *It looks as if the Irish weather is going to factor into our plans today. Do you fancy grabbing a cuppa at Bewley's?*

*That would be lovely. I would like it accompanied by another chat on Irish history.*

*Well, that might be a memory test. I will do my best, but I must confess that my A-levels were in math and economics.*

*And mine were in Philosophy and English, so that is why we are talking about history. I am now doing a refresher course.*

*Ah, we are well-blended, just like the tea we'll soon be sipping.* He smiled as he took the handlebars. *Given the winds are now picking up, I suggest that we make haste for Grafton Street so we can stay dry.*

We arrived at our destination just as the heavens opened and the rain and wind joined forces. I wrestled with my slicker, now slightly damp, as I slid into the booth. Looking around the stained-glass windows, I raised my hands as if embracing all around me. *I love it here, always have. It is the English major in me. I envision others sitting in these very same seats, Joyce plotting out Dubliners or Yeats mending his broken heart brought on by another of his mistress's rejection to be a proper wife. Did they talk about love or politics or war or their neighbors?*

*Oh, my darlin' Catherine. I am going to put good money, that like every Irishman and most women at that time, the conversation was Irish politics. Pretty much the same conversation you would be hearing at any of the local pubs today, only the names being cursed at have changed. For the treaty that Michael Collins brought home from London created a rupture across Ireland, separating parties, interests, and families that I fear may never mend. Our Civil War was its first victim.*

I had to remind myself that I had to listen to what he was saying. I kept looking at his eyes, like the skies at midnight. I became lost in their intensity. He had called me 'darling,' but for the Irish, that is a standard greeting. Nonetheless, it warmed my heart and, I feared, my cheeks. *Concentrate, Cate, concentrate* was my mantra.

John continued. *The War of Independence was all about self-definition from Britain, cultural and political. Once Collins brought that Anglo-Irish treaty back for ratification, sides were drawn. Passionate, unrelenting—often violent—views that came to blows at the kitchen table and on to the roads and fields throughout the land.*

*My mother's side was against the Treaty. Staunch supporters of the IRA, they wanted complete independence from Britain. Her family came from Cork City. To her da, this treaty was a betrayal of the dead, those who had fought and died for a Free State. He believed till the day he died that this country had to be one, there should be no dividing line between the North and the rest of this island. He couldn't accept that we would still be considered part of the British empire that the members of the Irish Parliament would have to take an oath of allegiance to the Crown. "Take a knee for the king? Never!" my granddad would shout, banging his fist on the table. "Collins took a bite of Lloyd George's tea and scones and seemed to like the taste. He gave us away."*

I raised my eyebrows; this was the first time he had mentioned any family. *And your da's side?*

John added a touch of milk to his brew. *Well, there are two sides to every issue.*

*Only two?* I responded as I reached for the same pitcher, our hands brushing against one another.

He took a sip of his tea. *You are a light in my life, Catherine with a C.*

My heart felt like it was going to burst.

*My grandad on that side of the family was a banker and while supporting the cause, he hadn't participated in the actual fighting. According to family lore, though without proof, he was responsible for raising the funds for the gunrunners for the IRA in its fight against the Crown. He agreed that Collins had negotiated a bad treaty, but he wanted the fighting to end. Granddad believed in compromise. He did it at work. He did it at home, which is why he and my granny celebrated their 50th wedding anniversary. He wanted the same for his country. Believed the treaty was a step in the right direction. It was time to get ourselves in order. Our men needed jobs. Their children needed schools. We were years behind in our manufacturing capability.*

*Come Christmas time, my own ma would start praying that our dinner would be devoid of politics.* John chuckled. *She never got her prayers answered; Michael Collins and the treaty cast a long shadow over the table. I was a young lad, but even I could feel the tension in the air. We were divided as a family. We were as divided as the nation. A nation that still draws this line in the sand.*

The rain had stopped. John looked at his watch. *How quickly the time goes when I am with you. Perhaps a wee bit earlier and without the chariot? The restaurant at the Shelburne has a lovely Saturday midday meal, if you would be inclined to accept my invitation.*

Wanting a bit more insight into who he is, I nodded and offered, perhaps *a conversation about books rather than politics?*

*Agreed.*

I smiled. *I will see you next Saturday, say at half eleven? Now, if I could retrieve my chariot, it would be time for me to return to the land of the cherubs.*

*I will count the hours*, and he doffed his cap.

*And I.*

The sun had now broken through, and its light was making prisms in the puddles we were carefully avoiding.

Handing me the bicycle, he cradled my face with his hands.

*Until next Saturday.* I simply nodded, unable to catch my breath.

———

Mam was asleep when I came in.

Joseph joined me at her bedside. *How was your outing?*

*The very best, Joseph, the very best. Let me change, and pour me a glass of Mam's best Irish whiskey. I want to talk to you about the Irish Civil War.*

Joseph stepped back. *The Irish Civil War? Well, I have not given much thought as to where you are on these Saturdays, but going back to the time before you were born would not have been my guess.*

I gave him a quick hug and ran up to my room. I needed a moment to savor the day. Then I joined Joseph, two glasses filled with golden amber awaited my arrival. We each picked up one. I asked him to begin.

*I was a young lad and fairly sheltered from most of what was happening. What I do remember is not so much about the about politics, but how that time broke our brothers, Liam and Andrew. The two of them had always been thick as thieves as far back as I can remember. Our da wasn't around that much, he spent most of his time at the mill. We were living with my own mother's parents, who, having lost their youngest daughter the day I was born, had pretty much given up their will to live. They simply had no energy left to supervise teenage boys, particularly those two.*

*Liam and Andrew were just lads when they joined the IRA, Liam was always a fighter, reckless and strong, he was looking for adventure. He was the perfect recruit; not afraid to get hurt or hurt others. I think with Andrew it was the love of country. He idolized Michael Collins, saw him as a hero who drove men harder but no harder than he drove himself.*

*It was after Collin's return with the Treaty that the two of them split along the same lines as the rest of the country. Everyone thought they knew best for Ireland's future, and there was a surplus of opinions. One has never been enough. Such was politics in those days, and as such, it was in our family as well. Andrew thought the treaty was the best option and said so. Thought it was the best first step. Liam was just the opposite; he saw the world in black and white, always did. There were never shades of gray in his worldview.*

I had to smile. *Not sure much has changed. Either in the land or at home.*

*Fair enough,* was Joseph's reply. Sipping the first of his drink, he closed his eyes. *I was coming down the stairs when I heard their voices. It was fairly early in the morning, and I was the first to rise. Andrew had been staying in the house, but we hadn't seen Liam for months. The wind was howling, so I couldn't catch all their words, but could tell from the tone that it was best if I stayed seated on the stairs.*

*I could see their shadows, they faced each other off. Andrew was the taller of the two, but Liam had him by a good twenty pounds, all of it muscle. Andrew's voice was quiet, I had to strain to hear him, but I knew the message. It was the same one he had talked about at dinner the night before. He knew the treaty that Collins had negotiated wasn't perfect, but he saw it as a foothold to a free Ireland. Liam saw it as a surrender dressed up as a victory. Said it smelled of betrayal and sullied the names of those who had fought and died alongside them. There were plenty of words but no fists that morning.*

*Andrew had a calm steadiness about him that seemed to disarm Liam's temper. Or so I mistakenly thought. Liam left the house without a word to say where he was going. He didn't bother to say goodbye to either me or our da. The next day, Andrew came home with the news that he had joined the New Republic Army. Da didn't say much, but gave the response that he often did, that it was up to us to do what we thought was right. I wasn't sure what joining another army meant, but I was off to school the next day and not home again until the summer break.*

*I was back. It was summer. It was a day I will never forget. The violence ravaging this fair island found its way into our own home. I had been out with one of my mates; it was one of the few days that week that the weather didn't demand you take heed and stay inside. I came home to find Andrew on the floor in the kitchen. He was wearing the uniform of the Free Army State. He was moaning, his clothes torn and bloody. Liam stood over him, his hands tightly fisted, shouting 'traitor' as he spat on him. Our da walked in and quietly said Liam's name. Liam looked at him as if he were seeing a stranger; his eyes were glazed, his nostrils flared. Da knelt and took Andrew's hand, and looked back at Liam. "This is your brother. You could have killed him."*

*Liam's voice was wild. "He is no brother of mine. He shoulders the king's rifle and uses it to kill our comrades. He is no different from those that wore black and tan. May he rot in hell." And with that, Liam stormed out of the house.*

*Da finally realized I was a party to all of this and sent me to my room. Andrew was in hospital for weeks and entered the monastery upon his release. We saw him off at the train station; he looked old beyond his years. The next time I saw him was when you were baptized. Liam was there as well. It was the first time we had all been together since the fight. Neither one spoke to the other, only a nod of recognition before the service.*

*Liam would return home periodically, usually looking for food, liquor, and money, and in that order. He was never able to hold a job, even those that our da had gotten him at the mill. It would never work, and he never saw it as his fault. He would rail about his bosses or his fellow workers or the long hours. Then he would take off, and we wouldn't hear a word.*

*Liam came home when Da died, saying he was staying for good. Mam had him take a spot in the mill. It seemed to go well initially, but then the cycle started all over again. O'Reilly, the supervisor that Da had hired and trained, didn't show him the respect that he deserved and treated him as a worker rather than the rightful head of the business. His fellow workers were either ignorant or lazy, sometimes both.*

*He came home one day after having too many at the local. Mam had put you down for the night, and I was in my room studying for my A-levels. I heard Liam's voice shouting, his sentences slurred. I came downstairs and saw him standing over Mam, yelling that she had to fire O'Reilly and make him the boss. That it was his place to be giving orders, not receiving them. Mam said she wasn't going to do that, that his da had trusted O'Reilly in running the business, and she was going to do the same. She started to say that he had to earn his place when Liam lost control. He had his hands raised as if to hit her when I came into the room. Mam hadn't flinched. I remember what our da had done, I said his name, loudly but calmly. That stopped him from doing the unthinkable. He looked at the two of us, his eyes were darting every which way, his mouth open. He said nothing more, just grabbed his coat that he had tossed on the floor in his rage, slammed the door, and walked out. Mam just sat there. She thanked me for coming down the stairs, but that I should go back up and continue my studies.*

*Shortly thereafter, O'Reilly gave her an offer to buy the mill. I am not sure whether it was the confrontation with Liam or the energy that she needed to run two businesses, a house, and the two of us that made her take the offer. But within three months of our da's funeral, the mill was sold.*

*This is a long way around your question, Cate, but you had to see the effect this war had on us, on our family. This country not only lost the North but a whole generation of lads. Lads who grew up shooting guns, hiding in fields, hating someone else. When it was over, they had no place to go. No place where they fit. I believe that is what happened to Liam. Our own family tells the story of what happened after Collins signed that treaty.*

Joseph closed his eyes.

I could think of nothing to say. I remembered Elizabeth's line that war is never glamorous. I now recognize its casualties are not just left on the battlefields.

------

**War**

Listening to these stories, these stories not of the turmoil and bloodshed of war but of its victims—family ties severed and lingering. Bitterness is a difficult cup to drink from. Liam and Andrew were torn apart by a piece of paper, the Anglo-Irish Treaty. It wasn't just about the politics—it was about betrayal, trust, brotherhood. For Liam, the treaty had been a broken promise, a rejection of everything he believed he had fought for. For Andrew, it was a beacon of hope.

The Civil War ended, but Ireland has not fully recovered. The division still divides—this country, my brothers, John's Christmas table.

I wonder what price so many have paid for a world that now is seemingly at peace.

——

I put down the pen.

——

Saturday morning dawned bright and beautiful. Though not as clever as Mam with the needle and thread, I was able to transform one of her old dresses into a style befitting both my figure and modern times. The navy satin was taken from her closet, but its 1930s style was replaced with a bateau neckline that hinted at an understated elegance, and its delicate cap sleeves added just the right touch of sophistication. I added a pair of short white gloves and my New York red suede pumps to complete the look. I intended to look very different from the young lass in blue jeans on a bicycle who couldn't refuse the offer of an ice pop.

Mam was awake when I came down to say goodbye, impressed when she saw what I had done. She shook her head at my offer to move her to the chair.

Her voice was soft, *I think I'd rather stay here, my darling daughter, just for a while longer.*

She gave me a warm smile. *I remember wearing what once had been that frock to a luncheon in honor of De Valera. I had just been given the order to dress the women in the Irish military. Not exactly my specialty,* she smiled, *but it kept food in the pantry and kept the business afloat. Indeed, well-floated.* She took my hand.

*You look beautiful, my darling' daughter. You will turn the head of whoever it is you made this dress for.*

Even as ill as she is, Mam knew. She knew something was up. I just gave her a quick kiss on the cheek, waved goodbye to Joseph, and was off. I crossed my fingers that by the time I got home, Mam would be napping and Joseph, being Joseph, would never ask a question.

I got to St. Stephen's Green with plenty of time to spare. The early morning frost had turned the leaves a deep, blood red.

John was already there. I knew I looked good, and the smile that went from his eyes to his lips confirmed it. *Should we walk to the restaurant? It is a fine day, and you look so beautiful, I am a mind to show you off.*

He took my hand. Not my arm. Our fingers intertwined. It felt comfortable. I would have started to hum if only I could carry a tune.

We turned and found our way to the Shelburne Hotel, a mark of sophistication with its tuxedoed waiters and linen tablecloths. This is where the well-heeled dined and often sampled the wine list to an extreme. I was not intimidated. I have been here before. This is where Mam would take us to celebrate each of our university graduations.

Our champagne cocktails arrived, and our order taken when I raised my glass to give a toast. *I think it is time that in true Irish tradition to talk about our love of poetry and storytelling.*

John smiled and reached into his jacket, coming up with a book, its pages yellowing with age. *I couldn't agree more. I have brought the "Collected Works of William Butler Yeats." I would like to tell you because I envision myself a poet. Alas and alack, not the case. This is the only book review that I can remember writing. Yet, I remember reading him for the first time, it was as if I had found a secret that had been waiting just for me.*

I laughed out loud, gathering more than one displeased face from our fellow diners. *That is a lovely thought.* I paused for dramatic effect, *though I have always considered myself more of a Wilde girl.* I put my well-worn copy of *"The Importance of Being Ernest"* on the table.

Now it was John's turn to laugh; he raised an eyebrow. *Oscar Wilde? Really? I mean, Wilde is witty and dramatic, but Yeats is timeless; he gets into your bones.*

I was now totally engaged in the conversation. *There is no doubt that Yeats is masterful. But Wilde is just so full of contradictions. "I can resist anything except temptation." How can you not help adoring someone who understands the art of irony like that?*

John was not giving in. *I understand the appeal of Wilde, his sharpness, his flair for drama, not only with a pen, but also his life.*

I couldn't help but grin. *Well, he did say,* "We are all in the gutter, but some of us are looking at the stars."

John leaned forward, smiling widely. *So despite my best efforts, we still talk of battles.* He raised his glass. *Here's to literary battles. And to us.*

I thought my heart would jump out of its skin.

The rest of the meal turned into a discussion of poets and authors, playwrights, and artists. We had no concept of the time. The lunch crowd had dwindled, being replaced by those looking for the start of the cocktail hour.

John looked at his watch. *How quickly the hours go when I am with you. For now, I just want to hold your hand and walk with you by my side.*

We were just leaving the restaurant when John stopped and pulled me to him. He put his lips to my ear, *I would like to kiss you, Catherine. Oh, so very much. But want to be sure.*

Before he could finish the sentence, I put my lips on his and inhaled him. My heart and the world stopped at the same time. I was not sure I had ever been in love. I was not sure if I was in love now. I was only sure that I had never felt like this.

I stayed in his arms, the sun breaking the last of its beams upon us. Reluctantly, we broke apart. We walked near my street. *I can make it from here.* I wanted to kiss him goodbye. An act I was not prepared to do in front of the house I call home.

John stopped and looked down on me. *Next Saturday, could we start even a wee bit earlier? There is a bus to Howth that leaves O'Connell Station at 10:00 a.m., and we could go to the sea.*

*I love it.* Stopping short of adding I love you. *I will see you then.*

He squeezed my hand. *A final kiss?*

*Yes, but one that will not scandalize the passersby.* He cradled my head with his hands and kissed me gently.

I practically skipped home, though I vowed to wear more comfortable shoes the next time such an outing was suggested.

———

It was getting harder and harder to keep Mam awake. She was not eating and drinking very little. Bridget showed me how to wet her lips so that she could take in some water.

*She is fading,* Bridget said, her voice quiet.

*I know, but it is difficult to see her like this. She was so full of life, a force to be reckoned with, every moment. I am not sure how I can manage her not being here for me.*

*We manage, Miss. We learn how to manage.*

*I am sorry, Bridget, I know you lost your da. It must be very hard for you and your mam with so many still at home.*

*'Tis. But me mam's life has never been an easy one, and yet she made each day special for us. We were Travellers, ya know.*

My eyes opened wide. *I didn't know* and quickly added, *nor do I mind.* I remembered that the Irish Travellers were considered the lowest echelon of Irish society, living in caravans, moving from town to town, no real jobs, not much schooling.

*I am sorry, I've never met a Traveller before. I've heard others call them gypsies.*

*Ignorant fools,* Bridget shot back, her green eyes now on fire. *We are not gypsies; no Romanian blood flows through us. Me da told me that we were here before the English, before the Celts. We are the true Irish, with our own language and our own way of life. We didn't want to settle on one plot of land but saw the whole of the isle as our home. That is why we took to moving from one spot to the next.*

*How did you end up staying in Dublin?*

*Now there is a story. Me mam and me da are a true love story.*

*Can you share if you have time?*

*Always have a moment to tell this tale. It keeps me da alive for me and I have a few minutes to spare, unless there's something else you think your mam needs.*

*No, she's settled for the night. Please tell me more.*

Bridget began the tale. In the weeks that she had been with us, I had never seen her quiet. She was in perpetual motion. Not now. *She is lovely,* I thought. *Her raven hair and bronze colored skin seem more exotic in repose.*

Her green eyes opened slowly, and she started, *'Twas the Puck Fair in Kerry where their story begins. Ma always blamed the Fair's crowned goat for her fate of giving birth to so many.*

In response to my quizzical look, she added, *Puck Fair was a fete long before Patrick found his way to our shores. We were celebrating Lughnasadh even then, the beginning of the harvest season. The goat, the pagan fertility symbol, is the Fair's greatest attraction.*

*Me da was the oldest boy in his family; they were the Travellers. He was at the Fair to help his pa trade some horses with the local farmers. Me ma's family were farmers up the road and never bothered to see any reason to go and enjoy themselves.*

83

*They lived with my granny, who ran the family with a strong hand and a stronger will. Me ma was allowed to go to the Fair with one of her brothers, with the strict rules that she was to stay with him and be home prior to supper. Well, me ma's brother dropped her as soon as they set foot on the grounds, running off with his mates, leaving me ma to fend for herself.*

*Was she scared, so young and all alone?* I couldn't imagine such a fate.

*Not me ma,* smiled Bridget. *She's never been one to walk away from adventure.*

*She was walking near the area where the horses were tied when she heard me da singing. She always said that she had never heard anything sound so beautiful. And when she saw him, she added, or seen anyone so beautiful, all dark hair with skin that had been touched by the sun, bronzed and golden. The song was "The Minstrel Boy." Me ma's older brother had died during the First War, and when Ma heard the words, she started to cry. Me da heard her sobs, and as he told the story, he thought his singing had brought an angel down to earth. When he first laid his eyes upon her, he said she was the most beautiful creation he'd ever seen. He then would add with a smile, and that included the lovely chestnut mare he was bidding to take home.*

*Well, that was it, for the two of them. They kissed, vowed their love. The next day, me ma packed a small bag and met me da at the Travellers camp. His people wanted nothing to do with her, her being a buffer, I mean, an outsider and all. But me da was as strong as their love. Told his family that if they didn't accept her, both of them would be leaving.*

*Now, you need to understand,* Bridget continued, her voice the strongest I'd ever heard it. *Besides knowing his horses and with a voice that could open the hardest of hearts, me da was the best bare-knuckle fighter in the family. He was the one that defended the family honor and could resolve any business or personal disputes with his fists. So, the family had no choice but to bring her into the camp. Me ma has always been clear that she was never accepted. When me da wasn't there, the others would speak to each other in Shelta, their own secret language. Soon, me ma had her hands full and couldn't give two pence for what was going on around her, for I was born less than 12 months from that first kiss, and me twin brothers followed in less than a year. The Travellers like large families, so while still cold to me ma, the air was beginning to thaw.*

*Ma lost two bairns after that and was pretty sick. There was no sympathy or caring for her from those that rode the caravan. Then came another set of twins. Boys again. I was 5 years old at the time. Took on more of a mother role than a sister to those young'uns.*

*Ma's body was giving out. The endless moving about, the babes all needing her milk at the same time, was taking its toll on her. Me da, too, was beginning to slow down and found himself losing matches that two years before he would have won easily.*

*The caravan was back in Kerry, not far from the Puck Fair. Whether it was the hand of fate or the work of the fairies, me ma's granny, who she had always been close to, saw her by the fire in the camp. She had the babes cradled in her arms, and I was playing with the other two at her feet. Well, Granny, who was a force to be reckoned with, would do nothing less than to find her way into the camp and see us. She took one look at me ma, and said, "You are coming home and bring them with you." Me ma refused, saying she had a husband and was staying with him.*

*Me granny knew better than to accept their marital status, for there had been no sacrament pronouncing them as man and wife.*

*So, me granny responds, "Bring him with you. There is a smithy in town who could use a hand, and you need to have a roof over your head and peat in the fire. I am going to find him. You pack what you need and meet me when the sun is rising tomorrow morning. I am bringing you home, and that is the end of this discussion."*

*Ma knew better than to argue. The camp was looking on, but me ma didn't let on what the discussion was about. That night, me da came home from a fight, battered and bruised.*

*Me ma spoke to him, stronger and clearer than ever before. Her message was simple: "This fighting is going to kill ya, and then what will happen to me? The wee ones will be taken from me, and I will be left to who knows what else. Me granny is willing to give us a roof over our heads, bread and milk on the table, and a promise of steady work for you. It will be as different a life for you as it was for me to come here. But it is no longer about us; it is about them as well."*

*She wanted a life for us. She wanted us to go to school. To have friends. To have a future. She told him that he never had the chance to think about the future. But we should have the chance.*

*Ma always said that she didn't know if it was her arguments or if Granny had gotten to him, or perhaps it was his broken ribs and black eye that convinced him, but that morning, he was standing beside her and got into Granny's wagon. Their first stop was to the local parish, where the priest married them in the eyes of the church. Then Granny took them home.*

I had to ask. *Did your da ever get used to life that wasn't on the road?*

*He never glorified his life before they were in Kerry. Told us tales but not with longing, more just storytelling. He worked with the smithy, and I think he liked it well enough. As we got older, he also started to train horses again. He was a natural and soon had more offers than he could accept.*

*Two more of us, me youngest sisters, were born there, but more evenly spaced out.*

*Then, just a year ago, me da was kicked in the head by one of the horses that had gone crazy. He was brought home but didn't last the week. I had just finished nursing school. One of the twins had left for America, and the other had gotten accepted at the University College Dublin. The young'uns were still in school and quite a handful, particularly the girls. Too good-looking and too headstrong for their own good.*

*We made the decision to come to Dublin. I could get work here, and me older brother could go to school and work part-time. Me brother in Boston is a fireman and sends us money as well, so we are making ends meet. Ma is thinking about getting a job, but I think the younger ones still need her home. The younger twins are playing with a band at a local pub and still need to be looked after whilst they look for fame and glory. And the girls are just about the same age as her when she ran off with da. And though I love their story, we don't need history to repeat itself!*

With that, Bridget jumped up. *I must get back.*

*I am so happy you shared your story with me, Bridget. You and your ma are remarkable women. As is your granny, I would have loved to have met her.*

*And she, you, Miss.*

———

### Heart and Head

Bridget's story about her parents—and what I know of Mam and Billy Conlon—has me thinking about how the heart can bend logic, how it pulls us toward things we can't quite explain. What gives someone the courage to walk into the unknown, not knowing what's ahead?

Maybe it is love. Or maybe something else—some quiet stirring inside, restless and hungry for more than what was expected. A longing for a life not already written. Perhaps it is that same longing that pushed me to leave this house and make my way to New York.

Mam and Bridget's mother didn't have the freedom I have. They couldn't just step away and try something new. Their choices were fewer, and yet they followed something larger than themselves.

I wonder—would it be easier if I knew this was only about love? John is reaching a part of me I hadn't known was there. Is that what Mam felt once? That with the right person, your world might open?

Maybe the fairies have a hand in it—nudging hearts forward when reason holds them back. It makes the questions easier to ask.

Though I seem to be asking more questions than I am answering.

———

I put down the pen.

———

It was late afternoon, and the light from the window was soft. A rare day in Ireland; the weather was quiet, as if the world was on pause. It was Friday, and I hoped tomorrow would look the same.

For some reason I couldn't quite understand, Mam seemed stronger. The strength in her voice had returned. She seemed to be sitting up a little straighter, her breath a little less ragged.

*Mam, you're looking a bit stronger today.*

She gave a tired smile, the corners of her lips slightly lifting, but enough to remind me of the woman she had once been.

*I guess I am,* Mam replied softly. *I've been thinking. About some things.*

*Like what?* My voice was barely above a whisper, as though afraid the moment would shatter if I spoke too loudly.

Mam's eyes drifted towards the window, watching the light as it bathed the room in gold. *I've been thinking about the book, the book of tales. I am not sure where it is. I can't believe that I haven't thought about it before. You know the tales your great-grandfather wrote on his journey to America.*

*For sure, it is part of our family lore; it was how you would tell me about your own ma. Her family had come from Quebec and then found their way to New York, picking up a young lad named Mike Mooney along the way.*

Mam smiled. *You do remember well. Well, there is a book of Irish legends and stories that he wrote during that journey. That was the book I took to Nell's house.*

*You never showed it to me.*

*It is too fragile, and you were too young. The pages can't take much more wear and tear. Then, when you got old enough to hold it, I simply forgot to give it to you. I thought there would be more time.* Mam looked wistful.

I got up from the chair. *Tell me where it is. I will bring it down and will be very careful, promise.*

I got another Mam smile. *In my closet, there is a metal box. It has all my final papers and this book. Joseph knows about the papers.*

I found the journal, its leather cracked, the ink faded, but the elegant, looping script of her grandfather was still there, just as she had described. I brought it downstairs.

*I have it, Mam.*

*Be careful with it, love. For like the past, it is fragile, indeed.*

Mam ran her fingers over the worn leather cover. *He was a schoolteacher, and he recorded all he heard. The legends of the banshees, the tales of the kings and queens that ruled this land when it was ours. These were stories that were carried with those who were forced to leave this island, searching for a new life. We are all stories, Cate. Our dreams, our heartaches, our loves. And stories never die; they live with the telling.*

*Can I read you one, Mam? I think it is a perfect day for the telling of a tale.*

Mam smiled. *For sure, but I should be sitting in my chair for such a treat. And if you don't tell the good doctor when he comes by, either courting or checking, never quite sure what he is up to,* Mam smiled, *I'll take a wee glass of whiskey and pour yourself one as well.*

This was my mam. This day was a gift. I got her into her chair, poured us each a small glass, and reached for her hand. *I will try to find a story whose ink is still legible.* I opened the book. *Here is one that will do. The story of Queen Maeve, the warrior of great strength and power.*

*Perfect choice, Cate, for as you know, it was my own mam's name as well. It means intoxicating, which is quite fitting as I take my first sip.* She raised her glass in salute.

By the time the sun had dipped lower in the sky, the story was over. Mam wanted to rest, the result of the storytelling and the half-empty glass of whiskey. I tucked her in, thinking that these stories, like her legacy, will continue to live on. They are woven into the fabric of our world, our family, passed down from generation to generation. They are part of the blood that runs through our veins.

———

## The Villain Cancer

Mam's strength is slipping away. There are days when she is more like the Mam I remember, when she reacts to an article I've read or comments on a dress that I have altered. More and more often, there are bad days. Days when she sleeps most of the hours away or is lost somewhere else in her memories.

The cancer is stealing her, inch by inch. I want to be able to fight back, to scream at the unfairness of it all. But the villain never shows his face.

I am torn with grief and gratitude, love and fear. I am thankful that I have this time with her. With Joseph. To show them, to tell them, how much I love them. Grief is already gnawing at me, coupled with fear. Fear of what my life will be like without Mam in it. There is no manual for this. No book to tell you what you should be doing, how you should be feeling.

I am not ready for this. I am not sure I will ever be ready. I doubt whether anyone ever is.

———

I put down the pen.

———

Today's weather is uncertain as to what it should do–cloudy, sunny, cloudy again. I want either rain or sun. I am not of the mindset to deal with anything in between. And all down to yesterday.

Yesterday began by spending the day in Howth with John. Or the man I thought was John.

From the moment I met John, I felt like I had known him forever. He was easy for me to be with. He listened when I spoke. He was calm, strong, but not overpowering. He understood quiet, not needing to fill the moment with the sound of his own voice.

We held hands as we walked the shore. He pointed out the strange little island with the cleft in its cliff, known as "Ireland's Eye." John gazed northwards, where in the blue-gray sky the mountains of Ulster rose steeply. His voice broke. *There is too much trouble in that beautiful land. Too many sons will be killed. Too many brothers will never come home. It is Ireland's burden; the love of this land kills those who hold it closest to their heart.*

I turned to look at him. He pulled me in, resting his chin on my head, his arms folding me tightly. The hug was so close, I could hear his heartbeat. He whispered, *No talk of battles today, either literary or warfare. Only love.*

We found our way to one of the seaside cafés. Though too cold to sit outside, we could smell the sea. Sea lions bopped their greedy heads in the waves as the fisherman returning with their daily catch threw the unwanted to the surf.

At the end of the meal, over our final cup of tea, John asked if I could find my way to come with him to Kinsale for a weekend. He started to describe an old inn there, nestled in the cove that brags that it is the best food in all of Cork. He took my hand. *I want to be with you, Catherine. There is much I need to tell you. I want to tell you more about who I am. I want to hear your story, your dreams, your hopes. I want to do it when I can wake up with you at my side. I want to make love to you. It's not something I say lightly. It is something that comes from my heart.*

*I can't, John.* It came out quicker than I wanted.

*Is there another in your life?*

*Yes,* and when he pulled away, I quickly continued, *It's me mam. My mother is dying. I am here to take care of her, to be with her in her final days. I can find my way to be with you on days like today, as my brother stays with her. But not for an overnight. Not far away. I am not sure how much time we have left together. It is with her I must stay. No matter how much I want to be with you as well.*

John took his hand in mine. *Grieving is hard, my darlin' Cate. You are bearing the loss of seeing someone you love dearly about to leave you. And that loss will be indescribable. It is we, those left behind, who suffer. Kinsale will always be there. We'll find a time, another time. Until then, we have our Saturdays.*

I nodded. *To our Saturdays.*

We walked back to the bus stop, a couple, a couple in love. I didn't feel guilty about being in love when Mam was so ill. Then I started to feel guilty about not feeling guilty. That passed, and for a moment, all I could think of was that I was in love. And I would bet good money John was in love, too.

That evening, I was invited to Timmy's parents' house for a party. Timmy had asked me last week. His mother was having a small gathering of family and friends to celebrate both his birthday and his graduation from Trinity's Medical School. He thought it fitting that I should be there both as an 'old friend' and as one who could testify to his skills as a physician. He added that some of the students from our old school, St. Margaret's, had been invited, so it would be somewhat of a reunion. I readily agreed. He is a good person, and I was curious to see both the Murphy house and how some of my old chums had fared.

I got Mam ready for bed before I left, and Joseph was confident he could handle the rest. He even lent me his car to drive to the party. He handed me the keys with a stern smile, *Remember what side of the road you are to be driving on. This isn't America.* His eyes widened as I fiddled with the keys. *When was the last time you were behind the wheel of a car?*

I didn't dare tell him it was before I left for New York, so I simply smiled and off I went, wearing the shimmering silk dress that I had finally finished. Mam was right, the skirt looked like waves floating to the sand.

The Murphys had bought one of the old Great Houses, a house that a British lord had held title to for centuries. It was one of the estates the rebels in 1921 had attacked, forcing its previous occupants to flee to London. The Murphys were now the proud owners, with the claim that generations ago, according to Timmy, his mother's ancestors had owned the very same tract of land.

I was cautious as I drove up the long-curved driveway, set between a pair of identical iron railings. The house came into view, a handsome stone mansion, with numerous tall bushes bordered by old timbers, oak, and beech trees. Holly bushes were gathered in between. I was thinking that Mr. Murphy must have done very well in America to come back to take possession of such an imposing estate. The coldness and the grandeur of the outside were immediately transplanted by the feeling of welcome transmitted by the surroundings I entered. Fireplaces were burning bright, chintz sofas, plush velvet chairs, and Waterford Crystal lamps brought a warmth into the rooms that the previous owners could never have imagined. This redecorating had clearly been a work of love and an unlimited budget. I thought to myself, *Nell would love it here!*

Timmy came rushing to my side as I entered, handing off my coat to one of the hired helpers. He kissed me on the cheek. *You look beautiful, like a goddess from the sea.* I couldn't help but blush.

He brought me over to introduce me to his parents, taking my arm as he did so. Gracious and hospitable, his mam scrutinized me carefully.

*Yikes*, I thought, *she thinks I am important to him. Joseph may be right about the Valentine after all.*

There was a small group standing next to the bar area. I recognized almost immediately graduates from St. Margaret's Academy, and I found my way there. The years melted away. We quickly passed the awkward introductory stage of resumé sharing—where we were living, what we were doing, how we were surviving. We were on our way to storytelling, and I was regaling them with my struggles of learning US English, when I heard his voice.

*Sorry, Ma, Molly took a bit longer getting ready as she wanted to look 'pecial' for Uncle Timmy's party.*

It was John, holding the hand of a 6-year-old little girl who was about to be scooped up by Timmy's mother. *I was wondering what was keeping you. Come, my darlin' girl, I want you to meet Granny's 'pecial friends.'*

The little one, her mane of black curls flying, was whisked away.

John turned and saw me. Our eyes met before I turned away. Happily, one of my former classmates was delighting the group with his latest adventures in the south of France, so I had only to smile appropriately when cued by the others. Timmy came by my side as his father called the gathering into the dining room for dinner. I was seated between Timmy and his mother's sister, an aunt whose name I never quite captured. John was directly across from me, the little girl between him and his mother.

It was as if I was living a nightmare, Tim introducing me to his brother "Jack," a man whom just hours ago I passionately kissed goodbye with a promise of more to come.

*Cate, is it?* John, now Jack, questioned.

I, too, could rise to this occasion, whatever it was. *Yes,* I replied. *With a C. Short for Catherine, the saint.*

Timmy smiled and leaned towards his brother, pointing at me, *And we have a saint-in-the-making with this one, Jack. Came all the way back from the States to take care of her mam, who is quite ill.*

Before that conversation continued, a very precocious six-year-old piped up, *I have not been properly introduced, Uncle Timmy.*

*My apologies, love. Mary Ellen, better known as Molly, please meet my dear friend, Miss Clark.*

She nodded in my direction, her father and uncle both watching. *I like your lipstick. I wanted to wear lipstick because this is a grown-up party, and I wanted to look grown-up. But he won't let me,* looking disdainfully at her father.

I couldn't help but smile. *Oh, you are so beautiful just as you are. You are in no need of such frivolous things.*

Jack bent over and nuzzled her, whispering loud enough for everyone to hear, *See, I told you so.* She shrieked with laughter.

Tim never took his eyes off me as John, now Jack, continued. *Where in the States are you living?*

*New York. I understand from Timmy that your family spent some time in America, Chicago, was it not? Were you there as well?*

*I stayed in Ireland to finish my schooling here at Blackrock, which is how my parents found this house. I joined them when I began university at Stanford. California's sunshine was more to my liking than the cold winds of either Illinois or Ireland.*

His mother then steered the conversation to her falling in love with this house and the perils of buying property long distance. I was happy for the distraction.

Timmy then looked down at my plate. *Are you okay, Cate? You've eaten nothing of your dinner? Are you not well? Do you want something else? I am sure we ...*

*No, no.* I touched Tim's arm. *I am afraid I was tempted by too many nibbles during the drinks party. I am saving whatever I have left for the cake, which I'm sure is coming.*

Tim settled back, and I turned my attention to the aunt whose name I still couldn't remember. Cake and champagne were served, though I don't remember touching either.

The evening was drawing to a close. Looking at his watch, John leaned over to his daughter, who was relishing every last bite of birthday cake. *Granny needs to take you to your bed upstairs. This is way too late for you. I will be up in a minute to kiss you goodnight.*

Granny stood up at just that precise moment to whisk her away, but not before Molly proclaimed, pointing at me, *She is very nice, even though she has ginger hair.*

I laughed out loud. It had been years since someone called me a Ginger.

Finally, after the final glass had been raised both to Timmy's accomplishments and his birthday, the evening ended.

I was putting my coat on when John, returning from kissing Molly, found me. Tim was at his parents' side, bidding the other revelers and relatives a good evening and safe journey home. John came beside me, his dark eyes finding mine.

*Catherine, it never occurred ...*
I didn't dare look at him. *And now is not the time for any conversation.*
*Saturday? My mother always takes Molly for the day.*
Our eyes locked. *Saturday* was my only reply. But all I wanted to do was to fold myself into his arms.

———

## Turmoil

John is Jack. He is Timmy's brother. He has a daughter named Molly. He had a wife. He lives a life very different from the one I imagined.

I thought I knew him, or at least, was starting to know him. But tonight, seeing him with Molly, everything shifted.

I knew there was more to John. No one's life is as simple as I wanted to believe. But this is a new layer, one I didn't expect.

He's a father. A father who has a daughter whom he clearly adores.

I feel unsettled, a mix of emotions I can't untangle. I'm not angry. I don't feel like I've been lied to. I just never imagined that John would have a child. That he is someone's father.

If John and I were to have a future together, Molly would be part of it. My dreams have now changed into a new reality. I can't pretend it's just John and me anymore. I simply don't know what all that means.

What I do know is I have never felt like this before. What I do know is that the touch of his hand makes my heart race, and the sound of his laughter lightens my mood. What I do know is I have fallen in love with him.

That hasn't changed.

———

I put down the pen.

———

Mam was asleep when I found my way down the stairs the next morning. Joseph looked up from the table. He started to speak, but I did a quick shake of my head. *Off to Mass.* My voice must have given me away.

*Are you okay, Cate?*

*Timmy's party,* I spoke before he could finish the sentence ... *so much of the past appeared all at once. A bit much to take in.*

Joseph turned his eyes to the window, looking out at the foggy street. *The sun is higher now, breaking its way through. You might not need your slicker after all.*

I gave a quick smile. *I will take it with me as insurance that it will be a sunny day.*

I escaped to the ritual of the Mass, a time to be lost in my own thoughts, thoughts that remained jumbled. I still can't describe my feelings. It isn't betrayal. No lies have been told. Confusion. For sure, but that wouldn't make the pit of my stomach feel like it was finding its way to my throat.

By the time Father Flanagan gave the last blessing, I had no better idea of what I was going to do than the moment I first knelt down.

I walked home slowly. My world was tilted sideways. I was uncertain; the web had become too tangled. John is Jack. Jack is Timmy's brother. John has a daughter. John has been married. Timmy is falling in love with me. I am falling in love with John.

My mother is sick; my mother is dying. I am here to take care of her. I am not here to fall in love.

My thoughts spun in circles. For the moment, I don't even want to think.

I opened the door to the house. Joseph was in the parlor reading. Mam was asleep. I kissed her forehead, and my fingers traced the back of her hand. Her skin now paper-thin. Joseph looked up.

*I need to change, and then I'll make us some lunch. Did Mam eat?*

Joseph nodded. *She had a bit of tea and toast but didn't finish it. Said she wanted to close her eyes more than she wanted to eat.* He gave a sad smile. *Take your time, I just had a cuppa, so in no hurry.*

———

## My Oasis

I've always been able to talk to Mam about everything. She was my compass, my quiet place. There was never a feeling too tangled that she couldn't help me unravel.

I sit beside her bed and watch her chest rise and fall, slower than it used to, like time itself is winding down. I want to pour everything out—to tell her about John, about Jack, about how they're the same man and how I don't know what that means. I want to tell her how my heart races when I see him. How my breath catches when he looks at me. And he has a child. A life that is already in place. What does all this mean?

Mam would help me sort it through. She'd see what I can't. How do you find your way without the one who taught you how to see?

How will I go on without her guidance? How will I ever survive in a world without her? Once again, I have more questions than answers.

———

I put down the pen.

———

Mam had not stirred when I came downstairs. I brought Joseph a cup of tea, neither one of us wanting anything else. We sat for a while in silence. He was reading. I was staring out the window.

I told Joseph that I was going to sew for a while, but just to call up if he needed me.

———

## My Refuge

I walked up the steps to the third floor, to the sewing room. I picked up the dress I was working on, the seam ripped carefully along the old stitching. I was pulling apart the old work with precision. I could hear Mam's voice in my head, the need to focus on what I was doing. I was to make each stitch count.

My hands were steady. My heart wasn't. I couldn't stop my mind from swirling. Yet somehow, in this small room, surrounded by the soft hum of the sewing machine and the quiet rhythm of my fingers moving through the fabric, I found some measure of peace. I was transforming something, pulling pieces together to make something that didn't exist before. Maybe that was all I could do now, stitch together the pieces of my heart.

I looked at the finished skirt. The seams were neat, the lines artfully placed. This is what Mam taught me. And like these lessons of needle and thread, Mam's love and understanding will never go away. It isn't words that matter.

———

I put down the pen.

———

I came downstairs. Joseph was sitting next to Mam and got up from the chair to put the kettle on. As I sat down at the table, he put his hand on my shoulder. Startled, as this was so unlike Joseph, I jumped back in my chair, calling his name loudly.

He poured the tea. *I am sorry, Cate, I didn't mean to give you a fright, but* Joseph briefly closed his eyes. *I am not sure how much longer she'll be with us.*

Confusion turned to fear. I had been so lost in my thoughts, I had given no mind to Mam, not even stopping by her bed to see her before I went to Mass.

*Why? What happened? I know she hasn't been eating much, but she was more like her old self on Friday evening, wanting a taste of whiskey.*

*There is no one thing, Cate. It is almost as if she were somewhere between here and heaven. I heard her talking last night. It was after you came in, and I came downstairs to get a glass of water. I couldn't make heads or tails of the conversation, but her voice was animated. More like she was having a proper chat with an old friend. I think we should start keeping watch at her bedside. We could work it out today, and Mr. and Mrs. M could spell us starting tomorrow. I will need to leave for a bit to get my desk cleared but will be back by dinner. For now, I think we should take our cuppa and go in by her.*

*Yes, was my only response. Too much was happening to me all at once. I had gotten used to Mam being sick. But she was still with us, and she had looked better on Friday. The thought that this was coming to an end was unimaginable.*

I went to her and kissed her cheek. *Good afternoon, Mam. It is Sunday, and though Joseph had promised us a bright day, I think the skies have another thought in mind.*

Mam's eyes fluttered open. She reached for my hand. *I saw him last night.*

*Him?*

*Aye, the one who is coming for me. He's a quiet man, very intense as you would expect someone who does his kind of work to be. His eyes, however, are soft. He reached out and took my hand. There was a brightness about him, a warmth that emanated from him. It beckoned me, but something held me back. I told him I wasn't ready.*

*'Twas the two of you. I told him, I need to lay my eyes on Joseph and Cate. He gave me a knowing smile, "You will never have your eyes off them."*

*That may very well be, but it is in this life I want to see them. So, if you are listening to my soul, it is saying, "Not yet."*

*He gave me a nod, "When you are ready, your soul will say, 'Enough.' I will return." And he was gone. I figured some other soul was calling him.*

*It was all quite lovely, really. But now, I could have a sip of water and then let me rest my eyes.*

Joseph put a glass to Mam's lips. When she was finished, she lay her head back on the pillow.

I stood up, startled. *I am not sure what we just heard. Did Mam tell the angel of death she would let him know when she was ready?*

Joseph nodded. We looked at Mam sleeping so peacefully, and we both started to laugh. Joseph shook his head. *Only Mam could do that.*

Joseph told me that he would sit with Mam and read out loud. *I picked up Beckett's new play, "Waiting for Godot," and thought I would give it a go. I am fine down here if you need some time to recover from last night's craik.*

I looked at him with a half-smile, *Beckett, seriously?*

Joseph looked perplexed. *Well, it has been well received, though, having glanced through it, she may never forgive me.*

I couldn't help but smile. *Think I will stick with Yeats; even Oscar Wilde may not be fitting at the moment. And I will take you up on the offer to retreat for a bit.*

Given all that was going on in my head, thoughts of John, Mam's dialogue with the angel of death, I knew I could use a bit more time alone.

———

## This House

I closed the door to my room and leaned against it, as if pressing myself into memory.

This could be the day. This could be the moment my mother dies.

It was Mam who made this house more than walls and furniture. Her voice calling up to me, her hands setting the table, her footsteps in the early morning—that's what made it home.

And when she's gone ... what will this place become?

A shell. A before.

I want to stop time.

———

I put down the pen.

———

The next two days, the house was silent. Mam was no longer waking up. We spoke in whispers, no radios played, no conversations held. We simply took turns sitting by her, reading to her, wetting her lips with a cotton swab. Joseph had given up on the Theatre of the Absurd and joined me in the poetry of our infamous Nobel Prize winner, Yeats. Patricia and Sean came by, followed by Nora and Elizabeth, to say a last farewell. There were tears in their eyes as I walked them out the door. *We are here if you need us.* I held their hands tightly as I whispered, *I know.*

Timmy came but stayed for only a brief visit; he just wanted to be sure she was resting comfortably. He held me in his arms. *She is not in pain; there is nothing more we can do for her on Earth. It is in the Lord's hands now.* He kissed me gently on the cheek when he left.

Joseph looked up when I came back from walking Timmy to the door. *He's a good man, Cate.*

*I know.* I kissed Joseph on the cheek. *I am going to try to get some rest.* He nodded and began reading.

----

The next day, we called for Father Flanagan to come to the house. It was time to give Mam the sacrament for the dying. It would be her last sacrament.

----

### The Last Rites

It was the middle of the afternoon, but time was at a standstill.

I reached for the black dress, the one I had brought from New York. That life seemed as if it belonged to someone else. I was getting ready to watch my mother receive the last rites, Extreme Unction, the sacrament for the dying. I wondered how this could be happening. To her. To me.

I found my way down the stairs. Joseph was already at Mam's bedside, her breaths shallow but steady. I had to smile when I saw him. He was wearing a new suit, charcoal gray with wide lapels, made out of the finest of worsted wool, a crisp white shirt, and the current fashion trend of a narrow tie. It was as if he was presenting the very best of himself, a true mark of his love and respect for her.

There was a knock at the door. Father Flanagan stood on the stoop. He said my name as I let him in. I whispered, *I believe we have everything ready*. He approached Mam's bed, nodded to Joseph, and crossed himself.

Joseph and I held hands as the prayers began. The priest read the prayers of absolution and anointed Mam's head with the holy oil. I squeezed Joseph's hand; tears were flowing down both our cheeks.

When Father Flanagan closed his missal, he looked over at us. *The Lord will soon welcome her into his heavenly home. She will look over you from there.* He left, his footsteps echoing softly in the quiet hallway.

Joseph and I continued to stand at the foot of the bed. It was as if we were waiting for Mam to wake up, even though we knew it would never happen.

Only the silence would remain.

———

I put down the pen.

———

I woke up with a fright. It was dark, but a light was shining through the door. Then I heard Joseph's voice. *Come down, Cate. I think it is time.*

I don't remember going down the stairs, but suddenly, I was kneeling by her bed, Joseph beside me. Mam lay quiet, her breath slower, and we each took one of her hands. She opened her eyes, bright as ever, closing them once again. I believe I heard her say, *Enough.*

She took her last breath.

———

### Lilacs & Roses

It has been two days since Mam's burial, and I still expect her to be sitting at the kitchen table when I come down in the morning. Or bustling around getting ready to leave for her shop. It feels unreal. It is hard to believe that someone so loved, so deeply a part of who I am, could disappear, could fall so utterly silent in my life.

I cannot think of a word to describe what those last days were like, the feeling when someone you love is dying, when the days are the last days. It is an emotion born out of a strange mix of opposing desires. Of waiting and wanting the waiting to be over. Of wanting time slowed and wanting time quickened. Of wanting an end to what is happening and never wanting the end. All at the very same time. It is a feeling of being submerged in a world that is both real and unreal, where you know the ending but can't begin to fathom what the next page will be.

I wander back to her room, her scent escaping the closet's door. Lilacs with a touch of rose. She always smelled like a spring day.

I found the ledgers she kept for "O'Shea of New York," and my heart stopped beating to see her familiar handwriting. There were her notes, numbers carefully placed in columns, comments about material ordered but not meeting her expectations, and references to the reaction of a certain client to a certain dress. I close my eyes and see her writing at the desk, her glasses perched on her nose, her left hand running through her now loose hair when a particular number or comment caused her to frown. Her ballpoint jottings were in her own shorthand, her penmanship still a product of all those years at Catholic schools.

She was going to tell me the stories of her childhood, her years before she returned to Ireland. There is a whole life that I wish I knew. In my mind, I see her as she must have been in those days, young, fearless, determined. I create the memory like it's my own.

What no one tells you about death is how permanent it is. I knew that it was going to happen. I thought I was prepared. But this is too painful. I can't take a day off to escape, a day when it is not true, a day when she would make me my tea or smile approvingly at the way I had done my hair. There is no break from the loss; it is final and ever-present. The me that I was when she was with me is gone. I am now nobody's daughter.

The memory of the wake is like a quilt—a series of patchworks, some pieces more prominent than others, but all brought together to bring comfort and shelter during such a gut-wrenching time. Sean and Patrica, Mr. and Mrs. M, were everywhere all at once, the recurring pattern. There were chairs in the parlor because of them. There was more food than could be consumed because of them. The house was spotless because of them.

Joseph was the quilter; he had made the arrangements at the local funeral home for the wake, the old-world custom of having the body shown in the house having now been relegated to a third party. Andrew had been notified and was given permission to come home and assist at the funeral Mass. He would arrive the day of the Mass and leave following the burial. The monastery rules were strict, his vows of obedience now sorely tested. The address we had for Liam was no longer valid; the telegram could not be delivered. It would just be the two of us, Joseph, and me side-by-side, shaking hands, introducing ourselves to people we had never met, reassuring those that we did know that we would call them if we needed anything. An offering I knew we would not take, and those who offered never expected to be called in.

On the second day, the repetition of it all became quite overwhelming. I whispered to Joseph standing at my side, *I wish somebody would tell me something about Mam I didn't already know. Everyone starts with "I'm sorry." I just wish they would stop. Everybody is sorry that they have to come to a wake. So, why don't they just say, "Sorry I have to be here." My reply would be easy, "Me, too."*

The afternoon of the last day, a familiar voice whispered my name. I looked up to find Nell, standing next to her, the infamous O'Brien. Joseph had sent Teddy a telegram with the news of Mam's death, and we had gotten a reply back that he wasn't able to make the journey over but would be in touch soon. He was to tell Nell. She was wearing a long, oatmeal colored wool coat over an impressively expensive-looking black silk suit. In her left hand, she carried a pair of deerskin gloves. *This is what New York looks like,* I remember thinking, *this was the world I left behind to find my world here crumbling.* I hadn't realized how much I missed her until she reached her arms out to me. I fell into them sobbing.

She whispered in my ear, *I am here. Teddy sends his love.* When I looked up, tears were streaming down her face, and she repeated, *I am here.* O'Brien brought each of us a glass of water. Taking a sip, I remembered to introduce them both to Joseph. Joseph gave Nell a kiss on both cheeks. *This means more than words can say.*

Nell held his gaze. *Cate holds a special place in my heart, and Maude made a difference in my life. And from the crowd that continues to gather, it looks as if she had that same effect on so very many.* Taking each of our hands in hers continued, *O'Brien and I are still a bit lagging from the trip over, best if we say farewell for the moment. We will see you at the church tomorrow.*

And as quickly and as quietly as they came in, they were gone.

And not a moment too soon, as they had barely closed the door behind them when Nora and Elizabeth arrived with a "keener" tightly grasping the flask of whiskey as her compensation for the role she was to play.

Nora was the first to speak. *She needs a proper Irish send-off,* nodding to the keener who began her wailing, her cries sounding like they were coming from my heart. I didn't know whether to laugh or cry. This was my two worlds colliding, relishing the ancient traditions of this island while having just held on tight to the two New Yorkers who had flown over the Atlantic. There were nods and murmurs from those present, some invoking the Irish 'ag caoineadh ... *'tis how it should be, how it has been.*

Joseph whispered to me, *Pray that Andrew and his fellow priests do not stumble upon what the Church has now forbidden as a pagan ritual from years past.*

I, for one, was happy for the diversion.

Timmy came every night, standing beside me the entire time. It was the last hour of the last day. Timmy put his arm around me, and I allowed my head to rest on his shoulder. I knew it made us look like we were a couple, but I didn't care. I closed my eyes for a brief moment, opening them to find John's voice expressing his sympathies to Joseph while shaking his hand. I was next; our eyes met. John held my hand, his eyes never leaving my face. His voice was low. *Catherine, Tim told me about your mother. I am so very sorry.*

I didn't respond; I couldn't say a word. I didn't dare. Timmy took his hand and thanked him for coming. I was in a daze. It was as if I were watching this happen from a perch somewhere outside of me. I couldn't feel. I couldn't think.

We buried Mam the following morning. At the gravesite, Andrew began the final set of prayers. He was weeping. I wondered when the last time he wept. In the solitary world that he chose to live in, there seemed to be no allowance for tears. Just penance.

*Mam is one with the land now,* Joseph whispered as the final amen resounded.

I could only nod. This was Glasnevin Cemetery; there was a sea of Celtic Crosses, like the one that marks this spot. Soon her name, date of birth, and her last day on this earth would be chiseled into the fine stone so that strangers passing by would know something about her. Strangers who would walk past looking for the stones of the heroes of the Uprising. I wanted her stone to say that she, too, was a hero. I wanted to shout to anyone who would hear me that she made a difference in this world. She made a difference. I said nothing. I merely made the sign of the cross, gave Andrew a kiss goodbye, took Joseph's arm, and left.

A shroud of rain began to fall, silent and gentle, like a curtain at the end of a play. It was the last act.

We came back to the house. There was enough food spread out to feed a small army, and the array of drinks lined up on the kitchen counter would rival any of the local pubs. I shed my black dress and stockings. I put on the soft coral sweater with a pleated skirt in a floral pattern that I had made from one of Mam's old dresses. I tossed off the heels; the ballet flats looked and felt good. I was coming downstairs when I heard the call for a song to begin. I entered the parlor, and Elizabeth and Nora recognized the reincarnated skirt and nodded their approval.

I looked around and found O'Brien in the midst of it all. Though a New Yorker born and bred, he looked and acted like he belonged. He gave me a smile that must have melted Nell's heart when she first laid eyes on him, and I understood why she had waited for him all these years.

O'Brien looked over to me. *Can I do a song for all our mothers who have left us but whose love was unconditional and boundless, shaping our lives, and leaving an indelible mark on our hearts? A mark that will never leave us.*

I smiled, my first of the day. *Please.*

O'Brien nodded, someone produced a guitar, and his tenor voice brought the room to a hushed quiet.

> *'Tis the last rose of summer*
> *Left blooming all alone,*
> *All her lovely companions*
> *Are faded and gone.*
> *No flower of her kindred,*
> *No rose bud is nigh,*
> *To reflect back her blushes,*
> *And give sigh for sigh.*

By the time he had finished the second verse, there was not a dry eye to be seen. Nell held up her hand. *Thank you, my love, but I knew Maude from her New York days, and she preferred lively over melancholy.* There was a burst of laughter and agreement from those gathered.

*And I have a request for you from me, having waited all these years for you to come to your senses and settle down with me at your side. I believe "The Wild Rover" would be fitting.* She got up and gave him a kiss and flashed a large diamond ring gracing the finger of her left hand. The crowd clapped their approval, I jumped up and screamed: *It's about time*! O'Brien returned Nell's kiss and with a grin in his eyes and his voice, started the next song.

Soon, Bridget, our Traveller, joined in. I remembered her telling the story of how her da could sing, and clearly, she inherited the same gift. The two of them warmed up the crowd, and the rest of the evening was spent living up to the standard of a true Irish wake. Sean Quinn brought over his Bodhran, someone produced a fiddle, and the craik flowed. I was having fun. Joseph was tapping his feet. Nobody was looking to leave. The house once again filled with laughter and song. The only thing missing was Mam.

It was well past a reasonable hour, and Nell and O'Brien were the last to leave. We agreed that they would come for dinner at the house tomorrow evening. I was not yet ready to let her go.

She took her hands in mine. *Many years ago, I asked O'Brien to teach me what it meant to be Irish. He told me you couldn't teach it, you had to feel it. Both sadness and joy. Tears and laughter. This was today. This was Irish. This is the gift your mother gave to you, and this was the celebration that we gave to her. Go to sleep, my dear one. I know that Maude is smiling down upon us.*

---

I spent most of the next day aimlessly walking around the house. Moving a dish from one spot to the next, not wanting to put anything away, for then it would seem that Mam was truly gone. Keeping the vestiges of yesterday still around me brought a strange sense of comfort. Once all was put away, the house would look as empty as I felt.

The clock had just struck six when Nell arrived with two bottles of good white wine, a true victory in a city that was built on the pillars of Jameson and Guinness. O'Brien cradled bottles of lager, which Joseph eyed with nothing short of a lustful stare.

I couldn't help smiling, remembering the first time I met O'Brien. I had only recently arrived in New York when I went into the library and was startled to find myself face-to-face with a handsome, youthful gentle-man. He had a full head of hair, steel gray with just brush strokes of char-coal black drawn in, and the most extraordinary violet eyes. I knew immediately that this was O'Brien. He looked to be in his mid-sixties, and the lines on his ruddy face told a tale of a man who had laughed, lived, and seen the world. His smile was wide and genuine, his handshake firm. I could see why Nell loved him. I could see how I could fall in love with him. I was already starting to do so when Nell arrived. Seeing her, O'Brien's face shone with love, admiration, and joy. It was the only light the room needed.

This is what I was looking for. I couldn't describe it, but I could see it. Feel it. They were friends. They were lovers. They were two unique and special individuals who became a third, a couple. Not in each other's shadow but standing tall, erect, side-by-side.

Tonight, Joseph would see first hand how special they are, why I love them. This was to be an evening of conversation, no formal sit-down. We were to eat and drink in the sitting room. It would just be us. Joseph and O'Brien were deep in conversation when Nell and I arrived with the tray for what was to be our dinner for the evening. While neither one of us could boast of our culinary talents, Nell's eye for color and symmetry produced a platter of delights, with an array of colors and textures all from yesterday's pantry. Joseph paused the conversation just long enough to pour the drinks.

After the traditional *Sláinte*, O'Brien started the conversation. *I was just telling Joseph that I was in Ireland during the war, or what your countrymen termed the Emergency.* Nell raised her hand. *Give them all the details, my love. It is a story worth telling.*

O'Brien nodded. *Always best told if I have a pipe in my hand. Would you mind?* We quickly gave our consent, and the conversation paused as he went through the ritual of filling the bowl and lighting the match. The smell of vanilla with cherry filled the room, and Joseph looked over to where O'Brien was taking his second puff. *I remember that smell, our da smoked a pipe though Mam wouldn't let him do it in front of Cate. Said she only wanted her to breathe fresh air, not something that came out of a pouch from who knows where.*

Nell was the first to respond, *Well, that certainly sounds like the Maude I knew. She had an opinion and was never shy about sharing it.*

Joseph and I both smiled; we knew exactly what she meant. She looked over at O'Brien, his pipe still emanating the blended aroma. *Come on, O'Brien, take a sip of your lager and start your story.*

O'Brien rolled his lovely violet eyes. *I was only here for a short visit. It was the time I was on assignment with the Red Cross and had been given access to the prisoner of war camps, mostly in Germany. It was a pretty gruesome task. I believed I was being shown the whitewashed version to photograph. Men lying in their beds reading books, sitting down for meals; I kept thinking, they could start roasting marshmallows any moment now. I knew it wasn't real, but there was no way of*

*proving it. I let the folks at the Red Cross know my concern, and they had a prag-
matic response. Even if this wasn't how the prisoners were treated every day, at least
that was how they got treated for the day when I was there. I should think of it as a
gift we were giving them. Well, that made sense to me, so I would try to extend my
time a bit longer at each shoot.*

Nell broke in, *You should see the pictures he actually did take. And hear the
stories he was told. Extraordinary. Just like him.* Her face beamed with pride.

*Thank you, love. As I took the pictures of the men at the camp, I asked them
how they got there. What had they done, what had they seen. What has come out is
a book that Nell and I have produced and that will hit the bookshelves in about six
weeks. She did the story editing. And "Through Their Eyes" is in the process of its
first printing.*

Nell smiled. *It is the stories of heroes and those whose actions were not that
heroic.*

My question was quick. *Has Teddy seen it? Joseph, Teddy was a POW. His
plane was shot down towards the end of the war.*

Nell gave a rueful smile. *No, he said he wasn't ready yet. I am not sure he
ever will be. And may this book and these stories change people's hearts and minds so
that those who sit at the power tables can reconcile their differences without shed-
ding blood. When they no longer send young men, most no more than children, off to
kill other human beings in the name of peace and prosperity. And sometimes even in
the name of the god they worship.*

O'Brien took the last sip of his lager and raised his hand to let Joseph
know that another would be welcomed. Joseph fetched a refill for all as
O'Brien continued. *A lofty goal, but, and no pun intended, I fear it is nothing
more than a pipe dream. Now, back to my being here in Ireland.*

*I was about six months into the assignment and was beginning to feel the effects
of too much war and too little sleep. Ireland had proclaimed its neutrality, but there
were rumors that prisoners of war were being held on Irish soil. I thought that
would be an intriguing storyline and convinced my bosses that I should give it a go.
I also wanted to be the first of my family to visit since my grandfather sailed from
this land as a young lad. And Ireland's neutrality was quite the source of lively
debate at our Sunday dinner table.*

Joseph nodded. *I was in England during this time, sent by De Valera to help
the British decipher German codes. Churchill, never one of our fans, was outright
hostile about the decision not to choose sides, not to give British access to our seaports,
the only thing he ever really wanted from us besides our servitude.*

Joseph's voice became more animated. *I would hear hushed whispers
coming from my colleagues that Germany had U-boats docking on our west coast.*

*Rubbish. What role could the world expect us to play in this international game? We had no military strength, no strategic alliances, and had barely outgrown our own colonial status. I understand numbers; we had fewer than ten thousand soldiers who were better equipped to preside at a ceremony than venture into an armed battle. We are an island country, and our navy was but two motorized torpedo boats.*

I had no reply. This was the most political conversation I had ever heard Joseph speak. I thought to myself, *Still waters truly run deep.*

O'Brien nodded. *I think the world understands that now. But neutrality is a hard road to navigate, and my question was, how does a country that has not taken sides in a conflict deal with the soldiers who were fighting on behalf of their home-land but were captured on these neutral shores? Dublin had been bombed by the Nazis, either by mistake or by design. You weren't at war, so any rescued soldiers could not be categorized as POWs. So, what to call them, where to put them, how to manage them?*

Joseph rubbed his brow. *I have never thought of that. It was the time when the Irish press was being censored by our own government, and only a few of us had radios.*

O'Brien continued. *Well, the Irish have been underestimated for generations as to our savvy and guile. Here's what I learned: the American and British soldiers were simply returned to their countries, no fuss, no bother. The captured Germans became "Guests of the State." These were the soldiers I met up with at the local pub down in County Kerry. They were allowed to leave their barracks, with the stipula-tion that they had to return by 11:00 p.m. They were safe, free to walk the hills, have a pint, and flirt with the local lassies. The only complaint I heard from them was about your beer. I won't repeat the comments, but even your finest lagers would not be able to compete with the brews these men once knew! Their stories did not make the book, but it is a true Irish tale. After the war, some married and stayed on. I had breakfast with two of them this morning. They are the strongest Irish patriots I have met, and that includes my grandfather, who thought this island was a slice of heaven.*

The conversation continued, easy and relaxed, like a gently flowing stream. Joseph was a captive audience to O'Brien's tales of life seen through the lens of a camera. O'Brien wanted to know about the world of mathematics. O'Brien and Nell talked of Paris; they were sailing the next morning. O'Brien wasn't sure what they would find, given the horror of the Nazi occupation just a decade ago, but Nell was optimistic. *I need only to drink a leisurely cup of coffee in a sidewalk café and sip a glass of rosé after walking along the banks of the Seine to be happy. To say that I was in Paris.*

O'Brien raised his hand in a mock salute. *That, my love, will be no problem.*

It was getting late, the evening had been like a slow dance, each moment woven together to form a commonality, a shared memory. Nell took a look around the room, as if she were committing the setting to memory. *I am sorry to say goodnight, but I fear we must. Tomorrow will be a long day. I am so happy we were able to spend time with you, Joseph. You are an extraordinary young man. Please know that our home will always be open to you, and do visit us in New York.*

*And my dearest Cate, you are my family. Whatever you decide to do, whenever you decide to do it, you will always have my love and support. You are stronger than you know. You are loved more than you can imagine.*

She raised her glass; no more than a sip was left. *When someone you love dies, something inside of you changes. In ways that you can't describe, in ways you are not even sure of, you become different. You take on a part of them—thinking what they would have thought, saying what you think they would have said, acting like they would have acted. It is how you keep them alive.*

*To Maude, who will always live in our hearts.*

Joseph and I clinked our glasses: *To Mam.* And then we said our good-byes to Nell and O'Brien with promises to write often and soon.

I was tired, but it had been a perfect evening. I said as much to Joseph. He was quiet, even for him, and gave no response. I thought I might have misjudged the connection that had been made between them.

Minutes later, Joseph turned to me as he started up the stairs. *She is family, you know.*

*Oh, Nell? Oh yes, she has been like family since the day I met her.*

*No,* Joseph continued, *she is family.*

I looked at him quizzically.

*You have the same eyes. Mam's eyes as well. You come from one and the same.*

————

## Our Eyes

It took Joseph to uplift the veil. We share the same eyes: Mam, Teddy, Nell, and me. And they are unique, not blue, not green, yet both green and blue. I have never met anyone else who shared this trait, except us four. I never made the connection.

I loved Nell from the moment I met her, but now, in this quiet moment, something shifted. She was not just a friend; she was family. A thread that somehow has been woven through generations.

It was as if Mam had sent me a gift. Like the book that held the O'Shea stories, this was a bond of history, of a lineage that had come before.

I will sleep well tonight.

———

I put down the pen.

———

The night was as dark and as unpredictable as my spirit. I woke up with a fright. I wasn't sure if there was a banging on the door or just the wind beating against the shutters.

The pounding escalated.

I threw my robe around me and went downstairs. The light in the hallway was on, and I saw Joseph standing in the doorway. His one word said it all: *Liam.* Shock, worry, questioning, all communicated in a single word.

Liam pushed his way in. *She still here? Wicked as ever.* His words were slurred, fueled by bitterness and cheap whiskey. Joseph motioned me to go back upstairs; I shook my head *no.* I had seen Liam drunk by both alcohol and rage before. It was not new to me. Joseph and I would stand together.

I found my voice. *We buried her last week. She had been ill for months. Welcome home, Liam.* It took a minute for him to recognize me.

His words were like shredded glass, biting and hard. *No sorrow on my part that she is gone. Packing me off to New Zealand rather than taking my rightful place as the head of this family. I am the firstborn. I have certain rights and privileges that are mine. This house, for example. It now belongs to me, and I am going to take it.*

Joseph sighed. *Come in, Liam. It is late, and we are all tired. These are conversations best held in the daylight.*

Liam chortled. *Always the pacifier, Joseph. 'Tis a wonder that you didn't sign up for the monastery rather than that shadow of a man called Andrew. I may be going to hell, but he will meet me there. There is no penance that can take away the sins that man committed in the name of love for country.*

*So, pour me a drink, or give me the bottle, as I am now your host.*

Joseph handed him the bottle.

———

Joseph and I just sat quietly as we waited until Liam closed the door to his room before we went upstairs. I don't remember what we said to each other, if anything. It was as if a ghost of the past had appeared at the door.

I was in my early teens when Liam left for New Zealand. Said Ireland and this house no longer appreciated him, and he was off to claim the fame and success rightfully his.

During the last war, he had enlisted with the British army since Ireland had proclaimed its neutrality. It was an odd choice for someone who had fought so hard for Ireland's independence. Many of his old comrades accused him of being a traitor to Ireland. Liam shouted back that there was nothing in Ireland for him, that he was a grown man but had no job, no family, no roof to call his own. He said the world of opportunity was with the British, and he had already been sworn in to defend the king.

Words would escalate to fists. Liam would resort to any means to win, once even breaking a bottle to use as a weapon. His temper was fierce and uncontrollable.

He left within a week of his announcement to join the forces in the Pacific, and we heard nothing from him for years. Mam would light a candle every Sunday, praying for his safe return from the war.

After Lord Mountbatten co-signed the surrender treaty with Japan, Liam came home. He was not much more than skin and bones. I overheard the conversation that first night from my hallway hideaway, having been sent to bed as I was too young to hear the gruesome tale. Andrew had taken his vows by then and was leading a monastic life, sheltered from the troubles of the world he had escaped. Joseph was back at the university. So, it was just Liam and Mam at the table.

Liam told her that he had been in Burma. Mam knew from the New York papers that the men who had fought in the Pacific had witnessed cruelties beyond description. Liam had been captured and taken as a POW building the "Death Railway." His leg had been broken just days before the bombing of Hiroshima, an act that ended the war and brought doctors to the camp who saved his leg. He and Mam talked until the wee hours of the morning, long after I had given up and retreated to my bed.

Liam slept the next two days. I was home from school when he came down the stairs. He tousled my hair, just like when I was a child. *You are growing up, little sister. Soon you'll be as tall as me.*

Then he looked around the kitchen. *Where does your ma keep the whiskey? I need a bit to start my day.* I showed him the cupboard; he took the bottle and went back upstairs to his room. When Mam came home from the shop, I told her what had happened. *He's been through hell, Cate. Let's give him some time and our prayers.*

But it didn't get better. Within a week, every bottle of liquor that Mam had in the cupboard had been taken, including the rum she only used to feed her annual Christmas cake. Liam would leave the house as the sun was setting and wouldn't be home until the last drink had been poured.

It had been a month since he had returned, and Liam's behavior was getting more and more erratic. He stole money from Mam's purse and then denied taking it. He lifted his fists at Mam one Sunday morning when she asked if he was making any headway in finding a job. *Finding work in this pit of a town,* he shouted, his voice filled with rage. *They call me a turncoat, an ass-kisser to the Crown. I am a bloody war hero. Men in this country hid under De Valera's robes so they wouldn't have to do what I did, see what I saw. They call me a traitor. They are cowards.* And he stormed off.

One day shortly thereafter, I was home alone, and Liam came in unexpectedly with "his one true mate," who, like him, spent every waking moment at the local pub. The man's beard clung to his face like a spider's web, trapping the remnants of spilled pints and last night's dinner. The man came over and put his arm around me, slurring his words while his eyes and his hands were moving up and down my body. *Who is this one, Liam? A fine one she is, too.*

*A girl from the shop,* was Liam's response.

*I am his sister,* I shouted, pulling myself out of the man's grip. *I am your sister, Liam.*

Liam threw his head back in laughter, *Only half of you. Only half of you.*

The slobbering man joined in the laughter, *Can I take the other half, mate?*

I ran up to my room and shut the door. I put a chair against it. I didn't feel safe. Didn't feel safe in my own house, didn't feel safe with my own brother.

I told Mam what had happened over dinner. Her face turned red. It was minutes, or at least what seemed like minutes, before she spoke. *This must stop. Come to the shop after school from now on, Cate. We will then come home together. You are not to be alone here. I will deal with Liam.*

———

Sleep did not come easily. After much tossing and turning, my mind finally surrendered, and I fell into an uneasy slumber. I woke early the next morning to find the weather was not going to help my spirits. It seemed indifferent as to what it would do—rainy, sunny, rainy again. I wanted either sun or rain; I didn't have the energy to deal with anything in between.

I spent the day at my desk writing the first of the notes thanking friends and neighbors for the kindness they had shown at the time of Mam's illness and her funeral. Keeping busy helped me get through the day and blot out the memory of Liam's screaming, his face contorted, his veins bulging.

Joseph spent the day in the kitchen, going over Mam's papers. The sun had set when I entered. He raised his head, rubbing his forehead with his hands as I walked in. He looked up and met my gaze. *Should we attempt to have some supper?*

*Yes, I haven't really eaten all day, but a hot shower is first on my agenda. Then I may be a more fit companion.*

Joseph nodded. *That works. I'm almost finished here. Liam left about an hour ago without so much as a word to me. I don't think we'll be needing to set a plate for him.*

I took a long, hot shower, letting the pelting of the water ease the memory of Liam's face, a memory that was making the muscles in my neck tighten up like the flowers that close their petals at night. I was feeling better when I made my way downstairs, attired in my favorite pajamas. Joseph had left the table, the papers gone. I started making our tea.

Minutes later, the sound of the whistling kettle brought Joseph back to the table. The poured cup warmed our hands, the fragrance of the tea both familiar and soothing. I took a sip and looked over at Joseph, whose face had lost none of his concern. I raised my cup to him, *Of all the things the British took from us—our land, our language, our dignity—they did give us tea. And I, for one, am grateful.*

Joseph gave an unexpected laugh, a laugh that felt like a blanket, gently wrapping itself around me. He lifted his cup, returning the salute, adding, *I think tonight's dinner special should be brown bread and cheese. I am not sure my stomach can handle one more night of any of the casseroles, brought with love and concern, but a bit heavy as a regular repast.*

*I couldn't agree more. I'll get the plates if you can find the makings of this evening's entrée.*

Over dinner, Joseph shared what he had gathered from Mam's papers. *All is in order. The house is already in your name, and Mam added you to most of her banking accounts. It is all straightforward, leaving us very little to settle. The bank and Mam's solicitors have all the original documents. I just wanted to be sure that I understood them. Liam has no legal claim to this house. Our da was never a joint owner, and none of us three lads can assert ourselves as a natural heir.*

I held on tight to my teacup. *It is too much for me to think about, Joseph. And I am not thinking clearly at the moment. But what about you? This house is also your home. I think of it as our house, not just mine.*

*I am fine, Cate. What I learned today is that Mam set up a trust fund with the monies she made when she sold the shop. She lived off that trust and has left the monies remaining to both you and me. After Mam sold the mill, she never used those funds but deposited them in a special account. That account is divided among the four of us. Liam's share is to continue in the trust with the bank as its trustee. It should be enough to satisfy Liam, but I fear he never sees enough as enough.*

Joseph paused, and a faraway look passed over his face. *He has been that way for as long as I can remember, always seeing himself as the slighted one, never grateful for what he has been given. I'm not sure he has forgiven me for our own mam's death. He called me a murderer once; his fists were clenched and his breathing ragged. I was about five, and our da, overhearing his rampage, got off his chair faster than I had ever seen before or ever again. He pulled Liam by the shirt, lifted him off the ground, and told him he was talking nonsense. Told him if he ever heard him say anything like that again, he would raise his fists to him. I think Liam was stunned. Our da never raised a finger to any of us. Liam was told to apologize, and he did, but I can still see the blaze within his eyes. It was the same kind of look he had last night. It is as if the anger within him is a raging inferno, blocking out reason, logic, and constraint.*

I didn't or couldn't respond. As painful as it was to hear Liam talk about Mam last night, the scene that Joseph just painted struck a dagger in my heart. It was a moment or two before I spoke.

*And Andrew?*

*He took a vow of poverty, so any monies most probably goes to the order. I am not sure how all of that works, but I imagine the good abbot knows exactly how to get what is rightfully Andrew's in their hands. Given last night's unpleasantness, for lack of a better word, I think it best that we leave this discussion in the hands of the solicitor. I'll try to set up a time to meet later this week. I will leave a note for Liam telling him that I am arranging a meeting so that all this can be explained to the three of us at the same time in the same place.*

Joseph's face took on a thoughtful look. This was not a man who liked confrontation; his role was that of peacemaker. This was going to be difficult. That was the only thing we could be sure of.

I decided to change the course of the discussion.

*Speaking of lawyers, do you remember me telling you about my friend Faith, who was being brought in front of a government committee to question her supposed communist affiliations?*

*Of course.*

*Well, it is pure rubbish. It is all about making headlines in the newspapers' morning editions. Teddy is in the thick of it all, providing legal counsel to one of the government committees that is trying to sort out this mess. It was the reason that he couldn't fly over with Nell and O'Brien for Mam's funeral. He sent me a quick note with them, along with a promise of a long letter to follow.*

*And this is that letter?*

*Received in the post this morning and still unopened, I might add. I thought I would share its first reading with you. It should take our minds off what we are facing here. Let's adjourn to the parlor and put a log on the fire.*

Joseph nodded. Once settled and the fire lit, he stretched himself out and looked more relaxed than I had seen him in weeks.

I began reading.

*Dearest Cate,*

*I am remiss. My feelings of guilt and sadness are overwhelming. It is too soon after Mam's death to ask how you are doing. My mother wrote telling me how strong you were at the time of her passing. She remembers only too well how grief feels as you accept the words of so many trying to say the right thing. And there is no right thing.*

*I was too young to remember much when my father died. The feeling of loss was more acute when my mother's friend Henry passed. And then there was the war, too many of those I called my friends were taken. Some so quick that there was little or no time to say a final prayer; others lingering long enough to know that they would never be held or comforted by those they love. Death is an abstract concept. We, the living, talk about it, but it is not an experience we have. What we have is the loss, the never to be had again. The never to be seen again. What is left behind are memories. That is what keeps them alive for us.*

*Know that I think of you every day and wish there was more than I could say or do to ease the pain.*

My voice broke, and Joseph sat up quickly. I shook my head, mumbled that *I was fine,* and in a stronger voice, continued Teddy's tale.

*I am sorry that I wasn't able to make the trip to Ireland to be with you. It was the same time that Faith appeared before the Committee on Un-American Activities, and time and distance prevented me from coming over with her and O'Brien. Since I couldn't be with you, I thought I would take you with me to that hearing. I shall start with how our inimitable Faith prepared herself. She is unique, but I am sure I don't have to tell you why and how.*

*So, make a cup of tea or, better yet, pour yourself a bit of that fine Irish whiskey for this story. A story whose ending I will not divulge until I am ready to sign with love.*

Joseph stood up, *an excellent idea. I think I would like this chap. Pause reading while I pour. It sounds like this may be a whiskey fable indeed.*
Once settled back in, glasses poured, I continued.

*Faith has, at times, given me little or no hope. She seeks advice but takes her own counsel. So, sit back, my dearest sister, and close your eyes. Think of Faith, dressing like the star of a theatrical extravaganza in which she was playing the lead role, a woman falsely accused.*

No longer modeling the infamous "Rebel Without a Cause" look with her rolled blue jeans, white tee, and red nylon jacket, a day before the hearing, she arrives at my office donned in a black straight skirt, a striped jacket nipped at the waist, and a white blouse with a Peter Pan Collar. I had never seen her look quite like this, and the surprise look on my face must have given me away.

After the initial pleasantries had been made, she started rummaging through her purse, found what she was looking for, and took her seat across the desk from me, now wearing a pair of black rimmed glasses.

Here is the dialogue as I recall:

Faith: I think I would look smarter if I wore glasses.
Me: You are smart.
Faith: But people may not think I am smart.
Me: They will once you start to speak.
Faith: I may need time to think. So here is my prop.
Me: Glasses?
Faith: Yes, glasses. When I need to think, I take off my glasses. Purse my lips. Give a brief nod and start to speak.
Me: You could light a cigarette if Congress allowed it. It would take about the same amount of time.
Faith: I don't smoke.
Me: You also don't need glasses.
Faith: Yes, but only you and my ophthalmologist know that to be true!

Faith and I were bent over with laughter when Peter Reilly appeared. Peter and I were classmates at Harvard Law School. Preparing witnesses for such government hearings that would rival the Spanish Inquisition is his specialty. Peter is short and squat. Having inherited male pattern baldness from his father, he does nothing to compensate for his lack of hair. He is not a man who fashion calls. His shapeless suit tells you all you need to know. He is a man who is important because of what and who he knows, not because of the image he tries to project. A rare find in Washington. Faith couldn't get a better lawyer, and that includes me.

After a brief introduction, Peter looked Faith in the eye, the glasses now sitting forlorn on the desk. He was clear, offering her three options, his fingers raised.

First, take the Fifth; it is your right. Refuse to answer any questions, get held in contempt of Congress, and possibly sent to jail.

He raised two fingers: Be a "cooperative witness" and give up the name of those you either know or have reason to believe have been affiliated with the Communist Party at one time or another.

Faith's face fell at the offer. And the third?

Peter put his hand down. Tell them that you will only answer questions about yourself, but none about other people. If you do that, you have given up your rights under the Fifth Amendment and could be legally forced to name names. And remember, every moment that you are there, that is what they want. Names. Never answer any questions with a definitive no. Ted here can help you with that, and Peter gave me the nod to proceed.

It was my turn to add to the conversation. It is standard lawyer fare. Use "I don't recall" or "that was so long ago, I am afraid I don't remember."

Peter broke in. Remember, you don't know what others have testified, and you could be charged with perjury. Those seated at the table hold all the cards. You have to play your hand close to your chest. When they badger you, don't react. You make eye contact. I have arranged for you to appear before the Committee in a closed session. It will be easier but not easy. McCarthy only puts the timid and those with a guilty look on display. If you look like you can fight back, he doesn't want the cameras filming. I understand you are a fighter. A fighter for what you believe in. So, keep those dukes up and you should be all right.

And with that statement, Peter said he had to run to his next conference, as the list of those called to testify grows daily. You got the right name, young lady. Faith means believing and trusting. Believe in yourself. Trust in yourself. Prove your name worthy.

Then he was gone.

Faith looked at me, Oh, Teddy, how am I ever going to do this?

I gave her my best smile. Remember all those plays you have worked on? Those radio broadcasts.

She nodded, and maybe soon television programs ...

Indeed, well, you have fed lines to some of the greatest head-liners the American public recognizes. Now it is your turn to have the audience believe your every word.

I cleared my calendar so that I could go to the hearing. There were days that it was difficult to find a seat; that day was not one of them. McCarthy wasn't going to be there, so limited press and not nearly as much mayhem.

For a moment, let me pause to describe the set. The committee room where Faith was taken is in the Old House Office Building. It was completed in 1908, and the only thing that has changed since then is the cast of characters. And with them, only the names are different. The wood is dark, the wallpaper striped, and globed sconces, once lit by gas, now flicker with electricity that brings all this into a harsh light. The cast was in play when I arrived. The room slowly filled up with middle-aged men, their pinched faces giving them the appearance that collectively they were suffering the effects of having eaten bad fish at last night's fundraising dinner.

Sitting alone across from them was our Faith. I almost laughed out loud when I saw her. She was in petticoats and pearls, looking like the girl next door in her newest floral frock. Her hair was neatly brushed in what seemed an appropriate do for this environment. It was a page boy, all kept in place with a matching headband. Give her an apron and she would be an extra on tonight's episode of "Ozzie and Harriet."

Although she had her back to me, Faith looked poised and collected. No nervous twitching. No palms rubbing each other. No foot tapping. Her voice was clear and strong as she confirmed that she was indeed Faith Martin and that she lived in New York City, New York. She wished them all a good morning, and the questioning began. They asked where she went to school, Barnard College, she replied. Graduated with honors, her voice went up as if she were the one asking the questions.

Just answer the questions, Miss Martin.

Yes, sir, sorry. It was just that my folks were so proud. Her voice had a smile.

I sat back. I was beginning to enjoy myself.

The questioning continued. Were you ever a member of the Communist Party?

Faith slowly shook her head. Not that I recall. Her voice got lighter, and I detected a bit of southern twang. But sir, did you know, George Barnard Shaw was considered a socialist and shared many of those same beliefs. When he won the Nobel Prize, they said his work was marked by both idealism and humanity. He won the Oscar for his "Pygmalion," which I understand is being made into the most wonderful Broadway musical, "My Fair Lady." You gentlemen must try ...

There was a bit of tittering among the clerks present. The chairman hit his gavel. Once again, Miss Martin, please just answer the questions.

Frightfully sorry, sir.

And though I couldn't see her face, her body posture spoke the word, sheepish.

Then I got worried. Roy Cohn, McCarthy's lynch pin, took over the questioning. I have never met him, but he is a force to be reckoned with. I was taken aback when he started to speak. His voice was soft, not what I expected from reading the headlines about him. The room got even quieter; everyone was straining to hear his voice. Miss Martin, do you know anyone who has been a member of the Communist Party? A fellow traveler, if you will.

The room got quiet. I must confess, my palms started to sweat. Faith paused. Sir, I am more than willing to answer any questions about me. But I simply cannot name other people or answer any questions about their politics or their beliefs. I believe that is called hearsay information, and I am sure your committee wants only facts, not speculation.

Cate, I almost applauded. Faith was giving an award-winning performance.

After ten minutes of basically the same conversation being

repeated, Cohn shrugged his shoulders and looked at the congressman sitting next to him. Mr. Chairman, I suggest that we call the next witness. Faith was dismissed.

Faith and I agreed to meet around the corner at a coffee shop after the hearing. It was a precautionary move; the hallways of Congress have way too many eyes and ears, some friendly, some not so much. We arrived within minutes of each other and would have hooped and hollered had we been alone. We settled for a hug.

I sat across from her and clapped. You were brilliant. When did you decide to forego the Rosalind Russell role of "His Girl Friday" to be Debbie Reynolds?

Faith took a sip of her now delivered chocolate milkshake. I thought about what you said. It made me think about my audience ... men. Men in their forties and fifties who are still thinking that they are robust and a catch. Russell intimidates, Reynolds charms.

Well, you did it, you made it through a Congressional Investigative Hearing unscathed.

Faith gave her head a quick shake as she pulled off the confining headband, and her curls came free. I feel bad for him.

Him, who?

The last questioner, Cohn. How his eyes bulge out, and that awful scar that runs down the length of his nose. He must hate shaving that face every morning.

Faith, and only Faith, would be one of the few people in the United States to feel compassion for Roy Cohn.

We celebrated with Peter the next night at Old Ebbits Grill. But it is late and that is another missive that I promise to write *soon. Until then, please let me know how you are doing.*

*I am holding you close to my heart.*

*Love, Teddy*

———

I put the letter down. *I like her,* Joseph said, *and him.*
  *You would, they are the best of people.*
  *Do you miss them, Cate?*
  *Yes, terribly.*
  *Are you going back to New York?*
  *I don't know. For the moment, I am simply going back to bed.*

———

The next day brought a handful of weather. There was a wind outside that would cut you in two, so I decided against taking a walk. I had put the kettle on for tea, and it was starting to whistle when the letter arrived. It was from Faith. I turned off the gas. The tea could wait for my second reading. Knowing Faith, it would take me at least two or three reads to unravel where she is at and where she is planning to go.

*My most wonderful Cate,*

*I miss you terribly, more and more each day. I want you to come back to New York. I want to talk with you. Laugh with you. And now I feel guilty saying all of that. You are having the most heart-wrenching of times. And it is I who should be comforting you. I wish I could think of the right words to write that might help you in your sorrow. None comes. Know that I am with you in spirit. Even though an ocean separates us, my affection and love for you remain steadfast.*

*Teddy told me that he had written to you about my experience in Washington. It was the most awful time. Some of the* newspapers write that McCarthy's heart is in the right place; he doesn't want Communists to infiltrate our country and destroy democracy. I understand that. But those are headlines. I was brought up to believe that you can't go after people who are innocent just to scare others out of their wits. That is fear-mongering, that spreads hatred and distrust, fueled by a lust for money and power.

It's not just the stage lights that are going dark in American theatre. There's a fear creeping in, Cate-a deep, gnawing fear that's settled into the hearts of those of us who once saw this world as family. The Red Scare has found its way through our stage doors, carried in by these congressional investigations. It moves like a poisonous fog, seeping into dressing rooms, rehearsal halls, and even producers' offices. No one is safe. Accusations come fast, often baseless, and trust is unraveling. You can feel it-actors avoiding each other's gaze, whispers in the wings, silence where there used to be camaraderie. I don't know who named me. At this point, it hardly matters. What matters is that, thanks to Teddy and Peter, I got out in time. I was lucky. But sitting before that panel, watching them hang on every word I spoke-it was chilling. They weren't there for the truth, Cate. They were hunting. Predators in suits, hoping I'd slip, say something, anything, to justify branding me a traitor. They hoped for blood; they wanted a headline.

I smiled and thought. *It wasn't just Teddy and Peter who set you free. You figured out what you had to do, and then you did it. As only you could. I miss you, Faith. I miss your energy, your spirit, your willingness to take a risk.*

I put the kettle back on the flame. There was still more to read, and I wanted a cuppa to join me in the reading.

Faith's handwriting actually became more animated. Her voice came through the written words on the page.

Now that it is all behind me, I am back in New York. As

Shakespeare said, the play's the thing. I love the way the theatre comes together. How the magic of a play is brought to life. There are all these moving parts that seem disjointed and appear to have no relationship with each other. Then it slowly merges: the actors, the scenery, the sound, the lights. It is all meshed into one: the play. And then the performance begins. We are transported to another time or another place. Then the curtain falls. The audience claps. The actors bow. Then the lights are turned on, and stark reality forces our eyes to open once again to the world around us. But for moments or hours, our cares were forgotten, or intensified, or confused. It is magical. I love it.

The confusion and fear previously felt, forgotten. At least for the moment.

My good news is that I am about to venture forth into a new world. The world of television. It is not the theatre, but the programs being broadcast are exciting and innovative.

I start next week. The writers and directors I will be working with have a fierce desire to bring quality and originality to their work and the screen. It is not the theatre, but theatre-like. I will write more when I have put in a full week's worth of work. But for the moment, I am beside myself, so keep your fingers crossed that this is going to be the best.

Miss you. Write to me. Send me confidence and love.

Love and Peace,
Faith

———

We had not seen Liam since the first night, but there were remnants of his presence: dirty glasses left on the table and stale cigarette smoke in the kitchen. Liam had scrawled his response to Joseph's note about the meeting with Mam's solicitor by saying he would meet us there. I suspected that he would first want to find one of the pubs that catered to the night shift workers.

That morning, I found Joseph at the kitchen table looking out the window. I followed his gaze. The morning skies, dark and dreary, mirrored my mood. There would be no sun to lighten this day. Only storm clouds. Somehow, it seemed fitting.

Joseph stood up. *Best we get this started.* I nodded, clenching the strap of my purse to stop my hands from trembling. We made our way to the solicitor's office in silence. Each of us lost in our thoughts.

Liam arrived minutes after us. His words of greeting were slightly slurred, giving evidence that my assumption about his first stop of the day was correct. His suit no longer fit—the shoulders sagged, the pant legs puddled over scuffed shoes.

We were shown into the conference room, furnished with polished mahogany and understated leather chairs, light filtered through the narrow windows, casting long shadows across the floor. The walls held diplomas and awards that reinforced the firm's reputation of attendance at the best schools and the victory of hard-won cases. The air hung heavy and thick as if it were bracing for an impending impact. Liam took his seat at the head of the table; he sneered, *my rightful place.*

Mam's solicitor, a Mr. Sullivan, arrived, his face a mask of forced calmness. He shuffled the papers his assistant handed him. He sat down adjusting his tie for the third time since he had entered the room. Joseph must have warned him that this might be difficult. This was not the man who faced adversaries in court, who convinced judges as to the innocence of his clients. This was a man whose job was to tell you what the papers sitting in front of him meant. Papers that he had drafted. He wished us a stilted good morning and proceeded.

As soon as Liam comprehended the terms the solicitor was describing, he stood up, his fists clenched, his eyes darkened, his voice laced with venom and this morning's intake of cheap whiskey. He pointed at Joseph: *You did this. You took away what is rightfully mine. You are no better than she was to me.*

The solicitor tried to interject, saying that this was well within the framework of estate planning. Liam turned to him. *Who are you to talk to me like that? You know nothing. You are nothing. You are in cahoots with him. This was to be mine. I am the eldest. It is my right.*

Looking at Joseph, he raised his fist. *This is all down to you. You should rot in hell. The sooner, the better.* Liam stormed out. The silence following his departure was deafening.

Joseph was the first to speak. *Our brother is not well, Mr. Sullivan. As upsetting as this has been, you are now able to see that our mother's wish that his portion of the trust remain in the hands of the trustee at the bank is warranted. She wanted to be sure he was provided for but that the monies were controlled.*

Mr. Sullivan adjusted his tie again. I had stopped counting how many times that act had been performed. *I understand, Mr. Clark. And I will duly note it for the record. Shall we proceed?*

Joseph nodded. *Only for the record, Mr. Sullivan. My sister and I are fully aware of what the terms of the will are.*

Minutes later, we were out of the office, having been given the advice to meet with our bankers as soon as convenient.

We each took a deep breath of fresh air. It was not yet noon, but it seemed the day had already ended. *Joseph reached for my hand. I think a proper lunch and a double whiskey are what is needed.*

I tried my best smile. *Yes, but not in that order.*

---

I woke up to voices and the sound of shattering glass. I don't remember coming down the stairs. The kitchen. I walked into a room in disarray. Cabinet doors hung askew, the countertop strewn with a mix of broken plates and glasses. Drawers opened, their contents scattered like fallen leaves. In the center was Liam, kneeling over Joseph's still body, Mam's kitchen knife in his hand. Joseph was bleeding. There was blood all over the floor.

I said his name calmly, deliberately, loudly. *Liam.* He looked up. His eyes glowed with a wild, unhinged light, as though the essence of madness had taken possession of his very being. I willed myself to stay quiet, to not give in to the unthinkable that was playing out before me. I kept my eyes on him, an inner voice telling me, *Make him see you. Make him see you.* I said his name again. *It is me, Liam, Cate. I am your sister, remember.* He looked up at me. *You don't want to hurt Joseph anymore.* Liam looked down on Joseph's still body. *Joseph is your brother, Liam. You don't want to hurt him anymore.* Liam looked at me and shook his head. My voice got quiet. *Give me the knife, Liam. You don't want to hurt Joseph anymore.* Liam looked at the knife as if he were seeing it for the first time. I repeated, *Give me the knife, Liam.*

*You don't want to hurt Joseph anymore.* Liam stood up, his movements erratic and unsteady. I repeated, *Give me the knife, Liam.* He turned the knife over in his hands, Joseph's blood already drying on the blade. Liam took a step forward. I thought I might be next, that I would be his next victim. I kept my voice calm. *I am your sister, Liam. I am Cate. Give me the knife. You don't want to hurt me, Liam.* He let out a cry, raw and anguished. He dropped the knife and, like an animal that had gone mad, ran out the door, his footprints marked with Joseph's blood leaving their trail.

Joseph moaned. I knelt down beside him. *Don't leave me, Joseph.* I took a kitchen cloth and placed over the gaping wound on his stomach and continued my mantra: *Don't leave me, Joseph.*

I needed help. Joseph needed help. I ran next door to the Quinns and banged on their door, my hands covered in blood. Patricia answered, no sentences, just words. *Help. Joseph.*

Sean appeared at her side, the word *Help* being the only word my brain could remember. I pointed to the house and started to run. Sean ran with me. He knelt beside Joseph, taking off the one cloth I had placed on the wound. Sean told me to get more, more clean cloths. *We need to stop the bleeding.* I did as I was instructed. Sean took a sharp breath; his movements were purposeful, measured. Here was a man who had seen madness and danger before and faced it with an air of quiet competence.

Within minutes or hours, I had no recollection of time, the Gardaí arrived, followed by an ambulance. Patricia had made the call, and strangers well-versed in bringing order out of chaos were now in charge. Sean brought me into the sitting room. Joseph was taken to hospital. Patricia placed a cup of tea in my hands. She and Sean sat on either side of me as I described my tale of horror to the officers. It was surreal. This couldn't have happened here, to us. I was describing a nightmare.

As we were finishing, one of the more senior officers, or at least he looked to be more senior, came in. Liam had been found, huddled beneath a tree near a park where he had played as a child. He was incoherent. Babbling that he had to get his mates ready for the fight. They took him to the station. I would not have to worry for my safety.

I thanked the officer. It hadn't occurred to me to ask what would happen next. Too much had happened already. I could only think of Joseph. I needed to get to the hospital.

I assured Sean and Patricia that I would be alright. Patrica insisted that she would stay with me while I got ready. I understood. I took a shower. I was calmer when I came back downstairs. As per Patricia's last directive, I handed over the blood-stained nightclothes I had been wearing with the request that they be thrown out. I would need no reminder of what I saw that night.

Sean, now wearing his fireman's uniform, drove me to the hospital before leaving for the firehouse. I convinced both of them I was going to be okay, I just needed to see Joseph. That I was grateful beyond words.

And I was. And still am.

———

Seeing Joseph in hospital, lying still in the bed, his arm wrapped in bandages, his eyes closed, his face swollen, his body colored in black and blue, I started to shake. The thought of having lost him to Liam's rage hit me with the force of a heavy wooden door that slams shut in a storm. I couldn't catch my breath. Though the sun was now up, I felt that I was surrounded by darkness and an unrelenting wind. I closed my eyes, praying to Mam not to take him. Not now. I wasn't sure I could bear the loss.

I felt a hand touch mine and opened my eyes to find Timmy at my side. I mumbled his name, remembering where I was and who he was, said *Dr. Murphy*.

*Always Timmy to you, my dear Cate. And I know this looks bad, but Joseph is going to be alright. His left arm is broken, and his right leg is fractured from his fall, but the stab wounds he received did no permanent damage. He lost a great deal of blood, and his head took quite a whack when he hit the side of the kitchen table, but he will recover. I am scheduled to be at the hospital all this week, and Joseph will be my top priority. We plan to keep him sedated for the next three days to give his head time to heal. Then, in about a fortnight, you should be able to take him home. He will be sore but will be able to get around. I will come by then to see you both. I am as concerned for you as I am for Joseph.* He gave my arm a squeeze.

*Thank you, Timmy, that will be lovely.*

*As your doctor, I think you should go home and get some rest. You have experienced trauma, as well. Try to sleep. There is nothing you can do here. I will let you know if anything changes, but I am as certain as any doctor can be that Joseph will be fine. He is strong in body and spirit. You were the one who saved his life. Our job is merely to help it mend.*

I squeezed his hand. *Timmy, your words mean more to me than I can say. You are the best of friends. I will enlist Sean's help in getting him back home. Whenever you show up will be fine with us.*

I walked home. I needed to move, to escape the hospital with its green walls and somber faces. My pace was slow, the cobbles impeding a faster pace that I had neither the energy nor the intent to try. This was not my neighborhood. This street was strange, hushed, and secretive, as if its job was to guard its inhabitants' secrets. I found my way to the bottom of Bow Street. The air changed. The walls of Jameson's distillery surrounded me, the air smelling of fermenting barley. I picked up my pace. The bells of Christ Church had not called the faithful to evening prayers, yet my senses were aroused. I needed a glass of this cherished brew in my hands. I needed to be home.

I opened the door to the empty house. Patricia was my savior. All was back in order. There was no blood to remind me of the suffering that had been ours just hours ago. I went upstairs, found my favorite pair of pajamas and robe, and put them on.

I called Patricia and told her I was home safe. I was exhausted but was fine. We agreed that I would stop by the next day so she could see for herself.

Coming back to the kitchen, it was as it had always been; everything was back in place. I took my regular spot at the table. Less than 24 hours ago, this room had been a place of carnage. I wasn't sure I could ever forget what I saw here. Or fear what almost happened. I wasn't sure I was angry or relieved. More of a mixture of both.

I made myself a cup of tea, forgoing the whiskey.

I started to think about the young men who had fought for Ireland in the War of Independence and on either side of the Civil War. Could they ever forget what they saw or what they did? Or what others did? When does violence become acceptable? Was Liam's rage a seed that had been nourished by the years when he killed or was almost killed? I was deep in thought when there was a knock at the door. I was not expecting company and clearly not dressed to receive visitors. I was composing my "come back tomorrow" speech when I opened the door.

It was John. I took a small step closer to him and slipped my arms around his neck. John dropped whatever was clenched in his hand and pulled me tight against him. He whispered, *I had to come. I have to hold you.* He slammed the door shut with his foot.

He kissed me, and I him. I pulled his coat off and then his jacket, both landing in a heap on the floor. I needed to feel his arms around me. Finally, I pulled back.

*Good evening, John.* I smiled.

*Good evening, Catherine with a C.*

I picked up his coats, placing them on the entry hall hooks.

I tightened the sash of my robe. *As you can see, I was not expecting a guest.*

John pulled me to him again. *I want to be many things to you, Catherine, but a guest is not one of them.* This next kiss was long and deep; it unleashed my spirit.

I started to sob. Tears streamed down my face in a steady, unrelenting cascade. My weeping was like a low, aching wail looking to escape the pain that filled me.

John carried me into the sitting room, lifting me into the chair, cradling me in his arms. In the dim light of the room, the world outside seemed far away. I had cried when Mam died, but not like this. This was anger, despair, fear. I clung to him with a desperation that mirrored my shattered soul. My tears soaked his shirt.

John's arms, strong and unwavering, enveloped me. The steady rhythm of his heartbeat, a fragile anchor in the storm of my sorrow. He whispered my name, telling me he was here, soothing me with his presence. His voice gentle. His hands stroked my back.

Eventually, my sobs turned into sighs. The room was still silent except for my breath and the soft, shushing of his voice. Time stood still.

I fell asleep in his arms. I don't know for how long.

The sun was breaking with the dawn when I woke up, now lying on the divan with my head in John's lap. His eyes met mine as I lay there trying to get my bearings. We both smiled.

He asked: *Better?*

*Much. At least for the moment.* I sat up. *So, where were we?*

John pulled me closer. *If I recall, I was kissing you.*

*Ah, yes. And, if memory serves me correctly, I was kissing you back.*

He started to pick up where he had left off when I put my fingers to my lips. Taking his hand, I led him up the stairs to my bedroom. I motioned toward the bed, John's eyes never leaving my face. I untied my robe, stepping out of my nightclothes that fell in a crumpled pile at my feet. I had never acted like this before, so bold, so needy.

John took a step back and, with slow deliberation, looked me up and down. *More beautiful than I imagined. And trust me, I have imagined this moment.*

I couldn't speak. The air between us crackled, and I started to move forward, but John shook his head. *I just want to look at you.*

I stayed rooted. But then it was too much for me, I was drawn by a force I had never felt before. I moved to the bed. John took off his shirt, his eyes never leaving me. I reached out to him, and he lay down beside me. I closed my eyes. I was soon awakened by kisses, gentle touches, slowly, artfully placed, here and there. Then the rush, the haste to answer each urge with another urge. We became one. I ran my hands over his chest, feeling the strength in his arms that held me. He buried his fingers in my hair. I shivered. I gave myself up to him, to the moment.

Once again, I woke up in his arms. John was still sleeping. I studied every line of his face, the curvature of his nose, the unruliness of his eyebrows. The intensity of my stare must have woken him.

*Good morning, Cate.*

*Cate? What happened to Catherine with a C.*

*Oh, my darling,* pulling me towards him once again. *I need to shorten your name, as it appears I must preserve my energy to make love to you. Like this.*

And once again, I found myself transported into a world where every breath and touch was magnified. In this shared space, the world outside ceased to exist. It was just the two of us.

Waking up again, the sun shining through the window affirmed that the day was well underway.

John was propped up on one arm, looking at me. I found myself beginning to blush; his look was so intense. *You are more beautiful in the morning, and I didn't think that would be possible. It is as if your soul, refreshed, shines through your eyes.*

The blush now was firmly in place. *Once again, John the poet emerges.* I lightly kissed his nose, propping myself up on my arm, as well. *You forgot to tell me, and I forgot to ask how you knew to come last night, and where is Molly? Do you work? Is there an office you must go to? Or a meeting to attend? And would you like a cup of tea?*

John tossed his head back and roared with laughter. *Now that is the Catherine with a C that I love. The woman of a thousand questions, whose curiosity about all things excites and charms.*

My blush deepened hearing those words.

John sat up in the bed, and I nestled in his arms. *I spoke with Timmy yesterday afternoon. It is my parents' anniversary next month, and we are planning a surprise dinner party for them. I was calling to go over the details. You had just left the hospital, and he told me what had happened. I didn't want you to be alone. I called my mother to see if she would take Molly for the three nights, an offer she never refuses. Went home, packed my bag, and told the office that I was taking a few days off and would be back later this week. Yes, I do work; I am a senior officer in the same bank my grandfather owned. And I would love a cup of tea.*

*Me, too. About the tea that is. Let's go downstairs and put the kettle on.*

The tea now poured, John opened up the icebox. *You have the makings of a fine breakfast here. Can I take a hand with the skillet?*

*A poet and a chef? Will your talents never cease to amaze me?*

John came over and kissed me on top of my head. *And you, my dear, ain't seen nothing yet.*

I smiled. *One point of clarification, what does senior officer mean?*

John shrugged as the bacon began to fry. *I'm the president.*

*Now, besides my stomach growling by the smells emanating from the cooker, I am impressed.*

*And, as I said, my dearest Catherine, you ain't seen nothing yet.*

———

After breakfast, I stopped by to see Patricia. I am not sure what convinced her. It might have been the secret smile I couldn't contain or the softening of my voice when I described my recent breakfast, but she was assured that I would be okay. She and the boys were going to her mother's farm for a few days while Sean was on duty. She wanted to be sure I was comfortable being alone. I couldn't tell her that I wasn't alone. Some things are best unsaid, even to Patricia.

That afternoon, John looked over Mam's financial papers while I went to visit Joseph in the hospital. John met me at Bewley's, and I gave him the good news that Joseph was recovering. He was still in a coma, but his breathing was more regular. John, in his best banker's voice, advised me where best to invest the money for security and growth. We walked home holding hands. This was easy, communicating by touch as well as by voice. We were a couple.

The next morning, I lay on John's chest. All was quiet. The first streaks of morning light were filtering through the curtains, giving the room a soft, golden hue. John was starting to stir. It was the start of our second day together.

*It is time*, I thought. *It is time to ask.*

*Can you tell me about Molly's mother? What was she like? Where did you meet?*

John tightened his arm around me, and his voice became quiet.

*Yes, it is time you knew. I have tried to keep my life separated from what it was and what it is. But it is time you know. Time you know about what my life was like then.*

*We met the week we graduated from Stanford. There was a reception for the students who were receiving their diplomas with distinction. She was a pre-med student who had worked hard to get the recognition. I received mine more by luck than by sweat. It was our mothers who brought us together.*

He chuckled softly.

*Her name?* I asked.

*Oh, Caroline, but everyone called her Carrie. It was how we decided on Molly's name, a name for the certificates, she said, and a name for the lullabies.*

John's eyes closed as he became lost in his memories.

*Tell me more about how you met.* I was now fully awake, hanging onto every word.

*Our parents met at that reception. Carrie's family was from California, but her grandparents had come to the States from Limerick following the First World War. When Carrie's mother heard my ma's lilt, she immediately struck up a conversation. They connected and made plans for both families to meet for dinner after the graduation ceremony.*

*I was spending most of my time with my fraternity brothers. One last go-round until the real world hit, and I had to start whatever the next stage of my life was going to be. My parents, my da in particular, were encouraging me to have this final fling, to get it out of my system. My ma concurred, but with the clear caveat that I was to show up for the ceremony dressed in a suit and tie and have dinner with them afterwards.*

I began to shift around. *Sounds like your parents had the right touch, let you be you while not letting you forget the right thing to do.*

John nodded. *It is my father who let us test our wings, to learn to fly. With my mother, it is more about doing what is expected, maintaining the family name, keeping the legacy alive.*

I wanted the conversation to come back to Carrie. I needed to know more. *And that is when you and Carrie met, at that dinner?*

*Yes, but the night before was my one last outing with my mates, and I showed up at graduation dressed according to my mother's instructions but with a head that wouldn't stop throbbing. I am wearing sunglasses in all my commencement pictures. My excuse was the bright California sunshine rather than the need to mask my bloodshot eyes.*

*Later, it became one of Carrie's favorite stories, that I didn't care much about meeting her that day. She and Tim, however, became fast friends. He was beginning his pre-med studies at Trinity, and Carrie was starting med school there, a major accomplishment for an American girl despite her Irish ancestry. I was moving back to Dublin following a camping trip through South America. Much to our mams' delight, we exchanged contact information. An address I lost along the way.*

*So how did you end up together?* I wanted the whole story, though it was becoming increasingly difficult to hear.

*It was at an alumni party here in Dublin about two years later. I was consuming much less alcohol and recognized her as soon as she came through the door. The Irish winds were blowing furiously that night, and she was a breath of fresh summer air, so full of life and laughter. She was tall with a body that had been honed on the women's field hockey turf. Her black curls bobbed up and down when she spoke.*

I pulled myself up, resting on one elbow. *That sounds like Molly.*

*Yes, Molly looks like her mother, but with my eyes and temperament.*

*And?* I didn't want him to get sidetracked.

*It all stumbles together after that. I recognized her immediately and rushed to her side, reintroduced myself, got her address, and didn't lose it. Six months later, we were engaged and were married a year from that date. Molly came along just 12 months later, so there were no scandals to tarnish the family name.*

*We had so much, so soon, so many dreams, so many hopes. Then she was gone. It still feels like a blow to my chest.*

John sat up.

I did the same, pulling the quilt around my shoulders. I felt a tight ache settling in my chest.

John's voice was soft, now heavy with grief. *It was a brain aneurysm. We should have known. Carrie should have known. She was a doctor, for God's sake. She complained of bad headaches, which we blamed on her workload, the pressure of her upcoming medical boards. Then she was nauseous. We thought she might be pregnant, but it was too soon to go to any doctor. If only we had …* John's voice trailed off.

I said nothing. John continued.

*It came without any warning and was over in minutes. It was a regular night; there was no harbinger that my world was about to crumble. I had finished reading Molly her bedtime story, and she was down for the night. We had just celebrated her second birthday.*

*Carrie was in the living room, sorting out what sections of the paper we each laid claim to when I walked in. She stood up from the couch and began to sway. She said she was going to faint. I ran to her side. Her hand began to tremble as she reached for the side of her head, and then she slumped to the floor. I knelt down beside her, calling her name. Her breath sounded fragile as if it could shatter at any moment. Her eyes, wide with unspoken fear, stared at the ceiling. Her lips parted. I heard her whisper my name as her life slowly ebbed away. Her eyes closed, and then a final breath, not quite a gasp, more like a quiet surrender. Then silence.*

*I was frozen. I don't know for how long. I stumbled my way to our neighbor's and asked for help. I remember very little after that. An ambulance came, my parents showed up. Molly was still asleep. I felt like I was underwater and couldn't find air.*

*Those days are all a blur for me. When it was over, I couldn't think, I didn't want to feel. It was unbearable to know that I would never hear her voice again.*

*My ma took charge of both me and Molly. Slowly, I came back to the world of the living.*

*It was because of Molly.*

John took my hand and raised it to his lips. *And now I have you. I never thought I could love again.* Tears began to fall from his eyes.

He laid back down and I beside him. Soon, I heard the gentle breathing of a man asleep.

Listening to John speak of his wife, a woman, a doctor named Carrie, was like watching him in another time. A time when I didn't exist. I understood grief, and my heart broke for his pain, but I was edgy. I got up without disturbing him. I had to reconcile what I heard with what I was feeling.

I made my way to the kitchen. I needed a cup of tea.

Minutes later, the steam from the kettle rose in soft curls. The shrill of the whistle reminds me that there are some things in life that tell you when they are ready for the next step.

I cradled the cup in my hands, staring at the deep amber liquid before I took my first sip.

I shook my head, realizing I was jealous. Jealous of a memory, of a life, of a woman who had once been John's whole world. A woman who was the mother of his daughter. Could I fill the space she left behind? John's grief touched my heart. My emotions were a tangled web of compassion and insecurity. I looked at my now empty cup. I was lighting the flame under the kettle for a refill when I heard his footsteps.

He came up behind me, put his arms around me, and began to nuzzle my neck. I leaned into him, his presence coaxing the tension from my shoulders and quieting my restless mind.

He asked, *Are you okay?*

I turned to look at him. *I think you should answer that first.*

*It is hard, Cate, hard to remember. But it is the past. I loved Carrie. I will always love Carrie. I never thought I could find love like that again until I met you. You must know that I love you. I am not sure what the future holds …*

I put my fingers to his lips. *Let us have today.*

John nodded, kissing my fingers. And then the infamous grin appeared as he scrutinized the kitchen.

He arched his eyebrows. *I see my culinary skills are needed once again.*

I pushed him back and shook my hair vigorously. *Excuse me, Mr. Murphy, I can scramble an egg and make buttered toast.*

John bowed. *Well then, my love, give it a go.*

And so, I did. And so did we.

There was no rush in the day, no sharp edge to the weather. There was a stillness, one that was quieting my soul and filling my heart with love.

That afternoon, John went to the market while I visited Joseph. Later, we walked to the Liffey. The air was damp but comfortable. It carried the smell of earth and sea, a quiet reminder that this land is an island, the sea just beyond the horizon.

Over dinner, John raised his glass, as if making toast. *Your turn?*

I couldn't guess what he meant. *My turn?*

*Yes, you are now to tell me of your past loves, the broken hearts you left along the way. And please don't include my beloved brother in your recount.*

I raised my glass, returning his salute. *Mine is a very short story. No real loves. Good mates who became a bit more. A few who started as a bit more ending up as good mates. I loved them in their turn or at least liked them. But not until now. Not until you, have I given someone my heart to hold. I am in love with you, John.* It felt right to say it aloud. It felt right to say it to him.

John stood up. *The clean-up can wait till the morning. I am taking you to bed, Miss Catherine Clark.* John came to my side of the table and pulled my chair out with the skill of the finest waiter at the poshest of restaurants. He took my hand, and for the first time since I could remember, the kitchen table was left with half-empty glasses and dirty plates. The tell-tale sign of a hurried departure.

The next day, the pattern continued. A lazy morning, followed by my visit to the hospital, John's trek to the market, and a leisurely walk back home. I thought it wasn't right. It had to be a sin to be this happy. This happy was too much too soon after Mam's death. This happy was too much with Joseph in the hospital. This happiness was too much given all my questioning about where I was heading.

It was our last night. I had set the table with Mam's finest linen and crystal. John prepared a meal that was a feast for the senses. I sat at the kitchen table, my only task being successfully completed, and watched John fill the space around him. His hands moved with confident precision, each motion looked effortless. I was caught somewhere between awe and amusement as John hummed along to his own melody. The centerpiece to his work was a majestic rack of lamb, its golden-brown crust glistened under the candlelight now lighting the dining room. Carrots and potatoes had been caramelized to a sweet, golden perfection. This was not just a man who liked to cook, this man was a man who created a meal that would rival those served on silver platters at one of Dublin's most posh restaurants. He told me it was his therapy, the monotony of the chopping, the blending of spices and herbs, and the angst of the scheduling to ensure all would arrive at the table at the same time and the right temperature. It was teaching him to live in the moment, a lesson he had learned the hard way.

I took on my familiar role; I poured the wine.

I was savoring the last bite from my plate when John reached over and took my hand. *I am in love with you, Catherine. I never thought I would be able to say that again. But in love with you I am, hopelessly, completely, and fully.*

*And I, you, John*

John raised my hands to his lips. *And we need to talk about what that means. Let's leave the dishes here and retreat to the parlor.*

The dim glow of the evening sun filtered through the half-drawn curtains, casting soft shadows across the room. The clock in the hallway clicked steadily, one more reminder that time was slipping away. John sat slightly towards me, his hands resting on his knees, his eyes searching mine. My hands began to slightly twitch. I ran my fingers through my hair.

John started the conversation. *You know, Catherine, I'm not the only Murphy man who has designs on your affections. My brother Timmy is in love with you. Has been since he saw you in the hospital months ago. You are all he talks about, and my mother is convinced he will be asking you to marry him. She warned him it is not the time in his career to take such a major step. His response was to ask the whereabouts of our grandmother's diamond ring and whether it would be suitable for an engagement. Mother asked me to intervene.* Another smile, *trust me, this was not the plan.*

The tension I was feeling eased. *I love Timmy, I truly do, but I am not in love with him. I am in love with you. I never want to hurt him, to cause any falling out between you. He is kind, considerate, and caring. He will make a wonderful husband and father for someone who deserves him. And I should also mention he is more than just a bit good looking.*

John threw his head back, his black eyes filled with mirth as his laughter erupted. *Careful, Catherine, unless you want to make me jealous of my own brother. We can probably figure out how to manage this, and my mother will be on our side.* The laughter stopped and his voice grew serious. He bit his lower lip, something I had not seen him do before.

*It is about Molly. She is my whole life. When Carrie died, it was having Molly that saved me from despair. My parents and I have created a world for her to offset the void of not having her own mother tuck her in at night. It is a fragile life and one that is harder and harder to balance as she gets older.*

John's eyes gazed out the window; he was once again biting his lower lip as though searching for the right words to say.

*We have not talked about this,* his voice was low and careful, *but where are you? Where do you see your life? Are you staying in Ireland? In Dublin? Or going back to New York?*

He was putting into words the question, the question that I have been asking myself. My heart clenched at hearing it come from him. I wanted so badly to have the answer, to know exactly where my place in life was. To answer one way or the other with self-assurance, with confidence that I knew where I was going next.

I put my hand over his, my voice wavering. *I—I am still trying to figure it out. Mam's illness is what brought me back. It was not part of whatever plan I had. And now with her gone and Joseph in the hospital, I am more confused, more at odds than ever over where I should be. I feel like I am drowning in unanswered questions.*

My voice cracked, *I just can't make the commitment of where I will be, not today. And I am not sure about tomorrow. I wish I could. Oh, how I wish I could.*

My voice was now barely above a whisper. *The only thing I do know is I love you.*

Then there was silence. The silence that felt like a goodbye that neither one of us could say aloud.

John was the first to speak. *I love you, too.*

A tear slipped down my cheek. *So where does this leave us?*

*Not the place I would like to be. I would like to be planning a life with you, but I don't see how it comes together. I don't want to lose you, Catherine, and I don't see how we can go forward. I have to think of Molly. I can't risk bringing you into our world if you will not be staying in it. It would be too confusing for her, and it wouldn't be fair.*

John paused, *I am not sure I could manage it, either.*

I understood his fears—the love for his daughter, the need to protect her.

He took my hands in his, his voice now barely a whisper. *These days have given me a glimpse of what life would be like with you by my side. It is beyond wonderful.*

*But this is not real, John. We both know that. Maybe a different time but not now, not today. This should be our ending. I don't know what my tomorrows are going to look like. I wish I did. And I understand your love and concern for Molly. I wish I could say that I was staying in Ireland, in Dublin. But I can't. Not today. Not even having spent this time with you. It has been magical. But I just don't know. Oh, how I wish I did.* My cheeks were wet with tears.

We stood up, our arms tightened around each other. There was no need for more words, the silence spoke louder than anything we could say. This was goodbye. My cheek rested against his chest. I listened to the rhythm of his heart, a sound I would carry with me. The moment stretched on, fragile and fleeting, until at last John loosened his grip.

I pulled back and gently stroked his face. *Will you do one thing for me?*
John looked quizzical. *Of course.*
*No matter what I ask?*
There was a slight hesitation as he responded, *Yes.*
*Will you make love to me? And try not to think that it might be the last time.*
*That's two things*, he said, standing up he pulled me towards him once again. *I can only promise the first.*

Our eyes met with a blend of longing and resignation. We blew out the candles, leaving the dishes on the table; tomorrow will be soon enough to put the world back in order. For tonight was a bittersweet dance, pleasure and sorrow flowed together as we became one. No words were said; we were saying our farewells.

The rising of the sun brought a new day and an end to our shared world. John came slowly down the stairs, placing his case by the door. His hair still damp from the shower. I was back wearing my robe rescued from our first evening. I shook my head no to his offer to help clean up the remains of last night's dinner. *You were the chef; the role of scullery maid is now mine to perform.*

He took me back into his arms, our last kiss, one mixed with fresh toothpowder and salty tears. Then he kissed the top of my head, and I stepped away. *I am in love with you, Catherine with a C. And always will be.*

*And I with you, John. Remember me when you walk through St. Stephen's Green.*

*I will remember you every day of my life.* He turned and walked out the door.

———

## A Voice

I move from room to room, everywhere I look I see John or hear his voice. In the bedroom, it is him whispering my name, in the kitchen it is the tune he hums as he prepares breakfast, in the hallway, it is the question of where he left his scarf. His absence is loud. And still, beneath the ache, I hear another voice that won't be silent. It tells me I'm not ready.

I love him; that is undeniable, but love alone doesn't feel like it is enough.

I couldn't ask him to wait. I couldn't promise him a future I wasn't sure I could build. He deserves more. So does Molly. And if there's a version of me who can give them that, she is still in the making.

I feel like a puzzle still missing pieces.

———

I put down the pen.

———

Father Flanagan stopped me after Mass on Sunday. He told me he had heard about Joseph. This was clearly not a topic either one of us wanted to discuss with the ears of the "Church Ladies" hovering close by. We agreed that Tuesday morning would be best for him to come by the house. Mr. and Mrs. M would be back with us on Tuesday and Thursday mornings. I thought it best to have someone else in the house the morning we would be meeting as a precaution for keeping the tongues from wagging.

Mrs. M was just taking the scones out of the oven, the air filled with the warm, comforting scent of buttery dough with a hint of vanilla, when there was a knock at the door. Father Flanagan had arrived.

Mrs. M brought our tea, accompanied by the scones. The good priest wasted no time reaching for both.

I assumed he would start by asking how I was managing, his mission being to console the bereaved. I hear the same question over and over—mostly from the same people who asked it yesterday or last week. I know they mean well, and I give them my usual response and thank them for their concern. Sometimes, I can feel the muscles in my jaw tighten. I want to answer correctly. *Most days, I have to remember to breathe.*

But no one wants to hear that answer. So, I give them the polite one, the safe one. *I am managing, thank you for asking.*

I took a sip of my tea, waiting for the question.

Father Flanagan didn't ask. He simply looked straight at me and said, *I am here about Liam.*

My eyes opened wide. I gasped. *Liam? How do you know Liam? He never went to church. I am not sure what, if anything, he believes.*

*I visited him in that hospital. I will confess that I told a small lie, telling the matron I was his parish priest. Few argue with a man in a black suit with a white collar, particularly in that place.*

For a man of the cloth, I thought, he can be charming. I took another sip of my tea.

*The first time I saw him, he was not well. His hands trembled as he sat on the edge of his bed, he stared into space, not looking at anyone or anything in particular. Neither one of us said much of anything. Sometimes the best you can do for someone is to just sit with them and remain quiet.*

I nodded. I knew only too well what he meant. I thought about Joseph but turned my attention back to the conversation at hand.

The priest continued, *I asked him if he would like to pray with me. He said he didn't remember how. It had been too long. I started the rosary, told him to join me when he could. The prayers were pretty much mine to offer, but I noticed that his hands looked calmer. When I finished, I simply stood up and said that I would see him again soon. He just nodded.*

*I have seen him three times since. He now says the rosary with me.*

As angry as I was at Liam, an anger that I could not put into words, I asked, *Is he okay? They aren't hurting him?* It was both a question and a plea.

*The hurt Liam is facing is not caused by others. At least not those he is seeing today. His soul has been shattered by the wars. He was just a lad when he became a soldier. He saw his mates die in front of him. He killed. The weight of these memories crash into him, the violence overtakes him.*

I could feel my temperature rise. *But he tried to kill Joseph. He waved his knife at me. We are his family. We are not the enemy, but he treats us as such.*

*You're not wrong, Cate. And there is no excuse for violence.*

*And Liam is not new to violence, Father. Even as a boy.*

*You are right again, Cate. None of this is easy. None of this is simple. We cannot point to one thing and say this is the cause. Or blame one person. Or one war.*

Father Flanagan took another sip of tea, pausing as if in prayer to find the next words. *During the time I have been talking with him, there seems to be a recognition of what you describe.*

*Liam doesn't remember much about that night until he heard you call his name. In his nightmare, he sees you kneeling beside Joseph, who is on the floor. And the blood. He says he sees so much blood.*

I couldn't help it. I started to cry. *How is it that he is a stranger to his own violence? Is he a casualty of war, the war within himself?*

The priest handed me his handkerchief. *Guilt gnaws at him. It turns into rage, particularly when fueled by alcohol. Now he hasn't had a drink in over a week, and the fog in his head is lifting. We talk about him giving up the drink, which is hard to do. He is not sure he has the strength for it. That is what I want to talk to you about. And to Joseph, when he is able.*

The good priest continued. *I know an order of friars; they have an abbey in Kilkenny. It was built on farmland. Their mission is to heal the troubled, those who jump to anger too quickly, or raise their fists too often, or turn to alcohol for the answer. I think Liam should go there. I have mentioned it to Liam as a possibility. It would be a place where he might be able to reconcile his past and figure out how to live in the present.*

*I don't understand, Father. Why do you need to talk to Joseph and me about this?*

*Ah, the absolute right question and the one I also had to explain to Liam. First, in order to be accepted, there can be no legal charges pending against Liam. Right now, the Gardaí are waiting for Joseph to be well enough to bring his case forward. And then there is the question of money. Liam is unclear, but he believes he has money available to him that could be used for such a stay. He is unclear as to how much and when he receives it.*

I nodded. *He is right; our mother left us each some money. Liam's is held in trust. I don't know all the details, but I can assume that funds would be available for something such as this. I take it that these good friars have not taken the vow of poverty.*

Father Flanagan threw back his head in laughter. *Indeed not. But the place is expensive to run. There are doctors to heal the physical ailments and others better suited to deal with the demons that torment. It is not luxurious, but it is well-kept.*

*Do you think he can do it, Father? Do you think he can change? Can he save himself?*

*If I could answer that without a doubt, I would probably be better at explaining the Holy Trinity to our First Holy Communion class. It is about faith and hope. And love. But to answer your question, there are no guarantees, but alone I don't believe he can fix it. The demons are too strong.*

*So, what are Joseph and I to do?*

Father Flanagan gave a soft smile. *For the moment, just think about what I have said. Think about what you want to do about Liam. Consider the stay at the abbey. And pray. Pray for Liam. Pray to your mother for help in your decision.*

*Joseph is coming home tomorrow. I will talk with him then. And please do tell Liam that Joseph is coming home.*

Father Flanagan rose to leave. *I will be sure to do that. May God bless you both.*

And with that, Father Flanagan gave me his blessing. I, in turn, gave him the remaining scones.

———

Joseph recovered more quickly than the most optimistic doctors had predicted. His arm in a sling, he needed a cane to keep his gait steady, but within two weeks of his return, it was tossed to the side not to be picked up again. The first few days he was home, there was little conversation. Or at least little conversation about what we needed to talk about: Liam, the house, my future. It was as if we both needed the respite, the comfort of routine, the peace that silence can bring. Timmy came by to check on him and me, but there were no offers to stay for supper. We needed to be alone with ourselves and with each other.

It was a late afternoon, the time of the year when the daylight hours stretched eagerly towards summer. The early evening light was delicate blue, like the Wedgwood vases you see in the finer shops. The trees bore the harbingers of the season to come, the tender green buds just beginning to make their welcomed introduction to the world around us.

Joseph suggested that we walk to the Liffey. My face must have shown my concern. *I can do the walk, Cate. I am stronger than I look, and my stubbornness is more potent than any of the medications the local chemist provides.*

I smiled. *I'll get my coat.*

We strolled in silence, our steps in sync as well as our minds. We got to a bench, and Joseph sat down, gesturing towards me to take the spot next to him. *And you ...*

It was neither a statement nor a question. *I feel like a sheet of paper that has been thrown into the wind. Pieces of me are being blown six ways to Sunday. I don't know if I will ever feel whole again. There is a terrible gnawing ache inside me. It changes, evolves, but it never gives way.* I looked away. Joseph said nothing. He just held my hand.

Finally, he spoke. *When I was recovering in the hospital, Mam's death and Liam's outrage were all I could think about. Those were bad days and worse nights. Since I have been home, there have been moments when it feels like a weak sun has broken through the clouds. It has been a hard climb, and the path before us is windy and steep. But we must move forward. Even if it is just one step at a time. It is what she would want.* He paused. *Nah, it is what she would have demanded without making it sound like a demand.*

I couldn't help but smile. *Spot on. It's a skill I wish I had inherited.*

Joseph gave my hand a squeeze. *You'll get there. I'm sure of it. So, here is how we might be moving forward.*

And in his way, his mathematical, problem-solving mind took over. *First, we need to talk about your future, the basic proposition. Then the other variables: what to do with the house, and then, finally, Liam. This conversation would best be done over dinner along with a glass of whiskey.*

I clapped my hands in agreement. *I'm in. We should be getting home. I can do dinner if you pour the liquid with your one good hand.*

Once settled in, I thought the conversation about my future would take the longest, but actually, it was over in minutes. The ice in my glass had not yet melted.

Joseph just looked at me. *Where will you be happy?*

I had to smile, my second of the day. That was such a Joseph-type question. I *really don't know, but it is not here in Dublin. Not now. I miss New York. I really do. I miss its energy. I miss the range of possibilities. I even miss the noise: the honking of the cars, the cabbies' shouts, the blaring sirens. And I feel whatever it is, it is unfinished. I just can't define what the "it" is.*

*Then you should go back and give it another go.*

*But I will miss you.*

*And I you. If going back doesn't make you happy, if it isn't what you want or isn't what you need, you come back. I will still be here. Dublin will still be here. So will the four kingdoms of Ireland.*

I closed my eyes. *I will go back. And then take it from there.*

Joseph raised his glass. *Good. Plans to be finalized later, but let us move on. The house?*

*I do have an idea,* I said, mirroring his toast. *My thinking is you will want to go back to living near the university.*

*Indeed.*

*I believe we just agreed that I will be living in New York, and you will go back to your own place. I don't want the house to be empty. It should be kept alive with sounds of laughter and children's too-loud voices.*

Joseph looked intrigued. *Indeed. So* ... his voice trailed off.

*I was giving a think we could ask Bridget if she and her family would like to move in. They are proud people; they won't be wanting it as a charity. We could charge them the same rent they are paying for their apartment. You would be nearby if anything goes terribly wrong and needs to be checked on. Bridget was wonderful when Mam was ill, so it would also be another way to show our thanks.*

Joseph sat back in his chair and smiled. *You are your mother's daughter. That is the perfect solution. We can give them a time frame, say three years. Her sisters will be out of school by then, and you should have a clearer idea of where your life will be. It gives all of us a bit of breathing room. We don't have to get rid of furniture, but maybe give the old walls a new paint job to welcome the family.*

Joseph dropped his eyes. *Did I tell you that Bridget would come by to see me whilst I was in the hospital? Just a bit of a smile to brighten my day, but that it did. Perhaps it is best if you speak to her about the house.*

I swear that Joseph might have been blushing by the time he finished that sentence. I decided not to pursue it.

*I'll send her a note tomorrow and ask if she could come by for a cup of tea after she finishes at the hospital.*

Joseph simply nodded, the flush of his face now receding.

*Liam?* I asked.

Joseph shook his head.

I interrupted. *I tried to see him, you know. Went to the hospital where the police took him that night, and they wouldn't let me in. The place looked like a gaol, all gray brick with bars on the window. They told me that the patients were not allowed to see anyone for their own good and the safety of the visitor. I didn't push. I am ashamed to say. I was so frightened of him that night that he hurt you, and I was scared. I turned around and left as quickly as I could. I didn't even have the courage to tell you that I had gone.*

*It is all right, Cate, that would not be the place you would want to see him. I think Father Flanagan has the best and only solution. There are enough funds for Liam to go to the Abbey and stay for as long as should be needed. I got the numbers figured out. The monies that Mam left him would cover the fees at least for the next few years. If longer is needed, we can figure it out should the time come.*

I nodded. *No question. Are you sure it's the best for Liam?*

*Not sure at all, Cate, but it is the best and only real option we truly have. So, shall we give it a go?*

*Yes,* I took another sip, emptying my glass.

*I will reach out to Father Flanagan, as well. I think we should leave it all up to him. And speaking of people to thank, Tim makes the list as well.*

*I plan to send him a Valentine.*

Joseph chuckled, *as I predicted.*

———

I sent Timmy a note, hoping that we could meet for lunch the next week. I agonized over each word, not wanting it to sound either too inviting or too formal. On the growing list of people I had to let know of my plans, his name was first. It was only fair to him, and it was the way to get the message to John, as well.

Two days later, there was a knock at the door. I opened it to find Timmy standing there. He looked tired, his dark hair longer than usual, circles darkening the skin under his brown eyes, a faint stubble of a beard beginning to shadow his chin.

*Got your note and thought it was easier to stop by than compose one back. Plus, I wanted to see you.* He took me in his arms and kissed me before I could even respond to his greeting. I had a sinking feeling in my stomach. I wasn't sure I was going to be able to pull this off.

I pulled away as quickly as I could. *You are always welcome here.* I cringed inside, exactly the wrong thing to say. That sounded much too inviting. I needed to shut the door; I was leaving. *Let me put the kettle on for tea. I should be able to find a biscuit or two in the cupboard that isn't too stale.*

*A cuppa is fine. I have just finished two back-to-back 15-hour shifts.* He stretched his arms out in a large yawn. *What we never learned in medical school is how a body could feel this tired. But you, how are you? And Joseph, how is he faring?*

*He is truly something,* I thought. *Even with fatigue pressing on him, he is compassionate, caring about us. He has the heart of a healer.*

I tried to keep my voice light. The difficult words would come soon enough. They were weighing on my chest.

*Joseph is back at university but on a part-time schedule. He still tires quickly, but his leg is getting stronger every day, and his arm is almost fully healed. I think it is all down to strength of character and the best doctoring possible.*

Timmy smiled. *Always there for him and you.*

I poured our tea. Tim took off his jacket, putting it over the back of his chair, making himself comfortable. I sighed. This was going to be so much harder than I thought. And I thought it was going to be hard.

I passed him the plate of month-old biscuits. He had the good sense to wave them off.

I looked out the window. The wind was picking up; a small gust rattled the windowpane. I was trying to muster my courage. This was my chance to tell him. I just couldn't do it. Not then. He was too tired. It didn't feel right. And I needed more strength than I could muster at the moment.

*You are too kind, Doctor Murphy, and too tired. Please go home and get a proper night's sleep. When is your next day off?* I stood up, taking his jacket off the back of the chair.

Timmy yawned and stood up. *You are so right. While Timmy Murphy of St. Margaret's Academy would do everything in his power to spend more time with the lovely Cate Clark, the doctor in me can barely remember the last time he had 8 hours of uninterrupted sleep. Could we do lunch tomorrow? It is my first day off in two weeks, and the mere thought of sharing it with you will allow me to fall into a peaceful slumber.*

*Absolutely. Plan on lunch here.*

I walked him to the door. *Now go back to your flat, get some rest.*

*Good night, my dear Cate,* he murmured, stepping close.

I could feel the weight of his expectations as he stopped to face me.

*Good night, Timmy,* I echoed, my voice quiet. As he leaned in, I tilted my face just enough, enough to keep my cheek angled away, to avoid his lips. He was so tired, I am not sure he even noticed, the thought of sleep overpowering even a good night kiss.

At some point, I decided to go to bed. It was not my best decision. I kept tossing and turning, my mind buzzing like bees around their apiary. I knew I had to tell him I was going back to New York. I knew it since I told Joseph my decision, I knew it when he sat drinking his tea. I kept replaying the conversation. What should I say? When should I say it? I tried to anticipate what his reaction would be: hurt, surprise, maybe even disbelief.

I needed to be sure he accepted this was my decision, one that was not up for discussion or debate. Every time I closed my eyes, the conversation kept replaying in my head, like a broken record. Finally, a fitful sleep took over, but I was awake as soon as the dawn's light broke through my window.

Timmy arrived on schedule, looking more like the young man I knew, his thick black hair still damp from his shower, curled around his forehead. My heart stuttered in my chest, a twisted sense of déjà vu. They were brothers, John and Timmy. I had not seen it before or failed to recognize it. It was the jawline, the curve of the lips, the way the light caught his hair that seemed so familiar. I couldn't shake off the feeling that somehow I was betraying John at this moment.

I blinked, willing myself to focus only on Timmy, on the conversation I vowed would happen today.

Timmy had just finished commenting on the smell of the stew emanating from the kitchen, and we were back in the same seats we had sat in less than 24 hours earlier. He had brought wine that I had failed to open. I needed my senses sharp, and this was not going to be a meal either one of us would want to toast.

I had barely touched my food, and my hands began to tremble slightly. *There is something I need to tell you,* I said, my voice quieter than usual.

Timmy looked up from his plate.

*I am returning to New York. I am leaving in the next few weeks.*

Timmy's face paled; he looked like he had been struck.

*I don't understand,* his fork was still in mid-air. *I thought you were back in Dublin. I thought you were staying in Dublin.*

*I didn't come back to Dublin. I came back because of Mam, because she was sick, because she was dying. Now that she is gone, I need to return to the life I left behind. I need to figure out who I am to be, what I am to become. That is why I went there, that is why I need to go back.*

Timmy clenched his fists. *I know who I want you to become. I want you to become my wife. I love you. I want to marry you. I would have told you sooner.* He shook his head. *I shouldn't have waited. But with your mam dying and my work schedule at the hospital, I thought you needed more time.*

*Will you stay now? I want to be with you, Cate. I want you to be my wife.* Timmy's voice cracked, every word sounding like a plea.

I started to reach for his hand, but pulled back. I needed to keep my distance. *I love you, Timmy, but I am not in love with you. You deserve to be with a woman who loves you with every fiber of her being. And you will find such a woman. That woman is not me.*

He got up from the table. *I can't stay here any longer, Cate. I want to see you. I will need to see you. Can you promise me you will at least see me again before you go?* Tears started to fall down his cheeks.

*I am not sure that is wise, Timmy. I am not sure us seeing each other again will make this any easier.*

*I am not asking you to make it easier, Cate, I am just asking if I can see you before you leave. You can choose the spot and time. I will send you my schedule, and you can select the date.* He gave a brief smile. *I only ask that it is not a day I am coming off a double 15-hour shift.*

I didn't know what to say. So, I said yes.

Timmy said thank you and got up and left. I watched him leave, his back turned to me, his shoulders slumped.

———

## Loving is Hard

My heart is heavy, the air thick against my chest. The look in Timmy's eyes—the hurt, the disbelief—keeps replaying in my mind. I shattered something fragile, the dream he had about our life together, the future he had imagined.

Tears burned the corners of my eyes. I went into the parlor and sat in Mam's chair, wanting her arms to hold me, her voice to offer me comfort, to quiet the battle raging within me.

Loving is hard. I love John, but our future seems unattainable, like a distant star in a sky that remains out of reach.

Timmy loves me with a love that I cannot give back.

The end result is the same. I am on the search, the search to find out who I am.

A path I need to walk alone.

———

I put down the pen.

———

Four days later, this letter came in the mail:

*My Darling Cate,*

*I spent the last few days staring at this piece of paper, trying to make sense of the words I am about to write. No matter how hard I try, I don't know where to start.*

*I thought we were a couple or at least about to become one. I stood by your side when you were burying your mam, Joseph on one side, me on the other. I thought that was the message. The people you turn to when your heart is heavy, when the world is too much to carry alone. Joseph being one. Me, the other.*

*I wanted to be there for you then. I wanted to be there for you in all the days after.*

*I still don't know how I misread this. As a doctor, I am trained to examine, diagnose, and propose a remedy. That is what I have been trying to do when I think about our relationship. It is not working. While I spent hours examining it, I cannot render a diagnosis, and I don't think a cure has ever been found for a broken heart.*

*Despite my request, I think it is better that we not see each other again. I am not sure I could manage the mantra of "the last time" ringing in my head.*

*I love you, Cate. I wish you the best. I truly do. But I need to let you go. I hope you find whatever it is you are looking for.*

*Slán mo ghrá*
*Timmy*

———

I put the letter back in its envelope to tuck into my suitcase.

You are a wise man, Dr. Timothy Murphy. You deserve to find someone who loves you the way you deserve to be loved. It is just not me. I somehow wish it were.

I am ready to go back to New York.

# Book II

# 1955

I am on my way back to New York, this time by sea, wanting both the time and space the ocean crossing would give me. The ship has begun cutting its way through the Atlantic, the Irish coast fading into mist. I hoped the sea air and the quiet of the journey would ease the ache. I am not yet ready to accept this piece of emptiness within me. I went to the cemetery to say goodbye to Mam. As I looked at her name now etched on that cross, I realized I wasn't leaving my mother behind, resting in the soft Irish soil. I carry her with me. She is the way I put my trust in Joseph, in how I evaluate a piece of cloth in my hand, in every step I take toward a life she taught me to believe in. It is hard not to think about John. I close my eyes and see him sitting on the bench at St. Stephen's Green or taking my hand as we walk along the Liffey. It was my choice to take this journey back, back to New York. I knew when I made the decision to leave Ireland, I was leaving him, too. The decision my heart knew was right for me. And it is that very same heart that will carry him with me, no matter where I am. The memory of him. My love for him.

It was my second full day at sea. I was sitting on the deck, the day was bright, the air requiring only a sweater. I was reading *Auntie Mame*, a recommendation from Faith who had just seen the Broadway play based on the book, when I heard her voice.

*Are you enjoying your book? I know the author, and it is not an autobiography.* The words came from a woman of a certain age who appeared seemingly out of nowhere. She had thick, swept-up hair and a profile that belonged on a Greek coin. Even though her wrinkled skin was dotted with age spots, her eyes were bright and appeared to take in all around her with a single glance. She reminded me of Nell, a woman who could command others by her sheer presence, never having to raise her voice. She was pushing a man in a wheelchair. His face was long and thin, his spectacles perched somewhere between the start and the end of his bulbous nose. She didn't wait for my comment as she continued. *It is a blissfully easy-to-read, unapologetically American social comedy. There are enough perfectly timed, backhanded slaps at social snobbery, racism, and anti-Semitism to redeem it from total silliness.*

I smiled and gestured if they would like to sit and join me. She shook her head, *No, thank you, my dear. My husband, as you can see, is not well. He has lost his ability to walk and his ability to think. In days gone by, he was an expert at both.* Her eyes kept mine in their gaze. *Take life one day at a time. You cannot control the future, but you can live each day. And in the words of the memorable Mame, that is somewhere in the pages you are turning, "Life is a banquet, and most poor suckers are starving to death."*

The sound of our mixed laughter filled the air; even her husband's blank eyes seemed to twinkle. She gave his hand a squeeze. *We ate well. May you do the same.*

They left the deck. I didn't ask their name, and I never saw them again.

---

## At Sea

My cabin smells of polished wood and fresh linens. Everywhere I look, there are traces of elegance—from the thick, plush carpet to the brass and crystal chandelier commanding the center of the room. Grandeur. It is extravagant. It is a gift I gave myself.

Amidst all the finery, I can still hear the hum of the ship's engines while the vast Atlantic stretches in front of me. My thoughts, like the unruly waves, are ever churning.

I can't help thinking about the woman I met on the deck. Her face was kind, her eyes sharp, her smile genuine. She told me to live each day to the fullest. Years ago, the stranger on the tram told me to look for joy. His voice has echoed in my head all these years. Both messages resonate.

What does joy look like? How can I possibly find it when I am weighted down by the sorrow of loss?

How can I live life to the fullest? Is it the rush of excitement, the thrill of discovering something new or different? Or is it in the quiet moments when your life unfolds and your soul is at rest?

I am not sure what it means. Maybe I am not to know. Perhaps the answers lie not in the destination but in the journey itself. Perhaps we get guidance on how to manage our lives from the most unexpected sources. Strangers? Or fairies disguised as such.

———

I put down the pen.

———

It was the third day of my sailing when I met her. Teagan. She was standing on the deck, her coat and shoes carrying the message that she was not a first-class passenger. Her black hair was trying desperately to escape its knitted cap, which looked handmade and a bit worn from wear. She was alone. Her shoulders were shaking, her head was bent, and her hands were clenching the railing. My first thought was that she was sick. Though the seas were calm, the constant rolling of the ship could take command of even the strongest constitution. I don't know to this day why, but I felt I had to go to her, to stand next to her. I knew I didn't want her to be alone.

I went to her side and quietly placed my hand on her arm. She looked startled. I realized she was crying; tears were cascading down her cheeks from eyes that were as green as the fields back home. Her face bore the raw marks of anguish.

*Are you okay? Can I help?*

She pulled her coat closer around her, her voice breaking, words stumbled out, so quickly that I wasn't sure I got them all. *I'm not to be here. I just came to get air. I just needed to be alone …* and she started to sob. *It's just so hard to remember. I think I saw them. Or those that are like them. I don't want to get in trouble. I belong below.*

I recognized the lilt; she sounded like Mrs. M. *No, no, you can stay here as long as you need. No harm will come. Did someone frighten you? Are you in danger?*

She looked up as if she were seeing me for the first time, shaking her head that forced her hair to finally find its freedom from the too worn cap. *No, miss. I need to go back down, but there are so many people, so many words, so many with stories that they want to tell. It has only been three days, and I am exhausted by all the chatter.*

I laughed. *I agree. It doesn't matter where your cabin is located; I believe that anyone with a ticket on a steamer bound for America has a tale, one they want to share.*

I was greeted with a warm smile. *Me ma used to say that the closed mouth is the most melodious.*

*That's one I've not heard before. Your mam sounds like a font of wisdom.*

*That she is, miss.*

*How does she feel about you leaving home?*

The tears started again. She turned her head to the sea. *She doesn't know. I had to leave before she found out. I would have broken her heart, a heart that just loves. That loves as only a ma can.* She looked up at me, her eyes gleaming with tears. *Do you know what I mean, Miss?*

*I do. My own ma died a few months ago, and it is hard to think about my life without her in it.*

*Oh, Miss, I am so sorry. Must be so hard.*

I nodded my agreement and blurted out, *Would you like to have lunch with me?*

*I'm not allowed, Miss. I belong in third class, and we were given strict warnings about moving about the ship, particularly up here in first class. We were told to stay with our own. You might get in trouble if seen with the likes of me.*

*Well, first, my name is Cate, and that is what you should be calling me. Second, with what I am paying to travel the same distance as you, they wouldn't have the gumption to give me so much as a raised eyebrow, let alone tell me who I am allowed to eat with.*

*It is lovely to meet you, Cate. I am Teagan. But I wouldn't feel right, all that fine linen and turned-up noses would make me feel strange.*

*'Tis lovely to meet you, Teagan. I understand, and I have a solution. We can have lunch in my suite. The table and chairs there will do fine, and the lunch of our choice can be delivered. Will you accept my invitation? You are the first person I have met on this ship who I would like to continue to talk to.*

Another smile. *Then the invitation is accepted.*

*Grand.* I took her arm and off we went.

Teagan stood in the doorway, holding the windblown hat in her hand. She looked unsure as to whether she should step inside or retreat. *This is all a bit grand, Miss. A bit different from the rooms below.*

*That it is. I have stayed in those rooms, as well.* I smiled. *Let me hang your coat in the closet.*

Teagan took a tentative step forward, fingering the buttons of her coat, she handed it over. She took a look around, nodded ever so slightly, and gave me a smile. It was then I got my first good look at her. She was taller than me by two inches, with hazel eyes framed by the thickest of black lashes. Her long, dark hair, now loose, cascaded down her back. She would not be described as a traditional beauty; rather, there was something about her presence. She had the look of a warrior, fierce and determined. I sensed she would be a woman hard to ignore.

Any initial awkwardness dissipated as we sat down, I suggested that we order sandwiches and tea. Teagan agreed, saying that bread and cheese would be fine with her. Conversation flowed easily. She told me that she was hoping to find work in Manhattan. She had a friend, a colleague whom she had worked with who lived in Jackson Heights, Queens. She was going to stay with her until she found work. I shared that I was returning to New York and that I, too, was staying with a friend. I decided not to talk about Nell and where and how we lived. That would be better left for another time.

We had finished lunch when I asked her why she had been crying.

A cloud fell over her face. *It was the couple, the couple with the baby. I know why they came to Ireland. They came to buy a baby. To buy a baby from the nuns. A baby they had no right to sell, one that they stole from the mother's breast. But I had no choice. None of us had any choice.*

*I don't understand.* I couldn't grasp what Teagan was saying.

*Nah, 'tis all on the hush-hush. The Catholic Church and the Irish government are in cahoots. They put us away, tell us we are sinners. Then these so-called blessed nuns steal our babies, sell them off to rich Americans. They hold us hostage, afterwards, they make us pay them back with our labor.*

*I haven't heard about this.*

*It wouldn't have happened to you, Cate. It is only to the likes of us that it happens.*

*Did it happen to you, Teagan? Is that why you were crying? Can you tell me your story?*

*I've not told it before. It is my tale. One that I have not shared with anyone.*

*I will take your ma's advice and try to be melodious. Would it help you to talk about it?*

Teagan nodded. *Yes, if you are willing.*

*Aye, but first let me find a gift from the ship's captain that should help in the telling.* I found the bottle of fine Irish whiskey that had been in my "welcome aboard" basket and broke the seal, pouring each of us a glass.

Teagan began, her eyes clouded with a mixture of sorrow and anger.

*I thought we were in love. He worked for the same company; he was in accounting, and I was in the steno pool. We saw each other eating our lunches in the small park across from the office. He was tall with broad shoulders and carried himself like a man who could conquer the world. Some of the girls said he was a bit too full of himself to suit them, but I was taken. It started slow, walks in the park after lunch, a casual kiss, and then we got more serious. We would go to the room he was renting, where no one seemed to care who was visiting and what time they left.*

*He told me how pretty I was, how I was the prettiest girl in the steno pool and how lucky he was that I wanted to be with him. I wanted to introduce him to my ma, but he said that we had to wait. He was up for a bigger job, and he wanted it secured so he could impress her with his position. I think now he was probably afraid me ma could have sniffed him out. He told me about what our life was going to be like: a house outside of Wexford where we could take our babes to the sea. I thought he was wonderful. I was happy. Then I found out I was pregnant. I thought he would be thrilled. We could start our family now, the house in Wexford could wait a bit, but we would be happy. He got angry, called me a stupid girl. Said he could never marry me. That he was already married, and I should have figured that out. That was why we never saw each other on weekends. Said he needed to go back to Munster to help with the family farm, his mam being a widow and all. That was the lie he'd be telling me. I believed him. I loved him.*

*He was right. I was a stupid girl. I was young. I didn't know what to do. I went to my parish priest, Father Duffy, confessed my sins, and he told me he would help. I didn't want my ma to know. It would kill her. I was the second oldest girl and the one she pinned her hopes on for doing something more with her life than having babes. Made up the story I was moving to London with a mate, as I had an opportunity with my company that was too good to pass up. Ma has five others still at home, so while she was sad to see me go, she was proud of me, proud that I was doing something with my life. Told me to be a good girl and to write. I worked out with Father Duffy that I would write to him, and he would bring the letters to me ma. So that is the lie I told and keep telling.*

*That day, Father Duffy got a car to bring me. I didn't know where I was going until the car stopped and the driver told me to get out. The building was plain, a gray stone mansion, which hid the horrors transpiring within its walls. Three rows of windows stretching on either side of the front door let in the only light that ever entered. There were eight steps leading to the front door. I knocked. No one answered. I looked around, there was no sign of life. No voices of children. The only sound was the receding hum of the car that had made a deliberate and quick retreat once I shut its door.*

*I waited, not sure if I was to knock again. I couldn't catch my breath. The silence was deafening. Then I heard her, the heels of her black soled shoes tapping across the tiles. The door slowly opened. She was the memory incarnate of any nun I ever had. Her skin was translucent, and she had the cleanest hands I had ever seen. No dirt under the nails that were trimmed with just a scant bit of white showing. Her eyes and her mouth were what gave her away—menacing, calculating, unyielding. She would show no mercy, not that day, not in all the days to follow. There was no greeting, she said one word: "Yes."*

*I gave her my name and she squinted her eyes, inspecting every shred of me, stopping at my stomach that was stretching my coat. A sour look of resignation turned down the corners of her mouth. "I'm Sister Margaret Rose, come this way." I was led into a room not much bigger than a closet. A large wooden desk was its only furniture, behind it sat a nun so old and so severe looking, she made Sister Margaret Rose look like the welcoming committee at a school tea. I was introduced to the Reverend Mother, who did not look up. I began to feel more and more desperate. I wanted to run, truly I did, but I didn't even know where I was. My arm was aching from the suitcase I was still clutching, my dress began to feel damp with sweat. Finally, the Reverend Mother's head snapped up, "Can you tell me the date that you are due?"*

*I gave her my best estimate. Her response was chilling: "While you are here, you will be called Patricia."*

I started to say Patricia was not my name and that I wanted to be called by my own name. But the look on her face already told me that answer. By knocking on that door, I had already given up any right to be who I was, or at least, who I thought I was.

"Leave your case here. Sister Margaret Rose will show you to your room." I didn't ask when my things would be returned to me. I simply followed the first nun out the door. I was dismissed.

I was taken to a dormitory room and pointed to a cot under the window. There was a pinpoint of light being shed from its small glass panes, while the frigid air found its way through the cracks around its frame. A brown wrapper was at the foot of the bed. I was told to change into clothes provided. I looked around to where I was to undress, but there was no private space. I took off my coat and dress and put them under the bed. Inside the bag was a gray, stiff garment, and a white apron smock. The gray dress hung on me, and I had to use the ties of the smock to bring it to size. Sister Margaret Rose snapped that I was dawdling and should stop fussing. "No one cares what you look like. Take your shoes and stockings off and put on the socks in the wrapper. You only wear socks inside; we don't need you marking up the floors."

Within minutes, I was transformed. Patricia looked nothing like me. Or that is what I thought as there was no mirror to confirm or deny my suspicions.

Sister Margaret Rose continued my orientation. She pointed to the bathroom, "The privy when you need it. You share it with all the girls on the floor, so your time there is limited. Do you need to use it?" I shook my head no, I wasn't sure I would ever need to use it.

I reached out and took Teagan's hand in mind. I am sorry to interrupt you, but this is horrible. Did you ever find out where you were?

Oh, indeed, I had been taken to the Convent of the Sisters of the Dying Christ, which should tell you what an unhappy lot they were. They provided laundry services for the local shops and the Irish Aristocracy, though none of the good nuns did much of the scrubbing or the ironing.

I refilled our glasses as Teagan continued her tale.

We found our way down to Sister Augustine, a tall woman with an acne-scarred face and a twitch in the right eye. She glared at me with the left one. "You are a Magdalene, a fallen woman. You have sinned, a mortal sin, a deliberate and deceitful act. You are here to seek salvation. Our mission is to have you mend your ways."

I wanted to say that I knew who Mary Magdalene was. She was a woman whom Jesus saved; he had shown her compassion. Sister Augustine looked as if that word was not one she would have recognized. She continued, "You are to earn your keep here. You are to work hard, attend Mass, and keep silent. There is no talking *with the other girls. The only time we want to hear your voice is when you are on your knees asking God for forgiveness." She consulted her chart, told me I had been assigned cleaning and maintenance duties, and pointed to a row of Wellingtons against the far wall. She handed me a pair of scissors. "You will find the other girls outside. Just do what they do." She shoved me into the only chair in the room and grabbed my hair. I felt the pulling and twisted in the chair. She yelled for me to stay still. I had no mind as to what she was about to do until I saw my own hair falling to the floor. I grabbed her hands to make her stop, and the scissors fell to the floor. She pulled me up from the chair, kicked me in the shins, and screamed, "Sinner, outside, now!"*

*She pushed me out the door, and that is when I saw them, a sea of heads covered in shreds of hair in every color imaginable, kneeling in the grass. No one looked up. Each held a small pair of scissors, similar to the one that I had been given, and they were snipping the grass. I knelt down and joined them. No one said a word to me. There was no offering of a welcome. I knew there'd be no good news coming from a place like this. I was alone.*

*The next morning, I woke up hungry. Dinner the night before wasn't much: a piece of bread and a cup of weak tea. I was confused, trying to remember where I was, when a nun appeared and barked that it was time to get up. I followed the line to the bathroom. No one spoke; the only sound was the gulp of surprise as we splashed the icy water on our faces. It wasn't until we were at chapel that I saw every girl together. There were about fifty of us. I kept my head bowed until the priest found his way to the altar. Then I did a quick look around. Some were like me, flushed faces with growing bellies. Across the aisle were the others, thin, sad-faced girls with flat stomachs. The nuns looked on with serene reverence as the priest filled the chapel with his rants—sin, weakness, the evils of the flesh—his daily message. On Sundays, his one-hour tirade would go another 30 minutes. Most days, at least one girl would pass out from lack of food, exhaustion, or despair. Her head would often hit the floor. The nuns never moved, never tried to help her back up or offer her a glass of water. It would be left to the girls on either side of her to prop her back up.*

*Work began directly after breakfast, a breakfast once again of bread and tea. On Tuesday and Thursdays, the pregnant girls would get an egg and on Sunday, we each would get a sausage.*

*It 'twas later when I learned the truth. The truth that Father Duffy had failed to disclose. We were on our cots and the lights were out when I heard her sobbing. She was in the cot next to me. I walked quietly to her side and tried my best to soothe her. She found a handkerchief stained and crumpled and wiped it angrily across her face. "I miss my ma."*

I whispered, "I know this is hard, but you will be able to see her once your babe is born and you go home."

The girl, who was called Frances, stopped crying and looked at me, her eyes wide. "We're here for three years."

"Three years ...?"

No longer crying, Frances gave a snicker, "Unless you have one hundred pounds."

I couldn't help but gasp. "That is an extraordinary sum of money. And even if I had it, where would I go with my baby in my arms?"

"They didn't tell you, did they? You won't be keeping your baby. The nuns won't let you. They find good Catholic homes for them. Most from America. Our babes will have a better life. A better life than what we could give them. I need to sleep." And she rolled over, her tears dried up, her back to me.

I climbed into bed. My tears wouldn't stop. No one, not Father Duffy, not the nuns, no one had told me.

The days went on endlessly. The routine was monotonous: prayers, breakfast, work, meal, more work, tea, prayers, bed. Day after day. Week after week. Nothing changed as my baby was growing inside of me. The first time I felt the kick, like a soft flutter against my belly, I felt a sense of joy I never knew before. This was a new life. This was my baby. I already loved it.

Then one morning I couldn't stand. The pain was searing. I was taken to the infirmary. I screamed and shouted something was wrong. It was too early. The nun, this one unknown and wearing all white, hissed nothing was wrong. Nothing that I didn't bring upon myself. Nothing that couldn't have been avoided if I had kept my legs together.

"Is there nothing you can give me for the pain?"

The nun shoved a piece of paper in front of me with a pen in her fist. "Sign here by the cross. Sign with the name you came in with."

The pain was fierce; I never read the form. I signed it and reached out to the nun, the nun in white, "Now can you let me have something for the pain?"

She smiled, took the form, and left the room.

I don't know how long I was there. I came in and out of consciousness. I remember feeling like I was floating, I was high above my body looking down. I could hear mumbling, voices rushing. A new pain so sharp that it brought me back to the land of the living. I gritted my teeth; this was for my baby. I pushed and pushed again. My insides felt like they were splitting open. Then I heard a cry and the words, "A girl."

My baby was put in my arms, all blood, slime, and beauty. We looked into each other's eyes and fell in love.

I learned later that they had called in the priest, and I was given the last rites. It *was my baby that woke me up. It was my little girl who wanted to be born that saved my life. We are one and the same. I gave her life, and she saved mine. I named her Grace.*

*For six weeks, she lay beside me so that I could feed her. She was strong, she was hungry, she was a fighter. I changed her nappy, sang her lullabies, cuddled her. She was my daughter. I was her mam. I was healing. I knew it wouldn't last, but I kept praying that something would change. I would get my freedom, keep my baby, start a new life. I was regaining my strength and was told that I'd be returning to my duties shortly.*

*Then one day it was different. One of the nuns-in-white brought me into a small room where a glass contraption with a large suction cup attached to a bottle was on the table. I was instructed to sit in one chair, feed my daughter and then fill the bottle.*

*I started to rebel, but Grace reached up to me, she knew what was coming and was ready. I leaned over and brought her head to my nipple, and she started to suck. She looked up at me, her eyes filled with contentment and love. Unconditional love. I never understood what it meant until I looked at her face and my heart felt that it would break, it was so full.*

*The feeding lasted until Grace was satisfied and took her lips away. I raised her to my shoulder and patted her on the back. She let out a large burp. I laughed aloud, "That's my girl. Let 'em hear your voice."*

*The nun outside the door came in and waited for me to fill the container. When I was done, she reached for the baby that I was reluctant to give up. She grabbed her, muttering, "She is a beauty, amazing how good things come from bad. She'll make some family very happy, and that donation should fill our coffers nicely." With Grace in her arms, she turned her back and walked out the door.*

*I was instructed to go back to the dormitory. I was walking down the corridor when I glanced out the window as a car, big, black, and polished, pulled up. I froze in fear as the driver opened the passenger door and a young couple emerged. They were dressed in the latest fashion, and I thought to myself, Americans. No one in Ireland has that kind of money. Mother Superior came out and escorted them inside. It wasn't long before the three of them returned to the car, only now the young woman was carrying a baby. It was Grace. I didn't have to see her, I knew. I screamed her name and fell to the floor.*

*I woke up the next morning lying on the cot in the dormitory. My daughter was gone. My breasts ached with the milk that was intended for her. One of the nuns came in to check on me. I asked where my baby was. The nun smiled, "She is blessed. A good Catholic family from America has taken her home with them. She will be given a life that you would never have been able to provide her."*

*I screamed, "I am her mother."*

*The nun spat on me, "You are a sinner."*

*And that is how I was treated, with years of servitude to repay the debt of letting them sell my babe, my Grace.*

Teagan's face changed. She was back in the present, her face registering the anguish of those days, the devastation of being made a victim when you needed most to be sheltered.

She looked at the clock and gasped. *I must go. I've been gone too long.*

I stood up. *I understand, but will you come back tomorrow? Perhaps for lunch again? Here in my room?*

A smile crept over her face. *I would like that. And what will they be doing to me, throw me overboard? We're getting much too close to land for them to take the risk that I may make the shore.* And then a hesitation. *There is another one of us on board, I believe. We haven't said as much to each other, but she has a look about her. Would you be thinking you might like to talk to her, as well? I could chat her up tonight and see if I am right. Though I'm pretty good at figuring folks out.*

*That you are, Teagan. And I would love to have both of you for lunch tomorrow. I will be in my room from noon on, so whenever you can find the right time to come, I will be here.*

She stood up, *I'll being see you tomorrow. And I am going to have whatever you had on your plate. It looked delicious.*

*It is called Croque Monsieur, and I had never had it until I came on the ship. Basically, it is a fancy grilled cheese sandwich, but it is delicious. And it goes best with chilled white wine that we will have, as well.*

*Have not had that either, Cate. So, tomorrow will be many a first for me.*

I couldn't resist giving her a quick hug. *And, I trust, it will not be your last. Until tomorrow.*

And she was gone.

Long after Teagan had left, I just sat staring out my window at the unending gray waves beating against the ship. Unrelenting in their force, the steady rhythm of their hitting and retreating against the starboard became my mantra.

Remembering all Teagan told me, I was torn between shock and anger. And surprisingly, it was accompanied by a bit of warmth and anticipation. I like Teagan. Though we live in different worlds, she unprotected and I protected by so many, I feel a bond. She has an ease about her, coupled with a will of steel. Her smile is quick but genuine, and it moves swiftly from her mouth to her eyes. Even when telling of the horrors she has endured, there is a calmness about her that is coupled with the energy of intellect and the strength of survival.

It seems as if I had known her for years, even though this was our first meeting.

———

The sun set and I hadn't moved. I remained transfixed on Teagan's story. Her loneliness. Her commitment to overcome, to take a risk, to start a new life. And then it hit me. This was my mam's story. A story of a pregnant woman, alone. What if my own mother did not have a Nell in her life? What if she hadn't had the skills to make a life for herself? What if she didn't have the courage to bear the heartache of giving up her babe? Without the money, support, and friendship Mam had, what would have happened to her? To Teddy? And to me?

There might not even be a me.

Though the room was warm, I started to shiver. I put on my nightclothes and crawled under the comforter designed to ward off any of the cold ocean breezes that might find their way into these well-built walls. My mind was racing. I longed for mine to be quiet. I closed my eyes, willing for sleep to overtake me. When it finally did come, it did not bring the peace I sought.

———

## The Nightmare

I fell asleep thinking of Mam. And then I saw her. Her hair is flowing in the wind, dressed in green velvet, the sunlight casting a halo over her. She is young, free-spirited, dancing to the music only she and the fairies can hear. Then she stops in mid-motion. She looks lost, as if searching for someone; and in the distance, a rebel fighter approaches, his arms reaching out to her. She runs towards him, and just as they were about to embrace, he evaporates. Mam falls to the ground, the bright skies now replaced with dark clouds.

I heard a cry, not like one I have heard before, neither a scream nor a groan, but a mixture of both. It is coming from Mam; her gown is torn, her hair shorn. She has a babe in her arms. She offers it up to the skies and it, too, evaporates as she falls to her knees. Her head is buried in her hands.

I call her name. I tell her I am coming. She doesn't move.

I woke up hearing me shout, "Mam!" My heart was pounding, and I was in a cold sweat. The remnants of the nightmare clung to me like a dark shroud. This was not the mother I remembered. This woman was alone, unloved, and suffering.

The realization that it was a nightmare came slowly. I felt relieved, but my uneasiness wouldn't subside. It had all been real, too real. Tears were flowing down my cheeks. The nightmare was still chasing me, like a shadow that wouldn't let me go.

Something was still wrong. Something, I didn't know what, had shifted.

———

I put down the pen.

———

My restlessness continued throughout the morning, I wasn't sure whether Teagan would return, and I knew that my attempting to visit the third-class quarters would raise more flags than those waved down Fifth Avenue on St. Patrick's Day. I was devising my plan as to what to do next when there was a knock at the door. It was Teagan with another woman, about my height and clearly nervous. She was introduced to me as Margaret, but I was to call her Peggy. I couldn't take my eyes off her, she looked like a porcelain doll that you saw only in the finest of shops. Golden blonde hair framed her heart-shaped face in soft waves, her blue eyes mirrored the color of the summer sky. This was a woman, not much more than a girl, who would turn heads whenever she walked into a room. Both men and women would stare, she was that lovely. Yet, there seemed a sadness about her. Her eyes bore shadows; she kept looking at her hands clenched on her lap.

I wasn't sure what to do. I had no plan; food seemed the best alternative. I poured each of us a cup of freshly brewed tea and said that I was starving, and we should order lunch first thing. Peggy, not taking her eyes from her hands, said she wasn't hungry, but Teagan insisted that they both order the 'fancy ham and cheese.' Peggy didn't argue back.

Once all had been ordered, Teagan, no longer uncomfortable in these surroundings, did most of the talking, basically giving Peggy a recap of what we had talked about less than twenty-four hours ago. Peggy just sat and listened, never offering a comment one way or another.

While Teagan was taking a sip of her tea, I broke into the conversation and asked, *How did you know?*

Though I had not addressed the question to Teagan, it was Peggy who looked up and answered, *How did I know that Teagan was a Maggie?*

*I'm sorry I've not heard that term used. A Maggie?*

Once again, Teagan raised her voice. *It is what we call each other. To others, we are the Magdalene's sinners in need of penance.*

*And how could you tell that you both had been,* I struggled for the right words, *were Maggies?*

Peggy looked at Teagan. Her voice, quiet and firm, *You just know. 'Tis a sixth sense. The smell of the place never leaves. You carry it with you. The memories haunt you. You just know.*

Our food arrived, the wine was poured, and Teagan started the conversation. I thought to myself, *This is a woman who can lead; she has both the mind and the spirit to be in charge.*

*Peggy and I share the same memories, but our stories are different. Very different. We were not in the same place, but both are hell. All these places are evil, run by women in black who bowed their heads in prayer and then raised their hands to us every chance they got. They claimed to dedicate their lives to God, but we are children of God, and they showed us no mercy, no compassion, no love.*

I looked at Peggy. *Was your baby taken and adopted?*

Peggy shook her head. *I had no babe. No one ever told me why I was sent there, but I figured it out. It didn't matter; I was there and would still be there if it weren't for Peter and his twin brother, Paul. Twins in spirit and bond, but Pete was tall and had ginger hair like you, while Paul was thick and dark and could match strength with the best oxen on the farm. I am ... I was in love with Pete and he with me, but it was Paul who saved my life.*

*I am sorry, Peggy, I am confused. I thought girls were taken to these laundries because they were going to have a baby.*

*Not all,* said Teagan, *but some came because they were just too pretty. A near occasion of sin that had to be removed so as not to tempt. That is what happened to Peggy. Tell your story, just like you told me last night.*

Peggy began her tale. *Well, no one ever told me the truth, but I am pretty sure it was my own ma that sent me there, not that she drove me, mind ya. No, she had the parish priest to do that for her.*

*Me own da died when I was a wee lass, and me ma remarried soon after. I understand why. She had me and me two older brothers to care for and no way to manage. They say I look a lot like her, so she wasn't long waiting before an offer came her way. He was a merchant in town, well respected with a much larger house than what we were living in. As the only girl, I had my own room, a luxury that never was mine to have before.*

*For the first couple of years, all seemed fine. Me brothers and I were going to school, Ma had another couple of babies so that our stepfather, whom I was instructed to call "Father," seemed content. Father often stayed out late at night. Ma said it was to take care of business at the shop, but as I got older, I figured out he would be seeing other women. You see, one of my house chores was to do the laundry, and his shirts often had lipstick stains on them. Me ma never wore those shades, even on special occasions.*

*It was about five years ago, I had just met Pete. He was a couple of years older than me, and we started to spend time together. We weren't doing anything but talking, dancing at the church social, and holding hands. We liked each other, but we were still in school. I was good at my studies and had dreams of maybe even being a teacher someday. Father saw Pete and me walking home from school one day, holding hands and laughing. He didn't say anything, just stood in front of his store, and said my full name, Margaret, and nodded. I didn't think much about it at the time, cause I was with Pete and that was all that mattered.*

*That night, it was late, and everybody was asleep when I felt a hand on my leg. It was Father, and he was climbing into bed with me. "So, you got yourself a lad, hey, Peggy. Well, I bet he doesn't know how to do this,"and he started to kiss me. His lips were wet, and his hands were moving up and down my legs. I didn't know what to do, I lay there frozen, my stomach churning. Now I have always had a weak stomach,'tis where my nerves go, so me ma would say. When he stuck his tongue down my throat, I gagged and threw up. Well, whatever he was planning to do, he quickly stopped and jumped up. He shouted my name with some awful words attached and raised his hand to hit me when I heard me ma's voice. She told him to go to their room. Told me to change my night dress and go back to bed. And I did.*

*The next morning, no one said a word about what had happened the night before. That afternoon, as school was letting out and I was looking for Pete to walk me home, one of the nuns called me back into the classroom. Our parish priest was there. I had no idea what was happening and can't recall even now what was said; it is all foggy in my memory. The priest said that I was a bad influence and that my behavior made men, good men, act badly; and I needed to change my ways in order to be saved. He said he was taking me to a special school where the good nuns would see to both my education and my redemption. I remember saying that Pete was waiting to walk me home. And then the priest said, "That is what is wrong with you, Margaret. You think only about being with boys. That is sinful. You are sinful. You are to come with me. It is the only way that you will be saved."*

*I started to shake. "Go away. Does me ma know? I need to go home to me ma."*

*The priest shook his head. "No, you are to come with me. Your ma agrees that this is what we must do to save your soul."*

*I started to cry, "I don't want to go."*

*"Enough," said the nun. "Do as Father tells or you will have more than one sin to confess this week."*

*So, I left the school, my home, and Pete. Papers had been signed committing me to the Sisters of the Little Flower.*

Peggy settled in, her voice firmer, her eyes animated as she continued her story. Perhaps she was feeling more comfortable, perhaps it was the second glass of wine.

*The priest pulled up to what had once been a manor house. When the door opened, he tipped his hat to the nun and told me to pray for my redemption. The nun smiled at him. "We will see to that" and closed the door behind me.*

*I remember taking my first breath in the place. The smell of the place continues to haunt me: the smoky scent of burning candles, the stinging bite of bleach, the clean scent of laundry soap. I was assigned to the laundry room. The nun said the washing and scrubbing would show me how to cleanse my sins away, so that I could leave a new woman. A good woman! I said I had done nothing wrong. I was a good girl. Everyone said so. The nun slapped me across the face, so hard that I almost fell to the floor. She screamed, "Silence! If I hear your voice again, we will cut out your tongue."*

*I was not yet fourteen years old. I believed every word she said, every threat I heard her make. And it wasn't just me. About my second day, one of the girls got her monthly. She didn't realize it, but she left droplets of blood on the floor. One of the nuns, I can't remember her name, but she had a wart at the end of her nose that made her look as terrifying as she sounded, called this young girl a dog. A dog. She made her eat her dinner on the floor without any spoon. The girl started to whimper as they forced her to go down on her knees, and one of the other nuns kicked her. More than once saying, "If you act like a dog, we will treat you like a dog."*

*I vowed then I wouldn't say a word, raise my eyes, or make a sound that would direct their attention to me. I had done nothing wrong. No one seemed to care. If I was to survive, and survive I vowed myself I would do, I would play by their rules, act the part they wanted me to play. But my prayers would have them, these nuns, suffer the damning fires of hell. For they were sinners, not me.*

Teagan started to cry. *You were an innocent, and they stole your innocence from you. They were using God's name in vain.*

Peggy nodded and continued. *There were less than three dozen of us; all looked the same in our gray dresses and white muslin aprons. We were young, but you would not have known it. There were no smiles, no lilt of laughter, no story-telling. Our hair was clipped short, our names changed, given to us on the day we arrived, not on the day we were baptized. Some had swollen bellies, signaling that a new life was going to come into this world. Others were thin, bedraggled, with flat stomachs and a faraway look in their eyes. I learned they were the ones who had given up their babes but still couldn't leave. I was not one of them, I knew it and they knew it. Any reaching out was parceled out sparingly among them, and only to them who were on the same road to Calvary. I was alone. And alone I stayed.*

*I worked from 6:00 a.m. until dark, most days but Sunday. The laundry room was long and rectangular, barred windows, half below the ground, ran the length of the room, letting in no air and little light. The clothes were sorted into bins—cottons, fine silks, and the like. But it is the smell of those bins that I remember the most—rotten food, feces, dried blood, and stale perfumes. Other people's finery and it was up to us to make their world all clean and bright again. If we made a mistake, didn't scrub enough to get a stain out or scrubbed too much and damaged the fabric, we were punished. There was a room with no windows and little air where the worst offenders were sent to. The girls who came out of there had the look of one who had been brought to death's door and then forced back to the land of the living hell. I kept my head down, the only words I spoke were the prayers. I knew the only way to survive was to act as one of the "good girls." And survival was all I could think about.*

*One of the younger nuns took a liking to me; she gave me books to read. She had brought them with her when she entered the convent. She was kind. Though she was called Sister Ignatius, the name printed on the inside covers read Mary Cristina Kelly. It gave her address as Carlow, though I thought she looked more Spanish than Irish. I read and reread those treasures when no one was looking. Since I was the "quiet one" I was left alone most of the time. In the days in the laundry, I would remember what I had read the night before, recalling each of the characters, the words they had said. I lived in their world, not in mine.*

Peggy closed her eyes.

I could think of nothing to say. What I had just heard was too horrible to comprehend.

It was Teagan who broke the silence. *It was a lesson that I could have learned from you, Peggy. I was the one sent to that room more than once. Each of those places must have had their own chamber, a torture chamber, if you like. Mine was in the basement; there was no place to sit, a cold stone floor was my bed and my chair. There was a bucket to relieve yourself, but 'twas never emptied, and there was no air to relieve the smell. The only food I got was a cup of weak tea and a piece of stale bread twice a day. Everything around me was black, including any hope I had for the days ahead, but nothing could put a damper on me. I should have learned that my speaking out made no difference.*

Peggy opened her eyes and shook her head. *No, Teagan. It did make a difference, it made a difference to those who heard you, cheered you, wished they could be as strong as you. I was playing a part. I had been in a couple of school plays, even starred in the last one, and knew how to pretend I was someone else. And that is what I did. I played the one cast to be meek and mild and applauded those who could play the heroine.*

I could think of nothing to do but open up another bottle of wine. *I think you were both heroines. Each in your own way. Tell me how you left.*

Teagan was the first again. *I think the nuns just got tired of me. I had been there a bit over a year after my baby was gone, so my debt hadn't been paid, but I was taking up space. Space that could be filled by another poor soul whose babe they could sell. I was sent once again to Mother Superior's office. I had been on reasonably good behavior, so I couldn't think what she would be wanting with me. She offered no greeting when I went in, simply said, "You are to leave. There is a dress and shoes for you hanging in the closet next door. Put them on and place what you are wearing on the hooks near the door. There are three punts in the pocket. Then you are to go."*

*"Go where?" I asked.*

*"Wherever someone will take you in, but keep your legs closed this time. You'll not be wanting to come back here."*

*I did as I was told, my feelings all jumbled. I was free to leave, but didn't know where I was or where I was going. What I knew was that I didn't trust 'em a lick. They could be changing their mind, and back in the tomb I would be going for presuming I could leave without my debt being properly paid. I was about out the door when one of the Maggies I had worked with found me. She didn't say a word but handed me some bread and butter that I quickly put in the pocket of my dress. It was that act of kindness that gave me the courage I needed. I walked out that door and never looked back.*

I couldn't believe the story, to be thrown out without money or protection. It was like a story that Dickens might have written, but this was a true tale. Not something written to sell newspapers.

Teagan continued. *I knew I looked a fright, so I couldn't be going back to me home, me ma still thinking I was living a good life in London. So, I just started to walk, the fresh air and the sense of freedom making the path seem like it belonged to me, that it was taking me in the right direction. It took me about three days to find my way back to Dublin. The tinkers and the travelers I met along the way shared their food and let me stay the night, lending me their blankets to ward off the night chill. They restored my faith in humanity, a faith that had been greatly tested by those in black robes. I found my way back to the park in front of my old office building, and one of the girls from the steno pool recognized me as soon as the shock of how I looked wore off. She took me in and made me feel human again.*

Teagan's eyes showed a hint of merriment. *You wanna guess how that happened?*

Peggy nodded. *She let you have a bath and wash your hair.*

Teagan laughed. *'Tis what did it. Making up for all those months when the shower was cold and the soap a sliver in your hand. I sat and soaked. I am not sure what heaven will be about, but as long as the water is hot and the soap lathers you up, it will be fine with me.*

*Once I got cleaned up and me mate cut my hair into what she described as the latest trend, a pixie cut, I was able to take a look in the mirror. I could barely recognize my image, so I can't imagine what I looked like the day before. I was presentable. Skinny but walking all those miles had put color in my cheeks, so it wasn't as bad as I thought.*

*I found out that there was an opening in the steno pool, and happily, they took me back in. Me babe's father was no longer there. I learned he was thrown out when his reputation as a chancer became known. Just not soon enough for me. I found my way back to me ma's, told her that I missed home too much, and was back at my old job. She didn't press for more. 'Tis who she is. So, back at work I was, picking up my life where I had left it. But that was not the life I could live anymore. I saved my money until I got enough for passage to New York and some to tide me over. One of the other girls in the steno pool left a couple of months ago, and she wrote saying that there were jobs to be had in New York for the likes of us and could rent me out a room if needed. And so here I am.*

*And I am so glad you are.* I turned to Peggy, *and your story?*

*Not nearly as dramatic, though I like to think I have a flair for that. I was but a year or so in when I got the same summons, but the message was different. My debt had been paid, and I was free to go. Paul, Peter's brother, had found me and paid for my release. He was there, waiting for me. He told me straight away that Peter had died in an accident. He had become a fireman, just like he had dreamed, and there was a fire in one of the tenements. Pete was on the third floor when one of the beams broke, and he fell to the ground. He was called a hero, and his fellow firefighters all came to the funeral in their uniforms. 'Twas quite the event as Paul described. Their parents were gone by then, so 'twas just the two of them in the house. Paul said it was too much for him to stay; he was going to Cork City to find his way, so he sold the house. He took Pete's share of the sale and bought my freedom. I will never be able to pay him back for his kindness. He saved my life just as Pete saved the lives of those in that tenement house.* Peggy went back to staring at her hands.

Again, it was Teagan who spoke up, raising her glass to Peggy. *And what got you here?*

*The one good thing that came out of all those months of taking care of other ladies' dresses was that I have the makings of a seamstress in me. I told Paul that I know how to mend, thread a bobbin, and make stitches. I can use a needle. He found me a job with a dressmaker in Cork City. I found a room in a boarding house there, saved my money, and paid for my ticket. One of the shoppe's clients has moved to New York City and told me that she could find me similar work, along with a boarding house to stay at. I am going to see her as soon as I arrive. I need a fresh start. Ireland has too many bad memories. I am alone; me ma saw to that when she gave me up. I never plan to go back. I want a new life.*

I took Peggy's hand. *Me own ma had her own dress shoppe in Dublin. I could run a sewing machine from the time I could touch the pedals. I somehow feel that she has brought you*—looking up at Teagan, I continued—*both of you to me. I no longer feel as alone as I did when we first set sail. That is all down to the two of you.*

*We land tomorrow, and I imagine that confusion will reign supreme, and the two of you will need to find where next you are to go. I would like us to meet again.*

Both Peggy and Teagan nodded vigorously as I continued. *There is a restaurant near my neighborhood that serves the most wonderful pizza. It is a taste treat the likes you never had before. It should be fairly easy for you to find, even as a relative stranger. I will plan to meet you there a week from Sunday at 1:00 p.m. I will write it all down for you. And then our stories will be on the future, no more of the past. Let us toast to new beginnings.*

Teagan raised her glass. *And to new lives.*

Peggy raised her glass as well. *And new friends.*

Our glasses clinked.

———

### My Two Worlds

The morning air was crisp, the air tinged with the smell of salt-water and the ship's oil fumes. The dull roar of the foghorn competed with the shouts of family members trying to get the attention of their loved ones stumbling their way down the deck. The air was filled with excitement, the excitement of coming home, the excitement of new beginnings.

I was finding my way to the taxi station, my luggage to be delivered later in the afternoon when I saw her. It was Nell. She was wearing a wide-brimmed hat; a soft blue scarf around her neck caught the breeze. She was as beautiful as ever. I called her name. She opened her arms wide, and I rushed in. I felt the warmth and the strength of her embrace and the love in her message.

*Oh, I am so happy to have you back in New York. Are you exhausted?*

*Not at all, there is nothing much to do on such a crossing but read, eat, and sleep. And I have taken full advantage. It is not as quick as flying across the waters, but clearly better on my nerves and my sleep patterns.*

Nell chuckled and held me at arm's length. *You look wonderful. But more wonderful is to have you back with us. You have been missed more than words can say. I have held everyone at bay. Today it is just us. Tomorrow night is the celebration dinner. Teddy is coming home, Faith will join us, and O'Brien again resumes his residency. But first, let's get you home. My car is parked just down the block, away from the melee that will happen when the luggage appears.*

Home. I felt my worlds colliding. Was this bustling city truly home? But this woman, with her warmth, her charm, and her love, dissolved any concerns about starting anew. I just had to figure out where I was going to go from here.

I settled in. Unpacked. The house had not changed. Nell had not changed. I had changed.

———

I put down the pen.

———

We were in the library, Nell in her chair. Though it wasn't particularly chilly, Nell put a log on the fire. She gave me a quick smile. *I just love how it looks and smells.*

I nodded. *You know this is my favorite room.*

*Mine, too. It is why we bought this house. It was more space than Edward and I needed then, and clearly more space than I need now, but it was this room. This room told me it could be a home, and I was looking for a home.*

I took a sip of my wine. *Did you always know what it was you wanted? Or knew it when you saw it? I feel like I am drifting. Even before Mam died. But now it feels more like I am rudderless. Unsure of where I am heading.*

Nell's expression was thoughtful. *Oh my dearest, you are not lost. You are just looking for your path, and that can take time. It did for me. It was the sight of the Shirtwaist Factory fire that sparked my flame. Until then, I was attending meetings for organizations that I cared nothing for, and they felt the same way about me. Finding your way is a marathon, not a sprint.*

I gave a tight grin. *I met these two women on the ship. And they got me thinking about wanting to do something.* Over the next two hours, we talked about Teagan and Peggy, how we had met, and what they had endured.

Nell didn't say a word. She closed her eyes. *What you have described is heartbreaking. I have never heard such stories. I can't begin to imagine how these women survived. I know of one or two families who have adopted such children, have gone to Ireland, and come back with a baby. But we hear only the best. How the nuns were so supportive. How these young mothers were giving up their babies so that a better life would be theirs. How the Church ensured that the babies were only going to good Catholic families.*

I shook my head. *I don't believe we can trust that tale. These two women are both amazing. Teagan is strong, smart, and a force. She survived by her wits and determination. Peggy ...* I paused, I couldn't find the words ... *well, you will need to see for yourself. Peggy is beyond beautiful. She has a presence about her that is almost intangible. It is hard to explain because she is quiet and unpretentious, but with a grace that makes everything else in the room fade into the background.*

I took a sip of my wine. *I wish I could have helped them. I wish I could help other young women who are caught in the same web.*

Nell's voice grew more intense, *What exactly are you thinking of?*

*I am not really sure. But what if there were safe houses where these young women could go? Where they were provided with medical care, classrooms, and training. Where they could decide whether to raise the baby or willingly give the baby up for adoption. Where the choice would be theirs to make.*

Nell's eyes twinkled, as though recalling a long-lost memory. *Sounds a bit like Rachel's Hope that I helped launch years ago. Different population, but the same intent. A refuge and a launching pad. Let's give it some more thought. Teddy will be here for dinner tomorrow, and he may have some ideas as to what and how such things could happen. And I would like to meet Peggy and Teagan. But first, we need food. Rosita made a Shepherd's pie in your honor. It is ready to be popped in the oven, a feat even my limited culinary skills can master.*

I felt more relaxed than I had in months. Talking about 'what ifs' was invigorating. Being with Nell was comforting and safe.

———

## I Am Back

Tonight's welcome dinner was punctuated by current events, teasing remarks, and easy banter. Teddy talked about politicians, saying Mark Twain summed it up best with his quote: "Suppose you were an idiot and suppose you were a member of Congress; but I repeat myself." Faith held center court, sharing the latest celebrity scandals that never reach the tabloids, and O'Brien shared the news that his book had made the *New York Times* Best Seller list. At Nell's urging, I shared Teagan's and Peggy's stories.

This night was a gift.

The love I feel is piercing my heart and my soul.

I haven't thought about John since I arrived. Maybe the fairies are letting my heart mend.

———

I put down the pen.

———

Nell and Teddy weren't at the breakfast table the following morning. They were having their coffee in the room where Teddy's father, Edward, had his office. It was seldom used, remaining more of a shrine to the power and intellect of the man who once occupied it. I was finishing my second cup of tea when Nell came in and kissed me on the cheek. *When you are ready, Cate, Teddy and I would like to talk with you. We are in Edward's office.*

I stood up. *I can go now.* It was all quite strange.

The office was quiet, except for Teddy rustling the papers on the desk. I started to feel nervous and must have looked so.

Teddy gave a quiet chuckle. *No need to look alarmed, Cate. Mother and I have been talking, and we would like to include you in the conversation.*

Teddy, looking very much the lawyer, sounded quite prim and proper. I decided to poke him just a bit. *Should I go up and change? As you can see, I am still in my pajamas. Not all of us were up at the crack of dawn.*

It was Nell who responded. *Goodness gracious, no. So let me begin, you know that many years ago, I set up a foundation in the name of my husband, Teddy's father. Teddy has been going through all the papers, so that is why his lawyer voice has taken over.*

Teddy had the good grace to grimace just a tad as Nell continued. *We have been discussing the future of the foundation and believe it is time for it to be repositioned as a voice of change. It has basically just run on its own fumes these past ten years or so. There is money available to do something more. We just haven't done it.*

It was now Teddy's turn. *Basically, the board is my mother and me. We talked this morning and agreed it is time for a change. We would like to offer you the position to be its first executive director.*

I blinked, trying to digest what was being said. *But I don't have the experience. I have never run anything like this before.* I repeated. *I have never run anything.*

Teddy leaned forward, his eyes narrowing slightly. *That's true. You haven't. But you know us, and you know what things are important to us.*

Nell's voice came in. *Things like the home you described for those young women in need.*

It was back to Teddy. *We are not sure what the foundation should be doing. And we are open to learn. What do you say? You have our trust, and we believe that is as important as having held this job somewhere else.*

I was stunned. I stuttered. *I would love to. I just don't know where to begin.*

Nell came over and gave me a hug. *We will leave it to Teddy to work with the lawyers to develop a working paper on terms and responsibilities. If you don't like it or want to do something else, that will be fine with us. We are committed to moving the foundation forward. And we want you to do it with us.*

Hitching up my plaid pajamas to look as formal attired as possible, I gave the only response that came to mind, *Well then, let's give it a go.*

---

## And So It Begins

I am still reeling from this morning's conversation. Nell and Teddy want me to run the Walker Foundation, to be its first executive director. I am not even sure what that means, but I said yes.

I have never done anything like this. I am not even sure how to begin. Teddy said they trust me; that is reassuring. They know me well. They have seen me laugh and seen me cry. But trust is one thing. Leadership is quite another.

There is so much I have never done—balancing budgets, managing others, being a public voice. I believe the foundation can start to provide a sanctuary for young women like Teagan and Peggy who need help. I believe I have the mind to make that happen. And the heart.

I am afraid. But it is not the fear that paralyzes, but rather the kind that takes its place just behind the excitement. It will keep me moving forward.

Mam would be proud. That I know to be true.

This is the beginning. Perhaps the one I have been searching for. I will want to remember what this moment feels like—a combination of nerves, thrill, and resolve. When I doubt myself, question why I am doing this, or if I can do this, I will return to this page. I will remember why I chose to do this. I will remember that I believed I could make a difference.

---

I put down the pen.

————

On the appointed hour on the appointed day, I returned to my favorite Italian restaurant. The last time I had been here was with Faith, just before I returned to Ireland. It seemed like a lifetime ago.

Teagan and Peggy arrived within minutes. There was no awkwardness in our conversation, rather a gentle back-and-forth of questions on how our lives had moved forward since our days at sea. Peggy had found a room in a boarding house in lower Manhattan and was doing the finishing touches on ladies' dresses with the promise of more work to come. Teagan had become a fan of the city's subway system. Eyeing the last slice of pizza on the pan, she told of conquering this maze, a beast made of iron and concrete that was not for the faint of heart. I pushed the pan in her direction, and the slice moved to her plate.

*It took me a day or two, but I cracked the code. The numbers don't necessarily follow: the number 4 train doesn't go to the same places as the 3. The A and C trains are regular, but the B is an express train with no connection between it and its placement in the alphabet. I stick to the color codes, and the tangle of lines and numbers is becoming more familiar.*

*My first couple of days, I saw more of the city than I intended, and it all seemed too big, too loud, and too fast. Not sure I would be wanting to give directions to others, but for the likes of me and where I need to go, the subway is the only way to get from one place to another. I keep my shoulders squared away, don't make eye contact with my fellow riders, and do my very best to look like I belong.*

I laughed out loud. *You're braver than I, Teagan. I have to hold the map in my hand and question every conductor that I see. I have no sense of direction, so telling me to go east or west is only of help if the sun is either rising or setting.*

Peggy smiled. *You had to be out of luck in Ireland, where the sun is only an occasional visitor.*

By the time the chosen dessert arrived, a light cake, creamy with the rich aroma of coffee and an explosion of chocolate, I had given them an abbreviated version of my life. I was describing a life that they had not seen. Nell and Faith were keen to meet them, and I was to ask them to join us for dinner on Friday night. I wanted to be sure they understood what my life in New York looked like before they arrived.

Teagan picked up my hesitation as soon as I offered the invitation and put my fears to rest. *That will be great craic. And stop apologizing, Cate, we know you are posh. Remember, we had to climb stairs just to have lunch with you. We will put on our finest and meet you there. Peggy, I will pick you up and have a token for you to ride with me, to be my guest on the number 5.*

My face broke into a smile. *Perfect. Come around six.*

———

Friday came quickly, and I was a tad nervous. I was bringing my two worlds together, old and new. It was either going to blend well or be a disaster. I deferred to Nell to make all the preparations. She has the uncanny knack to make you feel like you are the only person in the room while making sure that everyone has what they need. We had spent most of the week talking about the Foundation and my new role. I shared with her that I was thinking of asking Teagan to join me. She had worked in an office, and I was comfortable with her. Nell counseled that we should bring up the Foundation and the direction we saw it taking as a response to the Magdalene Laundries.

*See how Teagan reacts to the ideas before you ask her. It may be too difficult for her, the memories too sharp and painful.*

*You are so wise, Nell. Thank you.*

*It comes from years of speaking too soon, too often. I learned my lessons the hard way.*

In retrospect, I can't remember why I was the least bit concerned about this gathering. O'Brien was not offered an invitation to join us; this was a "ladies only" dinner. The doorbell rang right at 6:00 p.m. Teagan and Peggy looked lovely and gave Nell a kiss on the cheek when I introduced them. We started the evening in the library. We had just poured the wine and Teagan's whiskey when the whirlwind we called Faith blew in. All conversation stopped.

*So, sorry I'm late. I had to go into the TV station this afternoon, as the producer for this week's show was sure the sponsors would go ballistic because our characters actually kiss. I couldn't believe it. This couple is married with kids, and the best they can do is a quick peck on the cheek. I reminded him that Lucy was pregnant on TV in 1952, and ratings soared. But nothing I could say or do could convince him. So, we had to call in the writers and redo the script.*

*I need a glass of wine. And I am so glad to meet you all.*

Teagan raised her hand. *I am Teagan, and Cate has already told us about you.*

Faith then looked over at Peggy and let out a small gasp. *You are perfect.*

*We need extras for the show we are doing, and you have just the right look. Have you ever thought about being on a TV show? It is filmed rather than a live production, so a bit easier.*

Peggy's eyes just got wider.

Nell stepped in. *Faith, slow down. This is Peggy. Peggy, let me introduce you to our Faith.*

Peggy smiled, shaking her head so that her soft yellow curls fell across her face like buttercups in a soft breeze. *A pleasure to meet you, Faith. And nay, I never thought of being on television. To be tellin' the truth, I've only seen a TV in a shop window. Televisions were a rare commodity where I come from.*

Faith was not to be deterred. *Do come on Monday. I will give you the address of the studio, and I will be there. If you get the part, you will be paid for your time.*

Peggy was calculating. *'Tis in the daytime that I might be needed?* Faith nodded in the affirmative. Peggy spoke as if only to herself. *I can be doing my sewing in the evening.* She paused for no more than a second. *Why not? I will give it a go, and Teagan can tell me what subway to take.*

*Yay* was Faith's reply. *Nell, I love these cheeses. I didn't have lunch, and I am famished.* Rushing over, she gave me a hug. *You look smashing, Cate. Everything you put on just works. I look like I was outfitted by my bedroom floor.*

Faith gulped down her wine.

Nell refilled any empty wine glasses, and conversation came easily.

Teagan's reaction to setting up the O'Shea Houses, named in honor of my mother who had also given up a child for adoption, was bittersweet. *This can make a difference. This would have made a difference for me.*

This was my opportunity to ask, *Will you help me?*

*Sure, what will you be needing?*

*I will be needing you to come to work at the Foundation as its executive assistant. It would be you and me together.*

*Are you offering me a job?* Teagan's voice sounded unsure.

*Indeed, I am. Will you come?*

*T'would be heaven, but are you sure?*

*Couldn't be more sure.*

Nell sealed the deal as she stood up to move us into the dining room. *You two are a great blend. The Edward Walker Foundation will grow to new heights with you both at its helm.*

I raised my glass. *Done. We can go over the details on Monday. For now, let us just celebrate new beginnings.*

---

## Friendship

The evening drew to a close, but no one wanted to leave. The last glass of wine was put down, coats were pulled on, and goodbyes lingered at the door. Even Faith had no dramatic moment, no grand gesture. There was a sense of comfort that whatever was going to happen next had already started to happen. We began as strangers, but as laughter filled the room, there was something in the air. Something that foretold what the future would hold. We will become friends, knowing each other better than most. We will become the kind of women who will show up for each other, without hesitation.

---

I put down the pen.

---

I was anxious to make it happen, to move into our first official offices, an empty floor previously occupied by *The Daily Sun*. This is the abandoned newspaper office where Nell had started her career as a journalist. This is where she first met O'Brien. I thought the stars were lining up; this is the right place for the next chapter of the Walker Foundation. I wanted it to feel like a place of change, of thought, of potential.

I needed legal advice and counsel, but I didn't want "big firm" help. Teddy had recommended a lawyer who might fit the bill. He had met Jake Bresky in Washington and liked him. Jake had returned to New York and opted out of big firm law to work with charities and foundations, a world that could not afford to subsidize all those pinstriped suits. I was meeting him in the office this morning. I arrived with hours to spare.

New York was just waking up. Early-bird commuters were rushing to make it to their workplaces when I opened the door to what was destined to become our offices. I shrank back in horror. The place was dark and dirty, with grimy windows, discarded ashtrays, and empty garbage bins that still captured the smells of their last occupants. I walked from room to room, taking notes. The décor didn't change. The desks were scratched and water-stained, and more than one cup of coffee had stayed in the same spot for far too long. The few chairs left were missing either a roller or an arm. There was no place to sit safely. Everything would need to be sanded down, refinished, and repolished. I was already on page three of my to-do list, hoping Teagan could create order out of all this chaos. I looked at my watch. It was 10:15 a.m., and this Jake Bresky had not yet shown up for his 10:00 a.m. appointment.

Then I heard him. *Wow! This place is a mess. Good thing you are not planning a grand opening anytime soon.* He extended his hand. *You must be Cate, I'm Jake.*

*I am, and you are late.*

He didn't look chagrined. *Sorry, there was this guy on the street who needed breakfast. The line at the deli took longer than I expected, as my new friend was very specific as to how his eggs should be cooked.* He looked around. *Why don't we go back there and grab a cup of coffee? Not sure there is a good spot here for the two of us to talk about what you may want me to do, and for me to figure out if I can help.* He gave a bit of a smile. *Or your call, if you even want me to.*

*Agreed. My to-do list is going to take me longer than I anticipated, and I could use the fresh air.*

*Then follow me*, was the response. I took a good look at him. He was tall and fair, with high cheekbones and a sharp jawline. His eyes were remarkably blue, so blue they seemed transparent. His blonde hair, slicked back, was overshadowed by a fedora perched precariously on top of his head. My immediate reaction was that this is a man who would rather not be dressed up, despite his expensively tailored suit and Yale degrees.

We found an empty table at the aforementioned deli. We were between the mania of the breakfast lines and the rush of the noon-to-two lunch crowd. It didn't take long for our order to arrive. His cup of coffee looked more like a cup of milk and sugar with a squirt of coffee. I got a cup of tepid water with a tea bag on the side. I rolled my eyes. *Someone needs to develop a training course in this country on how to serve tea. Tea is a dried herb. In order for it to be brought to life, it needs to be immersed in boiling water. This takes too much work, moving the bag up and down to achieve even the slightest change in color in a cup that is no more than warm to my touch.*

Jake burst out laughing. *I don't quite see where the mandate of the Edward Walker Foundation could encompass the education of the masses to proper tea brewing, but we could take a look.*

Now it was my turn to laugh. I thought, *I like this man.* But I needed to reassert myself; this was the first time I was acting in the capacity of the executive director of the Foundation. I needed to live up to the billing.

*I understand from my brother that when you were working at one of the big-name firms following law school, you were assigned to represent a company that was fighting against the right of its workers to join a union. And that you refused to take the case. That took a great deal of courage, perhaps some would even call it moxie.*

Jake shook his head. *Well, my father, who was and still is a senior partner at the firm, called it something else. And trust me, courage wasn't one of them.*

Now it was my turn to burst out laughing. *Why did you risk it? Particularly your father's wrath? Are you a champion of labor unions?*

Jake's smile was cockeyed. *Nope. I just don't like giving the big guy so much power over the little guy.*

*Is that why you left for Washington?*

*That is why I left to clerk for Earl Warren.*

I knew this felt right. *I believe I will like working with you, Jake.*

*Is it because I clerked for the Supreme Court Justice?*

*No, it is because you bought breakfast for someone in need.*

Jake walked me to the door of the building. *I'll draw up the terms of our agreement and send it over to you in the next day or two. Given the state of the mess you have upstairs, it will be a bit of time before you are ready to roll up your sleeves.*

Eyebrows raised, I tried to look every inch like an executive director. *It will be sooner than you think. And please just send it to my brother for his review. I would merely be doing that same, and this would save us time. Let me know if you need his address.*

Jake put his hat in his hand, looking at it with a lopsided grin. *I hate hats. I think they serve no useful purpose if you have a full head of hair.* He put his open hand out. *I have Edward's address.*

I took his hand, *Edward?*

*Yes, your brother is Edward Walker, correct.*

I laughed out loud. *Yes, that is correct, but we call him Teddy. So, please send the agreement to the Walker you have on your Rolodex.*

*I believe I am going to enjoy working with you, Cate.*

I shook my head and smiled. *Where I come from, we don't be making promises we might not be keeping.*

Now it was Jake's turn to laugh. I turned and gave him a quick wave as I walked through the door and up the stairs to the Walker Foundation.

---

All things considered, it had been a fairly calm week. Teagan was masterful in taking charge of the logistics for the new office, and I was attempting to get better acquainted with its financial pages.

I was hoping for the same type of weekend when the phone rang. It was Faith, out of breath, her sentences choppy. It took me three tries of *What? I don't understand* to finally get any semblance of the story straight. Faith's voice was registering three octaves higher than normal. *She is going to Hollywood, taking the train out next week, first class, all expenses paid.*

I didn't understand what she was saying. *Who is she?* My only response.

*Peggy.*

Now it was my turn to raise my voice. *Our Peggy?*

*Yes, our Peggy, fresh off the boat from Ireland. One of the talent scouts from MGM saw her in our show and wants to test her.*

*Test her? Test her for what?*

*To be an actress in Hollywood, to become a star. I am so excited I can barely breathe. This all just happened.*

I knew nothing about Hollywood, but I didn't think you go from being no more than an extra on a television drama to getting your name on the marquee, even if it is four or five lines below the box-office pulls. Faith agreed to come over for dinner to explain it all again. Nell would join us. I wanted to be sure there would be another sane voice seated around the table when Faith told Peggy's story. It sounded more like a tale conjured up by the fairies than real life.

We were back in the library, and though too warm for a fire, it was still a place of calm and serenity. Faith's energy was about to shift all of that.

Faith took center stage, Nell and I her captive and eager audience. *It happened so quickly, everybody but everybody is talking about it. It is what makes this world so magical; you can go from being invisible to being the name on every-one's lips.*

Nell smiled, her eyes twinkling. *My darling Faith. You are speaking like you are in a whirlwind, all energy and spirit, but your words are lost. What happened? Less than a week ago, you met Peggy for the first time and, if I recall correctly, you thought you could find her a part, non-speaking, in the television drama you were working on.*

Faith started to interrupt, but Nell raised her hand. *Not yet, dear, I need to get the sequence in order. This brain is too old to stitch together the bits and pieces for the entire story. So, take us back to your studio and Peggy's first day there.*

Faith did her best to look chagrined. *Sorry, but you know how I get.*

*Only too well, my love, so in Noel Coward's own words "Begin the Beguine," slow down and keep us in step and tempo.*

Faith took a deep breath. *The Monday Peggy came on set was pretty wild. To say it was not going well is an understatement. When I saw her at the stage door, I gave her a quick wave and probably pointed her to where she could sit down. I got distracted by watching our director and producer flailing their arms about. I had no idea what was causing the hullabaloo but thought it best if I wrangled the two of them down. By the time the issue—I can't even remember what it was—got resolved, I remembered to look for Peggy. It didn't take me long to locate her; she already had adoring fans at her side. One of the stagehands—who wouldn't give me the time of day—was handing her a cup of coffee, and an assistant producer, a young guy of about 22 and the cousin of the big-time sponsor of the show, was handing her a script. I could never remember his name. I referred to him as "rosy lips." His pair just doesn't belong to a too-skinny kid with a thatch of brown hair that could use a trip to a barber shop. Peggy called my name, and the two guys looked up, startled. Not sure whether they were surprised by having their fantasies interrupted or that I would be on a first-name basis with someone as lovely as Peggy.*

I smiled. *Really, Faith. Nell and I take exception that Peggy is the only looker who knows your first name.*

It was Faith's turn to smile. *You know what I mean. In my world, I am the glue that holds the production together. In the early hours such as this, I am lucky if I wash my hair, let alone hang around with the bright and the beautiful.*

*Well, that you do,* chimed in Nell. *But how did Peggy get from being adored to being on stage?*

*A bit of luck and a bit of kismet since that assistant producer's one task in the entire production was to find an extra or two for the second act.*

Nell nodded. *Isn't that what you had intended for her?*

Faith grimaced. *And so did I. But before I could even broach the subject and without hesitation, rosy lips offered one of those spots to Peggy. She said yes, no questions asked. She was to show up the following day to rehearse her role and would be given $15.00 for that week of work. I walked her to the door, and she was giggling. Catching her breath, she looked at me with a stunned look on her face. " 'Tis it true, Faith? They are going to give me that grand sum of money for just sitting there looking like I don't give a fig about what is happening? Willy (that was the name rosy lips had given her when she asked) said there was not much for me to do. I can do the mending I need to finish for the ladies at the shop in my room at the end of the day. But all that money. I will not have a worry about paying my board for the next month or so. I feel truly blessed. You are a saint, a saint for doing all of this for me. Someone you barely know."*

*I told her I was many things to many people, but few would put me in the saint category.*

*Peggy put on her gloves, gave me a quick kiss on the cheek, and was on her way back to her boarding house. I pulled myself to my full height to appear as intimidating as possible and stomped to where the now-named Willy was sitting. He confirmed that he had made Peggy the offer. He was looking for a beauty to sit at the adjoining table of the stars of the production in Act Two. Peggy would have no lines, merely reading a book while sipping a cup of coffee. I relaxed, no harm would come to her, as I had fished out that this said Willy had not gotten her last name or her address, so she was safe from this so-called producer who had potential predator written all over him.*

*The next day, we had our table read. That is when a scene is discussed and the characters dissected. Peggy came and sat at the far end of the table, reading the script she got after signing her one-week contract. The next day, we moved to the first rehearsal, when the actors take to their feet and stumble around the stage, scripts still in hand, and essentially making a mess of it all. This is the day I most dread because it is a train wreck, and the journey looks impossible. What became apparent that day and soon crystallized was that the supporting actress, the one who was playing the younger sister of the female lead, was simply awful. She couldn't remember a line, where she was to stand, or how to project a voice that was supposed to sound like an honors graduate of the finest finishing school. Her voice replicated the intonations of a conductor on the Lexington Avenue subway. Bronx born and bred, she could cheer the Yankees to yet another World Series but couldn't pronounce the 'th' to save her life or the script. The other actors were losing patience with her ruining every scene she was in.*

*The director finally had it. He looked over at Peggy and said, "Can she speak?"*

*I shook my head as if I didn't understand him. "You mean Peggy?"*

*He looked at me as if I was an imbecile. "Isn't she the one I am looking at?"*

*I practically stuttered, "Yes, she speaks, but she is from Ireland, just came over. She has an Irish accent."*

*The director wasn't taking my word for it. "Tell her to read this," pointing to the place on the script where the soon-to-be-canned younger sister had the most lines.*

*I went over to Peggy. "The director wants you to read from the script."*

*Her face crinkled up as she shook her head. "But you were saying I was to keep quiet and just sip my coffee."*

*"Well, that was before it all went to hell in a hand basket. This is for another part, but this character is a bit posh. A New York socialite and a snob, if you will. Her voice has to sound like years of inbreeding."*

*Peggy raised her eyebrows. "Is she to sound like the other two, the ones that have all the lines?"*

*"You mean the stars, yes. She is the younger sister of the female lead."*

*"I'll give it a go. I read all the lines and was listening while I sat. What is it he'll be wanting me to read?"*

*I pointed to the section, Peggy nodded, and we walked over to the director. Well, you could have knocked me over with a feather. She had the voice, well, almost the voice needed. She didn't sound at all like our Peggy, but like a guest for tea with Mrs. Vanderbilt. The director nodded, "You'll do. Work on your 'th's; they need to be more distinctly sounded out, and watch the 'r's.' Can you know the lines by tomorrow?"*

*Peggy, keeping the same accent, delivered a perfect thank-you and said she would know the part for tomorrow's practice.*

*The director shrugged, "Okay; the 'th' is fine, keep working on the r." He looked over at me. "Make sure she is ready." I nodded.*

*The director put on his jacket, instructing everybody to go home. He looked at the now-replaced sister and dismissed her with one sentence: "We won't be needing you again."*

*I regained my focus and assured the director I would take care of it all. I told Peggy to wait, that I would be back shortly.*

*Peggy just smiled as Willy came rushing to her side, looking like Little Jack Horner, who had just pulled out the plum with his thumb while eating the Christmas pie. By the time I got back from putting the never-to-be-a-star in a cab with her one week's wage and visions of stardom destroyed, Peggy was doing a line-by-line reading with the ever-so-accommodating Willy. I couldn't believe it was her. It looked like her, but it sure didn't sound like the young woman who was here for dinner last week.*

I stood up, trying to take this all in. *I clearly need to get us wine. I am not sure what we are celebrating, but it truly appears we should be celebrating something.*

After the glasses were poured, Faith picked up the tale. *Peggy is a natural. The next day, she knew her lines and had an instinct as to where to stand and when to turn. The camera loves her. Best, she was always Peggy: quiet, accommodating, and looking out for others. She was also getting paid $50.00 for the work. She said she had never known anyone to make that much money for something as fun as this.*

*On the final day of our shooting, there was a talent agent from MGM, one of the major studios, on set. We thought he was looking at the stars who, while poo-pooing Hollywood fame, were clearly looking to move to the western skies. We had finished up; the filming was done. It had all come together, and it was good. I was feeling quite pleased with myself. Much like a sculptor would feel when the ball of clay he had been working on turned into a recognizable object, one to be admired. Peggy was out of costume, looking and sounding more like herself when this man approached us. His suit was too tight and a bit too bright for the New York theatre crowd, with its yellow checks. His face was bright red. I blamed either the California sun or the third martini lunch.*

*He came up to Peggy and introduced himself. He explained his mission was to scout for new talent; fresh faces was the term he used. He told her that he was offering her the opportunity to be tested as an actress. A movie actress. He wanted her to come to Los Angeles, and he would arrange for her train ticket. There would be someone to meet her once she arrived in California and a place to stay at the studio's expense.*

*Peggy didn't respond. So, I stepped in. "What would she do at MGM, sir? Would she be put in movies right away?"*

*The scout had the good sense to treat me as a fellow professional. "No, ma'am. She needs to test first, and then the decision will be made as to what happens next."*

*I looked at Peggy and asked if she wanted to take time to think about the offer.*

*Peggy looked at the scout, her blue eyes never wavering, and in the same voice she had used in the play, asked, "And what am I to get paid?"*

*The scout looked nonplussed. "$300.00 a month to begin. That will increase once you begin to work in the movies."*

*Peggy continued. "I have obligations that need to be attended to. I can be on a train next week. If that is acceptable, my friend here, Miss Faith Martin, will review the terms of our agreement, and you should work with her directly."*

*The scout said he would draw up said agreement, and the two of us would meet in the morning to review. We agreed upon a time and a place, and he left with a firm handshake for me and a slight bow to Peggy.*

*Once he was out of sight and ear shot, I took Peggy by the hand, and we jumped up and down.*

*"Do you know what this means?" Was my only question.*

*Her reply was quick, "It means I can do more with my life than sew on other women's buttons."*

*Well, that all happened just 24 hours ago. Peggy refused my offer to have dinner to celebrate, saying she had to finish the work at the shop and tell them she would be leaving New York.*

*I asked if she was going to tell them she was going to Hollywood, and the Peggy we know returned. " 'Tis nobody's business where I am going and what I am about to do. Would like you to be telling Cate and Nell all that is happening. Teagan, too. They have been stars. And you are like a fairy godmother, sprinkling me with star-*

dust. *We could have lunch tomorrow, after you have met and reviewed the agreement. I'll be agreeing to whatever you think is right. For now, I need to be getting back and finish up what needs finishing up."*

I told Peggy that she was putting a lot of responsibility on me. She simply replied that she knew that.

Nell chuckled. *Well, in the short of 24 hours, Peggy has gone from seamstress to starlet, and you have moved from stage manager to agent. This is all very exciting.*

Faith shook her head. *Not a role I wish to play. I can barely manage my own life let alone someone else's. But the agreement I got looked pretty straightforward. I was ready for the conversation that happened this morning, but it seems like a month ago. We negotiated a timeline of three months. I figured that was long enough for Peggy to know if this was something she wanted to do and where she wanted to do it.*

Nell looked at the nearly empty bottle of wine. *I want to hear the rest of this but think we should move into the kitchen for some dinner. There is stew simmering on the stove. Faith, why don't you dish that out? I will slice bread, and Cate, you will continue your role as a sommelier.*

Once all our tasks had been accomplished, Faith finished her story. *Not much more to tell. I took the agreement back to the hotel where the scout was staying. He thanked me for my help, and I turned down his offer to join him for dinner after he patted me on my rear. Peggy and I met for lunch. It was not much of a celebration, a quick sandwich at the local deli. She signed the agreement and said she was going shopping for luggage. Peggy said she wasn't arriving in California the same way she did in New York. There would be no scuffed and worn-out tapestry bag with frayed edges and loose threads accompanying her on this journey. She was off to buy a two-piece set and gave me a quick wink. "I may not be able to fill them both up, but nobody will be the wiser."*

I asked, *When is she leaving?*

Faith sopped her remaining stew with the last piece of bread on the table. *She is on the 20ᵗʰ Century Limited, which leaves from Grand Central on Tuesday morning at 11:00.*

I looked over at Nell who smiled. *Are you thinking what I am?*

*If you are thinking we should give her a proper send-off, then you are correct.*

Teagan joined us on the train's platform Tuesday morning. Nell had the flowers, Teagan a box of good Irish tea, Faith the camera, and I, a bottle of champagne. Nell was the first to spot her. She already looked like a movie star wearing a green pistachio colored suit on top of a beautiful white silk halter top. Her only jewelry a strand of pearls and large pearl earrings. This woman of style and grace looked vastly different from the Peggy who would only look at her hands the first time we met. She turned as we called out her name, in unison. In the moments left, we hugged, embraced, and told her how proud we were of her. I put my hands on her shoulders, looking once again into those magnetic blue eyes. We made a promise to stay in touch.

The conductor called for boarding, and the porter took her matching luggage to the first-class car. She turned to wave as the train pulled away, the swaying of the cars carrying not only her luggage but a promise for her future.

The moment was bittersweet. I had said goodbye to too many in the preceding months, and Peggy was just one more. I would keep our vow. I would be there for her if and when she needed me.

———

A week later, a letter arrived. From Peggy. I tore the envelope open before I had even taken off my coat.

*Dearest Cate,*

*It was so lovely to have you, Teagan, and Nell be my last goodbyes in New York. I have not included Faith, as I believe I know her well enough that she would be there to wave me on.*

*If nothing else happens from my coming all this way, the trip alone was worth it. This is an amazing country; no part is the same. I think all of Ireland would be but a day's journey, but it took me three days to reach Los Angeles. This is another world, but more about that in a bit.*

*Within hours of being settled in my first-class cabin, though not as grand as the one you had on our steamer, I was being transported to another world, in more ways than one. Towns and neighborhoods along the river turned into green fields and farmhouses. I stayed in my room the first night, still pinching myself to be sure that I was truly on a train on my way to* perhaps a new life. It all happened so quickly, I just needed a moment to breathe.

I woke early the first morning. Dawn was rising but had its back to us. I was dying for a cup of tea, so up I got and cleaned up as best I could; even the finest cars are a bit tight on space. I found myself in the dining car that had a fair number of people already seated at this early hour. My thinking was the clatter of wheels on the tracks could put you to sleep when the sun was down, but it acted like an alarm clock at the first hint of light. The server came over, and I asked for tea and toast. I watched as those around me ate more eggs than the hens at Peter's farm produced in a month. I listened to their voices. Each so very different. I heard none like the posh character who brought me to this spot, so I decided to sit quietly and pay attention. They were speaking the same language, one that I understood but sounded different. Some were clipped and seldom used the 'r,' I learned later they were from Maine, the northern-most state. My soon-to-be-regular dinner companions were a couple from Kentucky, whose vowels were slow and drawn out.

I spent my days in the observation car, watching the world outside change colors. Miles of what I learned were wheat fields swayed in the wind while rugged mountains loomed in the distance. It was like moving postcards. Scene upon scene, ever changing, with the setting sun painting the sky in fiery reds and soft purples. It was as if the fairies were out with their paint boxes, coloring up the world.

On the afternoon of our third day, I stepped into the Los Angeles sunshine. The air here is warm and smells clean, the sky cloudless. No one carries an umbrella or looks to see if the sky is about to erupt. It is hard to believe that Ireland and California are even on the same planet. Palm trees sway, roses and wildflowers bloom everywhere. I think this must be a bit of what heaven will look like, minus the honking of cars. For, like New York, they are everywhere and demand to be heard.

I looked around, and there was someone holding an MGM sign. He drove me to the hotel, where a swarm of men in topcoats and tails, looking more like the Irish Aristocracy than anything I had seen in New York, ushered me in.

The next morning, I put on my freshly pressed green suit and got into the waiting car. We drove about 20 minutes and arrived at Culver City. If Los Angeles is modern, bright, and shiny, Culver City is a mix of farmland, dime stores, and ugly buildings. In the midst of all this hodgepodge is the white column fortress of Metro-Goldwyn-Mayer, looking like a palace, all white with columns.

I was taken to the office of Roger Smith, a dramatic coach. He wasn't at all what I expected. His suit didn't fit; it wore him rather than the other way around. In the land of handsome men, he was surely the outcast. His chin receded into his neck, and his one last strand of hair was wrapped around his head and then pasted in place. I was wondering what he was doing working in the movie business until he asked my name and told me to take a seat. His voice was firm and strong; I guessed that he had been a star on the radio. Unlike small children, he was a man who should be heard but not seen.

There was no exchange of pleasantries. He handed me a stack of bound white paper, which I knew was a script, said I was to memorize pages seventy-five through eighty, and be ready to test in two days. And I was sent on my way back to the hotel. And here I am writing to you.

This is a world I never knew existed. One where the sun shines every day. The sky in this city is filled with stars, the *sidewalks with those whose dreams and hopes have them searching for a spot in some constellation.*

*I close this wondering if I am going to be among them.*

*Know that I am safe.*

*Love,*
*Peggy*

———

The sign on the door, painted in plain block letters, read, "The Walker Foundation." I took a deep breath. There would be a formal opening of the office later in the week, but today was just about getting started. It was the first of whatever the next days might bring.

I was the first to arrive. I turned the key and opened the door. Taking a deep breath, my mind raced, flicking between excitement and self-doubt. How did I ever get here? Why me? What was I to do next? This was not what I expected. I knew I had gotten the role of executive director of the Walker Foundation because I was in the right place at the right time. Because I knew the right people.

At our last meeting, Jake tried to prepare me for what lay ahead. Without naming names, he talked about his other clients, the challenges they faced, and how they overcame their obstacles. I had to concentrate on the issues as he spoke. My mind kept envisioning who these people were, and the image was clear—older men, with decades of power, influence, and contacts.

Teagan had performed magic; the office was transformed. The walls were soft beiges and cool whites, and the morning sun had made the rooms feel larger and more open. The broken furniture was gone; the desks resurfaced and polished to a gleaming shine. The windows, now uncovered, let the sun shower the space with light and warmth. The cabinet drawers held our legal papers and files waiting to be filled.

I walked around, and it felt right. I could feel the energy. I stopped to read the small plaque in the reception area: *For those who think there is no hope in the future. For those who are seeking shelter from the rain. For those who think they are unworthy of love. You are welcome here.* It was the plaque we envisioned to be placed on each of the O'Shea Homes we intend to build.

I may be young and inexperienced, but I want to make a difference. I am not convinced that my colleagues at the other foundations can say the same. And I have an ace in my pocket. I have Teagan at my side. No matter how hard the route, together we will move forward. I put my gift to her on her desk. It was a framed picture of one of O'Brien's photographs—a woman with her back towards the camera, walking up a steep incline, her head held high, her shoulders squared. Underneath it was engraved, "And with a bit of bread and butter."

I sat down at my desk and closed my eyes. The buzzer rang, and I looked at my watch. It was not quite 8:00 a.m., too early for either Teagan or any potential visitor. I opened the door to find a deliveryman holding a bouquet of lovely red roses. The note read: *The Walker Foundation will bloom under your leadership. Jake.*

I put the flowers on my desk, the note in my purse. I was ready. It was time to begin.

———

## A Sighting

I was in a hurry. I told Faith I would meet her for dinner at 7:00 p.m., and my watch said 6:45 p.m.. I was only going to be on time if my fellow pedestrians moved at a New York City speed. In the midst of my hustle, I saw him. Just in front of me. Same black hair, same sure stride, same air of confidence. I stopped short, the world spinning around me.

He turned to face me. It wasn't John. I smiled. And then he turned the corner and was gone. *The fairies,* I thought, *up to their old tricks.* Reminding me that he had been real.

I shook my head. No need for that. I know only too well how real he is. Or how I love him.

———

I put down the pen.

———

Weeks turned into months before I heard from Peggy again. Faith would hear bits and pieces, so we knew she was well. Our lives were busy, all of our lives.

It was a cold and rainy day. My mood reflected the weather–unable to see the sun. I felt out of sorts. We were having problems securing the home. Neighbors were supportive in theory, but not anxious to have "unknowns" taking up residence on their streets. The mood lightened when I saw the envelope on the table; it was from Peggy. I called Faith and Teagan and told them to come for dinner. We would order pizza and listen to the glamorous tales of life in Hollywood. By 6:00 p.m., we had all gathered, Nell joined us, and I began.

*Dearest Cate,*

*First, you must not read this until you have Faith and Teagan with you. I close my eyes and see you sitting in the library, the wine poured, perhaps a log on the fire. Nell may join you, sitting in her chair. It is a scene from "Little Women." A book I never read, but I am now about to play the role of Beth. If you have not already done so, you must read the story. It is lovely, but alas! My poor character does not make the final scenes.*

*Now, to give you the update of my life among the stars, starlets, and handsome leading men, some of whom are seriously trying to lead me astray. So, take a sip of wine, my friends, and let me update you on the whirlwind that has been my life.*

*First, I am no longer to be known as Peggy Flaherty, born in County Mayo with a family history that these writers would love to get their pens and paws on. Not grand enough for MGM, my name and town. I am now known as MaryKate Donovan, an orphan who grew up in County Meath, in the shadow of the Hill of Tara, and whose family can be traced back to the high kings once crowned there. I was schooled by the good nuns, and still say my Hail Marys on my knees each evening. This is all part of* my "package"; it has very little to do with me, and no one has asked what it is that I want. But I am putting the cart before the horse, so let me go back to my first days. Days that are now a blur, so try to stay with me.

The day I was to read my lines, I arrived on time and was immediately jostled to a chair, where three women attacked my hair, my face, and my hands. Two hours later, I looked in the mirror and barely recognized me. My hair was lacquered, my cheeks pinker, and my nails polished to a shine. Once I was freed, I was taken to the stage and directed to stand here, walk there, look at this, flit around to that. I closed my eyes and thought about the lines, who I had envisioned saying them, what she would do, and how she would walk. When I was done, there was a pause and then a series of nods from those gathered around the set.

Then I was handed a contract. $1,200 a week, with the provision that it would be renegotiated at the end of three months. I was to accept all roles assigned to me, never refuse to sign an autograph, and not allowed to do any television work or any other profitable employment, which included theater, radio, and recordings. (Sorry, Faith, but I know you saw that coming!) There is also a "morals clause" stating that I was to project an appropriate image, appropriate subject to definition by the studio. All-in-all, I believe it says that the studio can pretty much dictate how I lead my life. I find that troubling, but I'm not in the position to argue. At least today.

So, my excuse as to why I haven't written all these weeks is that there are not enough hours in the day. I have been measured from head to toe, my chest is an asset, my thighs too thick. There is to be no bread in my diet, other than one piece of dry toast with my tea in the morning. My teeth, smile, nose, eyes, ears, and cheekbones have been examined by men whom I hope never to see again. They talked about me as if I wasn't there. My teeth are to be capped so my smile will show off perfectly white, even teeth. I wanted to tell them there was no Irish man or woman alive who had such a smile, but figured it would be of no avail. My eyebrows were plucked and arched, and I must admit, they do look considerably better. The color of my hair is acceptable. I have been given voice lessons. My Irish accent is both an asset and a curse. I am being taught when to use it and when not. Basically, I am to be Irish-on-demand.

All of this comes to playing a role, both on and off the screen.

Three weeks into all of this, I got the part of Beth.

This morning, I reported to the set, a jumble of wires and lights and people rushing this way and that. Tomorrow I start rehearsing. I am trying to remember all I have been taught, concentrating on my r's. All the voices in my head repeating: know when to speak, don't shout, don't whisper, don't look at the camera, don't fidget, be on time, know your lines, react, listen, be Beth.

So, there you have it, my dear friend. This is the first step in wherever this journey is going to take me. Pray for me that it goes well.

And in case you can't tell, I am loving it.

Love,
Peggy

———

Faith was the first one on her feet, shouting *I knew it from the moment I was her. She is going to be a star. The cameras are falling in love with her, and the audiences will follow.*

Nell got up and dusted off a copy of *Little Women* from its shelf. *I am going to read this again and pass it around. If Peggy is going to star in the film, we need to understand what Miss Alcott had intended for us. I will get extra copies for each of you, and two weeks from today, come to dinner and be prepared to discuss.*

Teagan lifted her glass: *To our beloved Peggy, may the road continue to rise up to meet her.*

Our glasses clicked.

——————

We were six months in. I thought it would get easier as the days went by, the laws and regulations, the formalities better known. That was the easy part. We were trying to help women, young women, girls, really, who needed our help. We had put together the plan, and it was simple: find a property, fix it up, open the doors, make our presence known. But the building would need to be more than just brick and mortar; it had to feel like a home.

Teagan and I were wearing out our walking shoes trying to find the right first spot. Every building felt wrong–too small or too big. Too impersonal and too cold.

We were out again on our search. That morning, we had looked at a worn-out Victorian. To call it a faded lady would be to stretch the compliment. Peeling paint and overgrown ivy made it look like a set of a Halloween thriller. The floors creaked with every step, and the air smelled of dampness and neglect.

I shuddered. Teagan shook her head, *Nah, I can't imagine how we could turn this into something that could nurture, unless you were a vampire.*

The day was getting progressively more humid. We walked past rows and rows of narrow row houses, each one a mirror of the other in brick and mortar. The stoops were scattered with stickballs, newspapers, and an occasional forgotten beer can. This was not what we were looking for. I looked over to Teagan. The summer heat clung to her like a second skin, beads of sweat gathering at her temple. *I need a cuppa.*

Teagan raised her hands as if in submission. *And I need to get off my feet and wipe my brow. I thought the days in the office were tiring; these scouting expe-*

*ditions are reminding me that I am better at hiking through the green fields of Wicklow than trudging on this city's broken concrete.*

I retrieved a handkerchief and wiped the sweat off my brow. *Aye. I suggest we take the rest of the day off. I need to get my hair cut. Teddy is coming home this weekend, and I don't want to look like I am Little Orphan Annie's older sister.*

We found a spot for our tea, and the waitress taking our order recognized our accents. She gave us a warm smile. *And where would you be calling home? It wouldn't be the likes of this city where you took your first steps.*

We told her she was right. The diner was empty, so she remained by our table talking to us. Her name was Deidre, and her parents had come over from Ireland when her mother was pregnant with her. Her smile and her teeth bespoke her heritage—a smile that came quickly and teeth that needed a good dentist. *So, while my seed was planted in Limerick, it was here that I grew up. And what brings you to this part of Queens?* Her eyes narrowed, scrutinizing me. *You don't be looking like this is the neighborhood you're liking to call your own.*

My smile was my only reply.

Teagan took over the conversation, and without giving away her story, told her about our mission and how we were looking to set up a home, a shelter if you will, for girls who found themselves without family support and with a baby on the way.

Deidre's smile disappeared. *Such a girl as you describe worked here for a short while. She was but sixteen and had to leave school to support her family. Her pa had up and left, leaving her ma with four little ones to tend. This lass was a beauty and got herself smitten with a lad who was all charm and not much else. Next thing you know, she's not showing up to work, saying that she has some kind of stomach upset and can't keep food down. When she finally comes back, she is all pale, and her uniform can't hide the growing tummy. It wasn't my place for making such talk, but one of the older women took her aside and got the story. She was going to have a baby, and she hadn't told her ma. The lass said she didn't know how. My mate told her that she had no choice, she had to let her ma know. It was the last time we saw her. We heard her ma threw her out of the house, calling her all kinds of names a daughter shouldn't have to hear. We don't know what happened to her.*

Deidre paused, biting her lip and nodding. *It would have been good to have such a place as you describe. A safe place where she could have had the babe.*

Teagan, a faraway look in her eyes that only I saw, added, *And decided whether to keep and raise it on her own.*

Deidre continued without a pause. *Aye, a tough lot for those so young. I think there may be just such a place as you may be looking for. 'Tis not far from here. The couple who owned the house died, and their two sons moved south years ago with no intention of coming back. I am not sure of the address, but I can get you close enough to find it. There is a For Sale sign in the front yard, so you won't be able to miss it.*

We got up, energized more by the conversation than the cup of tea. Hugs were given all around.

Leaving a tip larger than the bill, we left.

Our footsteps were lighter this time. I looked over at Teagan. *I think this may be the one. It feels right, and we haven't even seen it yet.*

We turned the corner. This was a tree-lined street with modest but well-kept homes. A mother pushed her baby carriage past us and waved at the older couple sitting on the porch across the street. This was a neighborhood. This is what we have been looking for. Teagan responded, *Aye. There it is.*

It was a white clapboard with a front porch. A large maple tree situated majestically on the lawn, providing both color and shade, served as the backdrop for the prominently displayed "For Sale" sign. It was nothing extravagant; it just looked like a home. I could feel it as I walked around back. The yard was small but inviting, a swing set still standing. Empty but not forgotten.

Teagan nodded. *I think this could be the one. It is a house that has known love and provided shelter. With a little care and a new coat of paint, it could do it again.*

*I agree, let's get back to the office. I will call Jake and see when we get inside and take a look.*

Teagan finished writing the contact information down. *Speaking of Jake, you know he fancies you, Miss Catherine Clark.*

I wrinkled my nose. *Stop it, Teagan. I have enough to think about right now. And Jake Bresky isn't making the list.*

Teagan shrugged her shoulders. *I was just saying.*

Within six weeks, 38 Mill Street was ours. It would be the first O'Shea House. Jake had checked the zoning restrictions, negotiated the price, and filed the paperwork. I signed the legal documents. Teagan started the renovations.

I took a deep breath. With one home underway, we could now begin looking for the next property. Then the backlash began.

The priest at the local Catholic Church warned his parishioners that such a place should not be allowed in the neighborhood. His message from the pulpit was chilling. Parents would be sending the message to their daughters that such behavior was being condoned and even accepted. The local town council guised their opposition more discreetly, voicing concern over so-called transients living side-by-side with long-standing, God-fearing citizens.

Nell shared a similar experience when she started Rachel's Hope during World War II. *We lost the battle. We couldn't win the hearts of the community with charts and data. This was about fear, fear of change. Fear these women were "the others"—too different to belong.*

We were having dinner, Jake and Teagan joining the usual trio of Nell, O'Brien, and me.

I asked, *What could you have done, if anything, to change their minds?*

Nell grimaced. *It would have been a hard fight. We were bringing Negro women into the neighborhood. It was too drastic and too visible of a change. So, we couldn't have done much about that. What we should have done, in retrospect, is to reach out to a local woman or two to help us. Women who lived in the town. Women who could quell the fears that we so-called "city folk" didn't care about their community. My voice was not the one the townspeople wanted to hear.*

Teagan spoke up and said one word, *Deidre.*

I almost jumped out of my chair with excitement. *Absolutely. We can hire Deidre to manage the Mill Street House.*

Jake's lawyer voice asked, *And Deidre is?*

Teagan, already onto next steps, quickly responded, *The waitress who told us where to find the house. She grew up in the neighborhood. Her parents came from Ireland, and she liked our idea. We need someone to manage the daily operations. The Foundation is providing food and medical care, but the residents will be given chores to do: cooking, cleaning, and the like. Someone has to have their eyes on all of this, and we are too far away and have more to do.*

It was Nell's voice to be heard next. *I think Deidre is the perfect choice.*

Jake raised his hands in mock defeat. *I will draft a job outline for you to review; she will be your first hire.*

Teagan shook her fist. *What about me?*

*You,* Jake bowed his head in mock reverence, *I believe you are not a hire but a gift.*

I raised my glass. *Amen. And speaking of an "amen," what about the priest?*

Now, it was O'Brien's turn to speak. *I know the archbishop.*

*Naturally*, was Nell's response, her eyes rolling to the top of her head.

O'Brien's violet eyes smiled back. *He went to school with my cousin. I play golf every spring with him at the Saints and Sinners Outing. I'll see if I can get you a meeting.*

_____

## Tomorrow

Tomorrow is a critical day. My mind is a whirlwind of "what ifs" and "let me understand." Two meetings. Both crucial. Both fraught with the potential to undermine the opening of the first O'Shea House. They shouldn't both be on the same day, but the Community Board's meeting was scheduled two weeks ago, and tomorrow at noon was the only time that Monsignor Sweeney, the emissary of the bishop and the force behind the pulpit pushing for community resistance, would meet with us. Then at 6:00 p.m., it's the local Community Board, the voice of the neighborhood where the O'Shea House is to be located. There, every word will be scrutinized and our value system challenged.

I am not sure I will sleep.

_____

I put down the pen.

_____

I woke up at the first light of dawn and turned on the radio. The weatherman was predicting a slight chance of showers, 10% chance during the day, with clear skies come nightfall. I envy his role, one where you are not challenged to be either right or wrong. According to Jake's prediction, we have about a 50/50 chance of getting the Community Board to endorse our proposal and a 100% chance of being able to move forward without their nod. The permits are in order, and we are doing nothing in violation of the local zoning laws. Their position is based on the need to preserve the integrity and sanctity of the neighborhood; the same argument was being made from the pulpit at Sunday Mass. We are on firm ground to move forward with the O'Shea House opening in December. Yet without community endorsement, we are at risk. We are to provide a safe sanctuary, but our residents could easily become a target for neighbors who are opposed to them being there. This is a fight we need to win. A fight for minds and hearts, not leases and court opinions.

My prediction of success with the Church's hierarchy is grim. We have a better chance of snow and ice on this early October day than having the bishop back away from his previous statements.

I opened the front door and, remembering the weatherman's warning, took my umbrella as a precautionary measure. No more than ten steps from the stoop, the sky opened and the predicted light showers became a torrent—sudden and wild, as if the heavens had decided to upend themselves without warning. Struggling to open the now reluctant brolly, I prayed that Jake's predictions were better than today's weatherman's forecast. I also hoped that the good priest wouldn't call off our meeting to start getting the animals in pairs.

I got to the office with only slight damage done to my chosen dress—navy blue, reaching just below my knees, an elegant lace collar softening its severity. I checked my hair in the mirror; the weather had ruined any hope of a sleek look. My mass of red curls looked like they could spring to life at any moment. I sighed, not knowing if my "good Catholic girl" look had retained its desired outcome of projecting both respectability and restraint.

Teagan had arrived, and the scent of freshly brewed coffee filled the office. She has acquired the New York habit of having a cup of coffee first thing in the morning. I remain a tea drinker, and she came into my office, handing me my first cuppa of the day. Her dress projected a quiet air of rebellion—the hemline above the knee, while a soft beige cardigan, the buttons undone, hung over her shoulders. Her hair, normally pulled back in a ponytail, was loose, with waves framing her face, more heavily made-up than usual. She looked like she was going on a much-anticipated first date.

My eyebrows arched, no question was needed.

Teagan answered. *Though I don't have Peggy's talent, I decided my role today might as well be that of a reformed sinner. Or at least a sinner the good monsignor might feel the need to reform. Thought we should be on our way shortly after 11:00 a.m., don't want to be late for our scolding.* Giving me a wink, she went back to her office.

I sat at the edge of my chair, my fingers trembling ever so slightly as I reviewed for the umpteenth time the papers we had submitted to both groups. Establishing the O'Shea House, my first initiative as the Foundation's director, was supposed to be simple—renovate a home, make it a safe space, provide a second chance for pregnant girls who had nowhere else to turn. We were reconditioning the home thanks to Teagan's organizational skills and Jake's legal expertise. It is making it a safe sanctuary that was proving to be a challenge. My challenge.

The clock on my desk was ticking, a reminder that time was running out. The road ahead would require everything falling into place at the right time.

I closed my eyes. I thought about Mam. She had overcome obstacles unheard of in her day and time. Nell had taken chances, putting her own life at risk in her mission to make the world a better place for working women and children. She had called last night with words of encouragement. Mam was with me in spirit.

I need their courage, their self-confidence to make this happen. I got up from my chair, looking in the mirror. My hair seemed much less unruly, my shoulders straighter, my gaze firmer. I bowed my head as if in prayer and whispered their names, *Help me, help me make them listen, help me make them see.*

I looked at the clock. Calling to Teagan, *It's time.* We were off.

We arrived at the diocese's office 10 minutes early and were taken without so much as a good morning to a waiting area that had all the warmth of a confessional. There was no offer of a cup of hot anything. A young priest with a pinched face served as our escort or guard. It was hard to tell what role he filled. He pointed to the empty chairs we were to occupy and said but one sentence, *I will let Monsignor know you are here.*

A distant bell was calling the faithful to noon prayer, breaking the only silence that filled the space. As the last chime rang, our escort opened the door, motioning for us to enter.

Monsignor Sweeney's office was the size of our conference room. It did not feel like an office. No phones were ringing, no files were piled neatly, no bustle of staff moving in and out. It was the kind of space where words were whispered rather than spoken out loud. At the end of the room sat Monsignor Sweeney, his posture rigid, his hands clasped before him on the polished desk—his look was that of a man used to unwavering power. His eyes were sharp, his mouth frozen in place. My first thought was he doesn't want to be here. His bishop told him to do it. It is only because of O'Brien we were given the audience.

I took a deep breath and looked up at the crucifix looming larger than life behind his chair, and said the only prayer I could think of—something like, *Here we go, Lord help us.*

I squared my shoulders. I was no longer a schoolgirl waiting for a priest's blessing. I had learned enough about the Church's hierarchy to no longer see its representative being holier than the rest of us. I nodded my head. *Monsignor Sweeney, thank you for taking the time to meet with us.*

There was no smile, no extension of his hand welcoming us to sit. I took a seat anyway, and Teagan did the same.

*Miss Clark, is it? And you are the executive director of the Walker Foundation?*

*That is correct, Father. And this is my associate, Miss Mooney. We come here today ...*

The "good priest" cut me off before I could finish the sentence. His voice spoke with the kind of resolute authority that comes from people accepting his decisions without discussion.

*I know why you are here.* His words sound like a warning. *Let me make our position clear. It is not for us to offer shelter to those who forsake the sanctity of the sacrament of marriage and succumb to the sins of the flesh. The gospel is clear—there is no compromise in matters of virtue.*

I was not to be lectured to. My blood began to simmer beneath the surface, the slow burn of my anger now threatening to bubble up. I took a deep breath, my eyes never leaving his gaze. *Let me also be clear. These are young women we are trying to help. Most are teenage girls who need a safe place to go. A place where they are not shamed but supported in their time of need.*

Sweeney's fingers started to tap against the desk. *There are homes for unwed mothers within the Church's care where they come to terms with their sins and the consequences of their actions. Your plan to move a refuge outside that framework.* Sweeney's voice was flat, stern, *it undermines the sanctity of the family, and the clear teachings of the Church. What you are proposing is not acceptable by either the faith that I understand you both practice or the neighborhood you propose to disrupt by bringing these sinners onto their streets.*

I started to speak but Teagan stood up, now looking down at the priest still seated. I realized I had not yet seen him blink.

*Have you ever been to one, Monsignor? One of those homes for girls about to give birth, homes under the care of the Catholic Church?*

Monsignor Sweeney seemed startled by the accusation. Here was a question he had clearly not anticipated. *No, no, we have others who are trained in such matters. It is not ...*

It was now Teagan who raised her hand to stop him.

*I was. I was in a Magdalene Laundry in Ireland. The priests who brought us to their doors, the nuns who bowed their heads in prayer, used us. Made us ... made me ... feel less than human. They called it discipline, but it was punishment. We were not there to atone; we were there to scrub floors, clean windows, and do other people's laundry. We were forced to work until our hands bled. When we were too tired to stand, they called us lazy. If we cried, they told us we were weak. If we were angry, they told us we were sinners. We were no more than slaves.*

*And then they sold our babies.*

Teagan's voice grew a bit loud. She was not done. *This was not a refuge. This was hell.*

Sweeney blinked.

I stood up next to her. Given our natural height, now augmented by three-inch heels, I hoped we looked like the Irish queens of ancient lore, formidable and tough. I was not backing down. *The O'Shea House will be different. We will offer compassion and try to heal both the physical and spiritual wounds these young girls have suffered.*

The priest said nothing.

Teagan looked over at me, a small smile now trying to escape her lips. We picked up our bags and started to leave.

Just as we got to the doors, we turned. Teagan, a smile now in her voice, began: *When we open the doors to the O'Shea House, Monsignor, please do stop by. We plan to have your name engraved on a plaque just as you enter. It will be attached to a basket of rocks with the words engraved: "In recognition of Monsignor Sweeney's support of the O'Shea House. And underneath the words will read: Let he who is without sin cast the first stone."*

We said our farewells in unison, but as we opened the door to leave, I turned once again.

*Monsignor Sweeney?*

His voice sounded less officious. *Yes, Miss Clark, I believe you and your associate have said enough.*

I gave him my best Catholic school smile. *Not quite. In reviewing our financial records, it appears the Walker Foundation has been most supportive of the bishop's capital campaign endeavors to move his residence to a more spacious, modern structure. Please be advised, we will be conducting an audit of all such donations in the next three months. I am sure we can count on your support and that of the bishop to open your books to our accountants. And our lawyers.*

He looked at me, no longer seeing a young woman with a mission but a woman with influence who controls the purse strings that fund his bishop's dreams.

His voice was quieter, *Is this a threat, Miss Clark?*

*No, Monsignor, it is a statement. Please remember Miss Mooney and me in your prayers.*

We closed the door behind us, Teagan whispering in my ear, *Fat chance of that happening.*

Jake was waiting when we got back to the office. After telling him all the details, in particular Teagan's rendering of the care the Catholic Church had shown her, he shook his head.

*Well done, both of you. It takes a lot to navigate opposition like that. May either the stones—that you will have to explain in more detail to me later this evening—or the fear of an audit change his position. If not personally, then at least publicly. Now onto the Community Board. We are going from religion to politics, and both provide division and conflict.*

I sighed. *This day can't end soon enough. I'll be meeting you at the Board hearing. I no longer want to look like a nice Catholic girl, though given my meeting with the good monsignor, I fear that description of me may no longer be accurate.*

Jake looked at me questioning, *Is that alright with you?*

I smiled back. *Not sure, but my mother might be rolling over in her grave. She spent a lot of time and effort to give me a "proper Catholic school" education. We were taught to respect those who wear black frocks with white collars. I think most still deserve that respect, but it is something earned. Respect does not come from the clothes you wear or any vows you may or may not have taken. Father Flanagan, our parish priest back home in Ireland, is kind and compassionate. I believe he saved my brother's life.*

*And yes, I'll be at the Mass this Sunday, as usual. For the moment, however, I may be a bit more discerning as to what confessional I chose to kneel in. I shudder to think of the penance the Reverend Monsignor Sweeney would throw my way.*

Jake gave my hand a squeeze. *I am going back to the office to prepare. I will see you later. Maybe grab a bite to eat afterwards?*

I grabbed the umbrella, remembering to bring it home. *Sounds like a plan. I will see you then and there.*

I went to give Teagan a hug goodbye. *You are a star. Describing your trauma at the hands of the nuns may have made the difference.*

*Thanks, but I am more pragmatic. My guess is either the basket of stones or the dollars might get his attention.*

I sighed, *if we got it at all.*

Teagan nodded. *I think we pierced him, and it matters not which arrow did it.*

She gave me a sly look. *You know he is besotted with you. Why not give it a go?*

I knew who she meant. Jake.

*Yes, and he is a great guy, but I have too much going on to add anything or anyone else to the mix of what can keep me up at night.* I wanted to add and he is not John.

I gave her a quick kiss on her cheek and left.

———

I spent more time deciding what to wear to the meeting than usual. I made the excuse that I wanted to make the right impression on the Community Board. I knew, however, it was Jake I wanted to impress. We had never been alone like this, and though tonight was business, I wanted to look different. It had been a long time since I cared about what a man might think of me. Might want me.

I put on the silk sapphire top, it's my best color, and it clings in just the right places. The realization of what I was doing and what I was thinking petrified me. "Not yet," both my head and my heart yelled. I changed into a black cowl neck sweater. The camel pants and black heels remained.

Jake was already seated when I arrived at the Committee Board meeting, which by day served as the local elementary school cafeteria. Hard metal chairs stretched in neat rows, six across, ten back was the seating area. The air was thick with the ghosts of today's lunch menu. The smell of greasy pizza crusts and spilled milk blended with the scent of cleaning chemicals.

A far cry from the polished, arrogant setting of my earlier meeting. The atmosphere spoke neighborhood–tight-knit, protective, familiar. This was a community. A community that perceived the O'Shea House not as a sanctuary but as a symbol of moral decay.

This was no legal battle. This was a battle for hearts and minds closed in fear. My stomach was in knots. My hands twitched.

I was glad to have Jake by my side. It would be up to him to have these people embrace our vision. According to Teddy, there were few better at winning a room.

We were last on the agenda. Thirty minutes in, the chairman, red-haired with a complexion to match, called our names. Around me, backs stiffened. Those who rose to speak were all in opposition. They spoke of zoning laws, of tradition, of maintaining the sanctity of their neighborhood. No one spoke of the quiet desperation of the girls we were trying to help. Girls who needed shelter, who needed hope.

It was now Jake's turn; he rose slowly and introduced himself. He took a deep breath, putting his hand through his hair. His voice softened, trying to bridge the gap between us and them. He smiled.

*I'm a good lawyer; my father was one, too. In truth, I didn't have much of a choice when it came to my career. Like many of you here tonight, I was expected to follow in my father's footsteps. There wasn't much of a choice.*

There was a tittering in the crowd, and a few of the men nodded their heads.

Jake's voice softened, *But standing before you this evening, I'm grateful. You see, I like defending people who believe in doing the right thing. In making a difference.*

He paused, letting his message resonate.

Jake's voice got slightly stronger. *I have done my research. I think I can safely say that I may be the only person here who isn't Catholic.* The confession was unexpected. Jake's eyes met each board member's in turn—open and honest.

I was shocked. I wasn't sure what Jake was preparing to say but it clearly wasn't this.

Jake continued, his posture relaxed, he loosened his tie. *But faith, any faith, teaches compassion. I ask you tonight to open your hearts, not just your minds.*

The room grew still. No comments being made under the breath. It felt like time had stopped. Jake knew that progress, real progress, was never born from comfort. It was born from discomfort, from the willingness to challenge old fears.

Slowly, one of the Board members, a middle-aged woman with silver streaks in her hair, shifted in her chair.

Jake caught her eye, *Ma'am, I am sorry, I don't know your name. Did you want to say something?*

Startled, she shook her head. *Not much of a talker.*

Laughter rippled through the audience.

Jake smiled warmly, keeping his eyes on her. *What's your name?*

*Regina.* Her voice broke. *My cousin was lost to us, lost to me. It was back home, before we came over.* Regina spoke with the warm, musical tones of her native Italy.

The chairman banged his gavel. *How is this relevant, Regina? We are talking about this house filled with unmarried pregnant girls going up in our neighborhood.*

Jake didn't flinch. *Please, Regina, go on.*

Regina nodded, her jaw now firmly set. She spoke about Angela, a party, a boy from the wrong side of town, a life destroyed by shame. Her story unfolded in haunting words, the memories evoked, painful to recall. The room listened. No one moved. Regina took a deep breath. *Maybe if such a place like this house were there for my Angela, she would still be with me. She would still be my best friend.* When she was finished, there was no sound but her breathing.

Jake stepped closer, his voice soft. *Thank you, Regina. Angela was blessed to have you in her life.* He gave a small smile. *I bet you still light a candle for her on her birthday.*

Regina laughed through her tears. *How did you know?* She shook her finger at him as if he were a child being naughty. *Not even my mother knows I do that. And at 92, she is still living with me, so nobody here needs to tell her.* Now the whole room was laughing. Me, included. The tension in the room had crumbled.

Jake, still standing, took off his jacket and rolled his shirt sleeves up. He was about to drive the point home when there was a rustle in the back of the room. I looked up to see the same priest who had been at Monsignor Sweeney's office entering. His black cassock was swaying as he ran to the front of the room. He dropped an envelope on the table, whispered something only the chairman could hear, and retreated as quickly as he had entered. The chairman took the envelope, looking both stunned and dismayed. He banged his gavel. *This is a letter from the bishop. The board will take a 20-minute recess to discuss, and we will reconvene this meeting at 7:05.*

I walked over to Jake. *Well, what do you think that is all about?*

*How about, great job, Jake. It must be hard to be this brilliant.*

I had to laugh. *Yes, great job indeed. And Regina was a turning point. Tears and laughter, a winning combination.*

Jake picked up his jacket. *Let me take the seat next to you. I am not sure my oratory skills will be needed again tonight.*

*How did you know everyone here was Catholic?*

*New York instinct. Irish or Italian surnames, tight-knit neighborhoods. This is a historic melting pot, and looking at the faces of those on the Board, it was a safe bet that they were either Irish or Italian. It was an easy jump to the Catholic connection. And with a last name like Bresky, I wanted to acknowledge that they were right. I am Jewish.*

My voice got more serious. *What do you think is going on?*

*My guess is your meeting with the good monsignor caused a bit of a stir. I am not sure what the result will be, but in my role as clairvoyant rather than that of a lawyer, I would bet that the diocese has reconsidered its position on the O'Shea*

*House, and the neighborhood will be blessed to have such a sanctuary grace their community. And it will not be for anything I said.*

Within 10 minutes, Jake's prediction proved accurate. The chairman and full board returned to their seats, and order was called once again. The chairman gave brief remarks that it had come to the attention of the board that the bishop had changed his position on the O'Shea House being located in the diocese. The letter read that the bishop had prayed for guidance and came to accept the need for these unfortunate girls to receive compassionate care. *Like Jesus*, the bishop wrote, *we should forgive those who have sinned and care for them as did the Good Samaritan.*

The chairman concluded that, given the bishop's approval, the Community Board will welcome the O'Shea House into the neighborhood. He thanked Jake for taking the time to appear before the board, and before a question could be raised, banged the gavel, and the meeting was over.

Jake and I hugged, a hug longer and firmer than one might normally expect between two colleagues.

I walked over to talk with Regina, and Jake went to shake hands with the chairman. I learned that Regina's family ran the local Italian bakery and made a mental note to have Teagan use her to cater the opening of O'Shea House. Jake then called me over to meet the board chairman.

*Cate, I would like you to meet Colin Finnegan, born in Kilkenny but a proud member of this community since his arrival some 40 years ago. Mr. Finnegan, the executive director of the Walker Foundation, Miss Catherine Clark.*

I took his hand, worn and leathery. *Lovely to meet you, Mr. Finnegan. Thank you for this evening.*

*You, too, miss. Please call me Red; it is the only name I answer to. I might be saying the same about you.*

*Nay, I get called ginger more than red and seldom to my face. Please call me Cate.*

*You are a bright young lass, and you have my full support. Anyone starts giving you trouble with the good work that you are doing, just tell them that they will have me to answer to. While the older folks care about what the bishop thinks, it is the young hooligans who understand that a right hook when you least expect it can change your mind faster than the threat of eternal damnation.*

*Go raibh maith agat, Dearg.*

My new best friend, Red, gave me a hug and a kiss on the cheek. *You're welcome, my darling girl.*

Jake and I walked out, him taking my arm. *Well, your troubles are over* here. *O'Shea House will open as planned, and the neighbors will be friendly. What-ever did you say to your new friend, Red?*

I batted my eyelashes. *I merely asked him if he would be the father of my children.*

Jake stopped short. *You did what?*

I took his arm back, *Seriously, Jake. I just thanked him in Irish. I'm not fluent but can make my voice heard when needed.*

Jake hailed a cab. *I think we should retreat to the more familiar lands of Manhattan. How about I buy you dinner at the 21 Club? I think tonight should be a celebration.*

We climbed into the back seat, and Jake stayed close enough that I could feel his warmth. I leaned back on the seat. *So what do you think changed the good bishop's mind?*

*Well, I could flatter you and say it was your persuasive argument. I could say that the stones in the basket got his attention. But, ...*

I closed my eyes. *Here comes the legal but. How much is this going to cost the Foundation?*

*Hey, hey, not so cynical, my dear Miss Clark. I am now off the clock, so any and all of my comments should be considered compliments of my benevolent nature.*

*My apologies, kind sir. What do you think?*

Jake caught my hand, threading his fingers lightly through mine. *My non-legal opinion is that you should continue donating to whatever cause the bishop has sought funding for in the past. Do not attempt to audit until the O'Shea Houses are well established and we can look to facts rather than battle unknown fears in presenting our defense. I am not, repeat, am not, saying that there is any misappro-priation of funds. But you, my dear, with that one comment, changed the course of where we were headed. Most times, when there is a real change in someone's posi-tion, it is either money or love at the cause. If I understand correctly, your priests take a vow of celibacy. So, I am going with money.*

*That makes sense. I may have to hold my nose, but I will just put it on my future to-do list.*

Once again, Jake leaned into me. *Now that I think about it, the ability to hold one's nose should perhaps be added to the job description of an executive direc-tor. And just a final note, celibacy is not one of the vows my faith practices.*

I smiled. *So, noted. And about the candles?*

Jake took a tighter hold of my hand. *A lucky guess. We had an Italian housekeeper for years. She went to daily Mass and lit a candle for everyone she loved on their birthday. I suspected Regina would do the same.*

Jake squeezed my hand, whispering in my ear, *I meant to tell you, you look beautiful tonight.*

I squeezed it back.

I closed my eyes. This felt good. It felt good to be the object of a man's attention. Particularly a man such as Jake.

The rest of the evening was taken with good food, fine wine, and great conversation. Jake offered to share a cab home. I declined, the wine and the events of the day were making my head spin. If I was to move on, it would be because of a decision not a moment.

————

## A Beginning

Tonight, something shifted. The O'Shea House found its place and is ready to move on. Perhaps the same can be said about me.

Jake stood beside me, and it felt right. When he held my hand, it felt right.

I am not sure I can ever let John truly go. I will always love him. But he is not here. And I am not there.

I think I could move forward with Jake. And if I do, it will be a choice that I make because it is what I want, not just because it is offered.

The fairies must be taking notes.

————

I put down the pen.

————

The weather was changing, as unpredictable as the forecast for an Irish day. We were looking for our second house, and Teagan had it all under control. The O'Shea Houses were going to make a difference. I was beginning to explore the next project we would be funding.

A light rain, not enough to warrant an umbrella but enough to dampen my hair, had just ended. I looked at my watch and picked up the pace, hoping that I didn't inadvertently step off the curb into a puddle and ruin my new suede shoes. The heels were much too high, particularly at the pace I was walking, but when I saw them in the deep rose color, they screamed that they belonged in my closet. I had no choice but to buy them.

The street lamps threw down shimmering ribbons of gold on the wet pavement as I hurried to meet up with Jake.

My decision to accept Jake's offer to have dinner had me second guessing. It was clear that this was a date, and I knew he was interested in being more than the Foundation's legal adviser. I wasn't sure what I wanted, but that wasn't really true. I wanted John. I just couldn't have him. I needed to move on. And Jake is a good choice. Actually, more than a good choice, he is a great choice.

Jake was waiting for me at the bar, looking completely relaxed, his charm apparent and effortless. I paused to take a good look, his blond hair a bit too long for today's crew cut look, framed blue eyes that could twinkle or glare depending on the occasion and the right response. Jake could command a room. I had seen him do it. Yet, there was a warmth about him. I had seen that, as well. He was a man who was as interested in listening as he was speaking. That is key for me. It is what made me fall in love with John; perhaps it could happen again. Perhaps I could fall in love with Jake. I know I like him.

He stood up when he saw me. I noticed that his fingers were restless, tapping on the bar. So, this is Jake nervous. And I am the cause. I was glad that I wore the new shoes.

Jake waved me to join him at the bar. He kissed me on the cheek. *You look lovely, as always. A glass of wine before we sit for dinner.*

*Of course.*

Jake gave the bartender our order. He took my hand, his eyes never leaving my face. *Cate, I think it is important that you understand why I asked you to have dinner with me tonight. Let me be clear, it was not and is not about talking with you about the work of the Edward Walker Foundation. Tonight is about us. And yes, I want the two of us to become an us. Or at least begin the path to potentially becoming an us.*

My heart started to hammer in my chest as he continued. *You are remarkable. Intelligent, interesting, determined, a force of nature with a lilt that makes me smile with your simplest greeting. I am smitten. I have been from the moment you complained about this country's inability to make a proper cup of tea. I want more from you than just being your adviser and even a friend. It is important that you understand that before we have dinner. I think you know me well enough that I try to get to the heart of the matter as quickly as possible.*

I took a sip of the recently arrived glass, my hand held a slight tremble. *I have had my heart broken.*

Jake nodded, *I suspected as much.*

I put my glass down. *Not just by a man, but also by mankind. Hearing the stories of the Magdalene Laundries, listening to what those women, no more than girls really, went through broke something in me.*

His eyes never wavered. *And you are doing everything you can to help others, so that the horrors you heard may no longer be repeated. That others have more choices. And, I have it on dependable authority, a broken bone heals stronger than before. Perhaps the same is true of the heart.*

He took my hand. *Cate, you must decide if this is a date that could start us on the path of something more. Let us have dinner and see where this evening and the two of us end up. If you are too unsure of either me or us and we are to be the clichéd "just friends," let us just finish our drinks and say good night. It is up to you.*

I found my answer without hesitation. *I am starving. I think we should eat.*

Jake stood up, I did as well. He took me in his arms and kissed me. A kiss that made it clear we were more than just friends. When we finally pulled away, I sighed, *I am not sure I am that hungry after all.*

Jake looked confused, as I took his hand, laughing. *At least not for food.*

He signaled to the bartender we were leaving, throwing down more money than what was needed to cover our bill. *I think I may have just what you need to spark your appetite,* he grabbed my hand, and we were out the door.

We went to his apartment. I kicked off my shoes, not caring where they might land. There were no words, no pretense. He took my hand and led me to the bedroom. There was a bouquet of red roses on the nightstand. I gave him a slight jab, pointing at the flowers. *A bit sure of yourself, are ye?*

He nuzzled my neck as he slowly unzipped my dress. It fell to the floor. *I am a man who likes to think positively, and I can think of nothing but you.* I lay down on the bed. Raising my arms, I whispered, *More than just friends.* He came to me, gently caressing me, and then his movements got stronger, more powerful. I lost all sense of time and place. It was just him and me. It was us.

———

## Moving Forward

I wasn't sure I'd ever be in this place again, opening myself up, letting someone in. And yet, here I am. It is easy. It is easy with Jake.

We laugh. We talk. We are quiet. I like him. He likes me.

We are living in the present. No promises. No pressure. Just two people willing to move from being friends to being an us.

Still, I know—I know—there's a part of my heart still in Ireland. With John. The memory of him, of what we shared, sits like sea glass in my chest—smoothed over time but no less sharp when I press too hard. What we had was real. I loved him. I still love him. I've accepted that love like that doesn't just fade.

Yet today, I'm stepping forward—not away from the past, but accepting what is mine to embrace today. This feels right for the moment.

For today, that's enough.

———

I put down the pen.

# 1958

## Yeats

The bell above the door gave a soft jangle as I stepped into the bookstore. Nestled in an alley on the outskirts of Greenwich Village, it is a timeworn place smelling of old paper and polished wood. I was looking to find a first edition of *Little Women*, a gift for Peggy on the premiere of her movie. Tall shelves loomed about me as I wandered slowly among the books of cracked spines and soft covers. Soon, I found what I was looking for, the muted red cover and gold lettering dulled with age but still prominent. I was making my way towards the shopkeeper when I saw it. *The Selected Poems of W. B. Yeats*. My hand shook as I opened its cover, half-expecting to find John's handwriting in the margins.

The air around me grew still, as if the world was holding its breath, waiting for me to remember. I did.

The fairies are spinning their mischief once again. I am moving on, but still remembering.

———

I put down the pen.

———

The night was a whirlwind of lights and energy. Peggy's, or MaryKate Donovan to her adoring fans, *Little Women* was opening in New York at Radio City Music Hall. Teagan and I were her guests for the event. Faith, much to her dismay, had to be in Washington finishing a week-long special assignment and would join us after the festivities.

The grand entrance of Radio City Music Hall blazed with light, the air thick with excitement, as a herd of movie stars and wannabes exited their shining limos. They posed for photographs and looked for someone to tell them what to do next. Reporters stood near the entrance broadcasting live. I was a little giddy; I had never seen anything like this. It was a contrived fantasy.

A man in charge of orchestrating the arrivals shouted over the deafening applause welcoming each and every star. Music added to the cacophony of sound, swelling from both in and outside the theatre. Teagan and I made our way to the lobby, waiting to be shown to our seats. A man standing next to me sighed. *I have been coming to these premieres for the past 10 years; they just get bigger and showier. Rubies and diamonds on loan from the jewelers while their insurance agents scan the crowd for would-be thieves. The only fake tonight is the smile of the actors who are pretending this is fun.* I asked if he thought that was good for the movie business, to see so many stars in the Hollywood galaxy gathered under the same roof. He gave me a shrewd smile as an usher approached him. He turned and whispered in my ear, *Very good for the business, less good for the art of filmmaking. All glitter and no substance.* I learned later that he was the script writer.

Teagan and I were shown to our seats. I was wearing a soft, lemon-yellow gown that fell in graceful waves to the floor, the fabric catching the light with every step I took. Mam's delicate pearl necklace was my only jewelry. She would have approved of the reflection I saw in my mirror. Teagan was dressed in floor-length ivory silk with a high neck and low-cut back. Her hair was styled in the newest chic French twist. She bore little resemblance to the woman wanting to try the fancy ham sandwich. Until she opened her mouth. *Wouldn't you be wanting our picture took and flashed all over the Irish papers. I'd be loving the girls from the steno pool to see me now*, she said as she copied the studied pose those preceding us down the aisle had displayed. I burst out laughing.

Inside the Music Hall, the opulence was overwhelming. Velvet curtains in rich reds and golds lined the walls. However, tonight, all eyes were focused on the giant screen that loomed at the front.

We were in our seats when Peggy arrived. It was hard to remember her as the girl from the ship. This woman defined effortless elegance. Her dress hugged her figure perfectly, its light blue color the same shade of her increasingly photographed eyes. This was a woman who exuded confidence and poise, the epitome of sophistication and style. Her bold red lips broke into a huge smile when she saw us. She whispered, *I am so glad you are here* just as the lights dimmed, and the projector roared to life.

The crowd went silent and the screen came to life, filling the room with the flickering images of the opening credits. There it was. Peggy's name, or her Hollywood name "MaryKate Donovan" following the words "And Introducing ." I reached over and squeezed her hand, just as her face appeared on the screen. I felt a wave of emotion—pride, awe, and a deep sense of joy. This was our Peggy. Her movements were elegant, her voice compelling, her very smile predicting she was going to be a star. And she was my friend.

―――――

Peggy bowed out of the after-party, and the three of us retreated to her suite at the Waldorf, a perk from her studio. I smiled remembering the young girl whom I met on our cross-Atlantic journey over two years ago.

Her world had changed completely but with us she was just Peggy. And like us, all she wanted to do was ease the ache in her toes. Peggy discarded her sky-high heels before she had taken off her coat. *My feet are begging for mercy. We should find the name of the inventor of three-inch heels and have him—cause you know it was him—tarred and feathered.* Our toes, now freed from their constraints, wriggled their concurrence.

We were tired but not ready to end the night; it had been too magical to leave abruptly, and we needed a slow unwind. We were deciding whether to order a pot of tea or have another glass of wine when Reception called. Faith had arrived.

Peggy gave permission for Faith to enter. *Well, the decision is now made for us. I will order the wine.*

Faith's verve was the spark that energized the room. She took one look around and spread her arms out, embracing us in one gesture. Her words came quickly, tumbling over each other in a rush to get out before another thought set them aside. *This is a movie set that would make the Golden Age of Hollywood designers go green with envy. Look at the three of you—a blonde, a redhead, and a brunette. And all true to the color that Mother Nature bequeathed you. Stunning. We just need to add Noel Coward and maybe Cary Grant into the tableau. Sophistication unbridled. Just be sure to clip your vowels.*

Our laughter didn't slow her down, as she continued without taking a breath. *But I have big news. At least, I think it is big news. About Teddy.*

I perked up. *Teddy? I haven't heard from him in a couple of weeks, but that is common when Congress is in session. Is he okay?*

*More than okay,* Faith finding a spot on the carpet, sprawled out. *I believe he is in love!*

Now she had my full attention. *You think he is what?*

*Yup, in love. I was having a drink with Peter at Ebbits Grill. I've stayed connected with him since he helped me at the time of the McCarthy hearing. And he is ...*

I put my hand in the air like a traffic cop telling the on-coming cars to make a full stop. *Later, Faith. Teddy, tell me about Teddy.*

*Well,* a sly smile fell over her face, *he didn't see me when I came into the bar. He was in a corner booth and he was with a woman. I could see them from the corner of my eye, so I took a long look. She was not what I would expect, though I never really thought of Teddy with anyone. Her hair was the color of sun-bleached wheat, and there was a wildness to it, as if it didn't like being controlled by today's pins and rollers. Her skin had a warm glow, which looked like it came from the sun rather than a bottle. Teddy's eyes were fixed on her, a slight smile tugging at the corners of his lips. It was then time for my entrance, I sauntered over to where they were seated and sweetly called his name. You would have loved to see his face, surprise, uncertainty and ...* Faith paused for effect ... *he was blushing.*

*Teddy, blushing. Are you sure it wasn't the lights in the restaurant?* I didn't know whether to laugh or cry. He had been in New York about six weeks ago and hadn't said a word to me about having anyone in his life.

Faith continued her tale. *He stumbled his way up from the booth to give me a quick kiss on the cheek. Then the Teddy we know took over. He introduced me to her. Her name is Mary Sienna Denton but goes by Sienna.*

*It was the mystery woman who spoke with a voice strong and clear, with no accent that would give away where she first called home. She knew that I was meeting Peter.*

*Now it was my turn to lose my footing, I wanted to know how she knew Peter. She told me she works with him; she is a lawyer in his practice. She went on to say that she had heard about me from both him and Ted.*

*Well, I couldn't help it, I rolled my eyes as Teddy gave me a poke on the shoulders. "Yes, Faith, to those over 25, I am called Ted."*

*I tossed my hair,* Faith mimicked the gesture. *I wasn't going to let him get away with that, so I countered, "and you should count better. I am over 25, and you will always be Teddy."*

*Sienna laughed out loud and offered to make room for me to join them. At that point, Peter arrived, who didn't seem the least bit surprised seeing them together.*

*I took Peter's arm and shook my head no at the offer to sit. I said that Peter and I were going to have a quick drink and then he was going to drive me to the airport. I bragged a bit about it being the opening of Peggy's film and that I wanted to be there to help her celebrate.*

*Sienna looked at me quizzically. I gave my best attempt with a woman-of-the world smile, "Oh, her stage name is MaryKate Donovan. She is practically family."*

*Ted picked up his coat and helped Sienna on with hers. Sienna said she had read about the excitement MaryKate was making in the movie world, and she couldn't wait to see the picture. Teddy gave me a hug.* Faith raised her glass in my direction, *told me to tell you he would call you tomorrow. Sienna smiled and off they went, arm-in-arm.*

*They hadn't even walked through the door when I began to badger Peter about her, about them. Peter is many things, but a gossip is not one of them. It was like pulling teeth to get any information.*

*So here is all I know. Sienna is from Colorado, comes from a family of ranchers who settled in the state when it was a territory. She came to Washington for law school, graduating at the top of her Georgetown class, and stayed on to work there.*

*Peter thinks she is one of the smartest, savviest lawyers he knows. I asked if he was comparing her to male lawyers or female lawyers. He got a bit terse with me and told me when he said lawyers, he means all lawyers.*

*That's all I got but I think our Teddy is smitten.*

Then the clock chimed midnight, and it was time for all us Cinderellas to find our slippers and go home. It was a night to remember. In so many ways.

———

## A New Chapter

I didn't know whether to be happy or sad. I had never thought of Teddy being with someone, having another family.

I want him to be happy. I just don't know how good I am at sharing.

———

I put down the pen.

———

The phone rang the next morning at 8:00 a.m. I knew who was going to be on the other end of the line. I picked up the receiver, and said *Teddy? Or am I now to call you Ted? Or Edward?*

He laughed. *Well, that answers my first question. You have clearly talked to Faith.*

*Yes, indeed.*

*Okay, this is all relatively new to me, but you and my mother need to meet Sienna. She is something else: smart, funny, driven, adventurous...a bit like all the women in my life.*

*So, when are we to meet?*

*Mother and O'Brien are back in New York later this week. I thought Sienna and I would drive up on Friday and spend the weekend. We will need to leave early Sunday after Mass.*

*That would be lovely. Should we be making up one room or two?*

Teddy almost stammered the response, *One will do.*

*I am looking forward to meeting her and seeing you. I love you, Teddy.*

*And I, you, Cate.*

————

When I hung up the phone, I knew this was serious. After all these years, I may be getting a sister.

————

The weekend went without a hitch. Sienna is the perfect complement to Teddy; it was evident the moment she entered the door. Tall, with an unspoken air of confidence, you can see her sitting comfortably on a horse, her golden hair blowing or arguing before the justices of the Supreme Court. This is a woman who can drive cattle across the range or take on a United States congressman. Both require skill and the ability to know how and when to rope the stray.

Dinner the first night was at home. The house smelled of baked salmon, rosemary and thyme. Nell was gracious and warm, yet her eyes were watchful. If this was the woman Teddy was choosing, she wanted to see for herself why she was so special. I felt the same way.

Sienna was relaxed; Teddy was the nervous one. Totally out of character, he began answering the questions addressed to Sienna—where had she grown up, what brought her to Washington, how did she find New York? Less than ten minutes into that discourse, Sienna leaned forward slightly, softly shaking her head but with tenderness in eyes that was unmistakable when she looked at him. and touched Teddy's hand. *I can answer for myself, Ted. I'm actually pretty good at it.* Her voice carried a smile that found its way to her lips. Teddy looked sheepish. Nell relaxed, her doubts resolved. Mine, too.

The conversation turned to life in Washington and the speculation that John Kennedy from Massachusetts, who had just won re-election to the U.S. Senate by landslide, was going to run for president. Teddy was enthusiastic, saying Kennedy was a beacon of hope, someone who could lift the darkness of the McCarthy era that still clouded the nation. Sienna was not as convinced. She agreed he was charismatic but felt he was inexperienced, with an East Coast-Harvard perspective that didn't represent the issues facing the majority of Americans. She winked at Teddy as she made her point. *There are those, however, who have that same pedigree whom I do love and admire.* Teddy bent over her and kissed on the cheek. *Good to know, my darling.*

The conversation was lively. We discussed politics, the work of the Foundation, Peggy's success on screen, and the whirlwind called Faith.

By the end of the weekend, Sienna had become part of the family. She listens. She cares about what she does. She cares about what other people do.

---

## A Sister

Teddy is in love. I can see why. And Sienna loves him. That is enough for me.

Nell gave Teddy the engagement ring his father had given her. He plans to propose to Sienna soon.

I am happy for him and more than a little envious.

---

I put down the pen.

---

A week later, I came home to find the rarest of all gifts. A letter from Joseph. I didn't even take off my coat before I tore open the envelope and started to read.

*My Dearest Sister,*

*I hope this letter finds you in good health. It has been too long since last I wrote, but you know better than most I am more comfortable with numbers than with words.*

*I write to tell you that I have seen Liam. Father Flanagan told me that Liam has been living on his own for the past three months and he is stronger, more at peace with himself. He said* that Liam thinks about us and wants to ask our forgiveness but doesn't think he deserves it.

It was Saturday last when I met him. I didn't write to let him know I was coming. If he didn't want to see me, to talk, I would just turn around and come home. And I would go again.

Liam is living on a small piece of land in the countryside, near the abbey where he had been staying. It is a secluded spot. The quiet there is thick, interrupted only by the rustle of wild grass in the wind.

He didn't hear me arrive and responded to my knock by opening the door but a crack. He looked more like our da than I remembered; his stature seemed broader, his eyes clearer.

I said his name. He responded with mine and opened the door wider. He made way for me to enter.

It was a fine day, so I said that it would be grand if we could just sit outside and enjoy the sun. He has a small bench, and there we sat. Mostly in silence.

I told him that you were in New York and we had a family renting the house. Liam asked if you were staying in the States or were looking to come back home to Ireland. I told him that I had given up predicting your behavior since you turned twelve. Liam laughed. It was good to hear that sound. He asked if I wanted tea, I said not that day, the next time perhaps.

I stood to leave, extending my hand to him. He didn't flinch or pull away. I told him that we are still his family. He took my hand in his.

We didn't say goodbye. There was no need for formalities or speeches. I simply got back in the car and pulled away. The past is the past, Cate. We cannot forget it, but we can move on. It is *what it means to be family. The door has been opened and shan't close again.*

*Mam would expect no less.*

*God bless you, Cate.*

*Joseph*

———

## Forgiveness

I thought about how, like Joseph, calculating the odds of success, having a strategy if the race wasn't won on the first meet.

I held the letter closer. I feel a sense of relief and a flicker of hope. Shaking each other's hands, after so many years, a simple gesture that speaks more than words.

I started to cry. Only Joseph could do this.

———

I put down the pen.

———

Jake was looking to take us to the next step, and I didn't resist. Perhaps it was seeing Teddy so happy. Perhaps it is recognizing that John is my past, Jake is my present, and potentially my future. It was time for me to meet his family. It was time to be introduced to his world. He was already a part of mine. We had become a couple. We were an us. It was comfortable. I was happy.

Fall had arrived, the air was cooler, the days shorter. Jake was taking me to join his family and their friends for the celebration of the Jewish New Year, Rosh Hashanah. This was a tradition.

Jake had not prepared me for the scene. The entry to his parents' house could rival the most sophisticated artist's gallery. The floors were marble, the chandelier a masterpiece of brass and crystal. A striking abstract painting dominated one wall, vibrant colors swirling in chaotic harmony. Smaller, framed works scattered across the other available spaces ranged from stunning to disturbing, all in sync with each other yet unique in their own way. It was quite extraordinary.

Jake, sensing my astonishment, raised his hands, circling the room. *I might have forgotten to tell you. My mother is an avid art collector with an eye for talent that even the most ardent gallery owner envies. She has a degree in art history from Smith and was pursuing a doctorate when she met my father.*

I raised my eyebrows. *Yes, a small point in the months we have been together that you have failed to mention.* I already felt like I didn't belong, and I had not yet taken off my coat. Jake reached into his pocket and placed a Yarmulke on his head. It was the first time I had seen him wear one. I knew he was Jewish. He knew I was Catholic.

I had no idea what to expect, and my first few seconds had confirmed that I was about to enter into a new world. Jake, sensing my wariness, took my hand in his, whispering, *You are lovely; you will capture everyone here with your grace and your style.*

I looked at him and winked. *Did you happen to tell them that I have an accent?*

He chuckled, *Don't worry, most of them gave up their Irish maids a generation ago. They won't ask you to bring coffee.*

I squeezed his hand. *And should that happen, I'll reply in Irish, and you should be hoping no one can translate.*

We entered the room laughing.

If the entry to the house intimidated me, the rooms we entered added to my discomfort. They had all the markings of Faith's award-winning sets. The sun in the final hour of its day cast the room in a golden hue. The air was infused with the sweet scent of honey and the warm spices of what I learned was a brisket simmering in the kitchen. The atmosphere in the room was not stilted but filled with muffled laughter and seemingly spirited conversation.

This was a different crowd than I was used to seeing. I couldn't describe it, but somehow it seemed scholarly. These could be the college professors Jake talked about who were his cousins, or the banking executive who just endowed a chair at Harvard's business school. Or the recent Pulitzer Prize nominee, his mother's best friend and college roommate, whom he called Aunt Goldie, though they shared no bloodline.

I took a deep breath as Jake walked me over to the couple who were clearly in command of it all. He wore a perfectly cut tuxedo, his fading blonde hair streaked with white, with just the appropriate amount of gel to keep it in place without looking as if he were trying too hard. I smiled to myself. This is what Jake would look like in thirty years. The woman next to him was stunning in an emerald green dress, the neckline cut to highlight a diamond necklace that glistened with her every breath. Jake gave the man a firm handshake and, not surprisingly, said but one word, *Father*. The woman called out *Jacob, my darling son*, her arms embracing him fervently and possessively. He pulled himself away and brought me forward, his mother coldly smiling while her eyes were assessing. I remember thinking this must be what one of those pieces of artwork feels like when this woman eyes it for the first time. To say I was scrutinized from head to toe would be an understatement. I said a quick thank you to Nell for lending me her aquamarine earrings that would be admired for both their cut and their size. I also knew they made my eyes sparkle.

I got the appropriate *Lovely to meet you, Cate. I am pleased you could join us for our Rosh Hashanah celebration. It is a family tradition that we bring together all the people who made last year full of memories and to whom we wish the greatest of blessings in the New Year ahead.*

I started to respond when Jake said, *I want Cate to meet Uncle Alan. She leads a foundation, and I believe they have a lot in common.*

It was his father who spoke. *Indeed. Alan was instrumental in setting up one of the foundations to garner support for the Israel state. David Ben-Gurion has singled him out as a true force in helping to create the path for our people to return to their rightful homeland.*

Jake's mother interrupted any further discussion. *Please excuse us, Cate. It is time for the hadlakat nerot.* Once again, I got the look as she continued. *I must light the candles. Jacob, please take my arm.* Jake did as he was told, accompanied by his father. I was left standing alone.

Jacob's mother was brought to a table where two unlit candles in gold candle holders were the only centerpiece. The guests gathered around, quietly, solemnly. With Jake and her husband at her side, she lit the candles and spread her hands in a circular motion, drawing them inwards toward her each time. My first impression was right, this setting was theatrical, and Mrs. Bresky was the star. She was mesmerizing. She covered her eyes and recited a blessing in Hebrew that Jake later translated. *Praised are you, Adonai, our God, Sovereign of the universe, who, sanctifying us with divine commandments, has commanded us to kindle the festival lamp.* She looked up to the crowd, *La China Tova*, and this Happy New Year wish was spoken to all, along with a kiss on the cheek.

Jake found his way to me, told me that his wish for the year involved me, and kissed me on the cheek. He took me by the hand and led me into the crowd that had gathered. I could feel his mother's eyes on my back.

The rest of the evening was a blend of traditional rituals, good food, and better conversation. Uncle Alan lived up to his billing as a font of knowledge on the perils of foundation leadership. He was on his way to Israel but promised to be in touch once he returned. "Aunt" Goldie was a force; I loved meeting her. A Smith College graduate, she raved about the work that one of the younger alumnae, Betty Friedan, was doing. She met Friedan at a college reunion where Goldie was being honored. Friedan was questioning why her fellow graduates, the independent, career-minded women of the 1920s and '30s, were now content to be the "Father Knows Best" poster girls of the postwar era. Goldie shared that Friedan had begun to survey these women and planned to author an article about her findings. She predicted it would shake the rafters. In the not-too-distant future, women will want more, demand more.

She looked at me, her eyes crinkling with humor. *Do you get asked why a nice girl like you isn't married? Have you ever been asked why you are not an executive in a major company? Or considering being elected to a political office?*

I chuckled. *Yes to the first and no to the second set of questions.*

Goldie gave a knowing smile. *Mark my words, women are soon to become rebels with a cause. And then watch out, a new world is dawning. I plan to be cheering it on. I hope that the same can be said for your generation of young women. Perhaps you could look at how that foundation you run could help. Jacob's uncle would never lift a finger or give a dime to such a cause.*

I nodded. *I think we might just be able to do that.*

*Good. La China Tova!* And she was gone.

Jake was soon by my side, taking me by the arm. *She is a powerhouse, isn't she? To think that she and my mother were college roommates seems unfathomable.*

I nodded. *Perhaps like Robert Frost, she took the road less traveled, and that is what made all the difference.*

---

## Life As It Might Be

Tonight was unsettling. Meeting Jake's parents, seeing the world he lives in, or at least is comfortably living in, has my mind twirling. The apartment where he grew up is beautiful. No, not the right word. It is impressive. It is a world where things are curated, intentional, and thought-provoking. I have never known such a world.

Jake's mother was gracious, but there is a chill under the silk. His father seemed accepting. The guests were welcoming. Yet, I was very aware of being an outsider. Jake was different there. Not in a bad way. It was just a version of him I hadn't met. Polished. At ease. That may not be fair. It could be that he just appeared to fit the space and knew all the hidden rules. And I didn't.

It doesn't make me love him less. If anything, I admire the way he moves through all of this without losing himself. But the question I can't answer is, could I ever belong? Even if given the choice.

We're still us. That hasn't changed. But tonight made me realize that "us" doesn't always fit neatly into the other worlds we orbit.

———

I put down the pen.

———

I was not surprised when a week later I received a handwritten invitation to join Jake's mother for lunch with instructions to reply only if the date and time were not convenient. I made sure I could attend.

I arrived at the appointed place on time and understood immediately why Jake's mother chose this restaurant. Like her, it spoke of understated sophistication, every detail a quiet testament to cultivated taste and exclusivity. Delicate cream-colored porcelain sat on tables dressed in crisp white linen; a single long-stemmed red rose provided the only break in color. The hum of classical music kept voices low. It was a place designed for privacy, not spectacle.

The afternoon sun streamed through the windows, adding to the only warmth I felt as the maître d' brought me to the table, where Mrs. Bresky was already seated, her napkin folded neatly in her lap. She looked as if she were posing for a formal portrait, her smile forced, her gaze firm and unwavering.

*Thank you for coming, Cate, particularly on such short notice.*

I nodded as I took my seat. *Your note said that it was important.*

*And so, it is.* She gestured to the table. *I hope you don't mind, but I took the liberty of ordering for both of us. The kitchen is known for its Dover sole, and the sommelier recommended a lovely Chardonnay to accompany the dish.* She managed a frozen smile. *I did not want to use our time together deciding what we should eat or drink.*

If this were to be a game, I would at least be a worthy opponent. I rose to the bait. *The sole will be lovely. I assume that it will be deboned?*

For a moment, the frozen smile thawed a bit. *Ah, the quick wit that Jacob speaks of. Not to worry, there will be no bones requiring us to lose our concentration or be distracted from our conversation.*

Before I could reply, our lunch appeared and the wine was poured; both lived up to Mrs. Bresky's recommendation. Our initial conversation was a polite veneer, a choreography of words and gestures. Mrs. Bresky shook her head no to the waiter's request for another glass of wine. I decided to do the same. So far, this was not the discussion I had been summoned to hear. My head needed to be clear for what I expected would be coming next. And then it began.

Mrs. Bresky cleared her throat; her voice was even. *Cate, you are a smart woman. You know that I did not ask you to join me today to review the chef's culinary skills. I want to speak candidly about your relationship with my son. Let me be clear. Our family's faith, our Judaism, is the cornerstone of our lives. It shapes who we are, and who the next generation must be.* Her eyes never left my face.

*And I am a Catholic. A Roman Catholic.*

She shook her head, *No, my dear, it is more than that. You are not Jewish. If you and Jacob were to have children, they would not be Jewish. In our faith, our Jewish identity is determined through the mother's lineage. This is called matrilineal descent and is based on the historical understanding that a mother's identity is more certain than the father's. It is also the mother who is given the primary responsibility for raising and transmitting Jewish traditions to the children.*

I started to speak, but Jake's mother shook her head quietly. *There is more. Hitler tried to obliterate us, and few tried to stop him from succeeding. My father's only brother was a well-respected banker in Berlin and refused to leave. He believed in Germany that reason would prevail and life as he knew it would return. He, his wife, and their children were taken to the camps. All but one died in Auschwitz. My one surviving cousin and his family have moved to Israel. We are blessed that he survived the terror.* Her voice got quiet, *though I can't imagine what his nightmares must be like.*

My hand started to slightly shake. *I am so sorry. Jake, I mean Jacob, never told me.*

*It is not something we speak of,* she said, her voice regaining its edge.

She continued. *The discrimination my son has faced is much more subtle: not being allowed membership in certain clubs, having important meetings scheduled on the highest of our holy days, recognizing that there are quotas for how many Jews will be admitted to the Ivy League schools. There are those, my dear, who believe that we got what we deserved because the Jews killed Jesus.* A small smile returned to her face, *though if you check your history books, I believe it was the Romans.*

I returned the smile, *or the government.*

Another fast smile as she continued, her tone measured and calm. *My son and my husband do not know that I am speaking with you today. I do not intend to tell them. I will leave it to you whether you share the conversation with Jacob. I respect you, Cate. My dear friend Goldie thinks you are a remarkable young woman. But I want you to know that should you marry Jacob, we will not dance at your wedding. Should you have children, they would not be recognized as our grandchildren. That would be a heavy burden for my husband and me to carry, but we must be true to our convictions and the life we lead.*

The room fell silent for a moment, the air thick with unspoken emotions.

I was the first to speak. *I have no response but to thank you for being honest with me.*

Mrs. Bresky's eyes held a flicker of sympathy. *You've been a lovely presence in Jacob's life. He cares for you deeply. Whatever you decide to do, I hope you find happiness.*

She offered a small nod of farewell.

I stood up and slowly stepped into the bright afternoon, the sunlight sharp against the weight pressing down on me.

---

## Is There a Way Forward?

I replay the conversation with Jake's mother over and over again. I try to breathe. I love Jake. I love his kindness, his compassion, his mind. I love the time we spend together.

But do I love him enough for him to have to give up his family, all he has known? Could I do the same? What would that life be like?

Jake hasn't asked me to marry him. His mother must believe he is going to do so. I don't know my answer to that question should he ask.

Is love enough?

I don't know what I am going to do.

———

I put down the pen.

———

The late afternoon sun filtered through the curtains, washing the library in its tired, fading light. I curled into my usual spot, shivering. The days were getting shorter, and soon the winter winds and biting cold would be at the door.

Nell sensed something was wrong as soon as she found me in the library. *What's wrong, Cate? You look troubled. Is Joseph okay?*

*No, no, Joseph is fine.* My voice was thinner than I intended.

*I assume it is your heart that has you looking so sad. Jake?*

*Yes, oh, I am all upside down. I am trying to sort out how I feel, what makes sense. Only the more I think about it, the less sense it makes, and my feelings just get more jumbled.* I raised my hands in surrender. *I met Jake's mother for lunch yesterday. Her invitation.*

Nell's face softened. *It appears it didn't go well.*

*Well, she was quite elegant in her delivery, but her message was clear: if Jake and I were to marry ... a topic by the way we have never discussed ... his parents would disown him and not recognize our children. Should we have children, another topic we have never discussed.*

Nell's eyebrows rose. *Goodness, she said all of that to you over one lunch. Is it because you are Catholic?*

*Yes and no. It is because I am not Jewish.*

Nell nodded thoughtfully. *And the children would not be seen as Jewish. My friend Rachel is Jewish. I know a bit about their faith. I went to her house for a*

*Passover and was deeply moved by their reverence for the rituals they hand down from generation to generation. From the lighting of the candles to the sharing of the meal, everything had meaning and significance.*

I nodded, shifting in my chair. *That is what Mrs. Bresky said. And the role of passing down those traditions is the role of the mother. A Jewish mother.*

Nell sighed. *And you can be many things, my dear girl, but you cannot become something you have never been.* She cocked her head. *Do you love Jake? Do you see yourself spending your life with him?*

*I do love him. I love his wit, his kindness. I love how he makes me laugh. How he believes in the good of people.* I hesitated. *But not like I love John. Or loved John.*

*Whoa, Cate. Who is John? You have never spoken his name before.*

*Because it still hurts. I met him when I was in Dublin. I never felt about anyone the way I felt about him. But there was too much going on in my life that I needed to sort out.*

Nell stood up and fed a log to the fire. The flames crackled to life, casting long shadows across the room. *I am trying to understand. Your mother was dying, and you needed time to grieve, to figure out what you were going to do next. That just required time.*

*Well, it is more complicated than that. John is a widower with a six-year-old daughter. His concern was for her. The risk of bringing someone into her life, particularly someone who didn't know where she wanted to be, was too great.*

Nell poked the log, staring into the blaze that now lit up the room. *I understand that as well. After my husband died, O'Brien came into my life. I loved him, and I was pretty sure he loved me. But he belonged to the road, to his camera, to telling his stories. He couldn't stay in one place, and that included being by my side. Teddy was young, a bit older than your John's daughter, but not old enough to have someone come in and out of his life. The life he and I had built together after his father had died. I walked away from the relationship. I had to protect Teddy. I made that decision then, and it would be the same decision I would make today. It wasn't until O'Brien could stay put that we came back together and started to live the life we now enjoy.*

Nell sighed. *So, my first question is, do you love Jake?*

*Yes, I love him.*

Nell sat back in her chair. *Do you love him enough to give up your dream of John?*

*It is hard to give up on a dream, Nell.*

*Yes, my love, I know that feeling well. But for the moment, let us be pragmatic. Does Jake know that his mother spoke to you?*

I shook my head. *She said she hadn't told either him or his father. It was my decision to make.*

*Well, perhaps that is the first decision you make. Should the answer be yes?*

I interrupted, *I know that answer. It is yes, that answer is yes. We have always been honest with each other. Jake is going to know something is different. He is away at a meeting now, but comes home tomorrow. I have not returned his calls. He will know something is up. I owe him the truth.*

Nell nodded. *So, you may want to think about choices. I can think of three. There may be more, but let's start with three. Stay together, knowing this cloud will always linger. Move forward, think about marriage and having a family, but recognizing your faith also puts restrictions on marrying someone who isn't Catholic. Jake would have to agree to raise his children Catholic. They would be baptized, receive communion, and pray to a savior that he has not recognized as the Messiah. Could he do that? And give up his family? And all that he has known? Or, three, and perhaps the hardest one of all, you may want to walk away, cherishing what you've had and understanding that any future together would be too difficult for you both.*

I sighed, *You are so wise, Nell. I am still not sure.*

*My darling Cate, I have just lived. So, listen to your heart and your head. And know I am here for you. I am always here for you.*

---

**Later, Alone**

This is so hard. I am still torn.

I don't know if I will ever truly give up the dream—the dream of John.

But Jake is here. And he is good. I like him. I like myself when I am with him. I like us. Still, what would a future look like? How could we navigate the differences in our faith and our families? Would I ever feel like I belong? Would Jake?

Mam had married Billy Conlon, a man who didn't share her faith. She said she believed their love could bridge the gap. Yet Mam knew, when she found out she was having their child, his family wouldn't accept her. Because she was Catholic.

Perhaps things haven't changed that much at all.

I have no answers, only an ache competing for space where a dream used to be.

———

I put down the pen.

———

The next morning, Jake appeared unannounced at the office. My face must have registered my dismay because he didn't say hello or try to kiss me. His first words were pointed and direct, *You are avoiding me.*

I nodded. *We need to talk.*

*Okay, but not here. Grab your coat, and we will go for a cuppa.*

I smiled at this attempt to calm the waters with a touch of the Irish.

The café was quiet, the air thick with unspoken words. I made my fingers trace the rim of my mug to stop their trembling. Jake's eyes were fixed on the table.

He let out a sigh. *My mother spoke to you, didn't she?*

*We had lunch last week.*

*I knew it. I saw her last week, and she never mentioned meeting you at Rosh Hashanah. I knew she would do something like this.*

*Jake, she is right.*

*No, she wants to run my life; she always has. I am not one of her paintings that she can reframe or donate to a museum, depending on what suits her at the moment.*

*No, Jake, that is not it. It's more than that.* My voice faltered as I said the words that I had been rehearsing all night. *I can't ask you to choose between me and your family. I care about you too much to want that for you.*

Jake's jaw tightened. *But why? We are good together. I love you. I want to be with you. I thought you were beginning to feel the same way about me.*

*Your mother was not unkind, but she was clear. If we were to marry, your parents would disown you. They will never see you again. They wouldn't accept our children. This would drive us apart. You know I'm right.*

Jake reached his hand across the table, looking for mine. I pulled it away, leaving a gap between us.

*I wish it were different.* My voice was breaking. *But I can't be the woman they want for you. The woman who takes her rightful place in the family. A woman who understands why certain things are important and keeps the traditions alive. You are wonderful. You deserve that woman. I am not her. And you shouldn't have to choose.*

*Is that what you told my mother?*

*No. I only thanked her for being honest with me.*

*I want to be with you, Cate, no matter what. I want us to have a life together.*

*But what would that life look like, Jake? It is not only your family and your faith. Should I have children, I would want to baptize them Catholic. That is what I know. That is how I was raised. What would such a life look like?*

The words hung in the air like an unspoken verdict. Seeing the pain in Jake's face, the lump in my throat became bigger. It was as if I had slapped him. Hard.

Jake's voice was low. *I don't know if there is a way that we can make this work. I don't like any of the choices.*

*I am not sure we have many choices, Jake. If we did, this conversation would sound different. We both know that. I love you, Jake, but the cost of this love is too great. Too great a price for either one of us to pay. It is better for us to stop being an us. I can think of no other way.*

My hand stopped trembling. I had made my decision, and it wasn't about giving up a dream. It was about recognizing reality.

Jake didn't respond. He nodded his head slowly.

The silence that followed was suffocating, as if the world outside had ceased to exist.

Jake was the first to stand. He ran his hand through his hair. *I will find you another lawyer. I can't work close to you without wanting you. Goodbye, Cate. I will miss you. I will miss us.*

He turned and left the café. I couldn't move.

———

## May the Fairies be Kind

I wonder if the fairies grieved for me the moment Jake got up and left.

Folklore has it that the fairies guide our steps, nudging us toward the path we should be following. But what happens when the world we live in makes that path too hard to walk? In the eyes of our families, Jake and I would be a house divided. Jewish and Catholic.

A faith I could never leave, and one that he could never forsake. That endless strain would have worn us down, piece by painful piece.

Yet, I feel empty. I go to the office thinking Jake should call or just show up, while knowing he will not.

Both my head and my heart tell me this is for the best. A future together is not for us; there would be too many obstacles to overcome.

I love him enough to walk away. I close my eyes and hope that fairies will be kind and walk beside him—even if I no longer can.

———

I put down the pen.

———

Joseph came for Christmas. It was December 23rd, and I was at the airport to greet him, a bit nervous about showing him this city and my life here. I wanted him to see it through my lens, knowing full well he would make up his own mind.

My eyes were darting at the sea of arrivals when I saw him. He was grinning, a rare treat given his quiet ways. I ran, throwing my arms around him. *You are here, you are here. This is the best gift anyone has ever given me. Come, we will get you into your hotel, and then you are to come to Nell's house for dinner. She and O'Brien are there waiting for you. And then tomorrow ...*

Joseph put his hand up. *Slow down, Cate, remember I just got off an airplane and am not even sure what time of day it is. So, first step back and let me take a look at ya.*

I did as I was told, saying a silent thank you that I had opted to wear my new green coat. While not as warm as my trusty tweed, I felt like a princess when I wore it. One that hadn't kissed the frog but ate it.

*You are lovely, little sister. Only, not really so little anymore.*

I could only smile. *Come, let me find us a cab. And brace yourself for the freezing wind; it can bring tears to the eyes of even the heartiest among us.*

*I'm prepared. I brought a scarf.*

*You'll be needing more than that, but let's get your holiday started.*

The taxi weaved through the traffic. Joseph stared out the window. I followed his gaze, seeing the sprawling mass of the city through his eyes—the towering buildings, the flashing lights, the sounds, the constant movement. We came to a standstill. This was New York traffic.

Joseph looked over at me. *Does this happen often? We move and then just stop.*

I shrugged. *Too many cars, all thinking that they belong on the road. It becomes an endless game of stop-and-go.*

Joseph grinned. *Same as in Ireland. Only it's the sheep. The horns don't matter; the sheep saunter, oblivious to raising voices and arms waving them forward. Best to sit back and wait. Sooner or later, we will get to where we need to be.*

Smiling, I leaned over and gave him a quick kiss on the cheek. *Oh, I have missed you. I am so happy you are here.*

*'Tis lovely to be with you, as well. And this city of yours seems to be more than I even imagined. And I imagined it to be big, noisy, and crowded. So, I am not disappointed, just a tad overwhelmed.*

Joseph opted to stay at a hotel, turning down Nell's offer of staying with us. I thought that made sense, and I was right. Joseph would need a respite from the constant comings and goings that the holidays brought. A place where he could step back from it all, even for just a few hours.

I had gotten him a room at the Gramercy Park Hotel, a short walk to Nell's. Earlier that week, when I told Nell of my choice, she suppressed a giggle. *Well, if you want to give Joseph a taste of New York, it is the spot. It is opulent and eclectic, a hangout for socialites and artists with a picture of Babe Ruth over the bar. A bit of something for everyone.*

*Well, it will be the thought that counts. And it is convenient.* My giggle now matched hers.

Joseph, now all checked in and freshened up, looked both pleased and amused by his accommodations. When I asked what he thought, he simply replied that it was grand.

The next five days were non-stop. Joseph was to see first-hand the magic of New York at Christmas. The city rose to the occasion, sprinkling its charm, from the towering tree at Rockefeller Center, glowing like a beacon with its pastel-colored lights, to the whimsical window displays at the Fifth Avenue stores. People hurried past us, bundled up in thick coats and wool hats, rushing between the glowing lights of Times Square to the quiet serenity of a snow-covered Central Park. The air smelled like Christmas—roasting chestnuts mingled with the sharp scent of pine trees waiting for a buyer—all carried by a burst of frosty winter wind. Joseph said it was like being in a postcard.

Nell and O'Brien continued to open up their hearts to him. Teddy, Sienna, and Faith came for Christmas Eve dinner, and we all went to Mass the following morning. Teddy and Sienna announced at breakfast that they plan to marry in February in a small town on the Chesapeake Bay. It is to be a small wedding, her parents and the family gathered at this table. This is family. I felt blessed. I felt loved. I thanked Mam for having given me this.

It was Joseph's last night, and just the two of us were out to dinner. He seemed quiet, even for him. I didn't know if it was because he was leaving.

I decided just to ask. *Joseph, I know you well enough that the furrowed brow means something is on your mind. Can you be lettin' me know what's got you troubled?*

Joseph shifted uneasily. *I'm at a bit of a loss. And I have tried to figure out what to do, but I just can't seem to come up with the answer.*

*And what, pray tell, has you in such a muddle?*

*I think it will surprise you to hear, it is Bridget Dolley. I love her.*

I lifted my glass. *I am not surprised at all. What I am surprised about is that it has taken you this long to admit it. Does she know how you feel, or are you being yourself and not saying a word?*

Joseph sighed, his shoulders dropping as if the weight of his thoughts was becoming unbearable. *I come back to the house each week to check on things, and we talk. Sometimes about the garden, sometimes about her work at the hospital, sometimes about almost nothing at all. I believe she looks forward to our conversations and to seeing me. But to answer your question, I have not told her how I feel, for she is so much younger. I have her by 17 years. And she seems to step back when I talk about my life at the university. Her life before Dublin was a very different world from ours.*

I reached for his hand. I know how difficult it is for him when he is dealing with factors that can't be calculated or codes that can't be deciphered.

*Joseph, you're not too old for her; she is about my age and not a little girl. She's a woman who can make her own choices. It is about time you throw caution to the wind and tell Bridget how you feel.*

Joseph shook his head, looking away. *But what if I'm just ... complicating her life? She's been so kind, so generous, and—*he laughed bitterly, almost to himself. *I don't want to ruin our friendship by telling her how I feel. I don't want to lose what I have.*

I raised my hand. *That is foolish talk. You are not complicating her life by loving her. And you have loved her from the moment she came to visit you when you were in the hospital. You need to let her know. Bridget may feel insecure being loved by someone like you, but you can work through that. You just need to show her how much you care for her. You need to show her, not just tell her, that she is all you want. And you want more than being her friend.*

I thought about Jake. *Tell her you want to be an "us."*

*That all adds up, little sister. You have inherited Mam's wisdom. I think she would be telling me the same thing. To stop holding back. To let Bridget know how I feel. To be courageous.*

I raised my glass as if in a toast, a gesture that has become a regular ritual. *You'll never know what could be if you don't take the chance. And here's to being happy. A happiness you both deserve.*

Joseph clicked my glass, a small but genuine smile tugging at the corners of his mouth. *And I do like the odds of that happening.*

———

## My Brother in Love

The winds of February are upon us. The days remain too dark and too short, but a bright spark came in the mail today. It was a card from Joseph. He wrote to tell me he and Bridget are "courting." Only Joseph would use such a term. She is lucky to be loved by someone as wonderful as he.

Next weekend, Teddy is getting married. I am to be the maid of honor.

February may indeed be the month when love is in the air. Air that does not appear to be mine to breathe.

I hear nothing from Jake.

———

I put down the pen.

———

The third of the O'Shea Houses was near ready. This one had only taken six months to complete and was our first in Manhattan, in an area rightfully called Hell's Kitchen. This was not a typical house remodel. Here, we had taken over a tenement in a neighborhood that was both hardened and crowded. It is a place where streets throb with life–kids play stickball, men in chalk stripe suits make deals in the shadows. A place where dreams of a better life are common but seldom come true. Getting support from the local neighbors was not a concern here. Here, providing a way to a new life was the challenge.

I walked into the building and found Teagan looking every bit in charge in her new role as director of operations. She had forsaken her standard three-inch heels for work boots. Her hair pulled back in a ponytail, her blue cotton shirt tucked into pleated khaki pants, she looked like Katherine Hepburn gone Irish. I couldn't help but smile.

She was standing tall in the midst of scaffolding and plastic sheeting. In the corner, piles of debris–broken floorboards, rusted pipes, bits of plaster–lay in chaotic heaps. The men with their power tools and hammers were paying no attention to her as she walked around. I thought to myself. "Big mistake, boys. Big mistake."

Teagan's voice, firm and loud, cut through the thick air now filled with a showering of fine dust and grit. *That is not the molding I wanted over the doors.*

One of them glanced up from his power saw for just a second, his brow furrowing, as if what she said didn't matter; it wasn't worth his time to respond. He went back to work, giving nothing more than a casual shrug to her request. His comrades followed his direction.

I leaned against the only spot in the wall I didn't think would collapse. This was going to be worth watching. All the while, the mantra continued: "Big mistake, boys. Big mistake."

Teagan went over to the one with the power saw, the one who didn't have time for her. She planted her feet firmly, pulling the saw's cord out of the plug. It stopped. Now she had his attention. The other men stopped working. Her next words were clear: *Can you hear me now?*

The man looked puzzled.

*You didn't seem to hear me when I first spoke to you. So, can you hear me now?*

*Yeah, I guess. What is your problem, little lady?*

Teagan tossed her head. *Well, this lady, my little man, has a problem. It is you. And you are fired. Pack your stuff up and leave.* She pointed to the saw, now resting on the floor, devoid of its power. *The saw belongs to me.*

The now former leader of the pack started to huff. *You can't do that.*

Teagan gave her brightest smile. *So wrong, little man. Because I just did.*

He left, sputtering and shaking his head. She spread her arms out as if embracing the workers around him. *If any of you would like to join your colleague here, please leave your tools on the floor and exit by the side door. If you would like to continue, will someone please find the 9-inch molding that is to be placed around these doors and start to do your jobs?*

*Any questions, gentlemen?* She gave them all her best Teagan I-am-so-charming smile and arched her eyebrows with the question.

No one said a word, and two of the workers went off to find the molding. Teagan saw me standing there and gave me a wink. *All in a day's work, Cate.*

I remembered Mam's story about when she was hiring men to remodel her house. Different time, different place, but the same kind of woman.

I gave Teagan a thumbs-up.

I was getting ready to leave when I saw her in the doorway. There was something about her that was different. Her eyes were darting as if she was expecting someone to show up. An uninvited guest. I walked over.

She asked the first question. *Are you involved here?*

*Yes, my name is Cate, and this will be, at some point soon, the O'Shea House. It is a home for unwed mothers, or to be exact, women who are not married but are pregnant.*

The unnamed woman moved her hands to her belly. *Is that the criteria? You can't be married?*

My eyes widened at the question; it was one we hadn't heard.

*Well, we don't have real criteria. We are here to help. Do you need help? Is that why you are here?*

She gave a laugh, a laugh that was not accompanied by a smile. *I need help. Have needed it for years. It is just now I am asking for it. My name is Elizabeth, but everyone calls me Liz.*

*Come with me, Liz. I'm not sure there is any spot here where we can talk, but perhaps we can find a place nearby. I would love another cup of tea. Could I interest you in the same?*

She gave me a brief smile. *I would prefer mine over ice, a preference from having grown up in the south.*

I grimaced. *Tea over ice. My mam would roll over in her grave at the mere thought. But let's see if we can find a spot that can accommodate both our desires.* I noticed her teeth were white and strong, and her voice had a slight drawl. She was not one of our usual residents. She was older, well-dressed, with a voice that spoke of having gone beyond the required number of school years.

We found a diner, an American institution I liked, with its clatter of plates and the sizzle of its grills. Dublin had not yet been introduced to such a place. Liz and I took a booth in the corner, its faux leather seat blotched with coffee stains had faded from a bright shade of red to a dull pink. It said that we were not the first to find our way here to have a conversation that needed to be had.

Liz shook her head to my offer to add something more than the iced drink to the check. Her posture was private school trained, spine straight, shoulders back, eyes forward. There was also something about her I recognized. I saw it in Teagan. I saw it in Peggy. Like them, there was a quiet dignity about her. It was as if she had already decided somewhere deep inside that whatever this moment was, it would not define her.

Liz started the conversation without my prompting. *You are probably asking why I need more than a glass of sweet tea. I will share my story. A story I have never told anyone. I will start with where I am today. I am pregnant. I have run away from my husband. We live in Atlanta. I think he may kill me. I have no place else to go.* Liz gave a quick smile, *which about sums it up. And now I will try to answer your questions of why and how.*

My eyes widened. I couldn't control my reaction. She did not look like a woman subject to domestic violence. I stayed still.

*I was a sophomore in college when we met. I was working towards my degree in nursing. Greg, that's his name, was an intern at the hospital. He became my prince charming, tall, dark, and handsome, and we got serious very quickly. My mother was thrilled. I had never dated much in high school, and here I was bringing home the son of a well-known real estate mogul who was going to be a doctor. For the first time in my life, I thought my parents were proud of me. They loved Gregory from the moment he met them. He was charming, he was smart, and he came from a family that had money. My father, who liked to spend more time at the racetrack than with the family, likened it to my hitting a trifecta.*

*We were married shortly after I graduated from college and he began his residency. Everything seemed perfect at first. He is the kind of man everyone admires. My mother still reminds me of how lucky I am.*

I took a sip of my tea. I didn't know what to say.

Liz continued. *The isolation started slowly. He didn't like this neighbor or that friend. He didn't want me to make friends with the nurses I was working with, saying it would be awkward since he was a doctor. Then he didn't want me to go out without him. My mother was the only one I could see. She is his greatest fan, and he knows that.*

Liz paused; she squeezed her eyes. *I started working extra shifts at the hospital just to keep myself busy. His life was absorbed by his work, but he wanted me home when he got home, though his schedule could be erratic. There was no excuse accepted if I wasn't there when he arrived. I cut back on my hours. He asked for my paycheck. I asked why. He said it was because he was the head of the house. I thought he was kidding, but when I tried to make a joke of it, his eyes got dark. He told me that I should do as he said and be grateful. That he was only thinking of our future. He would give me an allowance to buy groceries, pay for my gas, and parking at work. If I asked for extra money to get a haircut or buy a new dress for a party, he called me selfish and greedy. He said it often enough that I began to believe it.*

Liz took a deep breath. Her voice got quiet, as if she was talking to herself. *Two years ago, he started to hit me. He never left marks anyone could see, so nobody would know. When he was finished and the rage had passed, he would beg my forgiveness. He would tell me he was sorry, that it wouldn't happen again. That we both had to work harder on our marriage. I had to be more understanding; he was under so much pressure at work. I thought it was all my fault, and I needed to be a better wife.*

Liz looked at me. Hearing her story, I had forgotten to breathe. *Then six weeks ago, I found out I was pregnant. I had been careful, but sometimes after he was in a rage, I just let him do whatever he wanted to do, without thinking of the possible consequences. I knew Greg didn't want children. I thought maybe once he knew we were going to have a child, start a family, we could go back to the way we were. I was wrong. At first, he told me that it couldn't be his child, that I was a whore who would do anything for attention. Then he said that I should get rid of it; that was the term he used. That was the turning point for me. I didn't respond. I just stared at him. I think that unnerved him. Then he started hitting and punching. I ended up on the floor. I could barely move. He went to kick my stomach, but I rolled over. I had to protect my baby. He stormed out of the apartment. I lay there all night. He never came home. The next morning, I went to the bank and withdrew all the money we had in our savings account. I packed an overnight bag and got on a train. I didn't leave a note or call anyone. No one knows I am here.*

Now it was my turn to take a deep breath. *How did you find us, the O'Shea House?*

*I think through the grace of God. But in reality, I am staying at a hotel about three blocks away and went to a deli to get something to drink. As I was waiting to get coffee, some big guy started shouting that he had been kicked off his job. He muttered to his buddy that it was the house that was being built for girls who, and I quote, "got knocked up and can't remember the name of the guy who did it." I simply walked up and down the streets looking for buildings under construction and asked the same question I did of you. And here I am.*

I thought to myself, *I will need to thank Teagan.*

I reached over and touched her hand. *You are going to be okay, Liz. We are not ready for you here, but we have two other houses. I'll get the check and walk you back to the hotel to get your bag. I am going to take you to our first O'Shea House. It is in Queens, about a half-hour from here. You will be safe there.*

Liz nodded slowly. *I can pay.*

I stood up. *We don't take money, but we are always in need of good nursing care. I think you will find yourself very busy, very quickly.*

Fifteen minutes later, we were on our way. Deidre was slightly surprised when she saw me at the door, followed by Liz and her bag. I merely said, *We have a new resident. Liz is a nurse. Her baby is due in about 7 months. I thought we could use her skills while she stays with us.*

Deidre picked up the bag. *There is a room on the third floor that has an empty bed. We all share space here. Let me bring you up. And when you have a minute, I'd love to have you look at our medical closet. I am still not sure we have all the supplies we need to have on hand.*

I left. Liz will be cared for.

---

## A Shattered Life

Liz's words are like a broken record I keep replaying. Her bruises, both physical and emotional, were painful to hear about. It brought back the memory of my seeing Liam wielding his knife at me while Joseph lay bleeding on the kitchen floor.

Liz had lived with fear and uncertainty for years. How could her husband, who said he loved her, treat her like that? Tearing her down so completely, so relentlessly, that she no longer saw her own worth. He made her believe that she was the cause, not the victim, of his brutality.

May the child she is carrying someday know her mother's strength.

For it was the love and concern for her baby that freed the binds that tied Liz to that life. A life of pain and fear.

I pray that her future will hold the joy and love she so deserves.

I am so grateful that an O'Shea House was there for her. It will make a difference.

———

I put down the pen.

———

Spring had finally arrived, breaking through, painting the world with pinks and yellows. The scent of fresh blossoms filled the air. I had gone to the Bronx Botanical Gardens that day; it was like strolling through a Monet painting.

I had just fallen asleep when I heard the phone ringing. It took me a minute to realize that it wasn't a part of my dream. A dream I don't remember. A dream that became a nightmare. I was home alone. Nell and O'Brien had retreated for a long weekend in the Hamptons, wanting to enjoy that vacation mecca before the summer crowds descended.

I picked up the telephone. I gave a hesitant hello, more of a question than a greeting.

It was Teddy. I didn't recognize his voice; it was cracking as he spoke my name. I became fully awake, every sense sharpened.

He mumbled, *Cate?*

I responded, *I am here.*

*There has been an accident, a terrible accident,* his voice broke.

*Where, whom? Tell me, Teddy.*

*My mother and O'Brien.* The sound of muffled sobs followed, like a breath that couldn't be caught.

I clutched the phone tighter. *I am here, Teddy. I am here.*

His next words were measured, as if saying them confirmed the worst. Teddy repeated himself. *There has been an accident.*

I waited.

*They were on the expressway coming back to the City. A tractor-trailer jackknifed and hit their car. They were taken to a hospital on Long Island. They are*

... Teddy's voice became a whisper, *hurt. Very hurt. The police told me to come quickly, but it will be hours before I get there.*

*And Sienna.*

Teddy started to sob. *She is pregnant and having a tough time. The doctor says we are not to worry, but until we know ...*

*Oh, Teddy.*

His voice was cracking. *She was to be a grandmother. She never knew ... we thought it was too soon to tell her. She never knew...*

*Tell me where, Teddy. Tell me where they are, the name of the hospital. I will go now.*

*Manhasset Hospital*, each word sounding like it was being pulled from a place of unbearable sorrow.

*I will find it.*

There was a pause; we said nothing. The silence, a respite from all the terrible things that we could not say.

*Teddy?*

*I'm here, Cate. Call Faith and have her come with you. You shouldn't be alone.*

*I'll be okay, Teddy. I will reach out to Faith, but best if she stays at her house. I will call her with an update once I know more. And you can call her from the road to get my message.*

For the first time, Teddy's voice sounded like his own. *That makes perfect sense. I love you, Cate. This is hard. So very hard.*

I had no response; the horror of it all was overwhelming. *Drive safely. I love you, too.*

We said our goodbyes at the same time. I put the phone down.

I looked around the foyer. Nothing had changed. Its marble floors, veined in pale gray and cream, still stretched across the entryway. The console table, its smooth walnut surface, polished and gleaming, held fresh-cut flowers in an Irish crystal vase. Somehow, it needed to look different to me. Teddy's message to come quickly was the harbinger of life as we knew it could be coming to an end. I looked at the Erté clock sitting in its place of glory on the console. It was 3:18 in the morning, hours before dawn. Yet the day had begun, and how it would end was too awful to even imagine.

I called Faith, convinced her to stay put until Teddy arrived. I couldn't put my fears into words. It was as if an unbearable weight had taken hold of my body. I was afraid to say anything aloud that might make my sense of doom real. Silence while suffocating was better. It was better to have things unsaid than to speak the unimaginable.

The drive to the hospital seemed to take forever, but my watch said less than 45 minutes. Unlike Dublin, there was no matron to meet me at the door, to tell me to keep my place. This hospital was all white and efficient, including the nurses.

Teddy had given the hospital my name, explaining that I was his sister, so I was brought into the waiting room without question. Within minutes, a doctor appeared wearing green scrubs, his mask hanging on his neck, his hands clasped tightly in front of him. He called my name. I nodded as he introduced himself, not trusting myself to speak.

He shifted uncomfortably. My hands started to shake. This was different from what I had experienced before. I knew it. His voice, when it came, was low and measured, but even then, it seemed to crack under the weight of the words. *I'm so sorry*, his throat tightening as he tried to steady himself. *There was an accident. Mrs. Walker... didn't survive.*

I couldn't speak. The words in my throat wouldn't come out. I shouted in my head. *No, that's not possible. She is too much alive to be gone. We need her too much. This must be some mistake. She was just away for the weekend. It is less than a three-hour drive.* My eyes searched for his, looking for some glimmer of hope that he had misspoken. There was none.

A nurse appeared at his side. *Is there something I can get you? A glass of water? Do you want to sit down? Can I call someone for you?*

I stuttered, *My brother is on his way. He is driving up from Washington. O'Brien? What about O'Brien?*

The doctor's voice changed its tone, more efficient, now on safer ground. *Mr. O'Brien is in critical condition. His sister has been called, and a priest is on the way.*

*Can I see him? Does he know about ...* I didn't have the strength to end the sentence.

The doctor looked at the nurse and nodded. *Yes, to both your questions. I can only give you a few minutes, but I think it would be good for both of you. Nurse, please take Miss Clark into Mr. O'Brien's room.*

O'Brien's room continued the hospital's white palette. I gasped as I entered. O'Brien was motionless, lying on the sterile white bed. His face was drawn and pale, the once-robust color drained from his skin as though the very life of him had bled away. Tubes snaked from his arms and mouth, tethering him to machines that beeped in a rhythm both unnerving and monotonous. The steady hiss of oxygen and the quiet hum of the IV drip seemed louder than they ought to be. His head was bandaged and bruised. The monitors above his bed blinked constantly.

I walked to the side of the bed, took his hand, and softly whispered his name. One of his eyes slowly opened, and I felt his hand slightly squeeze mine. A tear started to fall from my cheek. His voice was labored, and I bent down, my ear close to his mouth. *No tears for me, darlin' Cate, but you can shed them for both of us for our beloved Nell. I knew as soon as the car spun out of control that we weren't going to make it. I saw the truck jackknife, and then everything seemed to go into slow motion, the car spinning, the back of the truck looming directly in front of us. Then the world erupted into a violent symphony of sound: steel crushing steel, glass cracking, Nell moaning. I was still conscious, calling her name, telling her I loved her. Then no response. A woman who was in constant motion became still. I couldn't move. I was pinned behind the steering wheel, but I was able to find her hand. It was still warm. At some point, the faint wail of sirens began to grow louder, but I knew it was too late to help her. And without her, I didn't want to be helped. I don't remember anything else until I was the center of attention here. And then nothing until I felt your touch.*

*O'Brien,* was all I could say.

*I waited too long to be at Nell's side. I was so intent on having to do my thing, take my pictures, tell my story that I left her here waiting. For too long.*

I started to interrupt, *But your pictures are ...*

O'Brien's eyes started to close. *Are just pictures.* His voice was no more than a whisper; I had to put my ear close to his mouth to hear him. *Life can be taken from you without notice. Live your life. Live every moment. Do that for Nell. She loved you so.*

I started to sob. O'Brien's breath became more labored, and a gurgling sound emanated from his lips. I let go of his hand as a woman who had all the earmarking of being a member of the O'Brien clan came to his bedside, along with a younger version of O'Brien himself wearing a policeman's uniform. She said she was Finn's sister. I had to pause to remember that was what O'Brien's family called him. For us, he was and always will be simply O'Brien.

I mumbled my name, how sorry I was, and walked backwards out the door. O'Brien was gone.

As I turned around, I was embraced by the softness of arms. It was Teagan. She kissed the top of my head, cradling me as unrelenting sobs racked my body. Teagan said nothing. Our shared grief spoke volumes.

———

## Loss Overwhelming

My sense of loss is overwhelming. Nell had been there for me, supportive, loving, challenging. I wasn't alone; my sorrow was shared by Teagan, Faith, and especially Teddy.

Grief has its own clock, measuring the hours, days, and months at its own pace. Ma's death was hard, but I was with her, spent time with her before she was gone. But the accident that took Nell and O'Brien opened a new wound before the first had healed. I wasn't prepared. The emptiness is crushing. So is the anger.

I thought I could press on. That coming to the office each day would keep them close to me. But it is not the case. My spirit feels worn thin. I have nothing left to give, not right now. I feel rudderless, at sea with the world without direction or purpose.

———

I put down the pen.

———

## Retreat

I am stepping back from my role at the Walker Foundation. Today is my last day sitting at this desk. The sun is pouring in through the windows, just as it did the first morning that I walked in. Much has changed, particularly me. I became a woman comfortable in making decisions.

The Foundation has grown, its work expanded. The O'Shea Houses provide the sanctuary we sought; they are doing the right thing for a population of women too often ignored and ostracized. Knowing of Liz's trauma, a shelter for victims of spousal abuse is being developed. Teagan has all of this under control as the new executive director. A new decade is dawning, and the call for change is growing louder with every drumbeat. The Walker Foundation won't just answer that call—it will help lead the charge. I will sit on its board with Teddy, taking Nell's seat but never her place.

I think about the women in my life. Mam started her own business in Ireland in the 1920s, an accomplishment for anyone, let alone a single woman. Nell exposed the horrors that women and children were experiencing in the hands of the factory owners at the turn of the century. These women were my two role models. I watch Teagan. She stands up even when others shout for her to sit down. I listen to Faith. Her energy, her compassion, her righteous indignation when others are treated badly. These are women who protect others in need of protection. These are women who shout to have their voices heard. I think of Peggy. A woman who creates herself to be a different person by a word or a glance, yet remains true to who she is.

These are women comfortable leading the parade. I am not the thoroughbred that they are, each in their own way, but a blend. I need to find a space outside of my sorrow and let the clock run down.

I have found a secluded cottage by a lake nestled in the hills of upstate New York. It will be my retreat. I will try to heal.

———

I put down the pen.

———

# 1960

I gaze out the window at the lake, its surface shimmering. On days when the sun breaks through a cloudless sky, the horizon blurs. The water and the heavens merge into one endless expanse of blue.

My thoughts drift like the waves lapping on the shore. I remember both the messengers and the messages I have received. They began with the man on the bus, the on with the cane. Then came the woman on the voyage back to New York. And finally, O'Brien's last words.

Each of them was in motion—journeying from one place to another, from one chapter of life to the next. Different faces, different times, yet their advice resonates. Find joy. Live each day. Listen to your heart.

———

## Decision

It is a soft rain, the kind that barely taps at the windowpane yet seeps into your very being. I sit by the window looking at the fog roll in, cloaking the lake in a soft blanket. The weight of missing Mam and Nell clings to me like this mist, refusing to let go.

My tea has grown cold. As has the air.

I feel restless.

My first day in New York, I questioned who I was to become. I now know that finding oneself is not about one single moment. Rather, a series of them. The death of a loved one changes you. A broken heart changes you. A beautiful sunset or a quiet walk on a beach changes you. You evolve, you adapt, you navigate. You rise to the occasion. You stumble and fall. You get up and start again. It is a voyage of self-discovery, where each step brings deeper insights and new layers of understanding about who you truly are. It is a journey, not a destination.

I open the journal that Nell gave me, and the words jump out at me. These pages tell stories. Stories about love of country, about the shattering cost of war, about forging one's own way. A wave of emotion follows. Grief for Mam, sharp and familiar. Pain for Liam and the demons he has never learned to name. Heartache in hearing John close the door and Jake leave the table. Anger at Nell dying without me being able to say goodbye. But there is also laughter and love. And hope and redemption.

I reread the stories, as a realization begins to creep in. These are not just words on a page, but stories that should be shared.

I found a yellow pad, and the words started to appear on the page. At first, a trickle. Then a downpour. It was as if the story was urging me to bring it to life. A place where my characters see what I see, feel what I feel, and maybe even heal what I cannot yet mend.

My table is littered with pages, some handwritten so poorly that I can barely discern my own scribblings. But it feels right.

I feel more at peace. I walk by the lake to say a fond farewell. I realize how much it reminds me of home. A shock runs through me. When I think of home, it is always Ireland.

My first decision is made; I am going back to Ireland. I am returning for me. This is not about obligation or longing. It is about belonging.

———

I put down the pen.

———

I just returned from Washington. I went down to say goodbye to Teddy and Sienna and to hold their baby girl once again in my arms. My goddaughter was baptized Eleanor O'Brien Walker. Our new Nell is a miracle. She is a new beginning.

I, too, am ready to begin, to remember, to carry forward.

———

## Friends

My plane leaves tomorrow. It will bring me back to cobble streets, green hills, and gray skies. Back to Ireland. Back home.

Teagan and Faith were taking me to dinner. I met them at Delmonico's, where I was ushered into a private room. Not only were Teagan and Faith there, but there stood Peggy, as well. She had flown in from California to say goodbye. I was both laughing and crying at the sight of them.

It was a night filled with deep, belly-holding laughter and tears no one tried to hide. We toasted, we hugged, we shared stories. It was well past midnight as we stood together on the sidewalk, arms wrapped around each other. No one wanted to break the embrace. We made a pact, one reunion each year, all four of us, no excuses. We will follow Peggy to wherever her next film takes her. We will meet there, whether it is Paris, Buenos Aires, or Boston. We will eat, drink, and laugh until it hurts. We will grow older but never apart.

These three women are my dearest friends. No, more than friends, they are my anchors, my beacons of light, my safe harbors. These are not friendships to fade over time or distance. Whatever comes—good, hard, messy, beautiful—I know they'll be there for me. And I'll be there for them. Always.

I kissed each of them goodbye and left.

———

I put down the pen.

———

# Book III

I had forgotten how sharp the wind off the Atlantic can be, how the Irish coast refuses to be tamed. Joseph found me a cottage in Howth, a small stone path from its front door leads to the sea. Time is slower here. The tide ebbs and flows. Even when the world around us howls its disdain, the waves rise up to greet the rocks as they have done for centuries. Everything is in constant motion, but nothing changes.

I am back in Ireland. Joseph is nearby. He and Bridget are to marry. It will be a small ceremony. Joseph thinks he is too old for the fanfare, and Bridget just wants to marry him. Teddy writes that he and Sienna are going to have another child. I believe saying hello to new life eases the pain of having had to say the final goodbye to those we love. I am happy for both my brothers.

I am content. I remember Mam telling about the first design she created, the dress for Delia Stein, how she talked to the dress, professing her undying love. I have done the same, only my object of affection is 210 pages of a printed and bound manuscript with my name on its spine. It is the story of a feisty and courageous woman who refuses to be confined by the norms of her time. It is the turn of the 20$^{\text{th}}$ Century, a time when women's voices were often silenced. My heroine is strong, defining life in her own terms, and she will be heard. She is not Ma, she is not Nell, but a combination of the two—a woman who carves out her own path. I have grown to love her as I write the words, creating her story.

The male character looks vaguely familiar. He is tall, dark-haired, with eyes to match, who loves Yeats and his time in the kitchen. I blinked at the page when I realized it was John. Perhaps if I can't have him as part of my life, I can have him in the one I create. The fairies would approve.

I have bought a typewriter.

———

I put down the pen.

———

The road was narrow and winding, unpaved and more fitting for sheep than my new car. My eyes were scanning the one-way path as my hands gripped the wheel. My mind was awhirl, I wasn't sure what I was doing was right, but knew that if I didn't at least try, I would regret it.

I want Liam to come to Joseph's wedding. I was going to see him and convince him to join us.

I am doing this on my own; neither Joseph nor Father Flanagan knows my plan. I wanted us to be reunited as a family. I wasn't sure what to expect. There has been too much loss. I need to recapture what we have left.

I found the cottage. Liam was in the garden; the only sounds I heard were the hoe attacking the soil, the chickens pecking at the corn, and two goats gnawing at the grass. I took a deep breath of the cool country air and called his name. He looked up, startled. His body appeared fit, his face weatherbeaten by the winds blowing off the hills.

*Cate?* his voice was low. *Is it really you?* His eyes flickered with surprise.

*Yes, Liam. I am home now, back home in Ireland. I wanted to see you.*

*I am not the same person ...*

*I know, Liam. I know. Joseph has told me.*

A smile stretched across his face. *Ay, Joseph. He comes regularly, doesn't stay long, and doesn't talk much. I think that suits us both.*

I reached for his hand, and Liam didn't pull it away. *Well, you'll be having no such luck with me. A talker, I am, and a talker, I will always be. These roads almost did me in. Could you be offering me a cup of tea?*

Liam kept my hand in his. *I can put a kettle on, and I baked a loaf of bread this morning, if you would like a bite to go with it. I have some fresh goat cheese, as well.*

We went inside. Liam found the matching chair to the one pushed into the table. I looked around. The cottage was small but neat. Here there was a calmness that soothes him.

I sat quietly while Liam prepared the tea. There were but two cups on the shelf; this was not a man who entertained.

After he sat down, I began. There was no reason to wait. *Joseph is being married next month. He is marrying a lovely woman named Bridget Dolley. She is a nurse and helped us when Mam was ill.*

Liam didn't respond.

I hesitated slightly and then blurted it out. *I want you to come to the wedding. I want you to be there.*

There was a long silence. Liam just looked at his tea and shook his head. *I am not one for being around folks anymore. I'm better off here. On the land and the quiet.*

I took a deep breath. My voice softened. *I understand, Liam. But you have a family; Joseph and I are your family. Soon, Bridget will be as well. Please come with me. I will be by your side the whole time. And Father Flanagan will be there. He is doing the marriage.*

I added quietly, *It would mean a lot to us, to Joseph and to me.*

Liam paused again. I thought to myself, *He makes Joseph look like a magpie,* but I sat still.

He continued. *I can't just slip back into that world, sit in a church with people I don't even know. I don't even own a tie. It wouldn't be fitting.*

*You know me. You know Joseph. You know Father Flanagan. This is going to be a small gathering. You remember Joseph well enough to know the spotlight is never something he's craved. The same can be said for the darling girl who has agreed to be his wife. And as for your outfit, I have you covered. You won't need to worry about a fancy suit.*

Liam's voice had a hint of disbelief. *What do you mean covered?*

I reached into my bag and pulled out my measuring tape. *I am my moth-*

*er's daughter and have a way with a needle and thread. I am sure I can find one of your old suits safely stored in one of the cedar closets and work my magic on it.*

There was a long pause. His voice quieter, *Alright. Alright. I'll come.*

---

## My Brother Liam

I found a suit. I wasn't sure it was Liam's or Joseph's. I had work to do. Men's clothing isn't my forte. It needed to fit both his body and his sense of belonging. Not too much, not too little. Just like Goldilocks, this suit had to fit just right.

I struggled with whether I should tell Joseph that Liam was coming. I wasn't sure I could trust Liam to make it, and I didn't want to disappoint. I took the coward's way out, I told Father Flanagan. He only shook his head, *It would be a gift, but I think it best to wait and see what the day will bring.*

It was the day before the wedding. My dress hung carefully on the door. Tea length and lavender in color, the fitted bodice was trimmed with an antique lace that I had taken from one of Mam's old dresses. She would be with us at the altar. I went with a fascinator. A hat, even one carefully placed and secured with pins, is always defeated by my crown of red curls.

I took the drive to get Liam. I breathed a sigh of relief when he met me at the door, ready to go. He was shaved and had gotten a haircut, a major step for him and no small task for the barber whose chair he found. He picked up a worn duffel bag containing the few items he was bringing for this overnight trip. We drove in silence and in darkness. Liam's hands rested nervously on his lap, his eyes fixed on the road ahead. The weather held; I didn't need rain and wind whipping about us to add to the uneasiness.

We arrived back in Howth safely. The sounds of the waves crashing against the shore greeted our arrival. I showed Liam to the extra bedroom; his suit hung on the door, neatly pressed and waiting. A white shirt and tie were on the bureau. He looked at me, uncertainty in his smile. *You made this just for me?*

I smiled, *Aye, for you. Go on. Give it a try.*

Minutes later, Liam emerged, the light wool fitting his body made him look strong; the light blue color made him look gentle.

I clapped. *You look good.*

He took another look in the mirror. Coming over to me, he kissed me on the cheek. *Thank you, sister.*

Liam's eyes said more than his words. It wasn't the clothes. It was the realization that people care about him. That he was part of a family. That he was loved.

May that continue through tomorrow.

———

I put down the pen.

———

The day was bright and beautiful. Mam had clearly answered my prayers and given us sunshine and blue skies as her wedding present.

Liam was wearing his new suit; his body looked less tense, as if it had found a strength that hadn't been there before.

Liam and I walked into the church just as Joseph stepped onto the altar. His face registering no surprise in seeing Liam, he crossed the space between us in a few long strides.

Looking directly at Liam, Joseph spoke, *I am glad you came.*

Liam's eyes welled with emotion. Joseph looked at me and nodded. He rested his hand gently on Liam's shoulder. Joseph's voice was low but clear, *I am about to take my vows. Would you walk our sister down the aisle and then come take your place beside me at the altar?*

Liam stepped forward, he put my arm through his, and smiled. No words were spoken, none were needed.

———

Joseph had warned me, but it was still a bit unnerving to see Timmy at the wedding. It made perfect sense. Timmy had been there for Mam and for Joseph and had introduced us to Bridget.

We were back at the house when he came up to me, giving me a kiss on the cheek. *You look beautiful as always.*

*And you don't look as tired as the last time I saw you.*

He smiled at the recollection. *The life of a resident. Not much better for me these days, but the 15-hour shifts are mostly a thing of the past.*

He paused. *You were right, you know. Even though hearing it broke my heart.*

I took his hand. *I am sorry I did that. It is not what I wanted. You deserve to be loved, not hurt. We loved each other. I still love you. But it is not the right kind of love.*

Timmy slowly shook his head. *I didn't understand it then. I just wanted it to be you.*

I grimaced.

*But I understand now. I am with someone. And it is different. It is too early for me to bring her into this tight-knit group, but I am thinking about introducing her to my family.*

I didn't have to hide my happiness for him. *Oh, Timmy, that is lovely to hear. Your family will love anyone you love, I am sure of that. Except, perhaps ...*

Timmy finished the sentence, *My mother.*

I laughed out loud. *No, not your mother. I am thinking of Miss Mary Ellen Murphy. Molly is the tough sale.*

Timmy joined in the laughter. *You are absolutely right on that account. And as she gets older, her opinions are clearly her own, and she has no problem making them heard. Much to the delight and sometimes the chagrin of her father.*

His voice got more serious, almost quizzical. *Jack was asking about you when I said I was coming to Joseph's wedding. Wanted to know if you were going to be here. If you were back in Ireland.*

I tried to keep my voice calm. *The answer to both those questions is yes. I have a place in Howth, and I am home. Ireland is home.*

———

## Look for Joy

I was grateful that Liam was a man of few words. On the drive back to the country—and again, alone on the return to the cottage—my thoughts wandered from the road to what Timmy had said.

John had been asking about me.

I hadn't found the courage to ask if he was with someone now. Timmy had moved on. John might have, as well.

But I hadn't come back to Ireland because of John. I came back because of me.

As I stood at the kitchen window, the kettle beginning to sing, a rainbow appeared across the morning sky. Was this a God wink? A quiet sign that I wasn't alone with all the questions stirring my heart?

Would he try to find me? Should I try to find him?

Like this cottage I've come to trust, I can weather more than one storm. I can stay calm, even when the clouds gather and the wind howls.

I will look for joy. I will take the chance that I might find it.

And I will trust that the path forward doesn't have to be certain—only mine.

———

I put down the pen.

———

It was the Saturday after the wedding. The morning sun rose, and with it came the promise of a bright sky. I took a deep breath, reminding myself, courage doesn't always roar. I drove into Dublin, my hands tight on the wheel to keep them from trembling. I made my way to what had once been our bench.

John was there.

He looked just the same. My heart caught in my chest.

He stood and said simply, *Catherine with a C.*

*John.*

Gently, he cupped my face in his hands and leaned in, his lips brushing mine. Then he held me close and whispered, *Tell me I'm not dreaming. Tell me you're truly here.*

I looked into his eyes. *I am here. I am home. This is home.*

He took my hand. *I have a plan.*

I leaned into his shoulder, shaking my head. *No plan. Just one day at a time.*

John smiled and echoed, *One day at a time.*

We began walking, neither leading, neither following. Just one step at a time.

The scent of lilacs and roses filled the air. Mam is smiling.

Or perhaps, it is the fairies.

# Irish Timeline

For the Readers of *Finding Herself*

**1905:** Sinn Féin (Irish for "We Ourselves") is founded.

**1916:** The Easter Rising. A rebellion against British rule takes place in Dublin. Though the uprising is swiftly suppressed, the execution of 16 of the rebel leaders and the subsequent imprisonment of over 1800 Irish men and women without trial ignites worldwide sympathy for Ireland's cause.

**1919:** The Irish Republican Army (IRA) is created as the successor to the Irish Volunteers. Known for its guerrilla tactics, the IRA becomes the armed force of the nationalist movement.

**1919:** The Irish War of Independence begins, led by figures like Michael Collins of County Cork.

**1920:** The British respond to IRA tactics by forming the Black and Tans, a brutal paramilitary force infamous for its cruelty. Their name comes from their mismatched uniforms.

**1921:** Facing mounting pressure, the British negotiate a ceasefire with the Irish rebels. The conflict ends with a truce.

**1922:** The Anglo-Irish Treaty is signed, creating the Irish Free State as a dominion within the British Empire. However, the six counties of Ulster remain part of the United Kingdom, and Ireland does not achieve full republic status.

**1922:** A bitter civil war erupts between pro- and anti-Treaty forces.

The first major battle occurs at the Four Courts in Dublin on June 23rd, fought between the Irish Free State National Army and anti-Treaty IRA.

**1922:** Michael Collins is assassinated.

**1923:** The Irish Civil War ends with a ceasefire. The anti-Treaty IRA leadership orders its fighters to stand down.

**1937:** Ireland adopts a new constitution, establishing Éire and bringing the country closer to full independence.

**1939:** At the outbreak of World War II, Ireland's Taoiseach (Prime Minister) announces that the Irish Free State will remain neutral.

**1949:** Ireland formally becomes a fully independent republic and leaves the British Commonwealth.

**1955:** Ireland joins the United Nations.

# Author's Note

F inding Herself is set in the 1950s—a time I find hard to think of as history. It was the first full decade of my childhood. We had black-and-white televisions that went off the air with a sound pattern. Married (and unmarried) women could vote, but they couldn't get a credit card without their husbands' approval. Teenage girls made scrapbooks of their favorite movie stars and cried for Debbie Reynolds when Eddie Fisher dumped her for Elizabeth Taylor. Boys wore their hair greased and their jeans rolled. McCarthy gave us the Red Scare. Great Britain crowned a queen. Ireland was admitted to the United Nations. It was the quiet before the storm of the 1960s.

Against this backdrop, Cate's story moves between New York City and Dublin. I've lived and worked in one city but only visited the other—and I knew that wasn't enough. So, I packed my bag and rented a flat in the heart of Dublin City for two months. I wanted to feel its pulse, walk its streets, and understand its history not just through books, but as someone who had been there. I was moderately successful. I found a local pub, a great bakery, and by the time I left, I could give directions to St. Stephen's Green.

But history is only part of Cate's story. Finding Herself is primarily a tale about love, forgiveness, and redemption. It's also about friendship—the friends who share your joy, lighten your darkest days, celebrate your victories, and hold you up when you stumble. These are my friends. They make a difference in my life.

Writing this book was a deeply personal journey. It began when the world I knew crumbled—when my husband's cancer returned. For twenty months, I watched as Russ left me, piece by piece. I mourned him while he was still here. I have learned that grief isn't a singular event—it's a territory you learn to navigate. It is raw and heart-wrenching. And how you survive is up to you.

There are moments in my life when a memory is jarred, a whisper is heard, an unmarked treasure is found. I wonder—who made this happen? Some may answer, *it was the fairies*. Others, *it was angels*. No matter their labels, they send reminders that mystery still surrounds us—and there are days when that is enough.

While this chapter of Cate's story is closing, I hope the women you've met through the *Herself* series stay with you. Women of courage and determination. Women of compassion, resilience, and grace. For they are like the women you know; the women you raise; the women you are.

Thank you for taking this journey with me.

Maureen

# A Lexicon

Terms, Places, and Phrases to Guide Your Reading of *Finding Herself*

**The Irish language**, once forbidden and nearly forgotten, has survived centuries of suppression. A Celtic tongue with only 18 letters—omitting J, K, Q, V, W, X, and Y— is now the national language of the Republic of Ireland and a vital part of its cultural revival.

Throughout this book, you'll encounter words and expressions that remain rooted in Irish soil. Some have made their way across oceans; others are still bound to the Emerald Isle. This lexicon provides a brief guide to some of these terms, with the intent to clarify and define.

**A-Levels** — Subject-based qualifications that lead to university, work, or further training. Assessed primarily by examinations.

**Anglo-Irish Treaty**--Ended Ireland's War of Independence and established the Irish Free State under the British Commonwealth, with six northeastern counties remaining under British rule. Negotiated by Michael Collins and others, it was highly controversial and the cause of political divide throughout Ireland.

**Ascendancy** — Refers to the Protestant Ascendancy, the small, elite Anglican ruling class that dominated Irish political, economic, and social life from the 17th to early 20th century.

**Bewley's** — A beloved Dublin landmark café.

**Craic** (Pronounced "crack")—Fun, gossip, good times, or lively conversation.

**Culchie** — A sometimes-pejorative term for someone from rural Ireland.

**Dutch Courage** — Bravery inspired by alcohol (not uniquely Irish).

**Eejit** — A foolish or senseless person.

**Four Courts** — Ireland's most prominent court building, heavily damaged during the Civil War.

**Free State Army** — The armed forces of the Irish Free State, primarily composed of pro-Treaty supporters during the Civil War.

**Gaol** — An old spelling of "jail."

**Gardaí** — The Irish police force.

**Glasnevin Cemetery** — A major cemetery in Dublin; resting place of famine victims and Easter Rising patriots.

**Go raibh maith agat dearg**--"Thank you Red."

**Ha'Penny Bridge** — A pedestrian bridge over the River Liffey, named after the halfpenny toll, once charged to cross it.

**Hospital Matron** — A senior female nurse managing hospital wards and staff.

**IRA (Irish Republican Army)** — A paramilitary organization central to Ireland's 20th-century conflicts with British rule.

**Is breá liom tú, a chara**-- "I love you, dear friend."

**Jumper** — A sweater.

**Keener** — A mourner who wails or sings laments at funerals.

**Kilmainham Gaol** — Historic prison where leaders of the 1916 Rising were executed.

**Nellie Bly** — A pioneering 19th-century investigative journalist (not Irish, but referenced).

**Newsboy Cap** — A flat cap more common in British fashion, also worn casually in Ireland.

**Orange Order** — A Protestant fraternal organization, largely based in Northern Ireland.

**Papist** — A historical (often derogatory) term for Roman Catholics.

**Privy** — An outdoor toilet.

**Shawlies** — Working-class women known for wearing black shawls, often seen into the 20th century.

**Slán mo ghrá**—Farewell my love.

**Solicitor** — A type of lawyer who handles legal matters outside of court.

**Taoiseach** — Pronounced "TEE-shock," this is the head of government or Prime Minister of Ireland. The President of Ireland serves a mostly ceremonial role.

**The Emergency** — Ireland's term for the World War II era, during which it maintained neutrality.

**Tongue Wags** — Gossip or idle chatter.

**Trainers** — Sneakers.

**Ulster** — One of the four traditional Irish provinces, consisting of nine counties—six of which form Northern Ireland.

# Acknowledgments

No book is written alone. The act of writing may be solitary, but the journey is anything but.

To my family and friends—thank you for listening patiently to my updates, offering encouragement when I stalled, and always believing in me. Your faith in this story, and in me, kept me going.

To my dear friends and beta readers—Candi, Carol, Colleen, Erin, Kathy, Louise, MaryEllen, Rolaine, Sandra, and Sandy—your insights, honesty, and time were invaluable. You helped me see Cate's story with fresh eyes, and I'm deeply grateful.

To my intern and granddaughter, Bridget—remember that life is meant to be an adventure. Be curious. Be courageous. Look for joy.

The Irish are known for their warmth and generosity, and my time in Dublin only deepened that truth. To Ken and Peggy Mooney—thank you for opening your hearts and your home. You showed me an Ireland I had never truly known—its stories, its spirit, and how to brew a proper pot of tea. It was your road that rose up to meet me.

The 1916 Rising is familiar to many of us with Irish ancestry, but I wanted to understand the scars left by the Irish Civil War. My gratitude to Dr. Brian Hanley, assistant professor of history at Trinity College Dublin, for generously sharing resources and insights into this turbulent time. Go raibh maith agat, Brian.

To my publisher, Stephanie Larkin, and her team—thank you for assisting and enlightening me. It's is a pleasure to work with you.

To Joan Tuley, a fellow upstate New York gal—you were able to gather my pages and drafts and shape them into a manuscript. Many thanks.

To my readers—thank you for following the *Herself* series and for taking your time to read these stories. You remind me why I write.

And finally, to all. Live each day fully. Make memories. Smile often. Be kind.

Until we meet again,
Maureen

# About the Author

Following a career that led her from managing colleges to Fortune-500 companies, to major international law firms, award winning author Maureen Reid began writing the kind of novels she loves to read. Blending fiction with historical facts, Maureen is inspired to write about strong women who by sheer will and spirit become the best that they can be. A storyteller, Maureen's characters have been described as flawed but determined as they try to make a difference in their lives and in the lives of others. The issues they confront are as current as today's headlines.

When she is not somewhere else, Maureen lives in the metropolitan New York surrounded by family and friends. She is blest that four of the world's most beautiful, smartest and kindest girls call her "Grandma."

Visit Maureen's website maureenreidauthor.com to check out her latest *Musings* and the date for the release of her next book.

# Also by Maureen Reid

*Becoming Herself*

*Choosing Herself*